5 Weeks

Of

Saturn

By:

Mike J. Kizman

ISBN: 978-1-966477-55-6

Table of Contents

About the Author

Mike J. Kizman was born in and lived all of his life in Northwest Indiana. He has been married for over 30 years and has one daughter away at college. Mike has always been the creative type, being the author of many unpublished short stories and poems. He is also a visual artist who creates mainly landscapes using acrylic paint on canvas or colored pencils. His work in that medium can be found at Simply99 Creations on Facebook and Instagram.

When Mike isn't creating, he can often be found walking his terrier mix dog, Kardashian, which he adopted from a shelter when the dog was seven years old. He volunteers for many different children's programs and is an award-winning Girl Scouts leader who led his daughter to earn the prestigious Girl Scouts Gold Award.

Chapter 1

New Beginnings

Oh, hi again. It's nice to see you back. It's been a rather busy week for me with the new job, new city, and potential new boyfriend. Today is Saturday, June 7, 2025, and unlike last week, it's sunny and clear, with a forecasted high of mid-70s all day. Beautiful. I can't wait to take advantage of that. It's just after noon, and I'm waiting for Janus to come pick me up for an all-day date. Until he arrives, let me catch you up on what has been happening with me while I pet my beautiful little kitten, Muffin.

My name is Saturn O Syres. Not Saturn O. Syres. O, without a period, is my full given middle name. I just moved to this city three weeks ago, exactly, on my 24th birthday. I'm 5'5" tall, of average weight, and am living on my own for the first time in my life. I moved to Oakfield in Central Indiana from Hohman, Indiana – about 150 miles away, bordering Chicago– to take my dream job in advertising, designing billboards. I am also a craft stick artist and sell my creations at various craft shows in Northern and Central Indiana. I have been working diligently over the past couple of years to get my life back on track.

I was raised in a Christian home with loving yet sometimes too lenient parents, who allowed us to make mistakes in hopes we would learn from them and come back to God on our own. I say "we" because I have an older sister, thirteen months my senior, named Venus. She was overbearing growing up, trying to force me to become more like her as she wore all of the latest trends and followed the latest fads, berating me for my obsession with looking at magazine advertisements and building with craft sticks while wearing loose-fitting clothing.

She had too many boyfriends to count in high school, attracting them mainly by wearing as little clothing as the dress codes would allow and acting all high and mighty. She is also a math genius who graduated from Indiana University with a degree in accounting during the COVID-19 pandemic shutdowns. Oh, and while there, she fell in love with a farmer from Omaha. She quit her accounting job in Chicago, married him about a year and a half ago, moved to Fremont, Nebraska, and works on the farm while also keeping the books. Now her clothing covers her entire body, loosely, I might add, and she only has eyes for Eric Brown, her cowboy husband. We had a contentious childhood growing up together, and now we're the best of friends, despite her overbearingness still shining through at times. She's also two months pregnant.

After she left for college, I tried to become more like her for some reason. I went from wearing my usual loose-fitting clothes to dressing with more skin than material showing on my body. The boys started hovering around me as they did her. When I went away to Ball State University in Muncie, Indiana, things took a turn for the worse. With the help of my roommate and her friends, I discovered the art of partying, that wine makes me frisky, and I lost my virginity while being propped up on a sink in a bathroom while a wild party was going on just outside the door. My "body count," if you will, went up to anywhere from 3 to around 5.75, depending on how you count it, before I graduated.

During my senior year of college, the year after COVID lockdowns, my roommate was Chloe Summers, an engineering major. She's a Christian woman from Michigan City, Indiana, not too far from Hohman, and after some deep conversations early in my senior year, she helped bring me back to God. Don't get me wrong, now. I'm no angel, and neither is Chloe. But now, we help keep each other in check and strive to bring out the best in one another. We both had our falls along the way, sure, but since iron sharpens iron, we try to hold each other accountable for our actions and keep our lives closer to how God wants us to live.

She went back to Michigan City after graduation and now works as a City Planner. We still keep in touch, trying to get in at least one Zoom call a week. During college, she helped me learn how to design better craft stick art, and she often accompanies me to craft fairs to sell them. For me, it's less about the money and more about the fact that I not only enjoy making the items, but also spending time with the person who has become my best friend in the world outside of Venus. There is one coming up that I wanted to go to, but the move has changed those plans, and Saturn Sticks will be sitting that one out.

I'm now back to being me, wearing the loose-fitting clothes I find to be comfortable, and I got my dream job working in advertising, with billboards as a specialty.

The day I moved into this town, I visited a local restoration shop and purchased furniture for my apartment. Mom didn't like that I was buying mismatched furniture, but I explained that if things didn't work out, I didn't want to have all this lovely, new furniture to try and resell. She also didn't like that I didn't buy a bed and am opting to sleep on my couch. I told her that it was to save money, which is partly true. The part she didn't have to know is that I didn't buy a bed to help ward off temptation. As I said, I'm no angel. I expect to date while living here, and if there's no bed, then the temptation to invite someone to stay over is minimized. I know that other places in the apartment would still be tempting, but I'm trying something here. Let me have this one.

I have dated a man a couple of times since being here. His name is Blake Boyd, and he was a barista at Jack's Coffee and Pastry, a place I've come to frequent. He's a nice guy who has ambitions of opening his own chain of coffee shops, which is excellent. What isn't great is that when he found out I was in advertising, he immediately talked about us opening a chain of shops together, with him operating them and me promoting them. He had us getting married, having lots of kids, and living happily ever after 'til death do us part. I've nothing against any of that, but he was talking like that on our second date. Too much, too soon, so I broke it off with him inside the coffee shop, then he was fired for harassing the customers once again.

After that happened, I immediately and literally bumped into Janus Rings, who was having coffee and donuts. Janus is 27 years old, works at the restoration shop, and delivered my furniture. While at my apartment, I tried sending signals to him to ask me out, but he didn't seem interested. I was disappointed, but I didn't let that bring me down… too much.

After the coffee shop owner and another employee helped clean up the mess I just made, Janus and I got to talking. He holds a Bachelor of Science in Business from the University of Notre Dame and has taken a Furniture Finishing and Repair class at Ivy Tech Community College. He works at his dad's restoration and resale shop and plans to take over the business one day.

We talked for a while, and he invited me to his church the next morning, as I hadn't found one yet in town. I went. He was charming as he introduced me to others there, calling me only by name with no pretenses about any relationship we may now or soon will be in. We then went on a date following the church's coffee hour.

He took me to a local diner, where he treated me to a gyro and French fries before we took a walk down the trails at the forest preserve. I had hoped to walk there the day before, but the rain had made other plans for me.

As we walked, we also talked. I learned that he was a deacon at Oakfield Second Christian Church and served on the outreach committee. He told me a little about what he does for that, and after I mentioned it sounded a little like advertising for the church, he chuckled and agreed. He didn't immediately assume I'd help him with it, nor did he make plans for our next sixty years together. This man may be a keeper.

When we were about to part ways, I asked if he'd like to kiss me. He was hesitant, saying that he usually doesn't kiss on first dates. I told him that if we counted the furniture delivery, the coffee shop, the church, and then the lunch after church, this might have been our fifth date, so it's okay. He again chuckled at that, then leaned down to kiss me. It was short, barely a peck as his lips barely brushed mine. It was brief, soft, sweet, and perfect. I wanted him to kiss me again, but the moment was too perfect, so I didn't attempt to, which may have ruined our time together.

We agreed to go out again, and he said that he'd call me. I daydreamed about him and that kiss all evening while working on a big craft stick project that's been going on for a couple of years now.

A few weeks before graduation, Chloe used her engineering tools to create designs for me to build a model of the Shafer Bell Tower at Ball State University, the tallest collegiate bell tower in the state of Indiana. It's a big and ambitious project, and since I enjoy attending craft fairs to sell my goods, I've been working on it alongside other smaller projects. It's been almost two years since I glued the first two sticks together for this project, and I'm finally close to getting it done. I don't think I'll sell it, though. This is probably a keeper, or possibly a gift for Chloe. Or maybe I'll donate it to a charity. I'll decide that later. In the meantime, I think I'll put Muffin down and work on it a little now.

As I said, I came to town to start a job at a smaller advertising agency located here. After graduation, I secured a position in Chicago at a major firm with a global reach. However, once they found out that I could do voices and imitate almost anybody, thanks to a ventriloquist doll Dad gave me for Christmas when I was a young teenager, I spent the next year and a quarter in a recording studio doing voices for all sorts of ads. Don't get me wrong, I liked doing it, and it paid well, but I felt I wasn't putting my degree in marketing to good use, and, at the urging of Venus, I started my search for a new job.

I soon landed one at All-Ways Advertising, a smaller Midwest agency. When I interviewed for the job, I made it clear that while I wouldn't mind doing voiceovers on occasion when needed, I really wanted to work on creating ads, designing them, and applying the skills I learned in college. After the owner and boss, Gretchen Gillmore, had me make a mock campaign for a pizza restaurant they were hosting, she was impressed. It was based on the billboard that inspired me to pursue a career in marketing. It was a billboard advertising for the billboard itself, saying "Your ad here." I drew a concept on a yellow sheet of paper that showed a pizza with only cheese, and a caption next to it saying "Your toppings here."

I was hired immediately and was to start a few weeks later. We presented my design to the client, Rodney Phelps, owner of Here and There Pizza, and he loved it. We started building a campaign for multiple billboards around my "Your toppings here" concept, and soon my billboards – MY billboards – will be seen all over the county. That is literally one of my biggest dreams coming true!

When I showed up for work bright and early last Monday at 9:00 a.m., I was surprised by many things. First, I came to learn that the owner, Gretchen, isn't always as stern as she presented herself to be during my interview. While she is a hands-on boss, wanting to be in on the loop of everything, and always trying to undercut the competition, she also believes in allowing her employees to do what they do best, and she doesn't interfere with their processes. As long as the work is getting done and on time, she doesn't care if you bounce a ball against a wall while thinking or purposely make bad ads on your way to the final project. It's a job that requires lots of creativity, and everybody seems to have their own process, whatever that is.

It's also a lot smaller than I thought it would be. I mean, I knew it wasn't going to be anywhere near as large as the agency in Chicago, but I believe there are fewer employees here than were in the recording department back in Chicago.

My job is also a bit different from what I expected. After Gretchen offered me the job creating billboards, which at the time she didn't know was my dream job, she said that I would also be expected to help in other departments if needed. She even said that I may be asked to do voices for campaigns that needed them, and I told her I was okay with that as long as I also get to actually work on creating the ads.

When she said that I'd be working in the billboards department and helping others when needed, that was a bit vague, as I came to learn.

While All-Ways Advertising may be small, it's also a full-service ad agency, which means we'll handle it all for you. We do everything from creating and printing flyers to pass out door-to-door, to radio and TV ads, as well as, you guessed it, BILLBOARDS! Yes, billboards! Although we won't actually go door-to-door handing out flyers, we pretty much do everything else.

As I mentioned, I was assigned to the billboards department. What I came to learn quickly is that, for the most part, I WAS the billboards department, and what a department it is. With the county, two major US highways running close to Oakfield, and Indianapolis nearby, there is no shortage of billboards that need advertisements. We're the biggest advertising agency in the area outside of Indy, and ninety percent of those seeking advertisement in the county come to us for that job, and we all strive to keep them coming back. Sure, it's a smaller county, nowhere near the size of Cook County, Illinois, or Marion County, Indiana, but it's still big enough to keep us busy.

At All-Ways Advertising, we all have our specialties. Karen Keyes specializes in newspaper and print ads, John Brady handles radio, and Diane Finley mainly produces television commercials. Gene Wright is the on-staff artist who spends most of his time in the art studio at the agency, but also assists in other departments when needed. There's a large meeting room with a big table where we all gather every morning. There, we update everybody on what is going on with our departments. We brainstorm ideas, everybody helping where they can. If one department is all caught up, they will routinely help others when needed. As my pizza billboard campaign was coming to life, I also helped John with a project he had for a local electronics store, and, yes, I helped come up with voices for him. As I said, I don't mind doing that as long as I get to mainly focus on billboards.

A couple of days ago, the owner of Here and There Pizza came into the office to check on the progress of his campaign. He wanted five different billboards, one for each direction of the two US routes and one in town near his restaurant. We showed him the ads, explained the concept, provided an analysis of how well we projected the campaign would perform, and suggested which billboard should be placed where. The owner was reluctant to the crudeness of how they looked, but when Gretchen not only assured him of her confidence in these ads, but also that if they didn't hit the mark, she'd refund him twenty-five percent of the campaign cost, he immediately agreed to the campaign. It was a huge confidence booster for me, but also a little stressful. I mean, if they didn't hit the mark, would she refund him the cost by firing me? No, I don't think so. I mean, she did approve the concept and made that guarantee herself. Still, it is a little nerve-wracking to think about whether this, my first campaign, has failed.

We didn't have time to think about that. We had a bit of a celebration for the newbie's first success. Gretchen and Karen congratulated me and told me not to rest on my laurels, as it's usually not that easy, but they had confidence in my ability to do the job. I was over the moon and close to Saturn up above in delight.

That evening, Janus came by my apartment to take me out on a date to the pizza place that had just bought my account. Janus was a true gentleman, and when it came time to order, he told me that since I had suggested "Your toppings here," I should choose the toppings for our large pie. I went with sausage, fresh tomatoes, and, since I was hoping to kiss him later, mushrooms in place of onions, which I usually choose.

"You must be so excited to see your work come to life soon," he told me.

"Yeah," I said, with excitement that quickly dissipated. "I just hope I wasn't a one-trick pony. You know, this campaign was just an off-the-cuff fluke. They usually don't come that easily. I was at the company for all of four days. This can't be normal."

"Maybe not," Janus said, then took a big bite of pizza, leaving a little sauce on his chin. "Tell me. Do you believe in yourself?"

This was getting pretty deep for a third-date conversation (I'm not counting the coffee shop, furniture delivery, or church in this count), so I looked at him again, closely. Was he looking at me the same way Eric looks at Venus? Not yet, but it's getting there, I think. After that long pause, I answered.

"Yes. I really do believe that I can."

"Believing in yourself is half the battle, Saturn. I'm glad you said that, now I feel better about what I've been wanting to ask you."

I braced myself, silently praying he wasn't about to take our relationship past the entry level it was then.

"Which is?"

"We talked about this at the coffee shop last Saturday. When do you think I could schedule an appointment to discuss advertising for the resale shop? I know we discussed billboards a little, but if you don't mind, we – Dad and I – would like to see other options."

"Oh, after all of that 'believing in yourself talk,' now you don't trust me," I teased, hoping he'd get that.

"No, no, no… of course I do… It's just that, with the business and all…"

"No, it's okay," I said, laughing a little while trying to be flirty as I ate a mozzarella cheese stick. "Honestly, that's the best way to do it. Can you come in on Monday morning, around 10:00 a.m.? We can discuss your needs and see what best suits you. If it's a billboard, then that's great. If door-to-door flyers seem more sensible, we can refer you to Karen Keyes. She usually handles printed ads."

"That sounds like a good plan, Saturn. Let's not talk business all night, though. I'm sorry I brought it up."

"Actually, I'm glad you did," I said, then reached to touch his hand, but he took a cheese stick before I could make contact. Drat! "I wanted to bring that up, too. I just didn't want you to think that I was dating you to drum up some business."

"Well, now that that's out of the way, how about we put the refurbishing furniture and advertising talk to the side for now? Let's talk about something else, like how Muffin is doing?" Janus smiled when he finished talking, then reached over to touch my hand for a moment. I think I felt like a lightning bolt went through my body.

Muffin is the black and while kitten I found outside my apartment window last Saturday when I stayed home due to the rain. I took him to the vet, and they found out he's nine weeks old and in perfect health. He is the first pet I have ever owned, and I plan on pampering and spoiling him for the next fifteen years.

"He likes batting craft sticks around," I joked, and he laughed along.

We sat, ate, and talked a little more until most of the pizza and all of the cheese sticks were gone. It was getting somewhat late, and we both had work in the morning, so he took me straight home. We said goodnight in the parking lot of my building, promising he'd call for another date before Monday.

"Well, goodnight," he said, then leaned down and gave me a slight peck to the lips. This was our third official date, and seventh if you did barista Blake Boyd's math.

"Wait," I said as he started to stand. I looked up at him, as he looked down on me, standing about 6'0" tall, I think. I wrapped my arms around him to give him a bigger kiss. Nothing too, too passionate. Just a lip-to-lip kiss that lasted much longer than the simple one he just gave me. We parted, and he stayed close, looking me straight in the eyes. I wanted to kiss him again, but I also didn't want to give him any wrong ideas. I just took his hand in mine, smiled as I said goodnight, and then walked away while holding his hand in mine for as long as I could. I went to bed, said my usual nighttime prayers, hoping Janus would be in my dreams. When I woke the next morning, I had a sore neck, and I couldn't recall anything I had dreamt the night before. Drat!

Chapter 2

The Week's End

I'm still waiting for Janus to arrive. He hasn't texted or called, but I'm sure he'll be here soon. We scheduled a meet-up after lunch, so that's a bit vague, if you will. Maybe he's making sure I have enough time to clean up after lunch, since that was ingrained in me by Mom, and he knows it. Maybe he's treating our last Saturday at the coffee shop as the start of our relationship and stopping to buy me flowers for our one-week anniversary. That would make more sense if we were in high school and celebrating weekly milestones, and if we were actually in a relationship. I mean, going out a few times this past week doesn't exactly make us a couple. Does it? We never really discussed that or any commitment. I hope we don't. Not today, anyway. Don't get me wrong, now. I honestly don't plan to look for someone new to date right now, but you never know. I wasn't looking for anyone when I met him. Okay, I was, but that was just a coincidence.

I wasn't looking for a pet either when I found Muffin outside my window, but here we are. Now, I think my small six-hundred-square-foot apartment has more stuff for him than for me, except for my craft stick supplies. We seem to share those, too.

Well, he may still be a while, so I may as well get you caught up some more.

I arrived at work at 9:00 a.m. the next day, feeling like I was floating on clouds. My ad campaign was greenlit, and I can't get the kiss out of my mind. Yes, I've kissed boys before, many times, as well as done … well, all there is to do with them, but somehow this was different. He's not some teenage football star groping me in the car because he thinks his status allows that, or some college guy looking for a one-semester fling. He is an adult who has likely been in relationships before and is looking for this one to grow naturally, without rushing into anything before its time. It may be like Venus on the farm. She and Eric grow corn, but won't harvest them until it's ripe. I still can't get over the high school homecoming queen now wearing overalls while feeding chickens.

Anyway, once I got settled in for the day after the morning staff meeting, Gretchen called me into her office. I hadn't been in there with her since my job interview last May, when I was offered the job. It still looked the same. I'm not sure why that surprised me. She asked me to sit down and then poured me a cup of coffee.

"Do you still take it black with a stirrer?" she asked.

"Yes," I answered. I take it that way because, at first, having a stirrer in black coffee annoyed Venus, and now it's more out of habit. "Thank you."

"You're welcome. How are things going with you? I mean, around here. Do you feel as though you're fitting in?" she asked.

"Yes." I hope she wasn't about to say I didn't fit in and fire me.

"Great. I wanted to discuss how we do things around here. You were hired pretty quickly and were immediately put on that pizza campaign. Things usually don't move that fast or easily here."

"I didn't think so," I answered honestly, then stirred my black coffee.

"You handle it brilliantly."

"Thank you." Now I was nervous. Was she about to drop the ball at any minute?

"As you're aware, we're a full-service ad agency. We may be small compared to your last job, but I like to think we're pretty big, especially around here."

"I agree," I said.

"Once you're more settled, you'll be expected to manage multiple clients simultaneously. As you can see, there are numerous billboards around, and we'd like our name on all of them."

"I'm sure," I answered, then sipped my coffee.

"We're also a small company that is expanding beyond this area and may eventually open branches in other markets. I want to keep that small-company, personal touch, no matter how large we grow."

"That sounds nice," I answered, though I wasn't sure what she meant.

"We like to get to know our clients' business. We just don't invite them into the office, sit with them, then record a radio ad or put up a billboard. We want our clients to succeed. The more they succeed, the more they maintain a professionally strong relationship with us."

"I'm sure," I said again, now feeling like a dope.

"Anyway," Gretchen stretches out. "We like to get to know our customers' business. We will, with the client's permission, of course, go to their place of business if we can. We look around, see what they do there, try to imagine ourselves as a customer, and then try to come up with a campaign based on that. Your 'Your topping here' thing was brilliant, but if Rodney didn't like it, you would have had to visit his restaurant, sample the food, and get a feel for the place."

"I did that yesterday," I told her. "I went on a date there. It was nice."

"Oh?" she said, sounding like my senior year roommate, Chloe. "What did you think?"

"It was delicious. I'd definitely go again."

"How would you convince someone else to?" she asked.

"I'd flat out tell them to go, but I think you're asking now that I've seen the place, what ad would I have come up with?" She nodded at that.

"Well…" I thought for a moment, feeling the pressure.

"Well, if it were for a billboard, I'd…" I gave it some more thought. Surely she can't expect me to do this every time. "I'd show a table where the customer finished their meal, but it wasn't cleared. There'd be a little pizza crust left, maybe an almost empty marinara sauce bowl, and bits of other food items.

Nothing whole, just crumbs and pieces. I'd have the restaurant name and location, of course, and have it say, 'We offer carry-out boxes, but you won't need them.' Or something like that."

Gretchen looked into space for a moment, smiling a little as she does, visualizing what I just said.

"I love it," she finally said, much to my relief.

"Thank you," I said, my heart now pumping at a normal rate.

"As I said, we like to visit our clients when we can; sometimes it's a little distance away. You may be spending a lot of time out of the office some days, and you should keep track of your mileage because you will be reimbursed. Keep the client updated, and ask how often they want to hear from you. Most prefer daily updates, but for some, weekly is fine. A lot of that depends on the campaign itself. Keep your team in the loop, and the teams that you're on will keep you in the loop. Never be afraid to bark out an idea, and try to find clients if you can. Any questions?"

"I'm seeing a man, and he wants to come in Monday morning to discuss a campaign. Is that okay?" I asked.

"Of course, it's what we do here," she said, almost laughing. "What is it for?"

"Rings and Sons Restoration and Resale Shop. He first asked about a billboard ad, but I said that a door-to-door flyer ad might work better for him. I know that's cheaper, so I hope saying that was okay."

Gretchen smiled and refreshed my coffee for me.

"That's more than okay; that's exactly how we want you to do things around here. Don't oversell. While it might lead to a quick financial boost, if we lose customers because of a failed campaign, we'll lose in the long run. Starting small and gradually building them up is a smarter approach. I know that store. I'd suggest beginning with a billboard, and once that proves successful, adding radio spots and some local TV ads. Wait... you're dating one of the sons of Rings and Sons?"

"We just went out a few times. I think he's the only son. Or, at least the only son who works there," I answered.

"Tall. Brown hair and a bit of stubble?" she asked.

"Yes. His name is Janus."

"Well, he'd look good on television for sure. Reel this one in, Saturn. You've got a really good potential catch for us."

"Thank you."

"We lost that farm account. Or, more accurately, he wants to wait a while before we get started. There are a lot of farms in the area and across the country. I'd like to start pursuing them more," she says.

"That would be big," I agreed, unsure of what else to say.

"It would," she agreed, but agreed more with herself. "Anything else?"

"No, I don't think so," I answered and then started to stand.

"Great. Go ask Karen if she needs help with her ice cream shop client. Most people don't even know there's one in town, so we need a catchy ad for that. It's due out in the newspaper starting the week after next. Go get that creative mind of yours flowing and see what you could come up with."

I left the office with a huge smile on my face. Not only am I close to landing my first client just a week after starting, but Gretchen also said I have a creative mind. I already loved that job and was sure that leaving Hohman for this was the best move I could have made.

Everyone here has their own office, or at least a small, private room that passes for an office. We have just what's needed to get the job done, and while personal effects are allowed, I don't see many in most of them, probably because of the space.

I go over to Karen's office workspace and knock a few times lightly. I wait outside for an invitation, then Karen finally calls out for whoever is outside to open the door.

"Oh, hi, Saturn," she said, looking up from her computer. She stands about an inch or so taller than I do, has long, straight red hair, and professional-looking glasses.

"Good morning. Gretchen said I should assist you a little with your ad. She mentioned it was for an ice cream shop in town?"

"Yes."

"I've been searching for one of those, but I couldn't find one," I said.

"That's the issue. It's been there for about a year, but it's not in the best location for an ice cream shop. We need to get a newspaper ad ready to go, and I've been stumped. Any ideas?"

"Well," I said as I took a seat across from her. "What is the name of the place?"

"Cheaper by the Frozen," Karen said with a straight face.

"Ikes," I responded. "Well, we can't change the name. Do you have pictures, a menu, anything like that?"

"Here are the specs," Karen said, and handed me some papers. I looked through them, trying my best to look like I knew what I was doing, but still remembered that I spent the last year and a half talking for ice cream cones, not actually creating the ads for them.

"It's a small ad, so we don't have much to work with," I said when I saw the specs on the job. "It needs to be striking to stand out."

"That it does," Karen said.

Karen's process is simple. We brainstorm a little, then chat a bit about whatever. She says that it restarts the creative process. If it works for her, then I'm fine with that.

I learned that she is a few years older than I am, has lived in the area her entire life, and earned her marketing degree from Purdue University, Lafayette. She's single, like me, and lives in a small apartment, like me. She isn't dating right now, but is in the market. I wanted to make an "advertise yourself more" joke, but I didn't think we were there yet.

Around 12:30, she suggested we take a break and go out to lunch. I ride with her to the same hot dog and gyros place that Janus took me to after church last Sunday. I had a Polish sausage with the works, and Karen ordered chicken strips, both served with fries and a soda.

"Have you been enjoying Oakfield so far?" she asked.

"Sure. I miss my family, of course, but it's all still been pretty good."

"Great," she said, then looked out the window. "It's a small town with not much to do. Yet, most who live here seem to like it."

"That's good to hear," I replied, unsure of what else to add.

"I understand you do voices," she asked.

"I do." Uh, oh. I could see where this was heading.

"And you could impersonate anybody?"

"Almost anybody. They have to be within my natural register, and I can't do all accents. Still, I spent the last year and a half doing that for the agency in Chicago, so I guess I could."

"Do me," she said with an anxious smile. Fine. I sipped my soda, massaged my throat a little, and looked her square in the eyes.

"This ice cream shop ad is one of my more difficult ones in recent months. I just can't seem to nail it," I said, even trying to mimic her mannerisms.

Karen laughs, removes her glasses, breathes onto them, and then wipes them with a napkin.

"That's what I sound like on a recording, alright," she said while still laughing.

"Thanks. Our voices are similar enough that it wasn't too hard."

"Still," she said, still chuckling a little as she put her glasses back on. "Got any plans for dessert?"

"Have a cookie here?" I asked.

"No. Let's go to the ice cream shop. Let's sample a few flavors, and if they charge us, we can just put it on the agency's tab," she explained.

"We can do that with ice cream?" I asked, hoping not to get into trouble.

"Sure. It's for an ongoing campaign. I mean, don't take advantage and order seven of their most expensive menu items, but asking for a couple of cones and maybe a banana split would be acceptable."

"Great," I said, smiling, then followed her out to her car to go to Cheaper by the Frozen.

Karen was right. Not only was the name not the best, but the location leaves something to be desired. It was nearer to the manufacturing section of the city, but being closer to where the shopping is would probably do them better. Karen and I went inside, introduced ourselves to the teen working the register, then she called the owner out.

"How are you doing, Khandi?" Karen asked.

"Great," Khandi said, then Karen introduced us.

We said hi, then Khandi gave us a quick tour of the shop. It was small and took only about five minutes, but it was informative. She then told Jinx, the girl running the register, to get us anything we wanted free of charge. I ordered a medium strawberry-kiwi shake, Karen wanted a rocky road ice cream cone, and we also shared a banana split. We enjoyed our treats at a table, watching as only a few other customers came in while we were there.

"What do you think?" Karen asked.

"She could surely use some advertising."

"Any ideas on how to go about that?"

I looked around a little, noticing more of the outside than the inside.

"Maybe find a way to show the location isn't as out of the way as it seems," I suggested.

"Interesting," Karen said, then scooped a liberal piece of banana and vanilla ice cream. "How would that go?"

"Well, I'm not sure now. Maybe we could think about it more and come up with something," I said, then scooped some ice cream with pineapple bits and chocolate sauce. "Wow, this is good. It was worth driving the extra mile for."

Karen was in the middle of eating a spoonful and nearly spat it out.

"That's it!" she declared.

"What?"

"Wow, this is good. 'It was worth driving the extra mile for!' That could be it!"

"You think?" I asked, not wanting to get too excited.

"Let's head back to the office and bang it out. See what else we can come up with, too."

We finished our desserts, then she drove us back, and we came up with a few rough ideas. Karen is pretty good at sketching with a number two pencil, and we had a few mockups finished by the end of the day.

"Let's mull this over during the weekend," Karen said as the clock ticked closer to five. "We can reconvene on Monday before presenting it to the rest of the staff."

I reminded her of my appointment with Janus, but mentioned that since he wouldn't arrive until ten, a nine-thirty presentation would suffice. We then said goodbye to each other and the other staff members as we passed them by and headed home.

I was tempted to stop by Cheaper by the Frozen on my way home for another treat, but I figured that one and a half in a day is more than enough if I want to keep the 140-pound figure that my driver's license lists. As it is, I'm really pushing the limits; there's no need to push them further.

I drove by there again just to see what billboards or other ads in the area might be showing. Ads often play off of one another, so I wanted to check if anything was trending nearby. There wasn't. There was an expired billboard for a sporting event that had already passed. That could be a good spot for Janus's advertisement. I made a mental note of that.

I'm back at my apartment just after 6:00 p.m. I first pet Muffin, who was sleeping in his cat bed, then put my purse down. I went to check what I could have for dinner, and settled on spaghetti with buttered white bread as a side.

After I ate and cleaned up the mess, I thought about what to do next. Janus and I didn't have plans for that night, and I didn't want to call him. I'd rather take things slow, especially since we had an all-day date planned for the next day, so I thought a call might be too much. If he called me, I'd talk to him all night if he wanted. Spoiler alert: he didn't call, text, or reach out in any way.

I don't watch much regular TV now, but I do enjoy watching movies on a streaming service occasionally or browsing YouTube. I check some streaming options, but nothing is catching my interest at the moment. Then I started browsing YouTube and found a two-hour video that features only classic ads from the 1970s. I turned it on and was amused by what they showed during that era. One of my favorites was for a mouthwash brand, where a young employee told his older boss that he had bad breath and needed to use the mouthwash, then slapped the bottle down on his desk.

What was also interesting about this was that every fifteen minutes or so, YouTube played an ad from today. Comparing then and now was fascinating, and I was hoping for a mouthwash ad from 2025 to show. It didn't. A classic ad for a national ice cream chain was shown. It was interesting, but I'm sure we'll be sticking with the "worth driving the extra mile for" concept. Or, maybe Karen will think of something better over the weekend. Either way, we won't be copying the one shown on YouTube.

I started working on the bell tower project for a while, switching between looking at craft sticks, glue, and the television. An ad aired for Lincoln Logs, a child's building toy that might be as interesting as craft sticks, and I noticed it.

After two hours and however many minutes, the video came to an end. I sat there thinking about it, and again realized the power of advertisement. Most of those ads and their jingles were still running through my head, and I really wanted to go to my bathroom and "plop plop fizz fizz" despite my not having indigestion at the moment.

Just after ten, I realized the time. I went to brush my teeth and do other bedtime preparations in the bathroom. I came back out, turned off the television, then knelt beside my couch, folded my hands, and prayed my nightly prayers. I lay back on the couch, said one more quick prayer, and closed my eyes.

Muffin jumped onto my stomach, and I drifted off to sleep with him purring, rolled up on my belly. "Life is good," was my final thought before being taken into dreamland.

Chapter 3

Weekend Wonders

I'm back to the present again, and I see from the window that Janus has just pulled into the apartment building's parking lot. He drives a relatively new red Chevrolet pickup truck of some sort. It's the traditional kind, with one bench seat and two doors, not one with a back seat and four doors. I give Muffin a quick scratch on his head, put the cap on my craft sticks bin, grab my purse, and go out to greet him.

I run up to his truck as he's getting out. He greets me with a simple "Hi," but doesn't kiss me hello. I suppose we're not quite there yet. He then reaches into his truck and presents me with a bouquet of flowers. Not roses, and I'm relieved about that. These were six carnations. Pretty pink carnations.

"I was driving past a flower shop, thought about you, and brought you these just because. I hope you like them," Janus says as he hands them to me.

"They're beautiful," I say as I take them, then give them a big sniff. I think about it for a moment, then figure it would be okay to invite him into my apartment for a little while before we leave. "Come on in with me so I can put them in some water."

I grab his hand and lead him into the building, down the stairs. I open the door and invite him inside.

"I'll only be a moment," I say as I close the door, and he sits. "Oh, this is Muffin. He likes to be petted. Have a seat if you like."

"Thanks. You look nice today, by the way," Janus says as he pets the cat's head.

"Oh, puh-lease," I say. My hair is in a tight ponytail, I'm wearing long, loose denim shorts, and a red T-shirt with some white stars that must be three years old by now. I'm almost embarrassed by how I look now that he mentioned it.

I run to the kitchen and try to find a vase. Realizing I had none, I took a pitcher from a cabinet to fill with water. I sniff the flowers again and feel a little emotion coming onto me. I set the flowers down, excuse myself, and run into the bathroom.

I close the door behind me and look at myself in a mirror. I see a single tear falling from my eye, and I use some toilet paper to wipe it away. I'm not wearing any makeup, so I don't have to worry about mascara running down my cheek. I'm not sure why I got so emotional. Guys have given me presents before. I suppose they were always a regular gift, like a birthday or Christmas. I think this is the first time a boyfriend gave me something like this just because I pull myself together and rejoin Janus, reminding myself that he's not actually my boyfriend.

"Thank you for these, they're beautiful," I say as I fill the container with water and admire the flowers.

"I'm glad you like them," he says back with a smile as he scratches Muffin's chin.

"I'll place them here on the table and pull the chairs back so Muffin can't climb and knock them over. They are definitely going to brighten up this dull place."

"It looks nice, your apartment," Janus says as he looks around. "I like how the furniture looks in here."

"You would," I say with a chuckle and walk over to him.

"Well, are you ready?" he asks.

"Not quite. I have to thank you for the gift first."

Before he could say anything, I pulled him down and gave him a quick, one-second kiss on his lips. He smiles at me. I think he wants to kiss again, but instead asks if I am ready to go again.

"I am," I answer as I pick my purse back up.

We decided to go hiking again. Instead of visiting the forest preserve we went to last Sunday, he took me to a slightly larger one, just a county over. It didn't take very long to get there, maybe about half an hour, and we didn't talk much on the way. He also didn't have the radio on, so we enjoyed the ride while I admired all the billboards along the way.

We get there, and there are just a few other vehicles in the lot. He says that the walk is a little bit longer and slightly more treacherous than the last. He says he was going to use the porta-potty first, and suggests I do the same. I really don't have to "go," but I try, anyway, just in case.

Janus stretches before we begin our walk, and I laugh a little as he does. He just smiles back and then says he'll lead the way as we start our trek.

He was right. These trails are a bit more challenging than I'm used to. I typically walk trails with slight hills and dips, but here, while I wouldn't go as far as calling them extreme, they are not too far from that.

We walk for about half an hour, much of it uphill, with my legs starting to feel the burn. We approach a sharp right turn, and Janus tells me we're almost there.

"Where?" I ask.

"You'll see," he says, smiling.

We finally arrive at the spot he was leading us to, and it is stunning. There is a low, wooden rail fence to keep hikers safe, as before us is one of the most beautiful sights I've ever seen. We are high above a prairie, looking down at the mostly grassy landscape below, with rows of pine trees in the distance. Any pain in my legs and body quickly disappeared as I breathed in the fresh air and gazed into the distance.

"I just love coming here," Janus says as he takes my hand in his. I'm actually wanting to put one arm around his back, one in front, and wrap him in a side hug as we look, but I'm having to keep reminding myself that we're not in a relationship, so I hold my urges back. We say nothing as we stand there for five minutes, admiring God's handiwork before us.

Janus finally takes my hand and begins to lead me further down the trail as we talk more about how beautiful this place is. It's easier now that we're mostly going downhill, and we reach his truck way too soon in my opinion.

"I'd love to come back again," I say as he opens my door for me.

"There are others around, too," Janus replies. I'm not sure if that was his intention to take me to all of them eventually, and I didn't want to ask.

"I hope to see them all someday." There, that was vague enough but still showed intent, I think.

Janus asked if I wanted to go out to dinner, and I said that it seemed a little early.

"I'll just have to drive slow and take the long way," he says.

"You do that," I say, smiling at him.

This time we talked a lot. I learned he also has a sister who is two years older than him, is married, and lives in Indianapolis. He said that when his dad opened the shop, he was expecting many sons, which is why the name includes 'Sons' instead of 'Son.'

I told him about Venus. How we were constantly at odds with each other growing up, and now it's like we're the best of friends. He asked me some questions about the farm, but I honestly couldn't answer most of them.

When we get back to Oakfield, he asks where I'd like to go for dinner. I told him that Here and There Pizza will do, but this time, he gets to pick the toppings. He must not be thinking like me, because he ordered one with pepperoni, onions, and peppers. We talk more through dinner, then he asks about dessert. I tell him I know a place.

I direct him to Cheaper by the Frozen, and while I so badly want to order one shake with two straws, I opt for a root beer float, and he orders the same. *Close enough,* I think.

I told him about the ad campaign and talked just a little about his upcoming meeting, but didn't want to get too deep into it. We finish our treats, and after he asks what we should do next, I suggest he bring me home. I really have been enjoying our day, but it's going on 8:00 p.m., and I feel we've already spent enough time together today.

He takes me back to my apartment and walks me to the door. I don't want to invite him inside since it's now technically nighttime, and I request we say goodnight where we are. He says he had a nice day and asks if I am coming to church tomorrow.

"I am. I really liked visiting last time," I answer.

"Wonderful. Please don't feel you have to sit by me. Well, I'll see you tomorrow, I guess."

"Were we going to do anything after the service?" I ask.

"How about we play that by ear?" he asks, and I nod and smile.

He starts to lean down a little, being careful not to move too fast. I ease him a little and wrap my arms around him and pull him down. I won't say it was the most passionate kiss I've ever given or had, but this time I definitely tasted the onions and peppers he ate earlier. We part, and he smiles at me, then goes back to his truck.

I go inside and immediately change for bed. I don't lie down just yet. I pet Muffin a little, then open my craft sticks bin to work on the bell tower some more. I keep the TV off as well as any music. I want to work in silence as I think about Janus and our day together. Is he the one, or just another passing fad? I don't want to think about that now. I just want to think about our walk, what we talked about, the flowers, and especially that kiss at the end.

When the time came, I brushed my teeth and prepared myself for bed. I give Muffin a few more pets and enjoy the purrs coming from him. I take a carnation from the pitcher, and after I say my prayers, I lie back with the flower in my hand, hoping the smell will sweeten my dreams tonight.

At 8:00 a.m., my alarm clock rings. You know, the kind with the hammer and two bells on top. I feel like throwing it across the room, but as I sat up to turn it off, the carnation fell from my chest onto my lap. I stop the ringing, then pick up the flower. I sniff it deeply, and I get reminded of yesterday. Well, the smell and my sore legs do.

I get up and put the flower in the pitcher with the other five. I take a very long, very hot shower and enjoy every second of it. After I towel off, I put the raggedy shorts back on that I wore to bed last night, wondering why I didn't bring my church clothes in with me. I also wonder why I don't walk to my bedroom wearing just my underwear, or nothing at all. I know I'm alone in here, but that's still something I can't bring myself to do.

While my bed is the sofa in the front room, I still use the closet in the bedroom for its intended purpose. I slide a few hangers and come across this nice, knee-length blue dress to wear to church. I put that on, along with white pumps. I comb my hair, parting it over my left brown eye and letting it hang down freely.

I look at myself in the mirror for a moment. Venus used to say I was the ugly sister and called me sloppy seconds. She apologized to me for that at her wedding, saying she was jealous of me and never considered me either of those. While I may not be "sloppy seconds" or "the ugly sister," I still believe my looks are average at best and wonder why someone like Janus wants anything to do with me. I push those thoughts out of my mind and pour some Cheerios for breakfast to go along with my coffee.

I arrive at Oakfield Second Christian Church about twenty minutes before the service begins. Janus is already there, and when he sees me, he excuses himself from the person he's talking to and comes over.

"Good morning, Saturn," he says. I silently prayed he wouldn't kiss me here and now.

"Good morning, Janus. I'm looking forward to church again," I say, sounding like a total dork.

"Me too. I always feel inspired at the end."

"Good morning," a man wearing Docker slacks and a white buttoned-up shirt with the top button undone asks as he walks toward us. "It's nice to see you again. Saturn O Syres is your name, correct? That's an interesting name."

"Thank you, Pastor Chalke. O is my full, given middle name. It's not short for anything."

"Interesting," the pastor says. "We didn't get much of a chance to chat last week. How do you two know each other?"

"Umm…" I start to say when Janus saves me.

"She's new in town, and we met when she bought some furniture from the store. We dated a couple of times, and we're just seeing where it's leading."

"Well, I'm glad to hear that," Steven Chalke says. "Just go the way God leads, and you'll get to where you belong in His timing."

"Thank you. I believe God brought me to Oakfield to work my dream job."

"What is that, may I ask?" the pastor asks.

"Advertising, specializing in billboards."

"Interesting," Pastor Chalke says with a smile.

"Whether or not Janus will be a part of my future, God hasn't revealed yet."

"Well, again, when it comes to that, trust His timing. It was very nice to see you again, Saturn. I'd like to talk to you more, but I have to get to work now."

Pastor Chalke walks away, leaving me feeling a bit uncomfortable next to Janus. He smiles at me, obviously thinking the same thing.

"Just so you know, Saturn, I'm not assuming anything between us. I'm not sure if we have a future together."

"I am," I smiled.

"You are?"

"Sure. Our future says we'll be sitting by each other during church. The timing is right, so let's go."

I hope my attempt at humor eased him a little, just as it did me, if only a little. We take bulletins and sit halfway back down in the left row of pews. We sit close to each other but not too close. We sing hymns, and his voice sounds nice. Not Ed Sheeran nice, but nice either way. After the service, we find ourselves back in the community room enjoying cookies and coffee.

We are chatting amongst ourselves, with Janus telling me more about the church and some of their outreach projects. *He'd do pretty well in advertising,* I was thinking, when a lady, about our age and quite attractive, came over to us.

"Good morning, Janus," she says, sounding very sunny.

"Oh, hi. Good morning," Janus says with a rather big smile. "I'd like you to meet Saturn Syres. She's new in town and is considering going to new churches. Saturn, this is Sunny Knight. She's another deacon, on the hospitality committee. She made that coffee you're drinking."

Her name is Sunny Knight? Drat! Janus also introduced me as someone new in town, not even a friend or anything close to that. Double drat! Well, I'd better be hospitable in return.

"Hi, good morning, Sunny," I say, offering my hand to shake. She does.

"Good morning, Saturn. Did you enjoy the service?"

"Very much, Sunny." I almost want to spit out 'Sunny,' but I hold back. "I hope to be a regular here."

"Well, we'd welcome that very much," she says, half-smiling at me, then turns to Janus and offers a full smile. "Do you have plans for lunch?"

"Well…" Janus begins to say, then looks at me.

"Because a few deacons were planning on going out to lunch to talk about the upcoming Independence Day Music, Food, and Crafts Fair," Sunny says. "We were going to discuss how to advertise our booth and try to come up with some ideas."

"It's just an informal meeting, right?" Janus asks.

"Yes."

"Well…" Janus stalls a little as he looks at me. I nod to answer his silent question. "Saturn should come with us. She's…"

"We'll be discussing advertising. You may get bored," Sunny says right at me.

"I promise I won't," I answer, trying to hold back my chuckle.

"Well, it's informal, so I guess that's okay. We're meeting at Second Street Wok at noon. I'll see you there." Sunny touches Janus's hand and walks away without saying anything more to me.

"Why didn't you tell her?" I ask.

"It'll be more fun if we don't. Not yet. We have time. Want to drive back to your apartment to drop off your car, then we can head to the restaurant together in my truck? The parking lot there is a little tight."

We do as Janus suggests, and while I'm home, I quickly change into loose-fitting jeans and my green "Craft Life" T-shirt. We arrive at the restaurant just before noon, and the rest of the committee is already there, sitting at a table for six. Sunny says that she saved a spot for Janus next to her, and I sit on his other side. Janus soon makes introductions.

"You already met Sunny. This is Tanner Bloom, and Gina Byrd is sitting next to you. We make up most of the deacons. Everybody, this is Saturn O Syres. She's from Northwest Indiana and just moved here about a month ago."

I greet everyone with a smile, and we order before discussing business. I got the chop suey, and Janus ordered Mongolian beef. There was general chit-chat happening while we waited for our lunch to be served, mostly talking about the service and Tanner's butcher shop.

Once the food came, Janus led us all in saying grace, then Sunny took over the meeting.

"We want to talk about how to advertise the upcoming fair in Oakfield Park this July Fourth. We have enough in the budget to take out a full-page ad in the newspaper, and I think that's the best way to go."

"Won't that eat up most of our budget?" Janus asks, and she lays her hand on his for a moment.

"It makes the most sense," she says, then eats a piece of noodle. "We need to get the word out there."

"I see," Gina says.

"Are there any questions?" Sunny asks. I hesitate, then look to Janus, who nods back at me.

"I have a suggestion…"

"This is a committee meeting, so outsiders can't speak," she snaps.

"This is informal. I really think we should listen to what she has to say," Janus says, and smiles at me while he uses chopsticks to eat a piece of beef.

"Go ahead," Tanner says, sounding a little disinterested.

"Well," I start, feeling a little nervous. "I wouldn't go with a full-page ad, especially if that's most of your budget. Most people, when they see that the page is only an ad, ignore it. It may not be prudent for you to do that."

"Well, what do you suggest then?" Sunny asks, then looks at Janus with bright eyes.

"Well, the city and other bigger businesses are already advertising this event, some taking out ads in the newspaper already, and others are putting flyers in storefronts. If you add to that, you'd just be spinning your wheels. You could simply allow them to advertise the event, and when people come, they will see your booth."

"Fine," Sunny says with a bit of attitude as she forks some rice. "But what would you suggest we do?"

"What do you do there? What happens at your booth?" I ask, and Janus answers.

"We have a couple of tables under a canopy. We have information about the church and upcoming events. We pass out candy to any kids who want some, and talk to anybody who wants to talk to us."

"That's about it," Gina agrees.

"Is that enough?" Sunny asks, glaring at me.

"No, it's not," I say, then all eyes are on me. "The candy and information are good, but you want to show the community that you are there for them. That you're not all talk, but also action."

"And what do you suggest?" Sunny asks with more attitude in her voice.

"May I ask what the budget for this is, please?"

"Should we tell her?" Sunny asks.

"Five hundred dollars," Janus answers, ignoring her.

"Well, first. I wouldn't just give the kids candy. I'd set up some easy games for them to play and win. Bozo buckets, picking up a rubber duck, and the number on its bottom is how many pieces of candy they would get, or even spinning the wheel would work. They're fun, and a guaranteed winner every time."

"Interesting," Gina says, and looks to Tanner for approval.

"You'd also want to consider offering a service right there for adults," I continue.

"Like what?" Sunny asks.

"How often does your church go out in public like this?"

"Five or six times a year, maybe," Gina answers.

"Great. Here's one thing that comes to mind," I say, and everyone looks at me curiously, except for Sunny. "Go to an outdoor store and buy a fully-enclosed tent, maybe ten by ten feet. Then go to a big box store or similar place and get plenty of supplies for changing a baby—diapers of all sizes, wipes, and anything else needed. I've never done that before, so I don't know exactly what it all involves."

"You never changed a diaper before?" Sunny asks. "Then how would you know about this?"

"I know that diapers are expensive, and most parents like a little privacy when changing their baby. You could provide it for them, free of charge."

"And what if nobody uses it?" Sunny asks.

"Most won't. Some may, but then nobody may. That doesn't matter so much."

"Why not?" Janus asks, fully invested in this now.

"First, the diapers and tent won't spoil, so you can bring them to each event. Wipes will expire, so you might want to find something to do with them before that happens. Replacing them would cost far less than the $500 budget you have for this event. The goal of this is not only to provide a place for baby changing and nursing to happen…"

"You want to offer breastfeeding now, too?" Sunny asks, still with a bit of attitude in her voice.

"Yes, but call it 'Nursing' on the sign, not breastfeeding. It's less controversial," I answer, and the men look a little uncomfortable over my wording, proving my point. "The point is, people will see it, even those without children, or older ones, who will have no use for it but see it to be a good idea, anyway. You'd be advertising to the community that you're more than Sunday morning worship. You care about the community and do what you can to provide for them."

"Do we charge for the service?" Gina asks.

"Of course not. It's within your budget, so it's no real loss to you. Sometimes, offering free, essential services will earn you more and serve as better advertising than charging and trying to turn a profit."

"I think it's a great idea," Tanner says as he finishes his dish.

"Me too," Gina agrees.

"Wait, wait, just wait," Sunny says, almost yelling. "Why are we listening to her? What does she even know about advertising?"

I look at Janus, he looks at me, and we silently discuss who should speak up. He nods that he will.

"Saturn has a degree in marketing from Ball State University and has worked in advertising for the past two years. Not only that, but she studied it since she was a young teenager. She moved here to work at All-Ways Advertising."

"That's how I know about the other businesses advertising for this. I also have a minor in psychology," I add.

"Well, how do we know she's any good?" Sunny asks.

"Have you ever seen the ad for Kitty Kitchen cat food? The one with the cat family discussing dinner options?"

"Yes," Sunny answers.

"That's my voice you hear."

"Which cat?" Gina asks.

"All of them. I also do voices," I then say some lines from the commercial using the characters' voices. Janus, Gina, and Tanner are all amused, while Sunny is less so.

"Anyway," she says. "That doesn't mean we have to do as she says."

"Sunny is right," Janus says, then looks at me. "We don't have to listen to her. However, we have a called meeting next week, and I plan to put it to the committee for approval. As you said, Sunny, this lunch is informal, so we won't be voting here."

"Well, this was fun," Tanner says as he stands. "It was nice meeting you, Saturn, and we hope to see you back next week."

Tanner and Gina leave and pay their bills on the way out. Sunny, Janus, and I stay for a bit, and it feels a little awkward. Sunny and Janus talk a little, ignoring me, looking almost lost in each other's gaze.

Janus eventually stands, and Sunny and I follow his lead. He leaves a rather generous tip on the table for everybody, then we leave, with everybody paying for their own meals. I don't mind, as it wasn't an actual date and Janus need not pay for me every time.

We go to the parking lot, and after Sunny says 'bye' to me, she turns to Janus. They say goodbye, then she wraps her arms around him in a big hug, and he hugs her back, not quite as tightly.

They separate, and as Janus drives me home, I don't say anything about that. We're not exclusive, so he can date or hug whoever he wants. I think. He asks about another date, and I just remind him about his meeting at the agency tomorrow. He leaves me with barely a peck on the lips, and I spend the rest of the day in my apartment, alternating between petting Muffin and working on the craft stick bell tower, all while wondering if there is something between Janus and Sunny.

Chapter 4

Mondays and More

Before going to bed last night, I had a nice chat with my sister, Venus, through a Zoom call. We discussed what to expect now that she's expecting and is due next January. We also talked about my career and Janus. She's still a little critical of me taking a job in a smaller city, even though it was she who urged me to find a new job, and she lives in a farm town with a population of just 68,000. Still, she wouldn't be Venus if she didn't act like that sometimes. I told her how I was helping the church advertise the event, and she advised that I speak with my boss about doing work outside of work hours, since they may frown upon that. She's a business major, so I took her advice seriously.

During the morning meetings, Karen and I present our idea about the "It's worth driving the extra mile for" ad for Cheaper by the Frozen. Everyone seems to like that concept, and Gretchen

Gilmore, the owner and office manager, tells us to go ahead with it.

"Whose idea was it?" she asks us.

"We came up with it together," I reply before Karen tries to give me credit for it. I'm not sure if she would have, but the way I see it, we're a team on this project, and that's how teams should work.

We hear what others are working on, and I remind them that Janus from Rings and Sons Restoration and Resale Shop is coming in this morning about a potential new campaign. I wondered whether I should disclose our relationship at this point, but the problem is I don't know what our relationship is right now, so I keep it to myself. As we were wrapping up to start our day and week, I asked Gretchen if she could stay behind.

Following Venus's advice, I tell her about the meeting with the church yesterday. She told me that it was fine, and since they're a church, if they need a little more, they can come in, and we can help and write it off as a charitable deduction.

"Just be careful not to give out too much free advertising advice," she tells me. "This is still a business, and we don't make money working for free."

I tell her that I'll just keep it at the church, and she smiles before telling me to get ready for my appointment with Janus.

"Oh," she says as I start to open the door. "Don't offer any discounts because of your relationship with him."

"I won't," I assure her before heading to my office.

I straighten a thing or two and make sure I look good. Or, at least as good as I can look. I'm wearing a slightly nicer skirt and blouse than I'd normally wear to work, and I hope nobody will notice I'm showing a little more leg than usual. At ten on the dot, Gretchen's assistant and office receptionist, Frida Small, calls me on the office speakerphone to tell me that Mr. Rings is here to see me. I tell her to have him come inside.

He opens the door, and when I see him, I'm surprised to see him in a suit and tie. He looks so, SO handsome, but I have to stay professional about this.

"Please, have a seat," I say, indicating the chair in front of my desk.

We discuss his store and advertising needs. When I asked him approximately how much his gross annual revenue is, he hesitated to tell me. I assure him it's for professional purposes, not personal, and he then tells me.

"Great. Most businesses of your size spend around 8.7% of their revenues on advertising, so we have some flexibility. Of course, you could spend more or less; that's just the average. If you don't believe me, feel free to do your own research."

"No, I believe you, Miss Syres," he answers.

I'm not sure how to respond to that since I'm being addressed so formally. I decide to face it head-on.

"Most clients call me Saturn."

"Okay, Saturn," he says, smiling a little.

"Here's what I suggest. This office feels pretty stuffy, and I think we both need a break. Let's head to your place of business now, and that will give me a better sense of what you do there so I can create better ads for you," I tell him.

"What? I don't want to get you in trouble by doing that," he says, genuinely concerned.

"No, it's okay. It's not only part of our service, but it's also recommended. Is it okay with you if we go now?"

Janus agrees, and I tell Frida that I'll be out of the office for a while, as I do a client visit. We take Janus's pickup truck, which has a couple of worn-out reclining chairs in the bed.

"I saw them in the alley on the way over. I just had to get them. They will fix up nicely," he says.

"Interesting," I say, and jot down some notes about that on my clipboard.

We chat a little on the way, and I avoid bringing up Sunny and her relationship with him. When we arrive at the resale shop and walk in, he reintroduces me to his dad, Jesse.

"I saw you at church yesterday. I'm sorry I wasn't able to come and say 'Hi,'" he says.

"That's okay. It's nice to see you again."

Janus leads me back to his workspace. It's a fairly large room, probably about half the size of my apartment. I was expecting it to be a bit messy, but I was surprised to find it clean, organized, and with every tool in its place.

"Does it always look like this, or did you clean it for my benefit?" I ask.

"You can't work in a messy area," he answers. "I worked hard at getting it like this. If I use a tool, I put it away right away, even if I know I'll use it again in a few minutes."

Oh my gosh. That's exactly what my mom says a kitchen should be like.

"Well, mostly. The tools I use all the time, like screwdrivers and certain wrenches, stay on this table near my workspace, and I put them away at the end of the day. I mean, there's neat, and then there's obsessive."

"I agree." I laugh a little, seeing how he's now more like me when it comes to that sort of thing.

He shows me some items in the store that don't need restoration, such as gold clubs, dishware, paintings, and similar things.

"We just clean these up and sell them as-is. However, the heart and soul, not to mention the biggest profits, come from the furniture sales. You paid for three truck payments for me when you bought your furniture."

"Funny," I say as I look around more. "Can your dad take a few minutes' break so we can discuss your advertising needs?"

Jesse doesn't want to leave the floor, so we sit and talk right there at a table Janus just finished. It's very nice.

For now, they decide to stick with the single billboard concept, and that's fine. That's what I do. I tell them that we'll develop a few concepts and present them when they're ready.

"You won't want anything too cluttered on the billboard," I tell them. "Your name, address, phone number, slogan, and photo of one of your nicer pieces should do well. Maybe even this table we're sitting at."

"We don't have a slogan," Jesse says, then looks at Janus. "Do we?"

"I don't think so."

"We'll also come up with slogan ideas. That will be free of charge. You can choose one of ours or create your own. If you don't mind, I'd like to take some pictures to bring back to the office. Nobody but representatives from All-Ways Advertising will see them, and we won't publish anything without your approval. Are we good?"

They agree, and then I take some photos and have them sign general contracts for their billboard.

Janus drives me back to the office after I decline his offer to go out to lunch with him. I wasn't sure that a date while working would be proper; besides, I wanted to get this campaign started right away.

I left work at the usual 5:00 p.m. after spending most of the afternoon working on the Rings and Sons campaign, and Karen and I discussed the ice cream shop ads further.

At home, I make spaghetti for dinner and eat it while watching a little TV. I only pay half attention to the antics of the dysfunctional family during their latest crisis, just to see everything return to normal before the show ends. I watch another with a similar theme, then a workplace comedy comes on that follows the same formula, but it uses coworkers instead of family members.

Of course, I pay attention to the ads, which I still often find more interesting than the show itself. The later the shows air, the more "adult" they seem to become. The first show featured ads for toys and fruity-tasting breakfast cereals, while the last had ads for cars and laundry detergent. Man, I just love this business!

I worked more on the bell tower project during the last show. After I brush my teeth and get ready for bed, I say a longer-than-usual nighttime prayer asking God for guidance regarding Janus, both in our personal and professional relationship, and other more personal matters.

The next day at work, Karen and I were finalizing ideas for the ice cream shop. It's a small ad, focusing on the remote location and emphasizing that it's worth the extra drive because they use higher-quality ingredients. It will feature a banana split topped with all the fixings and include the slogan, "It's worth driving the extra mile for."

When we're finished, I go back to my office and review Janus's project more. I have it all set, for the most part, except for the picture. It needs a good picture. I look at the ad, think of Janus, and call him.

"Hi, Saturn," he says.

"Hi, Janus. I'm working on your ad now."

"How's it going?" he asks.

"Pretty good. Karen and I make a good team, it seems," I say.

"That sounds good."

"Janus," I say, sounding a little distant.

"Yes?" he asks.

"I didn't call to talk about your ad. Not only, anyway," I confess.

"Then why?"

"Well," I say, feeling a little guilty now. "I don't want to smother you or anything, but can we go out tonight? To dinner? Nothing fancy. That Asian restaurant would do fine."

"Sure. I'd really like that. Should I pick you up at six?"

"I'll be waiting," I say, then hang up.

I go home and change, and my date is there just in time. I meet him again in the apartment parking lot, and this time, he comes empty-handed. He greets me with a smile, but not a kiss. I so want to kiss him, but I restrain myself.

We arrive at Second Street Wok and sit at a table near the windows, offering a view of passing traffic. I order the pepper steak while Janus gets Kung Pao chicken and 'Chinese buffet' green beans as a side for us to share. I thank him for the thought and plan to stay quiet, letting him take the lead in the conversation.

I update him on ad concepts, but we decide not to discuss that too much. He tells me a little more about his store, or more specifically, some of the customers who came in today. I chuckle as he shares their antics with me, and assume this wasn't meant to be put into any ads.

The waitress soon brings us our dinners, and once she leaves, Janus says grace for us. He does most of the talking while I mostly watch him, trying to give him my best "I'm here for you" look. I'm not sure he catches that, but he decides to break some tension, anyway.

"Let's have a chopsticks race. The first to eat ten green beans wins. Want to?" he asks with the enthusiasm of a ten-year-old.

"Sure, just one thing," I say, then call the waitress over. I ask her for another pair of chopsticks, and after giving me a "Why?" look, she does.

I unwrap the extra pair while Janus watches me like I'm a weirdo. I hold one in each hand and tell Janus I'm ready when he is. He counts down, and the race starts.

Using both pairs, one in each hand, to pick up the beans, I chew and swallow ten before Janus even gets his third to his mouth. He looks at me, stunned and amazed.

"I'm a craft stick artist, remember? I use both hands equally while crafting, and even when I'm bored, I use them for other things – like chopsticks. Don't be surprised. I mean, I'm sure you can use a screwdriver with either hand just as well."

"You're right," he smiles. "I just didn't expect that, not to mention how fast you ate."

"Well, I've been eating longer than I've been crafting," I joke, and he laughs at that.

"Speaking of crafting, did you want to help with the church's booth at the fair?" he asks.

"Honestly, I do want to, but I think I'm going to register my own booth and see how Saturn Sticks do here," I answer.

I'm sure very well. Your work is amazing and unique," he says. "Thanks for the help the other day, by the way. Are you available to talk with the whole committee this Sunday after church? I mean, assuming you're going to be there and don't mind, and... and..."

"I'd love to," I say, easing his nerves. "Are we going out afterward?"

"I'd like that," he says.

We finish our meals talking more about our lives and learning just who each other is. He drives me back to my apartment building, and I'm more comfortable inviting him inside, though I was in full cautious mode.

I make some microwave popcorn and make a point to smile at him as I stand by the flowers he gave me. Then he asks me to show him how to do craft sticks. We sit on opposite ends of the couch while I guide him on how to make a basic box, like Mom showed me all those years ago. It was good, better than I expected, but then again, he does stuff like this for a living.

While we were doing it, I kept thinking I'd rather be making out with him on the couch instead of crafting, but I held myself back, though I did steal a kiss or two along the way.

Around 8:45, I asked him to leave. I walked him out to his truck, then turned to face him as he was reaching for his keys.

"I really enjoy our time together," I say.

"Me, too," he answers. "Well, goodnight."

Janus leans down to kiss me, and when he tries to break it after two seconds, I pull him back in. Again, it wasn't as passionate as a kiss I could give, but I was trying to show him I'd like him to call me more often. I give him a bit of a squeeze before we let go. He smiles at me, then drives off to wherever it is he lives.

"Maybe I'll find out someday," I say to myself as he fades into the distance.

Chapter 5

Working for the Weekend

Wednesday at work is what I have found in my few weeks here to be a rather typical day. I meet with clients, some new and some ongoing, discussing their billboards, whether it's new designs or an analysis of how the campaign is going. Karen and I seem to have a good rapport with each other and have become somewhat of an unofficial team.

While we are discussing the ad for Janus's account, John Brady, the man who usually handles radio ads, knocks gently on my open door to get our attention.

"Excuse me, ladies. I hope I'm not interrupting," he says.

"We could use a break from restoration. What's up?" I ask.

"Well," John starts, then scratches the back of his head, looking visibly uncomfortable. "I'm working on a radio spot for Main Street Music. He wants the voiceover to sound like a conductor, but not a stereotypical conductor. I'm stumped. Do you think…?

"Do you have a copy with you?" I ask. He sorts through his files and hands me one. I look at it while Karen is peeking over my shoulder.

"I think when most people think of a conductor, they think of a European person. With that in mind, you should avoid that sort of accent. Maybe even consider using a female voice for this. This script looks rather straightforward, so that simplifies things. I'd say go with demos of a female who sounds like she's around 18, one in her 30s, and a senior citizen. Record them, and let the client choose."

"Interesting," John says as he looks at his copy of the script.

"You'll probably want a middle-aged man in the mix as well," I say, then massage my throat some.

I take a deep breath and read a line from the script in each of the voices I suggested. John and

Karen are both amused, even giving me a spattering of applause when I am done. I wish they wouldn't do that, but then again, it is nice.

John looks at me uncomfortably again and says, "Do you think…"

"I'd be happy to do the demos for you, John. Can we shoot for after lunch? Is the recording studio open then?"

"Yes, and thank you, Saturn. I'm hoping for the teen voice, as it's more amusing, but as you know, it's up to the client. Oh, one more thing…"

"Yes," I say, cutting him off. "I'll be happy to voice the ad for you, as well, if that's what the client wants. I'll see you in the studio a little after one. Karen and I really need to discuss our project now."

John leaves, and Karen and I do what we said we would. We go to Harry's Hamburgers and Hot Dogs for lunch and talk about everything except work. When we get back, I spend the rest of the afternoon in the studio, recording voices, helping to rewrite the script, and assisting with voices for a few other ads. I know this won't turn into a full-time position here as it did in Chicago, so I'm going to go with it, especially since I might need a favor from John someday.

After work, I head on over to Andrea's Arts and Crafts to speak with the owner, Andrea Collins, about teaching craft stick art there. When I get in, she's with another customer, so I nod a greeting her way, then go back to the "Kids section" and see if she restocked those little beauties. She did.

After she checks out the customer, she comes back over to me. We shake hands, then start discussing plans.

We decided to hold classes there on Thursdays from 6:00 to 7:00 p.m. It will be for all ages, all paying the same price. Students will have to buy their own supplies, whether from Andrea's or another place, and we agree to a 60-40 split in my favor. Pre-registration won't be required, but will be recommended.

"How do you think we should advertise this?" she asks.

"Well," I say, trying to be careful. "The best way is direct. Make a flyer on normal typing paper with what it is, the store's name, address, phone number, etc. In big letters at the top, say what it is you're advertising, and maybe put a picture of supplies needed so people understand what it is. While it's for all ages, I'm certain that most students will be elementary-age kids, so market to them. Hang copies here, of course, and see about other places that kids frequent. Oh, and before you start hanging in the park, check on local statutes about doing that sort of thing. Some cities don't allow that. Be careful not to oversaturate, either. For example, don't hang twenty copies here. One on the door, one by the register, and one by the craft sticks should do well."

"Can't your agency do this for us?" she asks.

"We could, sure, but we'd have to charge you normal rates. For now, though, if you do as I said, we should hit our target audience. From there, one of the most effective advertisements is word of mouth. Just don't tell anybody I said that." We both laugh, and after she gives me a couple of packages of craft sticks for the help, I go home.

On the way home, I wonder if I'd get in trouble for that at work. Then again, I'm sure that the agency could absorb the $6 in craft sticks payment I just received. If not, they could take it out of my check.

I spend the rest of the evening alone, eating oven-heated chicken nuggets and fries, and starting a new craft stick project I hope to sell at the upcoming craft fair.

I get up the next morning to find Muffin sleeping on me. I give him a few pets before I sit up, rub my sore neck, rise, and do my usual morning rituals. I make it to the office a little later than usual, but still in time for the morning briefings.

I show the concepts for Janus's store, and everybody likes all three. I was advised to bring them to the client and allow them to select one that they like best.

I call Janus and tell him. He says that any time I could make it today is fine with him. I look at my other projects and decide to close this one out first.

I pull up to the resale store around 10:30 and park in the back to leave the lot spots open for customers. I go inside with my briefcase and see Jesse Rings behind the register, looking over a newspaper. He greets me with a smile, then shouts over his shoulder for Janus to come out from the shop area. He looks handsome in his tight T-shirt and safety goggles. I smile at his look, then he removes the glasses, looking a little embarrassed.

"I have your ads ready," I say, and put the briefcase down on the same table we talked at the other day.

Jesse calls his wife, Angela, over, and after introductions, I show them the ads, and they look over them carefully. All three are close to the same thing, but each has a different slogan. After discussing it among themselves, they chose the one featuring the table and chairs that we are sitting at, with the slogan "Factory quality, thrift store prices." It even has the six-month guarantee written in a smaller yet still legible font.

"And this is still the same price you quoted?" Janus asks. "There are no hidden fees or any extras?"

"It is exactly as I quoted," I assure them. "Remember, the longer you commit to, the cheaper the per-day price is."

"And where will this billboard be?" Jesse asks.

"On 5th and Chesapeake," I answer. "That's close to both residential and business areas. Right now, there's an ad for a sporting event that passed."

"And when will ours go up?" Jesse asks.

"It should go up on July 1st and stay there for six months. It takes time to print and schedule their installation. We use outside firms for that."

"That sounds perfect," Janus says as he stands. "I should be getting back to the shop now. Saturn, do you have dinner plans tonight?"

"Not really," I say.

"Care to have it with me?"

"Sure," I say. "But, let me pick the place and pay. You don't have to every time."

I leave without a kiss, but since this was a business call, I don't let that bother me.

I stay at the office the rest of the day, and when I get home, I change into some khaki shorts and a red and yellow striped T-shirt. I pet Muffin while I wait, hoping and praying that Janus won't get mad at me and break off whatever there is between us right now if this ad campaign doesn't work.

Janus soon shows up, and he's surprised to see me come outside with a cooler in hand, the one I bought for my camping trip when I was 18. I told him that I had made some sandwiches and packed potato salad and coleslaw, which I bought from the grocery store, and we could have a picnic in the park where the Independence Day celebration is being held. He smiles at the suggestion and opens the truck door for me to get in.

We arrive at the park and find an empty table. I set the table with paper plates and cups, and put a couple of soda cans by them. I had made salami and cheese sandwiches, and brought Miracle Whip and mustard in case he prefers either of those on his sandwiches. He opts for both.

We sit, eat, talk, and watch kids play as parents diligently watch their every move. I wanted to ask him his opinion on having kids, but I also knew that it was way too early for that topic. He thanks me again for the billboard concept, and while I didn't want to discuss work all evening, I did point out a couple of billboards in sight and offer a critique of each one.

After dinner, we put the cooler back in his truck, and he suggests that we go for a walk around the trail once or twice. I agree to once, and am open to twice depending on the time.

We chat some more as we walk. I told him about the Indianapolis Speedway project we did in art class, and he said that he'd love to see it one day.

He told me more about how life at the University of Notre Dame was and the many antics he found himself in. I'm not sure what about his college life he was keeping out. I just know the fact of losing my virginity on a bathroom sink while drunk at a party wasn't going to be disclosed today. No way.

As we walk and talk, somewhere along the trail, he reaches for my hand, and we hold each other's for the rest of the walk. I wanted to stop a few times and kiss him, but there were too many people around, and I didn't want to put on some kind of show for them. We see another couple doing that, sitting on a bench as we pass by, and we both try our best to ignore them, focusing on each other instead.

One lap was enough for me, and when we got close to where his truck is parked, I asked him to take me home. We drive the short distance and hum along with the music. Janus seems to like adult contemporary, and I'm fine with that. He's also played contemporary Christian music before, which is a little new to me, but I still enjoy it.

I wasn't going to invite him in until he said that he had to use the bathroom. While I still don't know him too well, I can't imagine that this is some ploy to get me in a locked apartment, toss me onto the couch, and, well, you know. There was a time that I may have enjoyed that, to be honest, but now I'm at that point in my life where I'd rather build a relationship on mutual respect and love than on carnal passions.

I bring him inside and point to where the bathroom is, though it probably wasn't necessary. While he is in there, for some reason, I shut the door to the bedroom. Then, I go to the dining set table and change the water in the carnations he gave me. He comes out of the bathroom and sees me there sniffing the flowers with a goofy look on my face, so I put them down and walk over toward him.

"They still smell nice," I say.

"So do you," he says, then looks a little uncomfortable. "I mean…"

"I know what you mean."

I lose a little inhibition, pull him down to sit with me on the couch, and wrap my arm around him to kiss him. We end up kissing each other more than we ever have before, more passionately, but still not too, too, TOO extremely passionate. After a minute, we stand up, he puts his hands on my waist, and steps back a foot or so. He breathes heavily for a moment, then says he'd better get going. I ask if I did anything wrong, and he assures me that I didn't and asks if I want to go out tomorrow night.

"How does dancing at the civic club sound? The local band isn't the best, and they play mostly standards, but it's a nice time. We can go out to eat first, or they sell hot dogs and stuff like that there. I'll let you pick."

"Hot dogs and dancing sound perfect to me. And, Janus, I didn't mean to…"

"I'll pick you up around six again. It's casual, so your usual jeans and T-shirt are fine to wear."

Janus holds my waist and kisses me again, this time it is tamer and shorter. As he leaves, I watch him as he disappears down the road again. I think from now on I'll let him guide our kisses. Or maybe not. I'm so frazzled right now, I don't know what I want.

As I say my prayers that night, I delve heavily into my relationship with Janus, ask God for forgiveness if my kiss was a bit too much, and ask for His guidance as we proceed forward. I mean, we're just going on dates now. I'm not sure if we're "dating" or not, especially since it seems he may be seeing Sunny as well. I suppose that's okay, even if he is. May the best woman win. I pray to God for Janus to find that woman, whether it's me or not. I also pray for me to find the right man, whether it's Janus or not.

After I realize it's been twenty minutes since I started praying, I decide it's time for bed. Before I do so, I grab a carnation from the pitcher and hold it again while I sleep, hoping again that the sweet smell will trigger sweet dreams.

I wake up to my alarm ringing, and the carnation is still in my hand. After sitting up and seeing Muffin sleeping in his little cat bed, I sit back a moment and recall my dreams from last night.

I was back home in Hohman. I think I was a teenager, but you know how such details can be deceiving in dreams. Anyway, I was there, in my old room. I had a bowl of green onions on my dresser next to a craft stick pencil holder, and as I was getting dressed one morning, one of them stood up and started dancing. Yes! The green onion came to life, or at least a mammalian-like life, and started dancing right before me.

I grabbed my phone to either start recording or to stream live on some platform, but I don't remember which now. Suddenly, those who were watching were right there in my room, standing next to me. Oh, don't worry. Somehow, I was already dressed, so they didn't see... well, you know what they didn't see.

Some who watched were still doubting the authenticity of it, claiming it to be some sort of AI thing happening before them, despite that not being a thing when I was 17 years old. They told me it was fake, and somehow I knew how to make it dance. I mean, I do know some magic. On that camping trip I took, a man named Elliot showed me how to make things disappear with this sleight-of-hand trick, but this was different. No matter what they said, I knew that the onion was dancing on its own. How? I didn't know.

Anyway, some believed it was real, others didn't. The alarm woke me up as it was doing an exaggerated hip wiggle. I mean, if onions had hips, that's what it was doing, but in any case, I never learned how it was doing it or if all of the others somehow were eventually convinced that what they were seeing at that moment was what was happening.

I have no idea what, if anything, that dream meant. I just get dressed, have some cereal, pet Muffin, and make sure that his bowls are full. Before I leave for work, I take the carnation that is sitting on the coffee table in front of the sofa and bring it to work with me.

At 10:00 a.m., I'm sitting in my office looking over a new account that just came in this morning. I'm sipping a cup of black coffee with the usual stirrer in it when Karen knocks on my door and lets herself in without an invitation. I'm fine with that. On top of coworkers and the making of a great team, she and I are fast becoming friends outside the office.

"How's it going?" she asks as she takes a seat.

"Pretty good," I answer.

"Is that from Janus?" she asks, indicating the flower in a tall cup behind me.

"It is. It's one of six he gave me not too long ago."

"So, what's the deal with you two?"

"Honestly, Karen, I don't know. We're just dating now. Nothing exclusive, or at least I don't think so. We never discussed that. We're going dancing tonight, but after that I really don't know."

"Well, you'll get there someday. What are you working on now?" She asks, switching gears to work, thankfully.

"Billboards for an auto repair shop. They want three, one in each of the regions in Oakfield. They'd like five concepts minimum, then they'll choose from them. Do you know anything about auto repair?" I ask.

"Only to take it to them when mine needs fixing," Karen jokes, then asks to see the specs.

After lunch, Karen and I discuss the auto repair shop billboards more. We take the conversation out by the reception area to invite others in on it, and everyone seems to have an opinion about it. Some suggest having a handsome mechanic on them, while John suggests focusing more on the repairing of cars.

"I could draw up some animated cars or mechanics," Gene suggests.

"They want human models for this," Karen answers. "Handsome ones."

"People want their cars fixed right and don't care what the mechanic looks like," John says.

"Speak for yourself, John," Karen replies. "When mine leans over to look under my hood, I want to see a cute booty looking back at me."

"Karen!" I shout in surprise at her statements.

"Hey, lighten up," she says, then reminds me of the calendars seen in many shops across the country.

"Touché," I say.

"Tushy," she says, and we both laugh.

We actually accomplish quite a bit of work, even though most of us spend the afternoon hanging out in the reception area. Just before 5:00, we all head back to our offices to finish up and get ready for Monday morning. I check my appearance in the mirror for some reason, say goodbye to everyone, and then head home to change into something that will make Janus want to dance close to me. *Just not too close*, I remind myself as I go through my stuff looking for the right outfit to wear.

Chapter 6

Dancing, Putting, and Pondering

I'm busy getting dressed in my bedroom when I hear a knock at the door. I see by my watch that he's a little early, but that's okay. I go to the door, and I see him in Dockers and a blue polo shirt, while I have on some of my preferred loose-fitting jeans and a red Ball State University T-shirt. I invite him in, and again, he's empty-handed and offers no kiss.

"I'll be ready in a moment," I tell him. "Have a seat if you like."

Janus sits on a chair I bought from him and picks up a project I've been working on. He inspects it closely, nodding his head as he does. I come out of the bathroom and ask if what I'm wearing is okay.

"It's perfect," he says as he looks at me. Is it the same way Eric looks at Venus? No, but then again, I didn't see him until he and Venus were dating a while and already deep in love. "What's this going to be?"

"Oh," I say, snapping back to reality. "It's going to be a flower pot holder for an 8-inch pot. They are popular items at craft booths."

"I can't wait to see it finished," he says. He's talking about the future, which is a good thing.

I give Muffin some extra love before we leave, and Janus scratches his head, prompting a "Mew" from the feline.

We arrive at the civic club. It reminds me of the place where my sophomore-year college roommate, Heather Plant, took me for a mixer, which was nothing more than a hookup party. The room size I'm speaking of now, not the activities. I was happy she brought me there, not because of my anticipation of hooking up – I didn't from that party, by the way – but that inadvertently was the occasion that brought me back to my love of craft sticks.

Janus pays an entry fee, and I feel bad because I didn't know there was a cover charge for this. I offer to pay him back, and he tells me to put my money away.

"You're my guest tonight," he says. "Just have fun. There are some modest hors d'oeuvres, soft drinks, food, and a cash bar. This evening is on me, so have fun."

"I will," I assure him, then hook my arm into his as I take a look around.

There are more people here than I expected, but it's still not so crowded that you can't move. There is a live band, and I suppose Janus's idea of "Standards" is mostly soft rock from the '60s, '70s, and '80s. They're good, at least for Oakfield. They are a six-piece band with five male members and one female, all of whom look to be about thirty years old. All of the men play instruments, and three sing, while the lady only sings. I also see a tambourine close to her, so I assume she'll play that when the song demands.

There are couples dancing, some eating, and a few are parked at the bar. I see Janus is bopping a little to the song that's being played, so I give him a nod, and he leads me out to the dance floor.

The last time I danced was at Venus's wedding. I had a little too much wine, and I ended up making out with the best man while we danced. We even danced slowly to the upbeat songs just to keep the kissing going. While I am dying for an intense make-out session with Janus, I don't think here and now would be the proper place to do that.

We dance, and Janus even does that pointing thing you see on the cover of that '70s disco dancing movie poster. I laugh at his antics, but I can see he is relatively light on his feet. We dance a couple of songs like that, then decide to take a break and grab some snacks.

He buys us a couple of hot dogs, and we both load ours up and do a weird "clinking of the dogs" cheers before we bite into them. Mine was rather good. It's a better quality than you usually find at events like this. I go to buy another, but Janus reminds me that tonight is on him and buys two more for us, plus two bags of chips.

There are a few tables set out, meant to be used only while you're eating, since there is plenty of seating elsewhere without a table. I take my seat while Janus sets his plate down and grabs a couple of colas from a vendor. We talk a little over the music, and I thank him several times for bringing me here.

We return to the dance floor, and this time, the band is playing a synth-driven hit from the early '80s. We try to dance how we thought they did in that era, and laugh a little as we do. A love song starts to play next. Well, not a full-blown love song. This was one about wanting to find love. Janus looks at me with his arms out, inviting me to stay on the dance floor. I nod, and we hold hands while our other hands are touching each other's backs. We don't dance too close, but we also don't dance too far from each other. It seems to be the perfect distance as we dance and look into each other's eyes. I'm not sure what he is looking for, but I am seeing if I see Eric's eyes in him. I think I might. Or, at least a glimmer of that. I wanted to kiss him when the song was done, but he instead says he wants another break, and we go to a couple of chairs to sit.

We're mainly chatting about the band and how lovely the lady singer's voice is when Sunny, seemingly out of nowhere, comes over to us.

"Hi!" she says in her sunny voice.

"Oh, hi, Sunny," I say back.

The band starts playing a fun song that was a hit in the late '60s, and Sunny tries to pull Janus up to dance.

"I'm here with Saturn," he tells her, then looks at me.

"Oh, go ahead," I say, smiling, trying to hide some rage brewing inside of me.

They dance apart from one another, and I actually enjoy watching Janus move from this angle. You don't see that so much while you're dancing together, but I definitely see it now. Next, the band starts playing a slow love song. Not just any love song, but that one from that famous movie scene where the lady is making something using a pottery wheel and the man comes up to her from behind and they… well, let's just say they did one of the hottest movie scenes from that era. It's not as much of a "love song" as it is a "we're already in love, so let's go to the bedroom and prove it" song. It's slow, sweet, and sensual.

Janus tries to pull away from her, but she pulls him back in. She wraps her arms around him, tightly, and sways gently to the music. As I'm watching, reminding myself that he's not my boyfriend, so I suppose he's allowed to dance with her like that, Blake Boyd sits next to me. He's the man I dated a couple of times when I first arrived in town. Then I broke it off right there at the coffee shop where he worked. I immediately and literally bumped into Janus as I was switching seats. He's nice, but he just isn't for me.

"Hi," he says.

"Oh, hi," I say with a faint smile.

"Are you alone?" he asks.

"No. I came with him."

I point to Janus, who is busy trying to keep Sunny's hands where they'd be more appropriate. The song is about over, and it can't end soon enough for me.

"Oh," he says, then offers a hand to me. "Would you care to dance?"

I sit there looking at Janus and Sunny, almost ignoring Blake. The song ends, and another that's fast enough to be a fast dance, yet still slow enough to dance close together. Sunny tries to keep Janus close to her, and he struggles to break loose.

"Maybe another time," I tell Blake and then walk over to Janus.

"May I cut in?" I ask Sunny. She gives me a look, then relinquishes his hand. We start to dance, and as the music dictates, we dance neither slow nor fast. We just dance.

"Thanks," he says.

"Blake is here and asked me to dance," I tell him, though I don't know why.

Janus stops dancing, then suggests that we get a drink.

He leads me over to the bar and asks if I'd like a glass of wine. I never told him what wine does to me, how it makes me almost uncontrollably amorous, and I don't know what to do. It's too early in our relationship for us to discuss certain things like that, and since I could usually handle one, especially after eating, I accept a red wine.

We sit at a round table with a couple of other couples, sipping our wine. I tell him how much I've been enjoying the dance, and he says that he's glad to hear it. We finish our drinks, and he invites me back onto the dance floor.

We dance to a disco standard, then the DJ starts playing the Cha Cha Slide, and every dancer acts silly as the man in the song instructs our actions. The song ends, and Janus and I laugh. Another slow song comes on, and it's another "we're already in love song." I decide to let Janus choose whether we dance or not. We do.

We dance a little closer this time, but not nearly as tight as Sunny was with him. The song ends, and I just can't help it. It isn't the wine; it's too early for that to take effect. It's everything else. The music. The dancing. Janus. I look at him like I want to kiss him, and he does. He leans down, puts his lips to mine, holds it for a half a second, and makes a slight click sound as we part.

It's barely been two weeks, I remind myself. *Contain yourself.*

It's getting late, and it seems the right moment to ask Janus to take me home. We ride in silence as we both take in the evening. I'm hoping that Janus doesn't have to use the bathroom, because I don't think I want him inside my apartment tonight. Everything is just too perfect. He doesn't ask. He does ask if we could see each other tomorrow, and I asked for another evening date as I don't want to spend another Saturday all day with him. I need to pace myself better.

Janus leans down to kiss me, and we do, but it wasn't as passionate as before. Well, maybe it was, but in a different way.

Janus leans down, kisses me for a few seconds, then holds his head to mine so we're nose-to-nose. We rub noses for a few seconds, then he kisses me again. He brings me in to hug me tightly, and after about ten seconds of that, he gently kisses me a third time. He says he'll be by tomorrow around 4:30, and I say that's fine.

I decide on shorts and a tank top for bed that night. I kneel and say prayers for a long time. I so badly want to lead a life filled with Christ, but I can also be weak at times, very weak, and have no idea about Janus's history. He is a 27-year-old man, after all, so he must have one. Is Sunny a part of that history? I don't know. Will I be a part of his history? Well, I already am, but for how long?

I make sure the alarm is shut off before I go to sleep. I have a little trouble staying asleep, not only because I have a lot of things on my mind, but also, Muffin keeps jumping up on me, and this couch isn't the best for sleeping on.

I wake around 9:00 a.m. Saturday, and consider getting a regular bed. But then, do I want that temptation in my apartment? Maybe God will answer that next time I'm in Janus's store by showing me if there's one for sale in there. Or would that be Satan tempting me? Life as a Christian isn't always easy, and God doesn't always provide you with clear, easy-to-follow answers. Drat!

After breakfast, I log onto the city's website and fill out an application to have a booth at the upcoming music, food, and crafts fair. I decided to bring mostly smaller items, with just a couple of the bigger, more expensive ones. I found it's better to build a bit of a reputation selling smaller pieces before bringing out the bigger stuff. I'll probably have a couple of dozen basic boxes that go for $10, and a few slightly more intricate ones costing a little more, like flower pot holders and shoe boxes. I don't take special orders quite yet, but I have been considering that.

After entering my credit card numbers for the $50 booth fee, I texted my senior year college roommate, Chloe Summers, to see if she was available for a Zoom chat. She is, and a moment later, I see her on my screen.

"How's it going, Saturn?" she asks.

"Pretty good," I answer. "I really like this new town."

"Well, I already know you like your job, so what's his name?"

"What makes you think there is a 'his' to talk about?" I ask.

"Come on, Saturn. I know you better than that."

"Fine. It's Janus. Janus Rings. We've been dating for the past couple of weeks. Just dated. Nothing more. We go out, spend time together, kiss a little, and go home. No commitment. No, anything but that, actually."

"So, what's the problem?"

She knows me too well for me to hedge, so I tell her. I know that it's not love, but it's more than infatuation. I think there's something there, but so is Sunny.

"Have you considered talking to him?" Chloe asks.

"Yeah, but I don't want to seem obsessive, clingy, or like I'm smothering him."

"Do you want to continue dating him?"

"Yes. I do. I really do," I answer as a smile appears on my face.

"Then just do that. Date him. If he's also dating Sunny, so be it. One of you is bound to win in the end. If it's you, great. If it's her, do you really lose anything after a fort night together?"

"Nice language," I say, chuckling. "I suppose you're right. We have a date tonight. Oh, and Chloe?"

"Yes?"

"Do you have plans for Independence Day? There's a craft fair here that day, and if you'd like to come, that would be great. It's a Friday, so stay for the weekend if you want."

"I'll definitely let you know. I want to, but have to see if anything else comes up."

"That's good enough for me," I say, smiling at my friend. "Well, it was nice talking to you. If I want a booth at the fair, I need something to sell."

We log off, and I work on the sticks with classical music playing softly in the background. I make a couple of basic boxes, and am surprised that I haven't gotten bored yet with making the simple craft. I have a light lunch, and after cleaning up, I text Venus to see if she's available to talk.

"Hi, Big Sister," I say when her face appears. "How is my little niece or nephew doing?"

"Hi, Saturn. Junior is doing fine," she says as she pats her belly. "The doctor says it's about as healthy as an embryo at this age could be. He says the due date is January 18, so we've a long way to go."

"Just keep it and yourself healthy, Venus. I'm really looking forward to being a spoiling auntie," I say and laugh.

"I will, Saturn. Now, what do you really want? I know you didn't call just to check up on me. I mean, it would be nice if you ever did, but you never do. What's up?"

"You know me too well," I say, then get serious.

We talk about me and Janus, and what I'm feeling. I ask her how she knew it was love with Eric, and when he started looking at her like that.

"Honestly, I remember the moment," she says. "We started dating during our first semester of college. It was going well. Normal dating, I suppose.

I stopped wearing my clothes that barely covered my body and started dressing more like you."

"And that was a bad thing?" I ask, trying to lighten the mood.

"It was a wonderful thing. I don't think Eric would have wanted to date anybody with their boobs hanging out like I used to wear. Believe me, in private, he really likes them and…"

"TMI, Sis. Just get on with it."

"Well," she says, then takes a sip from a milk glass. "When COVID-19 hit, and we knew we were going to be separated, we thought it was just going to be weeks, not years. We vowed to keep our romance going and declared our love for one another, saying it for the first time. In fact, it was the first time I ever said that to any guy."

"No kidding?" I ask.

"Why. Have you?"

"On with your story," I say, realizing the answer is no.

"Well, we ended up spending the night together…"

"Venus!"

"No, not what you're thinking. We mostly sat on a couch, just holding on to one another. We kissed some – okay, a lot – but that was it. We sat there, two bodies as one, fully clothed, just holding on to one another. I may have enjoyed that more than our wedding night. Well, no. That isn't true. But it surely comes close."

"That is so sweet," I say. "So, hoping another pandemic doesn't happen anytime soon, how will I know?"

"I'm no psychologist, and I thought you minored in that," she says.

"Very minored," I answer, not sure what that means. "I must have missed the day they discussed true love."

"Then here's a free lesson for you. You saw what I went through when Eric and I were apart. Are you willing to go through the same thing with Janus?"

I think about that for a few moments, and never verbally answer. We talk a little about how my job is going and how life on the farm is. I demand that she tell me absolutely EVERYTHING when it comes to her baby growing inside of her, and I even insist that she email or text me pictures of the ultrasound. She promises to keep me in the loop, then I log off and get back to my project, all the while thinking about what would happen in the case of a new virus terrorizing the world.

I lose myself in my craft stick building again, pondering everything that Chloe and Venus said. I haven't looked at the clock in likely hours, and am surprised when I hear a knock at the door. I don't bother looking at a clock now and am surprised to see Janus there in denim shorts and a yellow T-shirt with what I think is some sort of superhero logo. I look down at myself and see the mess I look like.

"Come in, sit. I'll be right back."

I rush to the bathroom to run a comb through my hair and wash my face. I quickly change into similar shorts as he is wearing, and since I don't have superhero clothing, I put on a "Cat Mom" shirt I bought a few days after finding Muffin. I think we'll look cute together now, so I return to him to give him a proper greeting.

He again doesn't offer to kiss me, but gives me a paper bag and says there's a gift inside for me. I open it and see a beautiful flower vase inside. I thank him and ask why.

"For flowers, of course," he says with a chuckle in his voice. "It's something we've had in the store for a while now. I garbage-picked it and cleaned it up, but it's next to perfect now."

"It's absolutely perfect," I say, and give him a peck on the lips, then walk to the dining room table to transfer the remaining five carnations into it. "That's two gifts you gave me, and I gave you nothing so far."

"That's not true," Janus says. "You gave the committee a great idea for an outreach program."

"Well, I still want to give you something," I say, then return to where he's standing.

"How about another kiss?" he asks.

I wrap my arms around his neck and kiss him for three seconds, hoping we start to do this every time we meet.

"So, are you ready?" he asks.

"Where are we going?"

"A surprise."

He takes me to Mapletree, the city north of Oakfield and just ripe for some new advertising. After I ask for about the fifteenth time in the last fifteen minutes, we pull into a place called Putt and Swat, a mini golf and batting cages place with an arcade, go-karts, and a simple café.

We buy tickets for mini golf, and he hands me a pink ball while he opts for blue. That should make it easy for us to remember. It's not as crowded as one may expect for a perfect June Saturday night, but it may get more crowded later.

We take our time going through the course, sharing fun banter and trash talk. I was really hoping he'd do that thing where he tries to show me how to play by getting behind me, wrapping his hands around my waist to hold mine in his, and teaching me how to swing. He doesn't, maybe because I was a little bit better than he was. Or perhaps we're not there yet, though I still hope kissing hello was.

Anyway, by the time we played the tenth hole, we quit keeping score and just played for fun. We get to the last hole, one where if you get the ball into the next-to-impossible-to-get hole, you win a free game. Janus won the previous hole, so he shoots first. He aims, wiggles his rear a little, and shoots, missing by a few inches.

I go next and try to tease him by imitating his movements, except for the wiggling hind end. I shoot, and a second later, we hear bells and sirens going off. I won a coupon for a free round of golf!

"Next time we come, you're paying," he teases, but all I heard was "I want to date you some more."

"Fine," I say in an exaggerated, exasperated way.

"How about a pizza?" he asks.

We put our order in, and since it'll be about fifteen minutes, he challenges me to go-karts. He pays the teen at the booth, and after we're strapped in, we race eight other teens, pre-teens, and kids to the finish line. Janus easily wins the race while I come in sixth, just behind what looks to be a fifteen-year-old girl and her boyfriend, just in front of her.

I congratulate Janus on the win, but refrain from kissing him like the girl kissed her boyfriend. He thanks me, says I did well (he lied), and we go inside to enjoy our pizza and sodas.

While we eat, we get more serious as we discuss what to expect at the deacons' meeting tomorrow after church.

"You're just there to use your expertise for us to do it right," he says.

"I'll try," I answer, as I'm hardly an expert at church function planning.

We go into the arcade and play some games against each other. We went two games to one, his favor, beating me at air hockey. I was better at skee-ball, and we both crashed out playing a racing video game.

He asks if I want to try the batting cages, and I decline the offer as I've never done those before. He gets in a medium-speed one, dons a helmet, chooses a bat, and hits 11 of the 15 balls that are pitched to him. As he comes out, I tell him how good he was, and act like a teen and kiss him right there.

We hang out for a short time more, then around 10:00 p.m., he drives me home. We say goodbye at the apartment building door again. He asks if I want a ride to church, and I tell him I'd rather drive. He smiles, says good night, and gives me what I thought was a slightly tame kiss for the evening we just had. I don't want to ruin the moment, so I leave it at that.

It's nearly 11:00 before I'm ready for bed, and I don't think I've been up this late since college. My prayers are relatively short tonight, but I still ask for guidance on where Janus and I stand. I took one last look at the vase he gave me, then turned out the lights for what I hope will be a good night's sleep. Muffin jumps onto my stomach, I give him a pet, and drift off to sleep with the sounds of "Purring" in my ears. Sweet dreams, indeed.

Chapter 7

Sunday Slowdown

I go to church the next morning and sit by Janus again. Jesse and his wife sit next to him. Sunny decides to sit alone behind us, more towards Janus's side. She greets him as she takes her seat and gives me a simple nod. Not exactly very hospitable.

Pastor Steven Chalke's message really hits home for me as he preaches on 2 Timothy 2:22, "So flee youthful passions and pursue righteousness, faith, love, and peace, along with those who call on the Lord from a pure heart." I listen as he talks about leaving your youthful passions behind in pursuit of a relationship rooted in righteousness, faith, love, and peace, and wonder if he is speaking directly to me as the ninety-five or so others around me listen to him. A time or two, Sunny leans up and whispers something in Janus's ear. He smiled each time before turning his attention back to the pulpit.

We greet the pastor at the sanctuary door after he delivers his benediction, then go into the community room for refreshments. Janus reintroduces me to his mom, Angela, and we shake hands and chat briefly. She's a lovely woman who helps in the store when needed, usually tasked with cleaning up items like the vase Janus gave me yesterday or running the register.

When the room begins to clear, Janus excuses us from his parents because we have a deacons' meeting to attend. Janus leads me to a room down a hallway, and when we enter, I see a couple of people I don't recognize. They seem to be enjoying the conversation they're having, so Janus says he'll save introductions for when the meeting starts.

Soon, everyone who is expected is seated, and the woman I don't know leads us in prayer. Pastor Chalke asks Janus about my being there, so he makes introductions.

"This is Saturn O Syres," he says, and I like that this time he included my middle name. "She was invited to help us with the advertising of the upcoming Independence Day event, as she is an expert in that field. Saturn, I'd like you to meet Brynn Keigh and Joe Peppers."

I nod their way, and Brynn offers to shake my hand. Once things settle down again, the pastor proceeds before Sunny speaks up.

"Excuse me. She's neither a part of this board nor even a member of the church. Therefore, she's not allowed to speak unless she's specifically asked regarding her so-called expertise, and she's to have a seat over there while we go about our business." Sunny points to a chair at the corner of the table and gives me a look. "It's in the bylaws."

"Well," Pastor Chalke uncomfortably clears his throat. "While we are usually less formal about such things, Sunny is correct. Would you mind sitting there, Miss Syres?" he asks.

I get up to move and see Sunny place her hand on Janus's while smiling at him, then scooches her chair a couple of inches closer to him. I sit down, and they talk about their usual items before coming to the part for which I was invited. They discuss how they did it in the past, and then Janus eventually brings the discussion to me.

"Saturn has some good ideas about how to do it this year. We spoke last week about how to advertise for the event, and she used her expertise to help us come up with new ideas. To share her qualifications, she has a degree from Ball State University in marketing and has worked in advertising for over two years now." I think I see a hint of pride in Janus's eyes, but I'm not sure.

I was asked a couple of questions about my job and qualifications before my idea was discussed further.

"So, you believe this is a better way to advertise it?" the pastor asks.

"Technically, this is more marketing than advertising," I answer. "But, I'm sure this would be a wiser use of your resources."

"Have you done anything like this before?" Sunny asks.

"For a church, no," I answer.

"Then what makes you an expert?' she asks.

"Her degree and experience," Joe points out, and the rest of the room laughs at her. She puts her arm around Janus, whispers something to him, then puts her hand on top of his once again after the laughter dies down.

"Well, I think it's a wonderful idea," Brynn says. "Do you have any other suggestions?"

"May I see what you plan on handing out?"

Janus says he'll get it and excuses himself from the room. Sunny watches him from behind as he walks away, then gives me a look of some sort. I sit uncomfortably in the room of strangers as light conversations start. Janus soon returns, and the meeting is called back to order. He hands me some papers, and the room is silent as I look over them.

"Well," I say. "These are nice. Did you do them yourself?"

"Yes," Janus answers.

"They could be more eye-catching and less cluttered. Look at your upcoming events, for example."

I hold that up and show them what I was talking about, as well as the other handouts.

"As I said, these are good, but could use to be clearer. Would you mind if I take these back to the agency, have our print ad expert look at them, and bring something new back? You could then go with them or what you have here. Your choice."

"How much are you charging us?" Sunny asks.

"Nothing. The agency is willing to donate their time and resources helping you with this event," I answer.

It went to a vote, and my idea for the baby-changing station and other items passed, as did new promotional concepts, with only Sunny voting "No" on each item. She then says that since my time there is done, I should leave.

Janus walks me out to the hall, says I did a good job and he's proud of me, and asks if I want to go out to lunch with him once they're done. I tell him I'd rather go home myself and work on my crafts. He returns to his seat, and Sunny gives him a big smile, scooches a little closer, then puts her arm around his shoulder. He doesn't stop her and, in fact, smiles at her as the meeting is called back to order.

I go to my car and realize I'm not in the mood to go home for lunch. I'm also not in the mood for a full lunch. I drive to Jack's Coffee and Pastry and order a red velvet muffin and a latte of the day, whatever that is. I don't even bother to look.

I wait at the designated place for my order to come, then take my small tray to the end counter seat, looking out the window. I pick a piece of muffin and have a taste. Pretty good. I sip my drink and notice it has a chocolate flavor, too.

"Perfect," I say, minding my own business.

"It sure is," the man next to me says. I turn to look at him. Drat! It's Blake Boyd. Double, triple drat!

"Oh, hi," I say, hoping that will be our entire conversation.

"How have you been, Saturn? It's been a while," he says.

"I suppose," I answer. "I thought you got fired from here."

"I did. I just come here for coffee now. Blake's Beans will be opening soon."

"Oh, you found a place?" I ask.

"Not yet. By 'opening soon,' I mean hopefully within a year or two. Or three. Do you still do ads?"

"Yes. I have a lot to think about, Blake. Do you mind?" I ask.

"Not at all," he says, then sits quiet for thirty seconds. "So, what's on your mind?"

"Blake, I thought I made it clear. If not, listen. We are not dating. I just want to enjoy my muffin and drink, then go home. Please, leave me alone."

"But what we had was something special…"

"What we had were two dates. TWO! DATES! One kiss. That was it. Please, Blake. I really need to think."

"That's it," someone yells from behind. "I told you to stop bothering my customers before. You are hereby banned from this store, so kindly leave, or I will be calling the police."

"Come on, we were just talking," Blake says to him.

"Ma'am, did you invite him to talk to you?" the man asks.

"No, I did not," I answer, then take a sip.

"Leave!" he says.

Blake picks up his drink and asks if he can text me. Drat! I ignore his comment and take another piece of muffin.

"I think we met the last time he bothered you here," the man says to me. "I'm the owner, Jack Perry. I want to give you this coupon for a free drink and muffin next time you come in, and offer you my most sincere apologies."

"Thank you, but that's not necessary," I say, yet still accept the coupon.

"Here's my card, too."

I take it and look at it. Not bad, I suppose.

"Did you do this yourself? Design the card, that is," I ask.

"Yeah. I was hoping people would pass them around and bring some more business here. I really need to figure out how to advertise this place better."

"Really?" I say with a smile, then dig in my purse. "Here's my card. The seat next to me just became available in case you want to talk now."

Jack looks at it and smiles. We sit and talk for about fifteen minutes. He offers me a free pastry while we chat, but I decline. One muffin is enough.

I tell him to come to the agency whenever he can so we can discuss his advertising needs further. I stand and start to clear my spot, but Jack says that he'll take care of it. I thank him and leave on a half-filled stomach.

It's a nice day —too nice to stay at home —so I wonder what to do. I decide to drive my Beetle to a municipal lot down the street, a block or two, and walk around the downtown shopping area.

I think it's rather typical of a city of this size. There are lots of places to shop for all sorts of things, as well as many restaurants and places to eat. Most are either independently owned or are a part of a local chain, with very few national chain stores. In fact, aside from the requisite Dollar General store that are pretty much everywhere in Indiana, I can't think of another.

I'm not in the mood to buy anything, but if I see something I like, I may make a purchase. I just want to walk down the sidewalk and see what kinds of advertisements are in storefront windows. Yeah, I know. I could be with Janus, but I want to see what the local stores have in their windows instead. It helps me think, and I didn't get that done at Jack's as I expected.

The first store I see is Oakfield Shoes. They have a flip-flops sale going on, with a buy one, get one free deal. I'm considering buying some, but I'm more inclined toward the flyer in the window. It's dull, doesn't work hard to get your attention, and is a little cluttered with far too much information.

Next door is a low- to mid-range jewelry shop. It appears to be jewelry for teens and younger adults, but they also have items for older women and men. The flyer is neat, well-written, and clearly communicates to the customer what the sale entails and what they can expect. I can recognize Karen's work, for sure. I think she also handles their newspaper ads.

I roam the streets for a couple of hours, mostly looking at the flyers in the stores and going into a few.

I actually ended up going back to Oakfield Shoes to buy a pair of flip-flops and get my second pair for free. Hey, just because the flyer wasn't professionally done doesn't mean it doesn't work—just don't tell Gretchen that. I mean, I only saw it because I was looking for flyers in windows, but I don't expect them to get much business from that otherwise, if that's their only ad for the sale.

I take my flip-flops back to my apartment and try them on right away. I'm not in much of a mood to work with craft sticks, so I watch a baseball game on TV. I don't know much about the sport, just that the team that runs completely around the bases the most times wins. However, I enjoy the ambient sounds and the peaceful feeling I get from watching them play, as well as the ads around the playing area and other areas in the building.

I sit back, put my feet up on my couch, and drink some ice water from a glass. I wiggle my feet some as I watch an umpire call for an infield fly rule, whatever that means, when I discover that Muffin likes playing with bare toes. He nibbles at my right ones some, especially the little piggy who went to the market, causing me to laugh as his sandpaper tongue tickles. I sit up, pick him up, set him in my lap, and pet him for as long as he allows me to.

Around 5:00, I get hungry enough for some dinner. I'm not in the mood to cook, and I'm not going to call Janus, especially after declining his invitation earlier today. I think I have a taste for something American, so I drive downtown to Harry's Hot Dogs and Hamburgers. Before I go in, I take a closer look at the ads in their front window. They're simply typing paper with handwritten menu items and prices, using what appears to be a Sharpie marker. The crudeness of it actually helps in conveying that it's a simple restaurant with no frills, but the handwriting could be neater, and instead of crossing out mistakes, they should write a new sign.

I go in, and it's nearly half-filled, and the workers all look busy, so I suppose they're not hurting business at all.

While I've been to restaurants like this before, I'm still not familiar with their particular menu. I look up at the menu board as I walk to the counter, and accidentally walk too far and bump into the person waiting at the end of a very short line. I notice who it is when I look to apologize.

"Oh, hi Pastor Chalke," I say with a smile.

"Good afternoon, Saturn," he says.

"I'm sorry for bumping you like that, Pastor."

"Oh, don't pay that any mind, and while you're at it, call me Steven."

"I will," I say with a smile and look more at the board. Steven is next, and I decide to ask him something.

"Pastor… Steven," I say nervously. "Would you like to join me for dinner? I'll pay if you do."

"Well," he says, then walks to the counter to order, but finishes with me first. "Your help today was invaluable to us. How about I pay for your dinner instead, and we can sit at that booth over there in the corner?"

I agree to his counteroffer, and after ordering, I go and fill our drinks while he waits for the order to come up.

He brings a tray with his two hot dogs and my cheeseburger with all the fixings, both with fries, and sets our baskets before us. He says grace for us, then we enter into light conversation, with him asking me a few questions about where I came from and how I came to town. I think he knows I have something on my mind, so I bring it up when we're both about halfway done with our meals.

"Pastor Chalke, I know I'm not a member of your flock, but can we talk?"

"You're a child of God, so you are a member of the flock, and we are talking," he answers.

"No, I mean…"

"I know what you mean, Saturn," he says, cutting me off. "I just want you to relax; you look nervous. What's on your mind?"

"Can we make this one of those clergy confidentiality things, where it stays between just us?" I ask.

"Of course," he says, then takes a big last bite of his first hot dog.

I tell the pastor how I grew up in a Christian household with my big sister, Venus. How her influence then changed me after she left for college, and while I wouldn't say I "left the faith," I definitely strayed from it. I didn't share my entire sexual history, but I mentioned some regrets and how I'm trying to improve. I talked about my growing relationship with Janus and how my feelings for him seem conflicted. While I had boyfriends before, and even "had" boyfriends, none of them ever made me feel like I do when I'm around him. I don't want to go too fast with Janus, either. I want to do what's right in God's eyes, but I'm not sure what that is.

Pastor Chalke didn't say anything the whole time I was talking, then he sat silent for about thirty seconds as he ate a couple of French fries.

"You say you just moved to town, right?" he asks. I answer, though he knows, and I assume he doesn't want to talk about this subject. "Where do you live, if you don't mind me asking?

"Umm… the Bluebird Apartments," I answer, then bite into my burger.

"That's on Field Street on the edge of town, right?"

"Yes," I answer.

"They're nice. What is it, about two miles away or so?" he asks, then sips his soda.

"I guess."

"If you don't mind me asking, how did you get here?"

"I drive a Volkswagen Beetle. It's right there," I say and point to the car in the small lot.

"That looks nice," Steven says as he looks out the window. "How fast did you drive here?"

"I don't know. Thirty miles per hour, I guess. Why?" I ask, and am now rather confused.

"How do you know how fast you were going?"

"By looking at the speedometer."

"Why didn't you drive seventy miles per hour?" he asks, and bit into his second hot dog.

"Well, it's illegal, so I don't want a ticket. Besides, it's mostly through residential areas, so it would be unsafe."

"What if your speedometer was broken? Would you drive that fast then?"

"No," I answer.

"How would you know how fast to go?"

"I'd just go the speed that seems right, making sure not to move too fast and get into trouble or hurt someone," I answer.

Pastor Chalke doesn't say anything. He just sits there, silently, sipping his soda while I process what I just said.

"Well played, Pastor," I say with a smirk on my face. "Thank you."

"You're welcome," he says, then gets serious. "About your past relationships, have you atoned and asked God for forgiveness?"

"I have, and am still working on that. God and I have long conversations often," I answer. "I hope He forgives me."

"I'm sure He has," Pastor Chalke says. "Let's pray for you now."

He reaches across the table to take my hands in his. He prays quietly so only he and I can hear, and not only prays for forgiveness for me, but for me to find direction when it comes to Janus. He lets go, and while I thought he was done, he says something more.

"Janus is a good man, Saturn, and you may be just what he needs. Now, how about telling me more about your job in advertising? That must be some fascinating work."

We talk a little bit, and of course, he wants to hear my voice impression of him. I quoted a passage I remembered from his sermon earlier today, and he smiled as I spoke. We part ways with a handshake, then I head home for the evening. I added a few more sticks to my current projects, but I just wasn't feeling it. Instead, I grab my study NIV Bible that Chloe gave me, and try to see what God has to say about love. When I finish, I pray extra-long before lying down, hoping for more dreams to help guide me down this weird path I seem to be on.

Chapter 8

Celebrating Firsts

The next day, I found myself standing in the middle of a golf course. Not mini golf, but the real thing. I wasn't playing golf, and I didn't have a bag. I was standing in the middle of the big, green lawn, alone, taking a shower. Yes! There was a square shower head just above me, pouring hot water onto me as I held soap and began bathing.

There were no curtains around me or anything else to give me even a hint of privacy. No. I was standing there, in the middle of this golf course, naked as the day I was born, showering in front of anybody who was there, giving them a show they probably weren't expecting to see.

I can see myself, and I look like I normally do when I'm, well, undressed. There was this older couple, maybe early sixties, who just hit their balls, and they rolled by me. The lady came walking up to me and asked if I had seen where her ball went. I figure she can see all there is to see of my body, so there was no sense in acting all modest and trying to cover up. I pointed to the few feet away where she and her presumably husband's balls were, and she thanked me like my taking a shower, totally naked, out in the open on that golf course was the most normal thing in the world. I continued to lather up, thinking I may as well finish the job, having no idea what to do when I was done, since I didn't see any of my clothes or even a towel near me.

I heard bells ringing. I get startled awake and realize that it was all a dream. I'm wearing pajamas, sleeping on my couch, and am thankful that what happened on the golf course was just a fantasy of mine. Wait! No, not a fantasy. It was a dream, but what, if anything, did it mean?

Janus and I played mini golf recently, and while I can't control his visions, I know for sure he didn't see me in the buff that night. The older couple in the dream looked a little like Janus's parents, Angela and Jesse. Did the dream mean they want to see me naked, showering on a golf course? I highly doubt that. Dreams aren't always literal, and neither should their interpretations be. Did it mean that I should bare my soul to Janus? We're barely a month in, so even if that's what the dream meant, it's still not happening any time soon. What I really think is that I should get up and get ready for work. With a stretch of the arms, I massage my neck a little, pat Muffin's head, stand up, and head for the bathroom. Soon, I'll be leaving for work.

It's a rather busy day for a Monday, but not in a good way. The county just held its primary elections, and the general elections are coming up in November. Many politicians call the office to inquire about extending their campaigns, while those who lost call to say they won't be renewing their ad campaigns. Company rules are that we treat all clients equally, regardless of whether we have voted for them or plan to vote for them. We also inform clients that we attach a disclaimer to all our political ads stating that All-Ways Advertising doesn't endorse any candidates or policies shown in the ads. I'm new to town and not sure who is who yet, so I believe I can help with their billboard needs impartially, as the case may be.

Karen's newspaper ad for Cheaper by the Frozen came out today, so after work, she and I went down there to celebrate. No, we don't celebrate every time a new ad comes out, but in the case of ice cream, we figured, why not?

We go there after work, and I get myself another banana split while Karen gets a Cheaper by the Frozen Frenzee, which is a cup of ice cream with your choice of add-ins, including fruit, candy, and other flavorings. Karen has a medium with Oreos mixed in, and since this was her campaign, she paid for it.

"So, how do you like the agency so far?" she asks after we take a seat.

"I really enjoy doing it. It's been my dream job since I was around thirteen."

"Well, prepare yourself. The political ad season could be rather hectic. I just started four years ago during the last cycle, and it was maddening."

"Do they get upset if the ads aren't perfect?" I ask.

"No more than a normal client. They're mostly in 'campaign mode,' so they will be nice to you for the most part. Some have trouble understanding that we can't publish what we know to be untruths about their opponents. Most are reasonable with their requests, but just be careful, Saturn. If you're not sure, ask anyone for help. We can't be getting the agency sued over anything like that." She takes a spoonful of her treat while I process what she just said, then changes the subject. "So, how's Janus been?"

"Good, I suppose. He didn't call today, but I don't think we're on a 'talk every day' basis yet, so that's fine."

We talk more about us, and her love life as well. She's not seeing anybody steadily right now, but will go out on dates a few times a month, or look for men to dance with at the civic club on some Friday nights.

The next day was full of surprises. We do have a few politicians coming in, wanting to rush their next ad campaign. This is when we all work as a team, making sure that the billboard, print, radio, television, and any other ads we run all have the same message for the same candidate. I've been asked to do voiceovers for these, giving them the tone needed for the ad. Negative ads, which I hate, have to sound confrontational, while those for the candidate need to be done using a more reasoned voice, almost like you're trying to convince a five-year-old to eat her peas.

We do get a nice surprise around lunchtime. Today is the day that the Here and There Pizza billboard campaign starts, so they sent over enough free pizzas to last us a week. Okay, maybe just enough for the day with plenty of leftovers, but still. This was my first ad – and I mean ever – so a big fuss was made over me, including the requisite "Speech! Speech!" cry from the other employees. I wasn't sure if they were serious, so I gave a mock Oscar acceptance speech, exaggerating everything. They all get a kick from it, and Karen even hugs me when I step down from the chair they had me stand on.

I asked if I could keep all of the leftovers, and since it was my campaign, everybody agreed to let me have them. Once the party, if you will, is over, I return to my office, close the door, and make a call.

"Hi, Saturn," Janus says in a happy voice.

"Do you have plans for dinner?" I ask.

"Nothing solid," he answers.

"Good. I want to take you out for dinner. My treat."

"Great. Should I pick you up at 6:00?" He asks.

"No," I almost shout. "I mean, I want to pick you up. I can leave after work; there's no need for me to go home and change. Should I pick you up from where you live?"

"You get off at 5:00, right?"

"Yes."

"Okay, just come to the store. I'll be outside waiting for you."

We hang up, and I wonder if I should be worried that he doesn't want me to pick him up from home. Does Sunny live nearby, or possibly with him, and does he want to keep me hidden from her? No, that's nonsense. She saw me with him at the dance. So why the store and not his place? Well, I have to worry about that later. Right now, I have work to do for a mayoral wannabe that I know very little about.

I get to Janus's store a little after five. He is waiting outside just as he said he would be, and I get out to greet him. He says hi, again offers no kiss, but now, after talking with Pastor Chalke yesterday, I'm okay with that. We get into my car, and I drive to the location of our date, not telling Janus where we are going or what we are doing.

I pull over to a street curb in the middle of a block and announce that we're here. Janus is confused as he doesn't see a restaurant anywhere.

"There," I say, pointing.

"Where?" he asks.

"That bench. That is where we're having dinner. I brought leftover pizza, but I forgot drinks, so we'll have to eat it dry."

"Wait," he says, then goes into a hardware store. He comes out a minute later with a couple of bottles of water. He hands me one, and when I couldn't get it uncapped, I hand it back to him for him to do it for me.

"I didn't know they had a pop machine in there," I say.

"They don't. I do a lot of business with them and know the owner. He was happy to sacrifice a little water for one of his best customers," he explains, then he hands me my bottle.

We sit on the bench, eating pizza, and I'm being quiet. I want to burst, but I also want to wait for him to ask. He finally does, and not a moment too soon.

"So, why are we eating here?" he asks, then bites into his second piece.

"Well," I say, then sigh heavily. "It's a big day for me. I wanted to share it with someone. I hope… I hope by inviting you here, you don't think… You don't think… don't think that I think that we're more than… well… I needed to share it with someone."

"What?" he asks, looking a little amused and a little concerned.

"Turn around."

He does, then I point in the distance about a half a block away.

"Is that?" he asks.

"It is!" I shout. "It's my billboard. MY BILLBOARD! My very first billboard! My very first ad, ever! I've been waiting for this moment for a long time, and it's finally happened!"

I start to tear up a little, feeling a little silly over a billboard. Still, it was MY billboard.

Janus stares at it, and a smile comes to his face. "That is wonderful," he says.

"Thanks. There are four others in the area. I won't bore you with them, so this one is good enough," I say.

"Oh, no, you don't. Tonight, when we're done eating, I want you to take me to see all of them. I am so proud of you, Saturn. I hope mine looks just as good."

"Me, too," I say.

While we eat, I stand with a pizza in hand, and Janus uses my phone to take several pictures of me with the billboard in the background. We even walk closer to it to take some shots, and when a couple about our age sees us, I say, "That's my billboard," and they just walk away looking funny at me. I don't care.

I immediately texted some pictures to my family and friends and posted them on my social media accounts. Mom asked why Janus wasn't in the pictures, and I said he'd taken them. Also, it was because this was my moment. I don't know what the future holds for me and him, and I didn't want my first pictures in my first ads to be tainted by an ex. I'm not hoping for that to happen. I'm just being pragmatic. Don't judge me.

We clean our messes, then I drive Janus to the other four. I asked him which one he liked best, and of course, he said all of them. He'd be right, too. They are all masterpieces, but the first one we went to was the first one I helped design. My firstborn. My legacy. Okay, I'm being silly now, but come on. I've worked hard for this, and it finally happened!

I asked if I should take him home, and he said to bring him back to the store. I do, and by the time we got there, it was closed.

"Well, goodnight," he says, "and congratulations again. Tonight was your special night, and I'm happy you chose to share it with me."

He puts his hands on my waist, leans down, and plants a big kiss on my lips. It wasn't our biggest, but for some reason, it was more than I was expecting, especially since it seems I'm the one usually initiating bigger kisses. He releases the kiss, and I want to hold him for a little while longer. We stand on the sidewalk by the store's front door, arms around each other, just hanging on to each other. I finally loosen up, say goodnight again, and give him another peck on his lips.

I leave for work extra early the next morning. I don't need gas or to stop for breakfast. No, I just want to drive past the billboards again. I know soon this will all be old hat to me, that seeing my billboards and other ads will give a "Been there, done that" feeling, but for now, I plan to enjoy this feeling for all its worth.

It was a typical day. Phone calls, emails, ads, client meetings. All of those were happening. Karen and I spent lunch together at Taco Tom, and I regret those three tacos with hot sauce for the rest of the day. I'm sure those in the recording studio also weren't too pleased with my dining option.

Janus doesn't call, and that's fine. I come home tired, needing an evening to myself to catch up on crafts for the upcoming show and on the Gospel of

Matthew. I read the first couple of chapters, trying my best to understand and incorporate what I learned into my nightly prayers.

Thursday is a lot like Wednesday, just this time I bring lunch from home instead of going out with a co-worker. I keep my office door closed for my meal, just wanting some more alone time.

I go home and have a frozen dinner. Mom never cared for us having those, calling it the lazy way out, but I am tired and need something quick and easy before I need to leave again.

I get to Andrea's Arts and Crafts fifteen minutes before 6:00 p.m., which is when the first craft sticks class is to start. I see in the window some of her crude advertising for it, and I have to stop and look. It's crude, but not bad for an amateur. It may get some students, but hopefully not too many. I'm not sure if I can teach, so I guess we're all finding out tonight.

I set things up in the back classroom and even bring some of my past projects so they can see what can be built with a little patience and know-how.

The class begins, and three kids —Johnny, Maryann, and Katelyn —and one adult, Gloria, sign in. Gloria looks a little uncomfortable, but I assure her that she'll be fine, as this is a hobby for all ages.

I first introduce myself, then tell them a little about how I got started. I showed them some of my early pieces and a couple more recent ones. They "Ooh" and "Ahh" as they get passed around, and I can't help but smile a bit.

I then discuss the sticks a little, how to tell the good ones from the bad ones, and that the bad ones need not be thrown away, but can be cut down and used as good, shorter ones. I show them how to hold the glue bottle and how to distribute the white goo evenly.

"Don't worry too much if it drips down," I tell them. "It dries colorless. You may want to wipe down any extreme excess so it's not bumpy, but don't get too obsessed with it. With time and practice, you'll have your dripping down to a minimum."

"Do you ever drip, Miss Saturn?" Katelyn asks.

"Yes, I do," I answer honestly. "I just wipe it like I showed you and try not to do it again."

We begin by building a base for a basic box. It's not rocket science, and you hardly need a teacher to do it, but having one motivates you more, and being in a group offers encouragement from others.

We start building the box's walls, which takes patience. You can only put up two or three layers before having to stop for a while, wait for the glue to dry, and then proceed. If you try to do it too soon, the sticks are very slippery and hard to handle. We get the first layers done before class is dismissed for the week. The students left their projects behind and promised to return next week to finish. I stayed, started cleaning up the mess, when Andrea came in.

"How'd it go?" she asked.

"Pretty good. Gloria, the adult, felt out of place at first, but that soon passed. They all said that they'll be back next week."

"Well, that's good. Are you planning to show them how to do it like this?" she asks as she picks up a rather involved piece.

"Well, more of the techniques on how to do something like that. Doing that would take half a year of classes."

"What if we get new students next week? Will you be able to handle new students with old?" she asks, then puts the piece down.

"I should. I guess we'll see how it goes, really. I enjoyed this and am looking forward to next week."

"Well, here's your cut," she says, then hands me $24. "I hope this catches on."

I take the money and thank her. I'd like to stay and chat some more, but I really need to get home and rest before I turn in for the night. Karen was right about this being a crazy time at the agency. Still, dreams can be crazy sometimes. That golf course shower one the other night proves that.

I just want some mindless entertainment for tonight, so once I settle in, I turn on YouTube and play an hour-long video that is nothing but news bloopers. I laugh at the reporters as they fall, say the wrong things, and, at times, do not realize that the camera is on and the world could see them. Most seem to be good sports about it, but several are filled with beeps as the person doesn't like their current situation.

When it's done, I turn it off, then read a little more from Matthew, holding my Bible in my right hand and petting Muffin, who's sitting on my lap, with my left. He purrs a bit, and each time I smile down at him and pet him a little more firmly.

I get to the part in Matthew where John the Baptist prepares the way, and think that's a good place to mark the page and pick it up later. As I pray, I say extra sentiments for Venus and the child she is carrying, Pastor Chalke, and Sunny Knight. Yes, I say a prayer for Sunny. I pray to hope to get to know her better one day, and for Janus, as he is possibly dealing with dating more than one woman at the current time. That's his business, I suppose, and his right. Should I be open to dating other men? For the time being, let's just say I'm not entirely, one hundred percent closed to the idea. Drat! Drat! DRAT!

Chapter 9
Friday Homecoming

I arrive at work Friday morning at my usual time with a couple of dozen donuts in hand.

"Did you land a new account?" Diane Finley, who mostly handles television ads, asks.

"No. I just thought we'd all enjoy some for an end-of-the-week treat," I answer.

We bring them into our usual 9:30 morning meeting, which seemed to be a bit of a distraction, but a welcome one. We discuss all of the political ads that will be planned through November, and I tell them that Jack Perry of Jack's Coffee and Pastry will be there at 10:00, and that Karen will be joining us for the meeting.

The meeting is soon adjourned, and Gretchen takes the last donut in the box. She's the owner, so I suppose that's her right. Karen and I go into my office and compare notes until the time that Jack shows up.

He arrives a few minutes late, apologizes for it, we tell him it's no big deal, and then get down to business.

Jack's Coffee and Pastry is a part of a six-store strip mall that is near the outer edge of Oakfield's modest downtown. Oakfield, along with Mapletree, makes up most of the 50,000 residents of Kardi County, with the rest of the cities being smaller in population and mainly farming towns.

"First. I suggest changing your sign to your shop," I say.

"Why? What's wrong with it?" he asks.

"Nothing, if it were alone. There are six stores, and your sign is the middle one on the right. The ones above and below it are the same red color, so it looks like it's all part of Eddie's Electronics and not three separate stores. If yours is a different color, say yellow, then not only will yours stand out, but

Eddie's and Oakfield Auto Parts will as well," I explain.

"I see," he says.

"A lot of your business comes from impulse buying," Karen explains. "There are many who might already be shopping at the other stores in the strip mall and will stop in yours for a coffee or treat on a whim."

"What do you mean?" he asks.

"Well, it's more likely for someone going to purchase a new battery for their car to buy coffee or treats from you than someone coming for a medium decaf will end up buying a flat screen television on a whim. I mean, I suppose it could happen, but coffee and donuts are more impulsive purchases than wiper blades or a new e-reader," Karen explains.

"You may also want to add something below Jack's Coffee and Pastry. Something like, in smaller letters, 'Tea Lattes Cappuccinos' will show that you offer more than just coffee and baked goods," I add.

"Wait. You guys do signs out front?" Jack asks, a little confused.

"The sign out front is a main way to advertise, so of course we do. Now, about your other advertising needs. We'd think that one billboard on the main road from the residential part of Oakfield leading to the shopping district would be ideal. Depending on your budget, a radio or television ad could be done. That's up to you," I say.

"How much is a television ad?" he asks.

We go over a budget with him. Since few would be coming in from Indianapolis or other cities just for coffee, we recommend that he buy ad space on the local county's TV station during the morning news program. The agency could produce the ad, and we could start him on a month-long campaign.

"Who will be the face of these ads?" Jack asks. "I'm not sure I could afford a professional actor."

"Well," Karen starts, knowing that this part always gets a little uncomfortable. "Are there any employees of yours that you think would look good on camera? That would make a good face for Jack's Coffee and Pastry?"

"Well, there is this… one… she's young, nineteen… and she's… well…"

"Mr. Perry," I say, hoping to put him at ease. "We're not asking who you think would look good in a small bikini, looking seductively at the camera. She'd wear her normal uniform, looking like she normally does, with a bit of makeup enhancements to look better for the cameras. She'd do as she normally would during the course of her shift. Nobody will force her to do what she doesn't want to do, and she has the right to refuse, of course. We're not asking you who you think is 'hot' or would like to date, just who you think would make a good face for your campaign. If you like, we could hire somebody, but the prices go up for that."

"Well," Jack says as he runs his hand through his hair. "Her name is Sindi Green. I think she may make a very good face for Jack's. She's good with the customers and has a bubbly personality."

"Perfect," Karen says. "That's exactly what you want. Is she there now?"

"I believe so," he answers.

"Let's take this meeting there and have some lattes," Karen says. "Would that be okay with you, Mr. Perry?"

"Jack. And that would be fine. Let's go."

I ride with Karen, and we get to Jack's Coffee and Pastry soon after. Jack instructs the barista on duty to prepare for us any latte of our choosing and a piece of pastry, if we like. I take the latte of the day, this time it's some white chocolate thing, and a piece of chocolate cake, and Karen has the same. Jack asks us to take a seat at a table out of the way while he goes and gets Sindi.

She approaches us, walking next to Jack, and I thought that she'd be perfect for the ad—strawberry blonde hair to her shoulders, and just wavy enough. The apron over her uniform fits her perfectly, and the black framed glasses add that something special. She smiles when she gets close, and I know that she's the perfect face for Jack's Coffee and Pastry. She sits, and introductions are made.

"It's nice to meet you, Saturn," she says, and to my relief, her voice also fits the image that we were looking for.

"Good morning, Sindi. I can call you Sindi, is that okay?" I ask, and she nods. "Great. We'd like to speak with you about doing a television ad for the coffee shop."

We sit and talk, and as we do, she asks all of the right questions. I thought she'd be good in advertising, but I kept that opinion to myself. We told her our vision for the ad, which would basically be her serving some coffee and pastries to a customer, just as she does all day. We told her that the spot wouldn't pay anything extra, but she'd be pampered for about half a day, and the extra customers expected to come will amount to more tips for her, especially if they recognize her as the one from the ad.

"And seeing myself on TV would be fun," she adds.

"Yes, it is," I agreed.

We told her that we'd have a standard contract for her to sign when we shoot the commercial, which would be the following Monday. It would be written in simple English that she'd easily understand. Still, it would basically state that she'd appear in that and possibly other advertisements for the coffee shop, whether on television or in print. It also clarifies that neither the pictures nor any private information she provides will be shared or sold to anyone else, including any company, entity, or corporation.

"You could retain a lawyer and have him check it out, either in person or we could fax it to him," Karen says.

"I think I could understand it," Sindi answers.

"Great," I say. "Well, if that's it, we'll be back on Monday around 2:00 p.m. and get this ad on camera."

We all shake hands, then Karen and I go back to the agency and update Gretchen on what is happening. She liked my initiative and said there may be a bonus in my future. I smile at that, then we go to our separate offices.

I work through lunch again with the door closed. I actually think about bringing some craft sticks and supplies to the office to help me think, but I will contemplate that more later.

I'm lost in my work, trying to get a soft script set for Monday's shoot at Jack's, when my phone rings. I look at the caller ID and see that it's Janus.

"Hi," I answer.

"How are you doing?" he asks.

"I'm very busy right now. Is there something important you need?" I ask, then realize how harsh that may have sounded. "I mean, I hope I didn't sound rude, and I didn't mean to be…"

"Saturn, I just called to see if you wanted to go out on a date tonight," he says.

"Well…" I think about it for a moment, then I say something that really surprises even me. "I think I'm going home to Hohman tonight and will be staying at my parents' house."

"Oh," he replies.

"Just overnight. I'd invite you, and you could stay in Venus's room, but I don't think we're there yet."

"No, that's fine. You're right, we're not. How about tomorrow night? A good old-fashioned movie and dinner? I'm sure something is playing at the Twinplex downtown. If we don't like one movie, I'm sure the other will be… well, let's just see," Janus answers.

"That sounds fun," I say.

"How about we take in the early show at five, then dinner across the street at Taste of Italy. Do you like Italian food?" he asks.

"I sure do," I say, almost tasting the lasagna.

"Should I pick you up at 4:30?" he asks.

"How about I meet you there instead? I'm not sure how long I'm staying in Hohman, but I'll make sure to be back in time for the movie."

"Great. I'll see you then," Janus says. "And, Saturn…"

"Yes?" I ask after an awkward pause.

There is another awkward pause, then Janus finally speaks. "Have fun."

"I will," I say, then hang up. I feel a little distracted for the rest of the workday, thinking about whether I'm actually going to be going home for the night.

"Well, if I lied, then I'd have to say extra prayers tonight," I say to myself.

I call home, and Dad answers. I tell him I'm coming home overnight, and he sounds happy. "We can look through the telescopes," I tell him. He says that he's looking forward to it and will see me tonight.

When five comes around, I couldn't leave quickly enough. I hurry home, throw some clothes into a shopping bag, make sure Muffin is fed and his litter box clean, and I make the two and a half or so hour trip back to Hohman.

Because of the time difference, I pull in front of my old house around 7:00 p.m. Mom and Dad come out to greet me, and both hug me extra hard.

"It's barely been two months," I tell Mom mid-squeeze.

"And your point is?" she asks. "Come on in, dinner is ready."

We eat chicken, mashed potatoes, and corn, all of which are on my plate get smothered in gravy. They ask about my work, and I can't sound more excited as I talk about my accounts and my new billboard.

"We saw the picture," Dad says, then points to a wall in the front room.

He had a picture of me next to my billboard developed into an 8 X 10, and has it hanging next to Venus and Eric's wedding picture. While I do love my job, I hardly love it as much as she loves him. I hope they're not thinking that's as close to a wedding photo as they will get with me.

"Are you still dating that man?" Mom asks. "The junk dealer?"

"He works in restoration, not junk, Mom," I correct. "He has a better degree than I or Venus have."

"Right," Mom says. "So, are you still seeing him?"

"Yes. Just dating. It's nothing serious," I answer.

"Do you see a future with him?" Mom asks.

"We have a date for tomorrow night. Dinner and a movie. He may be going out with someone else tonight. We're not exclusive or anything, so it's fine."

But is it fine? I ask myself. It nearly crushed me saying that, but I didn't want Mom to think we are more than we are. I suppose it's good to remind myself of that, as well. I need to stop thinking about it.

"Can we look into space after dinner dishes are done?" I ask Dad.

"You two go ahead," Mom answers for him. "I can take care of these dishes myself."

I pull my telescope out from the garage and get it set up next to Dad's. He asks what we should look at first, assuming I'd say Saturn, as he starts to point his telescope in that direction.

"Venus," I answer. "I want to see Venus."

Dad is surprised, then adjusts his telescope without asking why. This time, I try hard to really focus on Venus and notice something. When it's not focused correctly, it looks like a white smudge. However, when you take the extra time that's needed to focus just right, something amazing happens. You see Venus for what it really is. It's not some white, blobby-looking thing, but a beautiful, almost indescribable, orange and yellow planetary beauty. It's amazing what happens when you take the time to really discover the intricacies of something, as it's just like my sister – a blobby mess at first glance, but something of understated beauty once you take the time to look at her properly.

"Wow," I whisper.

"What?" Dad asks.

"Oh, nothing. Let's look at Saturn now."

We adjust our telescopes, and I focus mine in. Yes, I still think Saturn is more beautiful than Venus, and you can take that however you like. I ask Dad about Janus and if we could see it through our telescopes.

"Let me try," he says, then takes over mine.

He moves it slightly, adjusts the focus, and says it's the thing in the middle. I look and laugh. Now THAT is a blobby mess. It's oblong, full of craters, and lacks any color. But I don't know. Upon closer look, it's ruggedly handsome, just like the man.

I stare at it for longer than I probably should have, both amazed by its looks and thinking about what he may be doing tonight. Is he out with Sunny now? I didn't know. I had a chance to be with him but declined, so now he's free to do as he wishes.

Dad and I look at Jupiter and then Neptune before I say I've had enough. We leave our telescopes out, go inside, and play Sorry with Mom. We pay half attention to the game, while the other half of the time we discuss my career choice and my new town.

"I like the city, even the county, and I really love my job. Remember, Mom? We saw that billboard that said, 'Do you need a sign from God? Here it is,' and the one next to it that said 'Your ad here'? God gave me a sign, Mom. I truly believe that. I am where He wants me to be. I'm even going to a church and am a little involved in their outreach committee. I know you miss Venus and me – I miss her too, if truth be known – but we're both where we belong for now."

I win at Sorry, and then Dad wins a game of Yahtzee. I say goodnight, then go to my old room. I must say, it is nice sleeping in a regular bed again, but I think I'll still delay the purchase of one for my apartment. I say my prayers, again asking God for some guidance when it comes to Janus, and ask Him to keep me from moving too fast. I sleep through the night, only stirring awake once or twice and noticing how much I miss Muffin being close to me as I sleep.

I wake around 8:00 a.m. without an alarm. It seems that my body has gotten used to that time and, despite the time change, it just knows when to get up.

I go into the kitchen area wearing shorts and a long T-shirt, expecting to pour a bowl of Raisin Bran for breakfast, when I discover that Dad had prepared a large breakfast that he usually reserved for Christmas or other special events.

"You're home, so it is a special event." Mom reasons as she sets the table.

To Mom's surprise, I asked to say grace for us, and she actually approved not only for me to do it, but for what I said. As we feast, the conversation goes more toward my new town and what there is to do there.

"Not a whole lot," I admit. "But, honestly, I prefer the slower pace. Around here, it seems everybody acts as if they're perpetually ten minutes late for wherever it is they are going. It's different there. People drive closer to the speed limit and spend more time in restaurants and at parks. Not everything is scheduled with a hard time limit, and I find that rather refreshing."

"You mean you go to work whenever you want to?" Dad asks.

"No, some things are scheduled, like work days. Of course, it's not that free. But when I leave to visit a place to create a better ad for them, it's more relaxed. Sure, there may be time limits, to a point, but it's not like every last thing is scheduled. I wonder if life on the farm is that way for Venus." I say that last part, trying to hint that I don't want to discuss my work anymore. It doesn't work.

"Do you still do voices?" Mom asks.

"Yes. Speaking of which, I want to take my ventriloquist dummy back home with me," I say, seeing Mom squirm a little when I refer to my apartment as home. "My telescope, too. I bet the night sky looks so much different there."

"Sure," Dad answers. "I'll help you pack it so it won't get damaged during the ride."

I helped Mom with washing the dishes, putting them and everything else away right away, as she always insisted, and then we discussed what to do for the rest of the morning.

"Let's see if Venus is available," I suggest.

We get her and Eric on a Zoom call. They sit close to one another and constantly smile at each other. We ask how their farm and wedding business are doing, and they said that the farm is flourishing, but the wedding events could be more regular.

"Have you tried advertising?" I ask.

"Always with the ads," Venus says with a bit of attitude. Ahh, the good old days.

"How else are people to learn that you offer them?" I ask. "Word of mouth is good, but I bet a well-designed, well-placed billboard would do wonders for the business."

"And I suppose you want to do that through your company?" she asks.

"We can, sure. At least I think we can. Or I could find a good advertising agency near Omaha for you. It's up to you, sis and bro-in-law. How are things otherwise?"

They say that Venus is still keeping up with her farm duties, but they will be looking into extra help come the harvest season, as she'll be further along by then. That was Mom's cue to jump in, and they spent the next half an hour discussing everything from baby names to diaper changing to what you do when the baby gets fussy.

"Have you considered any names?" Mom asks.

"Well, we're still deciding if it's a boy. If it's a girl, then Phoebe, which is a moon of Saturn. Her full name would be Phoebe O Brown."

"O? You mean, O, as in…?" I ask, or more stammer out.

"Of course," Venus says. "That was Eric's idea."

Venus looks at Eric, smiles, then gives him a little kiss. I am so shocked by what she just said that I have to excuse myself and lock myself in the bathroom.

I think about that for a moment. Here is Venus Birchard Syres, as a teen, who thought mainly about herself and constantly tried to change me, now wanting to name her firstborn after me. Well, partially after me, anyway. And don't think that that "moon of Saturn" thing escaped me. It didn't. If Janus and I make it, will he change me that much? No time to think about that now. I wipe my eyes, flush the toilet to make it seem like… well, I suppose you could guess that part, and return to the Zoom chat.

Mom is giving Venus more parenting advice as I take my seat back. I let them talk and look at Venus in a whole new way, and I think she notices. Eric looks at his watch, then announces that he hates to do this, but there are chores around the farm that need tending. A round of goodbyes follows, then I close the laptop, thinking about the name thing, but not bringing it up again. It is Venus, after all. She may change her mind a few hundred times before mid-January comes, so I'd better not go out and buy blankets and other baby items with that name on them. Not yet, anyway.

Mom prepares a light lunch consisting of mac and cheese and hot dogs before my trip home. Dad checks the oil on my bug, asks when the last time I had it changed. I just give him a look, then realize I probably should be getting that done pretty soon. I hug them both. Mom says a traveling prayer for me, and when she is done, I hug them both again and wave out the window to them as I head back to Oakfield to get ready for my date with Janus tonight.

193

Chapter 10

Weekend Woes

I get back into Oakfield around 2:00 p.m. local time, a few hours before Janus's and my date. I don't feel like going home quite yet, and decide to maybe cash in that coupon that Jack gave me and get myself a latte and a pastry.

I pull into the lot for the strip mall and see it's rather busy. I'm sort of hoping it's not all for Jack's because I'm not in the mood for a crowd now, and if it's too busy, he may decide he doesn't need advertising after all. I park in a spot on the other side of Oakfield Auto Parts, and check my look in the mirror before exiting my car.

I begin walking toward Jack's when I see Janus coming out of the coffee shop. I consider walking over to him to see if he wants to start our date early, but I also notice him hesitating a bit. He holds the door open, then a rather attractive woman who looks about our age steps out.

They walk a few steps out of the doorway, away from me, and Janus takes her by both hands, smiling at her as he talks. I notice that she is also smiling back at him, clearly enjoying holding hands. Janus then nods, leans down, and gives her a little kiss. It looked like either a peck on the corner of her mouth or maybe on her cheek, but they clearly kissed before letting go of each other's hands and parting ways. Janus watches her walk to her little blue car, waves at her as she drives away, then gets into his truck and drives away after her.

Were they just on a date? I ask myself as I try to process what I just saw. He's allowed to date someone else, as I am, too, but does he have to date someone on the same day that he makes a date with me? Well, I'm no longer in the mood for a treat, so I'm just going to head home and sulk a little bit.

I get home and plop down on my couch. Muffin was sleeping, and when I walked in, he woke up, looked at me, yawned, then went back to sleep. I turn the TV on and see what can be suitable as background noise while I work more with my craft sticks. I settle on a channel that specializes in showing old game shows, and I answer trivia questions along with contestants as I glue more sticks together.

Soon, a show that's a version of tic-tac-toe goes to a commercial break, and as I look to see one of the classic ads they show before showing the current ones, I notice the time. I stayed seated and watched as this baker seemed to be working 24 hours a day, saying "Time to make the donuts" often, before I changed for my date.

I slip into a pair of knee-length red shorts and a blue T-shirt that says "Take My Ad-vice" and wonder once again if I should go, do a last-minute breaking of the date, or just ghost him. Options two and three seem very rude, especially since I don't even know the whole story, so I leave my apartment, hoping to get to the theater ten minutes early.

I get there eight minutes before five and see Janus sitting on a bench, presumably waiting for me. He stands when he sees me, takes both my hands in the same manner as he did the other woman earlier today, and says he's happy to see me.

"A movie and a date?" I say, trying to sound giddy. "Who can resist?"

The Downtown Twinplex, which is what the place is called, has two screens, both with movies starting at 5:15. We look, trying to decide. There's "The Perfect Couple," a rated PG-13 rom-com starring a couple about our ages who were just starting out dating. That seems so familiar to me. The other was "Life With and Without Me," a PG-rated show that is a coming-of-age story of a thirteen-year-old girl from the big city who recently moved to a farming town. That's not exactly what Venus is going through, but it's awfully close.

"What do you think?" Janus asks.

"They both look... good. I can see either. How about you choose?" This will be interesting, putting him on the spot to pick a film out of two that I doubt he'd actually want to see if I film if I wasn't weren't with him.

"Well," he says as he cups his chin with his hand, helping him think. "How about this one?"

Drat! He went for The Perfect Couple. Drat! Drat! Drat! I was hoping he'd pick the other one.

I smile, tell him that's a nice choice, then say that since he's buying the tickets, I will get the snacks. He reluctantly agrees to that.

As we wait in the concessions stand line, we discuss what we'd like. Since we're going out to dinner in a couple of hours after the movie, neither of us wants to fill up on snacks. We settle on a tub of popcorn and two small sodas, which look like they hold about a gallon each. I almost wanted to suggest one soda, two straws, but I definitely know that we're not there yet. The snacks probably cost more than what a meal will cost later today, but I suppose that's fine. Before we go into the theater, I ask Janus to wait for a moment. I have to look around and see what the ads look like first. He snickers at that, but if we're going to date, it's something he'll have to put up with. They all look typical of a movie theater lobby, showing what movies are expected to be there in the future, but the concessions stand menu board needs work.

We find seats about halfway back on the aisle. Janus takes the inner seat, leaving me to sit beside him in the end chair. They are plush, comfortable, but maybe a little too bouncy. We small-talk a little bit, talking about a whole lot of nothing when the lights dim. I tell him to hush, it's starting.

"It's just the ads," Janus says. "Nobody pays attention to them."

I give him a look that says, "You better rephrase what you just said," and he quickly realizes his error.

"I mean… I don't mean that nobody pays attention… It's just that…"

"Quiet!" I whisper-shout, then lay my hand on his, showing him I'm just kidding. But I do want to see the ads.

There was one for a national beverage company, a mall in Indianapolis, and an online hotel-booking site. I liked them. They all had movie themes, so they understood their audience, told mini-stories, and managed to hold viewers' attention.

"Those were good," I tell Janus, and a person sitting across the aisle from me gives me a funny look.

After an endless number of trailers for upcoming movies, The Perfect Couple starts. The audience goes to a hush, and soon the opening sequence of a man stuck in traffic for five minutes as the opening credits roll is shown.

Halfway through, we're having fun watching as the couple on the screen mirrors us in many ways. But in some other ways, they didn't. There are a few misunderstandings and even a sequence where both are getting aggravated waiting for their date to show, only to realize that there were two places in town with the same name, and each of them went to a different one.

Once they found each other again, the romantic part of the rom-com started happening. After they had dinner, they went back to his apartment, where he invited her to sit on the couch while he went and got the wine. "Uh, oh," I think, remembering what wine does to me.

After a few glasses, they… well, let's just say, we soon see them lying in bed next to each other. What I could never understand was why, except maybe to keep their PG-13 rating, the man lies there with the covers down to his waist, showing his well-chiseled body, while she has them up covering everything just below her neck. I mean, they just did – well, you know what they did, so why the sudden modesty on her part?

I felt uncomfortable watching with Janus sitting next to me. I leaned a little away from him, and I think he did the same. During that scene, we sat there quietly, eyes forward, trying to pretend that the other wasn't a mere two inches away.

The movie gets back to their day-to-day lives filled with mini-adventures and a few more misunderstandings before they decide to move in together at the end. I'm not sure how well the film mirrored Janus and me, but I know for sure that we won't be moving in together except in the case of marriage.

We toss our snack trash away and leave our cars parked on the street as we walk across the street to Taste of Italy. The hostess greets us, and we are taken to a booth by a front window.

"I enjoyed that movie," I say, looking at the menu.

"Me, too," Janus agrees, then reaches across the table to touch my hand. "They seemed to have found their happily ever after."

"Yes," I answer, hoping he's not thinking that we'll have a similar happily ever after. "This looks good."

I pulled my hand away as I said that and pointed to the menu at nothing. I just wanted him to stop touching my hand.

"What does?" he asks.

"Umm, the lasagna." I look quickly to make sure it's on the menu, and thankfully, it is. "It's one of my favorite dishes, but I never make it at home since it's so complex and most recipes I find are for a dozen servings, not one."

"Just divide the ingredients by 12," Janus suggests.

"Sure, that's easy for Venus to do. I was never that good at math."

"I thought you were a college graduate," he teases.

"So are you," I say, glaring at him. "And from a better one than me. Tell me, how would you suggest advertising a restaurant like this?"

"Well… I'd… ummm… I didn't really take classes on…"

"You have a degree in business. Surely, marketing was a part of that."

"It was, just not, that I didn't really…" Janus starts to stumble a little, then looks at me, smirking at him. "Okay, you made your point." We both laugh, then turn our attention back to the menus.

Our server comes and asks if we'd like wine. I tell Janus that since I'm driving, I'd rather not drink. Not even one glass. While that is valid, it's not the only reason why I declined the wine. Janus did, too, though I think a little more reluctantly than I do.

I'm soon enjoying my lasagna with garlic bread while Janus has basic spaghetti and meatballs. We split an order of roasted cauliflower with capers and almonds and talked during dinner. He tells me more about his business, how he makes old items new again, and I find it fascinating. Not just for his upcoming ad, but it really is interesting.

We both enjoy spumoni for dessert, then I use the ladies' room while Janus takes care of the check and tip.

We walk across the street to our vehicles, which are parked just a few spots apart.

"Well, I'd better be going home," I say, noticing the time.

"It's only 8:30," Janus replies.

"I know, but we have church tomorrow."

"Would you like to do something after the meeting?" he asks.

"Well," I say, then think about his date earlier today. Am I the other woman in a long-standing relationship? Well, I doubt that, but he did kiss some other woman earlier today. "Let's play that by ear."

He smiles, then leans down for a kiss. I look around and tell him that people are looking, and I don't want us to put on a show for them. I just pecked him on the corner of his mouth like he did her, then turned to leave for the night.

I get home, change into something to sleep in tonight, and sit on the couch for a little while, petting Muffin as I think. "Lord, show me the way," I say as a simple prayer before lying down and trying to sleep for the night.

I wake up to the alarm, startling myself from a dream I forget within seconds of it going off, and massage my neck to relieve some of its soreness. I make a couple of pancakes for breakfast and eat them with a few slices of bacon while watching a local Sunday morning news show on TV.

I do the dishes, get dressed in dress slacks and a button-up blue blouse, and wrap my hair in a ponytail using a scrunchie. I now realize that Janus didn't offer to drive me to church like he did every other time. Did he realize I like driving myself, or is there another reason? No matter, church is starting soon, and I do NOT want to be late. I'm starting to feel more at home there, and I'd like to pray a little before the service starts.

I sit next to Janus where we usually sit, and this time, Sunny decides to sit next to him. She engages him in conversation and barely gives me a "Hello" in acknowledgement. "Have you thought about more of what we talked about?" she asks just as the service is starting.

"Shhhh," I say to her, feeling quite satisfied over that. Yes, that's petty, but also satisfying. I'm still in transition to becoming a Christian again, so give me a little grace here.

Sunny glares at me for a moment, then we all stand as the preacher welcomes us, and the praise band begins to play their song.

The pastor preached on pacing yourself in life. He advised not to move too fast, but if you go too slow, then you may miss out on important things. He used Jesus, of course, as an example. "When He got word that Lazarus was dead, He took four days before he got there, enjoying the trip along the way. Many around said that He was too late, and His lollygagging meant that Lazarus would be in that tomb forever now."

I look over, and I see that Sunny has moved closer to Janus, her hand practically on his leg and her head nearly on his shoulder. I lose track momentarily of what is being said from the pulpit as I try to determine whether or not Janus is inviting this behavior from her.

"Lazarus, come out," Pastor Chalke said rather loudly, seemingly waking up many in the congregation. After brief laughter, he finishes his sermon, which again really hit home for me.

After the service, I go into the community room for some coffee and cookies. I'm talking with Janus's mom, Angela, about nothing much. She asks me about Hohman, and I make comparisons to that and Oakfield. I know it's still new, but I prefer Oakfield to the two, hands down.

Janus comes over and tells me that it's time for the special committee meeting. We go to the same room as we were in last week, this time I'm allowed to sit next to Janus as I'm a part of this committee of the deacons. Sunny objects, but the pastor points out that the bylaws allow me to sit where I am.

Tanner Bloom opens the meeting with a prayer, then we get right down to business.

Brynn submits receipts for the diapers and other baby changing items she bought for the church, and Joe Peppers turns in one for the tent. They start discussing how to set it up when I ask permission to speak. Pastor Chalke grants it. Then, Sunny puts her arm around Janus, leans in close, and whispers something in his ear. I see that, and try to keep myself composed.

"I had an artist at the agency draw up how he thought it would best work, both for aesthetics in the space being used, and for advertising purposes."

I hold the drawing up, and after people have a chance to soak it in, Brynn asks if I could hand it to her to pass around.

"Of course," I say, and hand it to her. "I also have these handouts for the event. They're basically what yours was, just a little cleaned up."

"I did them," Sunny says as she glimpses the drawing.

"Feel free to use yours," I say. "I'm just…"

"Demonstrating her expertise," Joe says, cutting me off, causing the other to laugh. "I move we go with what Saturn had submitted."

"I have a question," Sunny says. She whispers something close into Janus's ear again, then takes his hand in hers and holds it. "I thought you did voices and billboards, and these aren't either."

"That's not a question," Pastor Chalke answers. "Last week, Saturn's credentials were made perfectly clear to this committee. We all, or most of us," the pastor pauses to look at Sunny, "accepted her credentials. I can't vote, but there's a motion on the table. Is there a second?"

"Second," Janus says. Sunny glares at him.

"Is there any more discussion?" Pastor Chalke asks. "Hearing none, let's put it to a vote."

It passed unanimously, with Sunny abstaining this time.

There is more talk about scheduling volunteers, and when the pastor asks if I want to help, I tell him that I would be having my own craft booth at the event.

"She won't even volunteer for her project?" Sunny states. "Well, then, I think Janus and I will take the first shift, and any others that we're needed."

A brief discussion about scheduling volunteers takes place, and then the meeting ends with Janus saying a closing prayer. As we're getting ready to leave, Sunny asks Janus if he'd like to go out to lunch to talk more about it.

"That won't be necessary," he says, then she leaves, again glaring at me as she does.

Janus then asks if I'd like to go out to lunch with him. I think for a moment and say that I will.

"Nothing fancy," I say. "Harry's Hamburgers and Hot Dogs?"

"Perfect," Janus says. "Meet you there?"

We arrive fifteen minutes later, with Janus having to stay behind to lock the church. We sit at a corner table, and as I eat, I wonder where I stand with Janus, who does most of the talking. Am I his girlfriend? A fling, of sorts? Friends? Well, I know we're more than friends, but how much more? I'd really like to learn, but I still heed Pastor Chalke's advice about not moving too fast.

"Want to do something else?" Janus asks as we clear the table.

I look him in the eyes, and still don't see how Eric looks at Venus.

"The park," I answer. "I want to go to the park."

"That sounds delightful," he says.

We get there and start walking around a trail. He tries to hold my hand a couple of times. But I swing my arms, pretending I'm not aware, not allowing him to do that. I'm still in deep thought when I see a bench coming up, with nobody around but the occasional walker-by.

"Let's sit," I say, then do. Janus sits next to me. I scoot away a little and urge him to do the same.

"What's wrong?" he asks.

"Janus," I say, then take a deep breath. I have to do this now.

"Yes?" he asks, sensing the seriousness in my voice.

"Janus," I say again, then hold up my finger when he tries to talk. "I know we've only been going out for a few weeks, and I have no right to…"

"To what?" he asks.

"Janus," I say again, then look him square in the eyes. "I know that we never agreed to be exclusive, and if you want to date other women, that's your right. Can I just ask that you, please, not flaunt that in front of me? It hurts when I see you like that, seeing you date others."

"Oh," Janus says, and looks down. "I did date another woman a couple of weeks ago, after our first several dates. We made the dates before you and I met. I kept them, but haven't seen her since. Even if you weren't in the picture, she just wasn't right for me."

"Oh," I say, not feeling more disappointed for some reason. "But what about…"

There is a long pause, then Janus asks me what about what? I again look him right in the eyes.

"You and Sunny are dating. I can see that. I'm okay with that, I suppose, but please quit displaying that in front of me."

Janus chuckles a little and shakes his head while looking down. He lifts his head and looks me right back in the eyes.

"I'll tell you the truth. Yes, Sunny and I dated in the past. Not in the too-long-ago past, I admit, but it's in the past. Sunny's a nice woman, but she isn't right for me. She's a dreamer. She's a candy maker – a very good one at that – who wants to open her own store. She wanted us to partner with my business, somehow bringing a resale shop together with sweet treats. I'm not sure how that would work, but she planned out our whole life after just a few dates. Yes, we dated. We kissed, and honestly, I did enjoy kissing her, but that's all over now. I promise."

"But what about… I see her putting her arms around you, you two holding hands, and how friendly she is with you," I ask.

"I've asked her several times to cool it down, honest," Janus says. "I don't want to cause a scene at church, so I allow it. You saw her hold my hand earlier today, but I didn't hold hers back. We only see each other at church and church events. I'll start being more assertive with her about her overfriendliness. I'm sorry you had to see that."

I look into his eyes, quietly. I think I see a glimmer of Eric. I decide to clear the air.

"Janus," I pause again, not liking this conversation. "I saw you on a date yesterday afternoon, before you and I went out."

"You what?" he asks. "I'm pretty sure I didn't date anybody but you yesterday."

"I saw you come out of Jack's Coffee with another woman. You held her hands, then kissed her. I mean, it's okay if you do, I'm just asking for you not to…"

"Saturn," he cuts me off. "You saw me then?"

"Yes," I say, feeling a tear fall down my cheek, but not sure why.

"Well, I wish you had come over."

"Why?" I ask.

"So I could have introduced you to Sabrina, my sister. She came in from Indianapolis for a short visit. I could show you a picture if you don't believe me."

"Your sister?" I ask, and my eyes suddenly dry up.

"Yes, my sister. Sabrina."

We sit quietly for a minute or so, then Janus takes my hand and breaks the silence.

"Saturn, I've moved too fast before. I entered into exclusive relationships too fast and said those three little words way too soon. I thought I meant them, but now I know it wasn't… that."

"Oh," I say, not knowing what else to say.

"Saturn," he says, and puts his other hand on top of mine that he's already holding. "I'm not ready for commitment with you now, but I'm also not actively looking to date anyone else, either. You are free to date whomever you want, and still date me. Let's just keep doing what we've been doing, maintaining a good speed about us, and see if we get there. Just promise me one thing."

"Yes," I say, then he squeezes my hands a little.

"If you start dating someone else, and you believe he's the one, break it off with me. I'll be fine. I promise to do the same for you. In the meantime, let's enjoy what we've got going here because, to be honest, this is the best start of any relationship I've ever had. What do you say?"

I think about it for a moment, then take my hands back.

"That sounds like a perfect plan, Janus," I say. "This also has been the best start of any of my relationships. Well, except for maybe this boy I met while on vacation in Wisconsin Dells."

"Hey!" Janus playfully jokes.

"I was seventeen. The relationship lasted two days, and he was my first kiss. It was perfect," I honestly say.

"It sounds that way," he says, smiling.

We sit there for a few more minutes, quietly looking at our surroundings, both taking in the conversation we just had. I'm the one who breaks it this time.

"You say that Sunny is a candy maker looking for a business and possibly a life partner?" I ask.

"That's one way of saying it," Janus says as he chuckles. I sit up and look at him.

"Want to play matchmaker? That just may solve a problem that we both have."

Chapter 11
Manic Monday

The alarm rings at 7:30 and wakes me up. Yeah, I had to set it for half an hour earlier to prevent me from having to rush around so much. I pet Muffin, who is lying on my belly, before I open my eyes. I eventually do and sit up, causing Muffin to run off, then turn off the alarm. I give my neck its usual rubbing, and this time include parts of my back that are also suffering from sleeping on this couch.

My mind immediately goes back to last night and what Janus and I talked about. Dating non-committally seems the best choice for us, though, to be honest, I don't plan on actively looking for anybody else to date. Janus could, but I honestly hope that he doesn't. I like the idea of a non-committed committed relationship. Drat! Dating could be unnecessarily complicated at times.

I also think about the other thing we talked about. He has a candy maker who is looking for a life and business partner who gets too cozy with him, and I have a coffee-mogul wannabe who is looking for something similar, who won't stop bugging me. Maybe if we get those two together, then… then… then I'd better get up and get ready for work.

I consider driving out of my way to see my billboards again, but I fight off the urge. Okay, I drove past one. Don't judge! It's still as beautiful as they get.

I get to work a little earlier than usual, so I get the coffee machine going before anything else. I go into my office and look at the grassy area outside my window, noticing how bare it looks. I sit and look to see what's on the schedule, and am reminded that today is another big day. It's the day we shoot the coffee commercial and take pictures for a potential billboard.

I make it to the morning meeting at 9:30, and since this is my first commercial shoot, we go over what to expect.

Since we're a small agency, and Gretchen likes to keep costs down so we can undercut the competition, we're expected to learn how to operate the cameras, lights, microphones, and other equipment used, as well as the makeup. I'm fine with that. As long as I don't sit in a recording studio doing voices all day, I'm open to whatever it takes to put these ads out there. Besides, learning how to run the equipment sounds like fun, and that may be a skill I could use someday to open my own agency. "Saturn O Syres Advertising, Marketing, and Sales" sounds good to me, and I bet it would look great on a letterhead. "If you need help, just signal SOS," could be the slogan. Well, if I want to do that, then first things first. Let's get the rest of this day started.

After the meeting, Karen and I touch base with Diane Finley, the television ads specialist, in her office. We show her a soft script we came up with, and she nods as she reads.

"Is this actress good at ad-libbing?" she asks.

"She's a barista from the coffee shop," I answer. "However, if her personality tells on her, then she probably will be good at ad-libbing and going with the flow."

"She's nineteen and will present perfectly on camera," Karen adds.

"Well, we'll have all afternoon, correct?" Diane looks at us, and we both nod. "Then we should be able to get usable footage today. Let's be there fifteen minutes early to have a look around. I'll tell Gene to grab his stuff and drive with me."

Karen and I leave her office, and as we go to get more coffee for ourselves, we agree to take her car.

"Cream and sugar are over there," Karen says after she sees me put a stirrer in my cup.

"I take mine black," I say, then take a sip and stir it.

"Why the stirrer?" she asks.

"It annoys my sister," I reply in the same way I have answered that question countless times before.

"Okay. Well, I have a business lunch, so I'll see you back here around 1:30."

I agree, then we both retreat to our own offices. I settle into mine, still ecstatic about being hired here not too long ago. I think about the conversation that we just had with Diane and start to get nervous about the shoot. I know I'm with experts and have to trust them, but this is my account, so I have to do all I can to make sure it succeeds.

I take out the Jack's Coffee and Pastry files and find the release that Sindi Green signed. I find her phone number and dial it up, hoping and praying it doesn't go straight to voicemail. It doesn't.

"Hi, Sindi. This is Saturn Syres from All-Ways Advertising. How are you doing today?" I ask after she answers.

"Pretty good, Ms. Syres. Nervous. Very nervous, but good," Sindi answers.

"That's normal," I say, having no idea if that's true or not. God will forgive me, hopefully. "Please, call me Saturn and the others by their first names; that should ease you a little."

"Thank you, Ms. Saturn," she answers, and I let it go.

"I wanted to touch base over this afternoon's shoot. We have a soft script here, which means it's written out, but if we – or you – come up with other ideas, just speak up and we'll see if it works. Do you have an email address?"

"Yes. Of course," she answers, and says it to me.

"Great. I'll send it via a PDF attachment for you to get familiar with. If you look it over, you'll probably be more at ease this afternoon." I scan the script, tap a few buttons on my keyboard, and hit send.

"Got it," she says, and I hear her clicking, likely to look at it right away.

"Also, please wear your normal uniform. No alterations. We'll have someone there to do your makeup, and we'll walk you through the whole thing."

"I usually don't wear a lot of makeup," she says.

"That's fine," I tell her. "It's just so the camera sees you better. With no makeup, you'd look like a ghost. We won't go overboard, I promise. Remember, we won't ask you to do anything you're not comfortable with, and that includes makeup."

"Thank you, Saturn. Is that your real name?" she asks.

"Yes, it is. And O, just the letter O, is my legal, birth certificate, middle name."

"No kidding?" she says, laughing.

I laugh along with her, then decide to end the conversation.

"Just be yourself, the person I'm talking to right now, Sindi. You'll do fine. Be there by two, and prepare for a long shoot. Believe it or not, it takes a lot longer than thirty seconds to make a thirty-second commercial."

"I figured so. I'll be prepared, promise. I'll see you there, Saturn."

With that, we hang up. I jot down a few notes to the script to better match her naturally engaging personality, then wonder whether I should wait or make that other phone call now. May as well do it now. I dial extra slow, just to delay it that much longer.

"Hi, Saturn!" I hear on the other end. This is not going to be easy.

"Hi, Blake. How are you?" I ask.

"Better now that you called," he says. "Did you change your mind about me?"

I think about how I could ask him this without giving him the complete information, but also not lying. Every lie adds minutes to my prayers, and they're already going to be long enough tonight.

"How would you like to go on a double date on Wednesday? Taste of Italy in Downtown Oakfield. Do you know where that is?"

"Yeah, I've been there before," he says rather enthusiastically. "A double date? Who else is going?"

"Ummm…." Drat! I wasn't prepared for this. "That's a surprise. Meet us there at 6:00. I promise all will have a good time."

"Great, I can't wait to see you."

"See you then," I quickly say, then hang up, thinking he wanted to talk more. Do I have to add that call to my prayers tonight? I suppose a slight mention wouldn't hurt. Hey, if nothing else, I get some more lasagna. That stuff is great from there!

I made some progress working on billboard ads for competing mayoral candidates. Both are men in their mid-40s, and I think both have a good shot at winning. I'm not the most political person around, but I do have opinions, and I'll reserve judgment until election day is around the corner; then I'll look into it more to ensure I cast an informed ballot.

I received a reply from Sindi. I'm hoping nerves didn't get to her and she decided to back out. "Drat!"

I say as those thoughts flood my brain. It is quite the opposite. She looked over the script and sent back a few notes about how she thinks it may work better. I smile as I read, hoping this afternoon will go smoothly.

I don't email her back, as we'll be meeting soon, and we could discuss those in person, though I did forward it to Karen, Gene, and Diane. Lunchtime arrives, so I figure now is the perfect time to call Janus to see if our plan is working.

We talked for a few minutes, and he said that he had asked Sunny to go out on a double date, and she accepted.

"Technically, it will be a double date," Janus says. "We didn't say that it was a setup and, hopefully, those two will attract and leave together."

"It's definitely a grey area when it comes to that whole 'Thou shalt not bear false witness' commandment," I say.

"Well, I guess we'll just have to stay after church this Sunday and pray at the altar, begging God for forgiveness," Janus says, then laughs a little.

"I'd like that," I say seriously. "I mean, not the begging God for forgiveness for a very, VERY, white lie – though we could do that too – I mean, praying at the altar with you on Sunday. It's a date."

"You got it," Janus says. "I'll let you have your lunch now. Want to go out before Wednesday? Just the two of us?"

"I'll let you know," I answer. "I'm not sure how beat I'm going to be after the filming today. Goodbye."

We hang up, then I have lunch in my office. I knew that I'd be nervous, so I just packed a couple of Granny Smith apples for lunch. If I get hungry later, I'll have a pastry or two at Jack's. I'm sure that would be allowed, though we'll be working.

After lunch, I get lost in my work again. I'm looking over the script, including the edits that Sindi suggested, when Karen knocks at my office door.

"Ready?" she asks.

"For what?" I reply without looking up.

"Your big shoot. Don't tell me you forgot about it, Saturn. I thought this was a dream come true for you," she answers, smiling.

"Wait, what?" I look at my watch and notice the time. "It sure is."

We leave my office and inform office assistant Frida Small that we'll be out for the rest of the day.

"Good luck," she says more to me, and I smile back as Karen leads the way.

We get to the coffee shop, and it's already hectic. Diane and Gene got there a few minutes before us in the agency van and were inside the shop talking with Jack about where to set up the equipment.

"Will the register at the end of the counter work?" he asks. "We rarely use it. I only had it installed to use when we got busy. I'm hoping once this ad airs, we'll have to use it more often."

"That's what we want too, Jack," Diane says. "That will work fine. Is the star here yet?"

"I think she's in the back getting herself mentally prepared," Jack answers.

"Perfect. We'll start getting the equipment in now."

Diane and Gene meet Karen and me at the front door just as we're entering. Diane says we can greet the staff later; right now, we need to get everything inside.

This is my first commercial shoot, and I'm surprised by everything involved. We set up two large floodlights and positioned them on either side of the register, facing the counter. There are also two cameras planned for use. One captures an angle almost straight ahead, and the other is for a side-angle shot. Diane says to place that camera anywhere, and we'll decide its best position once we figure out which side is Sindi's good side. There is also this long pole with a microphone with a fluffy cover that will be used.

The last thing we brought was a couple of large suitcases filled with makeup and other accessories. Jack goes back to see if Sindi is ready, and moments later, she emerges next to him, looking nervous but with a big smile on her face.

We introduce her to Diane and Gene, then she takes out some yellow tape as you'd see on a police procedural drama and tapes off the area where we are to film. Customers get curious about what is happening, and Jack is assigned to crowd control, simply telling the truth about what is happening while asking them to stay behind the tape and be quiet.

Diane helps Sindi into a chair and drapes a cape around her. She starts brushing Sindi's hair while Karen, whom I learned during the drive over, took classes to become a licensed makeup artist, starts working on Sindi's face. As Sindi is being pampered, the man and woman we hired as customers just arrived. They come over, say "Hi" to everyone, introduce themselves as Vince and Peg, and once she finishes with Sindi, Diane attends to those two.

"We're probably just going to see them from behind," Diane explains, so there's no need for a lot of makeup. We brought wigs, hats, and other accessories to help them appear as many different customers. After a few sound and light checks, we're ready to start filming.

Being a smaller agency, we all learn how to operate most of the equipment we use. Since I'm new and Karen is experienced, she, along with Diane, is handling the cameras, and I get to hold the microphone pole while the artist Gene takes turns operating the different equipment to ensure everything looks right. Drat! Well, I guess my turn to run the camera will come soon enough.

We review the concept with Jack and Sindi once more. Sindi will play "Counter Girl," the one who takes orders and then serves the customers. The two actors will play "Customers." They will walk to the counter, sometimes alone and sometimes as a couple, and place their orders. First, they'll order a pastry, then Sindi will ask them, "What will you stir?" and afterward, they'll order a drink. Sindi will serve them, making sure to make a big deal about handing them a stirrer for their drink.

Sindi stands nervously behind the counter, looking over at a crowd of seven customers watching her. Diane tells her that they will rehearse it a couple of times without filming, but I see her and Karen turn their cameras on. I learn later that it's common practice to tell them that to help the star be more at ease, but they like to record everything just in case something good happens during "rehearsals," which oftentimes it does. It's not really a lie, but more of a coping technique. I'm sure God is good with that.

Diane tells Sindi whenever she's ready, and after a deep breath, she nods her head and puts on a big, welcoming smile as the lady customer walks up.

"Hi, I'll have a bear claw," Peg says in a normal, boring voice.

"Sure, and what will you stir?" Sindi says with enough charm to light up brighter than the two spotlights shining on her.

"A medium Jack's latte," she says.

Sindi turns around, grabs the tray that already has those items on it, and sets it on the counter before her. She then takes a stirrer and dips it in the coffee with the finesse of a ballet dancer.

"Perfect," Diane shouts as the crowd claps. "Let's try it again. Peg, you're still up."

Peg goes through the bit, and again, Sindi is flawless in her delivery. There is more applause from the now growing crowd, and while I didn't think it was possible, Sindi's smile became bigger and brighter.

"Wonderful, let's do this next one with the cameras on."

Diane and Karen make exaggerated motions to make it look like they turned on the already rolling cameras, and Gene peeks through both to check the shots. Sindi takes a deep breath, and Peg waits for her cue to get the scene shot.

"I'll have a cherry Danish," she says.

"And what will you stir?" Sindi asks.

"Flat white espresso."

Sindi repeats her motions, and this time she picks up the stirrer with one hand, juggles it to the other, and dips it in the drink without missing a beat.

We go through the scene several times. Diane often puts wigs on the actors, has them change clothes, and even wears an oversized winter coat under their clothes to make them look bigger or stand on a box to seem taller, making it appear that there are several customers. Vince and Peg always stick to their script, but each time Sindi changes it up a bit, either exaggerating movements or changing how she asks them what they want, but always delivers the "What will you stir?" line flawlessly.

"She is absolutely perfect, Jack," Diane says as he walks over by her to see how things are going.

"I just hope the viewers will think so," he replies.

"They will," Karen says, then Diane calls for it to be done again.

"I think I need a break," I say after holding that pole for what seemed to be hours. I think it was.

"Actually, I think we're about done here," Diane says, and Gene agrees, then turns to the actors. "Thanks for coming out." She hands them both an envelope with their payment, and Jack tells them to go ahead and order any pastry and drink from the menu, on the house. They do, and another barista besides Sindi serves them. He failed to ask them what they would stir, which I think Jack notices.

I'm thinking we're about done when Karen says something.

"What about those who like regular coffee?" she asks.

"What about them?" I ask.

"They may seem alienated, or think that Jack's Coffee and Pastry doesn't cater to them. You take your coffee black with a stirrer, right, Saturn?"

"Well, usually, yes," I reluctantly answer.

"What do you think, Diane?"

Before I know what's happening, Diana pushes me into a chair, wraps a cape around me, and starts brushing my hair. Karen takes some makeup remover and puts it on my face. Gene repositions the cameras and signals to Sindi to wait. I'm not sure what they are thinking, but it isn't happening.

"Oh, no. I make ads, I don't star in them," I say.

"Sindi is the star," Karen retorts as she starts applying makeup on me. "You have to, the actors are gone."

I think back to high school when I was in that play. I couldn't go on stage because of stage fright, so I did the voices of the exchange student's parents, talking through a microphone in the sound booth out of sight of everyone.

"I don't act, I do voices," I object again.

"Have you ever ordered anything from here before?" Diane asks as she brushes my hair.

"Well, yes," I answer.

"How did she do, Jack?" Diane asks, looking right at him.

"Perfectly," he answers.

"See, you have experience. Is she ready?" Diane asks Karen.

"Just about," she answers, then adds a little lipstick. "There."

They tell Sindi to go back to her place, then lift me up from the chair.

"Just order a plain cake donut, and when asked 'What will you stir?', say a small black coffee." Diane gives me a look like I'd better or I'm fired, and I let out a deep sigh and get into place.

"Ready," Diane says, and I look at the crowd of maybe 14 now watching. "Action!"

I walk to the counter and see Sindi smiling back at me.

"What'll it be?" she asks, using a cowgirl accent. Why not?

"Rustle me up a plain cake donut," I say in a similar accent.

"What will you stir?"

"A small black coffee."

Sindi turns and serves them to me, then acts like she's about to lasso a bull before she drops the stirrer into my coffee. I turn to walk away with a huge smile on my face, trying not to laugh at the absurdity.

"Brilliant," Diane says, and she and Karen laugh. "Now, do it again. Normal voices this time."

We go through the scene once again, and this time I do it straight, the same way the actors did, but Sindi still added some flair to her part.

Diane declares that we are done for the day, and since it's 6:00, nobody argues with her. We get everything cleared out of the restaurant, tell Sindi again what a wonderful job she did, and Diane assures Jack that the ad will be edited and ready to roll for the morning news the following Monday.

We go back to the agency, and after getting everything put away per company policy, we call it a day. I stop to get a hamburger meal on the way home, and don't get there until close to 8:00. Not only will there be no date with Janus tonight, there won't even be a call or a text.

"That's okay," I say to Muffin as he tries to swat a fry from my hand.

I get everything cleaned up at home, make sure the cat bowls are full, then go and change into my most comfy pajamas. I kneel down at the side of my bed, saying my nightly prayers, adding the few white lies I've told recently just in case.

"I can't wait to see the finished ad," I say to the kitten as I lie down, and he takes his spot on top of my belly. "Good night, Muffin."

Chapter 12

Today is Tuesday

The next morning, I set the shower temperature just a bit hotter than the near-boiling temperature I already like. I let the drops fall on my skin, relaxing my muscles and waking me up at the same time. Once my hair is shampooed and I'm all rinsed off, I stay in the shower a few extra minutes just enjoying the feeling of the moment.

I reluctantly turn the water off and towel-dry my body. I use the towel to wipe the steam off the full-length mirror hanging on the door, then take a look at my reflection. I try to determine if the extra pizza, pastries, and fancy coffees have added any pounds. The visual says I'm fine, so I feel no need to buy a bathroom scale. Besides, they always seem to be off. Every time I stand on one, it says that I'm 5-10 pounds heavier than I actually am. Trust me, it's the scales that are defective.

I dress in a basic slacks and blouse ensemble, then go to the kitchen to see what I'll have for breakfast. A bowl of Cheerios sounds just about right with a cup or two of black coffee. I pour the cereal and milk into the bowl, grab a spoon, then pour some coffee into a large mug and slip in the requisite stirrer. Yeah, I know it's a waste of money buying these to stir nothing, but it's my nothing to stir.

I turn on the morning news from Indianapolis, and it's the same old thing. One political party bickers with the other while many crimes were committed overnight, local sports won or lost yesterday, and the temperature on this June 24th is going to be hot, just like every other June 24th in Central Indiana. Ugh, when are they getting to the good stuff? I take another sip of coffee and a couple of bites of cereal, watching a traffic report for roads I rarely drive on, wondering why people love living in big cities so much. Oh, here it is. Finally, my favorite segment of the morning news – THE COMMERCIALS!

I watched six ads for various products, a couple being excellent, and one making me NOT want to visit the store that much more. The one for a clothing store in Indiana looked familiar, and I wondered if Diane had anything to do with it. It was so well done, I just may go there this weekend for a shopping spree.

"Well, I'd better be getting to work now, Muffin," I say to my feline friend, who didn't even open an eye and acknowledge that he'll be missing me all day. I know he will, but I'm sure he'll find a way to cope. I clean up my dishes, turn the TV off, and make that drive to the agency to get there at pretty much the same time I do on a normal day.

I sit in the morning meeting, having little to say. Diane reports on my first on-site shoot, and she has very glowing things to say about me. She says that she liked the way I stayed professional the whole time, never complaining about holding that microphone pole despite it starting to get heavy after a while, and how I handled the thespians and client was done in the same manner as a seasoned pro.

"She even looks good on camera," she says, mentioning my part in the filming. After a light round of applause, I was asked to share my thoughts on it.

"Thanks," I said. "Diane and Karen are great managers, and Gene is a fantastic visionary. Oh, and thanks for the compliment, but I don't look that good on film."

Some chuckles follow my statement, and before the meeting adjourns, Diane asks if I had time this morning to help her with editing the commercial.

"It's your account," she reasons.

"Well, I never did that before, so…"

"So, there's no better time to learn," Diane cuts me off. "Be in film editing in half an hour."

I return to my office, check some emails, and since Janus's billboard is to go up in a week, I make sure that's on schedule. It is. Since I am sure that I will be doing some voiceover work for the coffee TV spot, I do some vocal exercises before heading for the editing room.

I walk in, and Diane is already in there, getting everything ready for editing.

"You've never done this, correct?" she asks.

"No. I mostly did voice work in Chicago. I've seen equipment like this before; it looks similar to what they had there, just not as much. I'm looking forward to learning," I answer.

"Great, then have a seat here."

"But that's where the editor sits," I say.

"I know," Diane says, then pulls the chair out. "What better way to learn than by doing?"

I sit down, run my hands lightly over the knobs and dials, and smile at the experience.

"Feels good, doesn't it?" she asks, and I nod in response.

"Now, I have notes here on everything that was filmed yesterday. It's all digital, so that makes for easier editing. There's really not a whole lot, only about 20 minutes of actual usable footage, which is plenty for a thirty-second spot. We hope, at least." Diane then shows me how to review the footage, and we watch all of it before we start editing. "That's typical, as you need to be fully informed. So, what do you think?"

"I think we should obviously alternate between the two actors, showing them as a couple just once, maybe twice, but separate each time. Can we watch them again, and I can take notes this time?" I ask.

"Of course," Diane says with a smile as she hands me a pencil and pad.

We watch them all again, a little slower this time, as I take furious notes. I'm almost getting writer's cramp when the last one, the one with me, shows.

"What are you thinking?" Diane asks.

"Well, they're all pretty much the same," I start, trying to gauge her reaction, then continue. "It looks like, besides the pastries and drinks, Sindi will be the breakout star here. Why not focus more on her cute ad-libs and less on the customers? We only see them from behind, except for me at the end, and I think more will focus on her rather than Vince and Peg, anyway."

"Good idea," Diane says. "What order would you think fits best?"

We work on editing for close to an hour, and while talking about the commercial, we get to know each other better. Diane has been with the company for 14 years, has a degree in marketing from the University of Evansville, and is from Muncie, Indiana.

"Advertising wasn't my goal in life," she confesses to me. "I'd much rather be on the marketing side of things. But I do like this job and this town, so it's all good. How about you?"

"I wanted to be in advertising since I was about 13, but I just didn't realize it then. Making billboards is, honestly, my dream job."

"No kidding?" she asks as she stops what she's doing to look at me. "I can't fire you, so you don't have to lie to me."

"It is the God-honest truth, Diane. Advertising is my life."

We get a crude video version of the ad together, then go into the recording room to record some voice-overs. We're not sure if we're going to use them, but covering all of the bases is how this all works. I record thirty seconds' worth using my almost natural voice, pretty much narrating what is happening in the ad. The last part is "Jack's Coffee and Pastry – What will you stir?"

It's getting close to lunch. Diane says I should take mine, and I learned enough for today, so she'll finish the ad without me. She still wants my approval once it's done, but she knows that I also have billboard work that is slightly behind schedule—just a little. Please don't panic, it will be done.

Karen and I take my Beetle and go to Doug's Deli, in the heart of the downtown area, close to Taste of Italy. Before we go in, Karen has a giggle at my expense as I look at the ads in their window.

"Not bad for an amateur," I say.

"I did them," Karen says in a serious tone, then, after my face goes into full horror mode, she laughs. "Just kidding. Come on, lunch is on me."

We both ordered the six-inch American sub with potato chips and a soda, then sat by the window. I'm not sure if Karen is Christian or not, but I say grace for us, and she folds her hands as I do so.

"How did you really like your first TV ad shoot?" she asks. "We're friends. You could be honest."

"Well," I start, hoping this isn't a trap. "It was a bit different from what I expected. I hope I get to run the camera soon."

"You will," Karen answers. "It's customary for the rookie to hold the boom pole the whole time. Maybe next time, you'll switch with the camera operator as the shoot progresses."

"That's good to know."

"You did look good on camera, too," she says. "Very natural."

"Thank you. I wasn't expecting that," I say.

"That's also part of the hazing of a new employee: putting them on camera to see how they react. I did that for a used car ad we shot, and I almost hit someone playing a customer with a used Ford Focus."

"No kidding," I say, laughing.

"That part didn't make the commercial. Usually, the employee doesn't. You just may," she explains.

"I wasn't that good," I laugh off.

"Yes, you were. I'm not talking to you as a friend now, but as a colleague and professional. You just may make the cut."

I sit and think about that for a moment, still thinking she's teasing me. Then something else she said comes back to my mind.

"Wait. I thought you told Dave we don't hire professional actors to keep the costs down, but two were there yesterday, and you said one was at the car ad shoot."

"Right," she says, then swallows the bite of the sub sandwich she just took. "We try not to. Those from yesterday's shoot and the car ad were members of a local community theatre troupe. They enjoy acting, and usually do it for free or, if it takes a long time, a rather small fee. Nothing close to if we did hire professionals, which we will do on occasion."

"Oh," I say, getting slightly overwhelmed.

"Don't worry, Saturn. You'll get this. Advertising is in your blood, right?"

"It's more of a passion," I correct. "Nobody else in my family likes them."

"It takes time, Saturn. So far, you are doing better than any other we hired, at least since I've been here. You have a very promising career ahead of you."

"Thank you," I say, smiling. We stay quiet for a while as she allows me to process everything we just talked about.

I drive us back to the agency, where I plan to stay locked in my office for the rest of the day. I first pour myself a cup of coffee and say, "What will you stir?" as I add a stirrer to the cup. I laugh at myself and give Frida a little smile as I walk past her.

I get immersed in my work, having to explain to the mayoral-wannabe that his billboard will be up when we said it would be, which is why it's not up now.

"These things take time," I try to reason with him.

"Don't you want me to win?" he practically yells at me, and I try to stay as professional as I can.

"I want to provide the best advertisements I could in the timeframe in the contract that you signed," I explained.

"It better not be even one second late," he barks, then hangs up. As I hang up, I decide that I do not want him to win. I mean, if this is the way he treats those working on his campaign, how will he treat strangers who reside in the city? He definitely will not be getting my vote, which reminds me; I'd better register before it's too late.

At 4:00 p.m., as I'm double-checking that the candidate's billboard will be up on time, my cell rings. It's Janus. I could use a few minutes' break before the last hour of the day, so I answered it.

"Hi, Janus."

"How are you doing, Saturn?" he asks.

"Well, I'm swamped at work. I don't have much time for small talk, so what's up?" I hope that didn't come off as rude, but I'm tired after these two days.

"I was wondering if you'd like to have dinner with me tonight. Your choice," he says cheerfully.

"Well," I think for a second. "I'd like to, but I have laundry that needs washing. I'll be going to the laundromat after dinner tonight, so I suppose the dinner will have to wait until tomorrow's double date.

"Oh," he says, disappointed. "You can come here. I can fix dinner, and you could use my laundry machines. I won't even charge you."

"Oh," I respond, a little surprised. I think about accepting, then remember what was in my laundry. Besides the usual pants and shirts, there are certain unmentionables that I don't want him seeing, either on or off of me. For some reason, I don't mind strangers in the laundromat seeing them, but Janus's eyes are strictly off limits. "I think I'd rather do them downtown. Thanks for the offer, though."

There is silence for several seconds before Janus speaks again.

"Saturn, this isn't about what we talked about the other day, is it? Just because I'm not ready for commitment doesn't mean…"

"I know," I say, cutting him off. "It's not about that. I'm not ready for that now, either, but honestly… I hope we do get there someday, and soon. I have to get back to work now, so I'll see you tomorrow. Oh, and just for some business…"

"Yes?" he asks, confused.

"Your billboard will be up as scheduled next Tuesday on the first."

"Great, can't wait to see it. Well, I'll talk to you later."

We hang up, then I sit and think about the conversation and whether or not our plan for tomorrow will work. We don't want commitment, but we want to conspire with each other to keep others from dating us. Should I switch my relationship status to "It's complicated" on my social media? No time to think about that if I want to be all caught up before five."

I do end up working a little past five, most of the extra time being spent filing papers and organizing my workspace. Once I'm happy with how everything looks and where everything is, I look out the window and take it in for a moment as I watch a few birds fluttering about, then leave for the day, waving at Gretchen as I go.

I get home, pet Muffin, notice my craft stick art inventory for the event coming up, then try to figure out what is fast and easy for dinner. I fry a pork chop and have that with instant mashed potatoes and some peas. I keep everything off while I cook and eat, wanting some quiet time for myself. Once I wash the dishes, I leave the pan on the stove for next time. I'm out the door with two large laundry baskets and a bag full of dirty clothes.

Before I walk into Clean as a Whistle, you should know me well enough by now to know I will be looking at the flyers in the window. It mentions the sizes of their machines, free dryer use, a frequent patron club card, and local sports teams for your kids to join. "Places where kids get their clothes dirty. Brilliant," I say as I walk in the door.

I grab one of the available carts and place my laundry on it. I purchase a small container of laundry soap and fabric softener, then take everything to a washing machine near the center of a wall, away from where several other washers are sitting. Most seem to be doing things to take their minds from waiting, like reading a book or playing on their phone. Me? I think just sitting and waiting sounds fine to me. At first, anyway. I have a lot on my mind, and here seems like a good place to mentally sort things out.

I load a machine, choosing to do my "unmentionables" first. I also run one machine at a time, for some reason. I guess it's to give me more time to relax, but either way, I opt to sit and wait it out.

Once the washer is done, I transfer the contents to a nearby dryer, glancing around and hoping no one else sees my undergarments. They're mostly basic, though I might have one or two fancier options that haven't been worn in a while at home, and I don't see myself slipping them on anytime soon. I turn to load the washer again when I accidentally bump into a man.

"I'm sorry," I say, then go about my business.

"That's okay," he says with a winning smile.

He loads a machine near mine, then sits in a seat close to me, leaving just one empty space between us. He has a book with him; it looks like a mystery. I nod at him as he opens it, then stare blankly ahead.

"I'm Chip," he says. "Chip Flanders."

"Saturn. Saturn O Syres."

"Saturn," he says with a smile. "I like that name." I nod at that, then look ahead again. He's handsome, I'll admit.

"Do you come here often?" he asks.

"No. It's my first time. I'm sort of new in town," I say, instantly regretting adding that last part.

"Oh," he says, then positions himself to face me better. "Where are you from?"

I don't want to be rude, and it's okay to talk to people, I suppose.

"Hohman. That's in the northwest part of Indiana, near Chicago," I answer.

"Oh, I go through there often. I'm a musician, and we do a concert in and around Chicago several times a year."

"You don't say?" I reply. "You don't look like much of a rock star."

He laughs at that, then looks me in the eye. "That's because I'm not. I play flute for the Central Indiana Symphony Orchestra. Usually, Metallica or Foo Fighters aren't on our set list. Now, if you're into Mozart or Rachmaninoff, then we're more your style."

"Oh," I say, laughing along with him. "So you don't like the Foo Fighters?"

"I love me some Dave Grohl, just not at work. So, what do you do?"

"I… um…." What to say, what to say, what to say… "I work in an office here in town." Technically, that's true.

"Nice," Chip replies.

We chatted a little longer with many pauses in the conversation. I enjoy his company, but I still want to stay cautious. My dryer buzzes, signaling it's time to switch out the loads. I stand up and turn my back to him deliberately. I hope he doesn't think I'm trying to show off my rear to him, because I'm not, and there's not much to show, I don't think. I just don't want him to see what goes on over it. I smile at him when it's halfway unloaded, and he smiles back. Drat! Am I giving him some signals with my…? I set the basket in a place I'm hoping he can't see, then put the freshly washed clothes in the dryer and start a last load for the night.

"You could use more than one machine at a time," Chip says to me.

"I'm just trying to burn some time. I haven't much else to do tonight."

"Oh," he says, then tends to his washing. It looks like he's doing just the one load, so he'll be out of here in fifteen minutes. Maybe.

"There's a pop machine over there, can I buy you a drink?' he asks. I'm tempted, but I decline the offer. He buys a Sprite, sits back down, uncaps it, takes a big swig, then lets out an extended "Ahhhhh" when he is done. I make a mental note in case this laundromat needs a TV ad in the future.

"Are you sure I can't get you one?" he asks again, flashing a sweet smile my way.

"You know, why not? That Sprite looks good."

He buys me one, uncaps it for me after sitting down, then offers to clink bottles before I drink. I say "cheers" after he does, smile at the gesture, then take a smaller swig than he did, but let out a similar "Ahhhhh" as him. We both laugh, and he touches his hand to my shoulder as we do. *Careful, Saturn,* I think as he faces me again.

"What else do you do for fun, besides laundry?"

I laugh at the way he asks that and answer, "I'm a craft stick artist."

"Those things you eat popsicles with?" he asks.

"Sort of," I answer. "How did you get into playing a flute? That's usually not a man's choice of instrument."

"Actually, about 37% of flautists are male. Not the majority, sure, but also not so unusual."

"Interesting," I say. "You still didn't answer. Why the flute?"

"It's long, slender, light, and has a nice, high-pitched tone. Why wouldn't I?" he asks.

"I like that," I say, then note that, as well, in case someone with a flute needs an ad.

We talk a little about orchestra life, then my dryer buzzes. I switch loads out, then his dryer buzzes, and he folds his laundry and puts it neatly in his basket. I like that he does that, and not just tosses them in like I see most men doing here.

"Well, I suppose I'm done," he says.

"I suppose," I agree.

"Are you hungry?" he asks.

"I… well…" I start before he speaks again.

"I saw these billboards for a pizza place here in town called Here and There Pizza. Since seeing them, I really want to try that place. Have you seen them?" he asks.

"The billboards?" I practically stutter out.

"Yeah, they are hilarious. They show a plain cheese pizza and have the caption 'Your toppings here.' It's brilliant, and makes me really want to try some. Would you like to join me?"

Oh! My! Gosh! He likes my billboards. What do I do? What do I do? Drat! What do I do?

"I have seen them, yes." Technically, that's not a lie. "I have other plans for tonight, though," which is sitting around and doing nothing here.

"Well, how about another time?" he asks.

I think for a minute. Janus says we're allowed to see other people, and having someone on reserve just in case Janus and I don't work out isn't against any dating rules. I don't think so, anyway. I look at him, see his smile, and decide what to do.

"I tell you what, Chip. Give me your number, and I'll call you if I decide to take you up on your offer. Does that sound good to you?"

"Well, that's not what I was hoping, but I'll take it."

He asks for my phone, but I keep it and ask him to give me his information. Once he is done, I turn the screen to face him to show him I did what I said I would. He looks at me for a moment, and I think he wants to hug me. I'm not sure. I think I want to hug him, too – just a little one, now – but I restrain myself. He picks up his basket, smiles at me, and then leaves the laundromat.

I look at the number in my contacts, wondering if I should delete it or not. I decided to keep it because, as I said, Janus and I are simply casually seeing each other now. I'll delete Chip's name if Janus ever starts looking at me the same way Eric looks at Venus.

I mind my own business for the rest of the time there. After folding my laundry and taking the baskets and duffel bag out to my car, I drive home. I put the freshly cleaned laundry away and consider calling Janus. I don't. I can wait until tomorrow to see him again, and besides, we're not on a 'talk every day' basis yet. I look at Chip's number again.

"I hope I never have to call him," I say to Muffin, then get ready for bed.

Chapter 13
Closings and Openings

On Wednesday, after the morning meeting, I checked on something that I looked into yesterday. There is good news in my inbox, and I hope this will bring a glimmer of happiness to the client.

I call the mayoral candidate and inform him that I offered to make a billboard swap with another ad agency. They had an ad lined up for one that is a little less trafficked than the one I had lined up for him, and if he's willing to make the swap, then his billboard could go up two days sooner than scheduled.

"It's still near downtown," I inform him. "It's closer to the manufacturing sector than the shopping sector. Still, people who work in plants vote, too, and the working class may be a better demographic for you. Fewer individuals may see it, but according to the research you provided to us, more voters are likely to see it. Maybe not a whole lot, but every vote does count."

"Do you think it's what I should do? Will I have a better chance of winning if we change the location?" he asks.

"It's what you've been asking for," I tell him, which is the truth. "I'm not a political analyst; you'd have to ask your team about that. You wanted your campaign to start sooner, and this is the only way to get that done."

"Hang on," he says, then puts me on hold. I wait a few minutes and hum along with the patriotic music that's playing.

The mayor in the city makes about $35,000 a year, and his campaign is paying significantly more for that in his ads, especially when you count in the primaries. I'm not sure why they always seem to spend far, far more to get the job than what it pays. I try not to think about that, as it's my job to provide said ads for him, not to do his books. Maybe I'll ask Venus about that one day.

"Fine, roll with that," he says, sounding a little out of breath.

"I will," I answer.

"And how is the TV ad coming along?"

I think for a moment, say "I'll transfer you to Diane," before hitting hold and sending him to her.

Moments later, I see an incoming call from Diane's office. Drat! Well, I have no choice but to answer it.

"Hi, Diane."

"Thanks for sending him to me," she says.

"Well, it was for a TV spot, so…" I say.

"You're learning quick," she says, then laughs. "Can you come to the editing room when you get a chance?"

"Sure."

I make some final arrangements for the late billboard switch, and once everything is confirmed, I go and meet Diane. She doesn't bring up the candidate, but tells me that the ad for Jack's Coffee is ready.

"We normally don't move this quickly around here," Diane says. "However, Gretchen put a top priority on this account. She thinks if it's successful, we'll have a client for life, looking to switch up campaigns monthly. This was a good catch, Saturn."

I smile at the compliment, knowing things won't always go this easily for me.

"Now, have a seat. I'm going to show you the ad before we take it to Gretchen and then Jack. She also likes to be more hands-on with newer accounts and newer employees."

"That's understandable," I say, then look up at the screen.

It wasn't what I expected, but it was still good. She mainly used Vince and Peg's parts, quickly swapping them as they ordered, then hearing one of Sindi's quips before she asks, "What will you stir?" The camera then zooms in on the tray.

"I like it," I say twenty seconds into the thirty-second spot.

"Just wait," Diane says, almost conspiratorially.

The last shot was of me ordering a plain cake donut, and when I am asked what I will stir, I say a small black coffee, then Sindi says, "That's stirrable," as she, in a somewhat exaggerated manner, places a stirrer into my cup. This time, the camera doesn't zoom in on the tray. Instead, it shows me turning around as you hear me say, "Jack's Coffee and Pastry, what will you stir?" by way of voiceover with the address superimposed at the bottom of the screen. At the end, you could see me standing with a tray in hand, and Sindi just behind, both of us smiling widely. I think that last part was from our first take when we were talking like cowboys, nearly laughing the whole time.

"What do you think?" Diane asks.

"I thought you normally don't use people from the agency for the ads," I question.

"Normally, we don't. But this time, it's too perfect. I won't use it if you don't want me to, but I guarantee, this will make Jack – and Gretchen – very happy."

"Well…"

"And look," Diane says. "I don't want to step on your toes, but you are still in training here, and we work collectively on most things. Here is a good shot for your billboard."

She displays on the screen the image from the end of the commercial, showing me standing, holding a tray, with Sindi smiling behind me. It says Jack's Coffee and Pastry in big letters at the top, just below Tea Lattes Cappuccinos, just like his new sign will say. At the bottom, in smaller yet still easy-to-read print, is "What will you stir?"

"I'm not sure I look good enough for this ad," I say.

"You look adorable," Diane assures.

"Isn't this a conflict of interest? I work for the ad agency, and…"

"And you're a customer of the shop. There is no deception, just a regular customer ordering some treats. I think Vince and Peg are more deceptive since they live in Indianapolis and probably never will go to Jack's again, unless they do more ads."

"Well…"

"Come on, let's go see what Gretchen has to say."

Diane leads me to her office, and after she is done with her phone call, she asks us to state our business. Diane speaks for us, and when she is done, we show her the ads, both for TV and the billboard.

"Brilliant," she says. "You and the blonde girl will sell a million cups of coffee. Get this to them now for approval, and let's get this going. When is the campaign to start?"

"Monday," Diane answers.

"Good. Now leave, and get this done."

We shut the door behind us, and I feel a little exhausted from that meeting.

"That's how she was when I interviewed," I say to Diane as we walk. "All business, not a second to spare."

"When she's in business mode, she turns it on. When she's like that, it means she approves of the job you're doing. If she doesn't like it, she'll sit you down and tell you what you're doing wrong. You may be in her office for hours."

"That sounds scary," I say.

"It is," Diane says, then stops and looks at me. "And you'll be thankful for every time she does that."

We get to Jack's, and he brings out a latte of the day and a chocolate iced donut for me, along with a blueberry Danish and toasted white chocolate mocha for Diane.

"I tried to guess, so I hope these are acceptable to you," he says.

"They're perfect," Diane says, then sips her drink. "Is Sindi here? She may want to see it. It'll only take a minute."

Jack signals to the young man working the counter now, and he waves over to Sindi to come and join us. She smiles at us as she walks, and I know Diane is thinking about the next commercial with her in it, because I certainly am. Jack stands and allows her to sit between Diane and me as he watches over her shoulder.

"This is your ad," I say, then Diane starts the video.

Diane gave me some advice on the way over. She says to watch their reactions closely as they watch, because that tells you a lot. Sindi watched with the predictable smile as Jack was more solemn. When it was done, Sindi clapped while Jack just sat there, thinking. Diane signals to me to remain silent until Jack speaks. It seemed like forever, but it was more like fifteen seconds later when he did.

"Perfect," he said, much to Diane's and my relief.

"What did you think, Sindi?" Diane asks.

"I loved it. Saturn looks so good. I can't believe you went with me instead of just her," she says, smiling up at me.

"Here is the billboard," I say, smiling down at her.

They are equally enthused with it, then Jack asks Sindi to return to work while we get some details ironed out.

"The TV ad will air during the morning local news starting Monday, and the billboard should be up later that day," Diane informs.

"I hope it works," Jack says.

"We have full confidence it will," Diane answers. "By the way, while we are an advertising agency, would you like some marketing advice, on the house?"

"Sure," Jack answers as he stands up.

"Many places like this display art on the walls curated by a local artists' guild. I recommend you contact them to see about having art for sale hung here, with themed shows every two months. The split could be up to you, but requesting thirty percent or a little more of the sales wouldn't be unreasonable."

"Thank you, Diane. I'll look into that. Once this campaign nears its end, if it's successful, I'll be contacting you to extend it. Would it be the same deal?" Jack asks.

"Let's just get through this one first," Diane answers. "If it's successful, then buying a year's worth of ads could save you money in the long run. We'll do a market analysis with you when this one is coming to a close, say in three weeks. If you see success earlier and want to extend, do not hesitate to call beforehand. Is there anything else you need right now?"

"No, I can't think of anything. Thank you, ladies. I'll make sure to be watching next Monday."

We grab our drinks, pastries, and equipment and hightail it out of there quickly.

"Once the client is happy and you close, don't dawdle. They may start thinking and want last-minute changes. They are less likely to call, so staying may add unnecessary work for you," Diane informs as she starts her car.

"I'll keep that in mind," I answer.

"Great. This is your client, and we just closed. Tradition says you buy lunch."

I'm not sure how accurate that is, or if she's just hazing the new guy again, but I happily buy us lunch at Harry's Hamburgers and Hot Dogs. As we eat, we discuss the last sale more. Diane tells me everything I did right, which was a lot, and all that I did wrong, which was, unfortunately, too much, in my opinion.

"You are doing fine," she encourages as I clean up. That's another tradition, or so I was told.

"Thanks, Diane. I can't wait to work on more projects with you."

We get back to the agency, and there are still several hours left in the day. I'm wondering how I'm going to be spending that time as we walk in, then Frida makes it easy on me.

"Gretchen wanted to see you once you got back," she says.

"Okay. I'll just put this in my office, then I'll be right…" I started to say.

"Gretchen wants you in her office once you get back," Frida says again.

"I'll take this for you," Diane says. "You'd better get in there, and good luck."

I walk toward the door, and once I get there, I turn to look at Frida. She signals for me to open the door and walk in, so I do.

"Sit," Gretchen says, and waits for me to do so. "How did it go?"

"They liked the ads," I answer.

"They?"

"Yes. Jack and his employee Sindi. She's the one who played the cashier in the ads."

"Sindi doesn't have a financial stake in this," Gretchen snaps. "What did Jack say?"

"Well," I hedge a little, hoping she doesn't yell at me. "At first, he was quiet, then he said that he liked it. He said if it's successful, then he'll extend his contract. Diane suggested for a year."

"What do you think? Will it be successful?" she asks, then stares at me.

"I think Diane and I gave it our all, and now success depends more on whether we hit the right demographics or not," I answer.

"Did you really give it your all, as you say?" Her stare seemed to have transformed into a glare.

"Well, not totally," I say honestly. Gretchen stays perfectly quiet. "I mean, I'm still in training. It was my account, but Diane did more of showing me how it's done than me actually doing. That's fine, as we were a team and it was a team effort."

"Do you believe that the right demographics will be reached?" she asks, then makes a note on what looks like my employee file.

"Yes, I do," I answer, and now I think I feel some sweat building on my forehead.

"Great. How is your boyfriend's billboard coming along?"

"Well," I think about whether or not I should correct her on the 'boyfriend' label, and I decide to do so without being confrontational. "The Rings and Sons Restoration and Resale Shop account is on schedule. It is set to go up on the first of next month. I also negotiated a deal with a competing agency, and we swapped billboards so my mayoral candidate will get his up two days earlier."

"Perfect," Gretchen says, then seems to relax a little. "How long have you been with the agency?" she asks.

"I started at the start of the month, so just over three weeks," I answer.

"How do you like it so far?" she asks.

"Do you want an honest answer, or do you want me to tell you what I think you want to hear?"

Gretchen glares at me again, almost to give me an 'I dare you' look. "Honest. I want to hear your honest answer."

"Okay, I'll be honest," I say, then take a deep breath. "It has been wonderful, a proverbial dream come true. I know that one day, the luster will wear off, and I may not be as enthused to be here."

Gretchen looks at me silently, makes a note in my file, and I feel uncomfortable again.

"Do you really think your passion for ads will start to wane?" she asks.

"I assume so," I answer.

"Saturn, I hired you because you and I have a lot in common. The rest of the team works here because they need a job. Don't get me wrong, they are great at it and deliver results. You, though… You live and breathe advertising. You have the same passion I had when I started in this business. Let me tell you something, Saturn…"

There's a long pause before I ask her what that is.

"The luster won't wear off any time soon. It hadn't for me, and I've been doing this for twenty-plus years. Keep learning from your colleagues, and one day you may be running this agency. If you tell anybody here that I said that, I will fire you."

"Okay," I say, then laugh. I notice she isn't laughing, so I stop.

"I'm not joking, Saturn. Keep that between you and me. Do you know of any other leads?"

I think for a moment, then remember the conversation I had with Venus during my trip back home.

"My sister lives on a farm, and she has a wedding business on the side called Brown Farms Weddings. She wants more business, and I suggested advertising, of course. I told her we can find an agency for her to use if she decides to pursue it," I answer.

"Why not suggest this one? I told you that we want to break into the farming industry," she says, the glare is now back.

"Well, because she lives in Omaha," I answer.

"Good. We've been looking to expand westward. I thought I told you that, too."

"Maybe you did," I say, slouching in my chair a little. "Maybe I forgot. I've been having to learn a lot since coming here."

"Get to your office, call your sister, and tell her that if she needs an ad, we will do it. Look into rates in Omaha, and offer fifteen percent below. Wait…" Gretchen sits, taps some computer keys, then looks up at me. "Fifteen percent works. Do you think her wedding business will catch on?"

"Yes," I say after thinking for a moment. "I really do."

"Good. That industry is always changing, which means so are its advertising needs. I'm glad I hired you, Saturn," she says, pauses, and I smile widely at that. "Now get out of here and tell me what your sister says, and try to remember everything we say at those meetings. We say them for a reason."

Gretchen turns to her laptop, then starts typing without so much as a goodbye. I stand, go to the door, look back at her once more to make sure I can leave, then open the door and exit. I tell Frida that I'll be in my office for likely the rest of the day. She is on the phone, so she gives me a hand signal saying she heard me, then I walk away, not without looking at Gretchen's office door one more time.

"She is scary," I mumble, hoping nobody heard me.

I sit behind my desk, replaying that conversation in my head. It was scary, as Diane told me. Will I ever be thankful for what just happened? I probably will, if I'm honest. For now, I need to process it before drawing any firm conclusions.

Before I call Venus, I look into advertising and billboard rates in and around Omaha. They are higher than they are here, but still far cheaper than Chicago. I checked to see what billboards in her area may be available in the coming weeks and months, and, not knowing the area too well, I wrote down several locations that look as if they may benefit her. I get all of the information organized, then dial up Venus's number.

After a little small talk, I tell Venus the reason for my call. She's reluctant at first, but once I convince her that listening is free, she quiets, for the most part, and listens.

"That much, you say?" she asks once I get to the cost.

"That's actually quite reasonable," I retort.

"You would say that," she answers, "you're not the one paying for it."

"Venus," I say, trying to get serious with her. "The cost of one billboard for a month is about half the price you charge for a wedding. Even considering your expenses, it would pay for itself after two events. Not a whole lot, sure. TV spots are also affordable for you," I continue. "Daytime ads, which may be your target audience, don't cost so much. Once one is produced, you can show that one for eternity if you like. Once your business expands, you may be able to do more than one wedding a week. Sure, you'd have to hire part-time help for them, but it may be worth it."

"I'm an accountant, Venus. Don't talk down to me about finances," she says, and I could just hear her restrain from hissing "little sister."

"I'm not, big sister." Hah! I got it in first! Score one for Saturn! "I'm the expert when it comes to advertising and brand building. Look, think about it for a while. I'm not sure how long that fifteen percent discount is good for, and while I don't think it will expire at the end of this phone call, it will eventually. Probably. I'll email you more details, so promise you'll look them over."

"I will," she promises.

"Thanks," I answer.

"No, thank you. I'm sorry for snapping at you. Junior in my belly has been doing that to me lately," she says more calmly.

"So, how is the future rugrat?"

We discuss that for a minute, then I remind her again to check her email and get back to me. I call Gretchen on the office phone and tell her how the conversation went.

"Perfect," she says after listening. "Start making designs when you can. We'll want that one up asap."

"Gretchen," I say nervously. "Venus – my sister – didn't say she'd want one or sign a contract yet."

"'Yet,' is the correct word. Just do it," she snaps, then hangs up.

I start doing what she said and get some early concepts sketched out. My art still hadn't improved much since high school art class, but I could still come up with enough for Gene to work with.

I work until 4:45 when I hear a knock at the door. When I ask who it was, Karen states her name.

"Come in," I say, then put the sketches down.

"How did it go with Diane at the coffee shop?" she asks.

I tell her, and she says that it is customary for someone who has just closed an account to buy lunch for the others involved at the time of closing.

"Don't worry. It all evens out, so you won't get a big hit to your wallet," she says.

"Good," I reply, then tell her how it went with Gretchen once I got back.

"That sounds about right," she says. "Diane is right. The more succinct Gretchen is, the happier she is with you. You did make that rookie mistake, though."

"You mean about my sister's billboard?" I ask.

"Yes. While we mainly operate in this region, we have accounts everywhere, and we could run ads worldwide, including Omaha," she explains. "Well, it's about that time. Big plans for tonight?"

"Just a double date," I answer.

"Well, have fun. I hope it goes well for you."

"I certainly do, too," I say. Diane says goodbye, then after I get my office set for tomorrow, I'm out the door, hoping to be on time for "Operation setup" tonight.

Chapter 14
Double Date

I make it home in record time. Well, probably not record time, but as quickly and safely as I possibly could. Admittedly, I didn't look at the speedometer too often, but I know I kept it at a reasonable speed, just as I talked with Pastor Chalke about. I hope and pray that conspiring with Janus in trying to get Sunny and Blake together isn't making the relationship go too fast. I don't think it is. Well, it's a done deal, so I'd better start getting ready.

After a quick scratch on Muffin's head, I go to the closet in the bedroom and see what is hanging up in there. I want something nice for Janus, but not too nice to give Blake the wrong idea. Maybe this simple knee-length basic blue dress paired with simple white flats will do the trick.

I wasn't planning on taking a shower when I got home, but after sweating it out in Gretchen's office, I think I want to. I slip into the shower and bathe as fast as I can, trying my best not to get my hair wet. After ninety seconds, I figure that was enough, so I turn the water off, towel-dry, and slip into my undergarments and dress. I wipe the mirror and apply a modest amount of makeup. When that's done, I look at the time. Perfect. Janus said that he'd be there at around this time, so I sit on the couch and will pet Muffin while I wait.

Minutes later, and mid-purr, I hear a knock at the door. I open it and see Janus smiling as he comes into view, wearing a stunning black suit with a navy-blue tie. Wow!

"Ready?" he asks.

"In a moment. Come in, don't sit," I answer.

"I won't," he replies, then looks over at Muffin.

"You could pet him if you like," I say from the dining area. "These flowers are almost dead." I put on a frown for him as I grab my purse, then walk over to him.

"I'll just have to bring you some more," he says, then leans down and offers me a kiss. After the basic peck, I wondered if we're on a kiss hello basis now. I sure hope we are! He looks at the blankets on the couch, then over to me. "Still sleeping out here?"

"Yeah. It's a little uncomfortable, but not the worst thing. I'll buy a bed someday, I hope."

"I picked up a twin today. It needs work, but should turn out fine," he informs.

"Are you trying to get some more business from me?" I jokingly ask.

"Free delivery," he tempts, then smiles from the conversation.

"I'll keep that in mind," I say as I lead the way out. "Let's go."

The ride there was nice. He told me about some of the furniture he worked on today. I pointed out a billboard or two (or three or four) along the way, and each time he seemed interested in what I had to say about them.

We get to the restaurant, and after parking in the lot, Janus does a quick scan and says he doesn't see Sunny's car anywhere.

"I don't remember what Blake drives," I tell him. "I know it's a car. A blue car, or maybe red."

"Could it be brown?" he asks jokingly.

"It could be all the colors of the rainbow as far as I remember," I answer. "Well, maybe not. I'd probably remember that."

We both laugh a little as we walk toward the front door of Taste of Italy. Janus holds the door open for me, but I pause first to look at the ads on their front window.

"Anything interesting?" Janus asks.

"This one, for their food truck that's going to be at the Independence Day crafts and food fair. It is very well done."

Janus takes a look, puts his right hand to his chin, and examines it like he's an art critic.

"It looks like a normal flyer in a window," he says. "Am I missing anything?"

"Not in the least," I reply, then walk inside with Janus following.

The hostess greets us and asks how many people are with us. I answer four.

She asks, "Would you like a booth or a table?"

"We're waiting for the rest of our party," Janus answers. "Can we wait for them to arrive and choose then?"

"Certainly," she answers. "Have a seat on the furniture if you like."

There is a couch and a couple of chairs near the front. I sit in a chair, and Janus sits in the other one. We chat for a few minutes before Sunny shows up wearing a lovely canary yellow dress with white trim.

"It looks like I'm on," Janus says as he stands to greet her.

He says, "Hi," and she takes his hand. He frees himself from her and tells her that I'm one of the others joining them on the double date.

"Oh, hi," she says, then turns her attention back to him.

Janus tries to keep the small talk as small as possible, and minutes later, Blake arrives wearing Dockers and a green polo shirt. I introduce him to the rest, and they say they recognize each other from the civic club dances, but they have never formally met before. Once we all know each other's names, we agree on a booth near a window.

The hostess leads us there, and Sunny decides that Janus will sit on the inside near the window, with her next to him. Blake follows their lead and takes the inside seat across from Janus, inviting me to sit next to him.

The hostess leaves menus behind, and we all fall silent as we look at them. I already know I want the lasagna, but I look through the menu anyway, just in case. As we're looking, our waitress introduces herself as Sofia Moretti and asks if we'd like to see a wine list. Drat!

"Is anybody wanting some?" Janus asks.

"I'm not sure…" Blake says, then looks into his wallet. Janus notices and eases the situation.

"I tell you what," he says. "The shop had a pretty good quarter, so this evening is on me. Get what you like, and I'll pick up the tab for all of us."

"And I'll take care of the tip," I added. Janus and I give each other a mental high five as the waitress waits.

"I'd like a Chianti," Blake says.

"Me, too," Sunny smiles.

"I don't want wine, and will decide on my drink later," Janus says, and I say the same thing. Sofia writes that down and says she'll be back to take our orders.

The conversation begins with Sunny asking Janus how business is going. Although we want this evening to focus on Sunny and Blake getting to know each other, maybe getting our stuff out of the way first will help that happen during the meal.

Janus talks a little about the good quarter, what he's been doing at work, and even mentions the billboard that will be going up next week. Sunny seems bored at that part, then Janus starts to turn the conversation toward Blake.

"Have we decided yet?" Sofia asks as she comes back.

We all look around, and I start by ordering the lasagna and milk. Sofia then looks at Janus.

"I have a taste for fettuccine alfredo, for some reason," Janus says. "I'll have that with garlic bread and milk. In fact, bring enough garlic bread for everybody at the table. Mozzarella cheese sticks, too, with that red sauce."

"Mozzarella cheese sticks with marinara sauce," Sofia replies, stating what that red sauce is called, then looks at Sunny.

"I'll have the shrimp scampi," she says.

"That's what I was wanting, too," Blake says, then he and Sunny exchange glances. Yes!

Sofia leaves, and the table is quiet again, so I decide it's a good time to tease Janus.

"How often do you order that dish?" I ask him.

"Rarely," he answers. "This may be my first time ordering that here, actually."

"Why do you think that is?" I ask.

Janus thinks for a moment, then I could see the look on his face when he realizes that was the dish in the ad near the front door.

"Anywayyyyy," he stretches out, smiling at me the whole time. "Blake, what do you do?"

"Well, I'm between jobs now. I'm hoping to open a coffee shop one day and expand it throughout the United States and beyond."

"That sounds wonderful," Janus says. "Do you have a plan in mind?"

"Well, first, I'd need an investor. I think a partner may work well, too. Coffee is good, but something to complement it would be better," he explains.

"You may consider nothing done before," I add. "Coffee and pastries have been done to death. It may be hard to penetrate that market. What else have you considered?"

"I actually haven't, Saturn," he says, then touches my hand with his. I try not to wince and look at Janus. He knows the plan, so we stay on track.

"I wouldn't be of any help," Janus says. "Coffee and restoration wouldn't go together. I restore coffee tables and sell them, but that's about as close as I could get."

"Here are your mozzarella sticks and marinara sauce," Sofia says, looking at Janus as she speaks. "I brought your Chianti, shall I pour it for you?"

"Just leave the bottle, please. Add it to the check. I'm paying for everybody," Janus says to Sophia, who nods, sets the bottle down, then leaves.

"Saturn, you're in the business. Sort of. Do you have anything to offer Blake on how to get started?" Janus asks, then pours the wine for Blake and Sunny. I take two cheese sticks, set them on a small plate, then pass the rest to Blake.

"You'd want to start small. Have you considered buying a used food truck or van, or even a tent, and selling at events like the upcoming crafts and food fair?" I ask, genuinely wanting to see him succeed.

"I hadn't considered that," he answers. "Do you think that would work?"

"Well, marketing and advertising are different, but also cousins, if you will. Market your truck, and it could act as advertising with a well-done paint job or a sign for a tent. Maybe find someone to go in with you on the truck to cut costs. Also, coffee is good, but if customers see coffee and something to go with it, they're more likely to buy from your truck, even if it's just coffee. Something to complement it, as you've said."

"Really?" Sunny asks, unconvinced.

"You'll see that yourself soon. Not many will likely use your church's diaper changing station, but it will attract those who think it's a good idea, and you will see more attendance at your other events, and possibly Sunday morning," I explain.

"How do you know that?"

"The person I bought my degree from told me," I joke, and Janus and I laugh. We stop, not wanting to get her upset tonight. "It's marketing 101, Sunny."

"I see," she says, then chomps into a cheese stick.

"So, Blake," I say and look at him, wanting to get back on topic. "Will you be using the same recipes that Jack's Coffee uses?"

"Yes. Well, no and yes," he says, then takes a sip of wine. "I mean… it'll have lattes, cappuccinos, and the other drink he has, but my recipes are different. Better, I think. I've been tinkering with recipes quite a lot and have most of them perfected."

"That's great," Janus says. "Do you have the same machines he has?"

"No, I can't afford them yet," Blake answers. "I do have good quality coffee and espresso makers, but not the top of the line, which a coffee shop would require. That's where an investor would come in. Does your agency do that, Saturn?"

"No, we only do advertising. How much are you talking about, though?"

Blake tells us, and while it's not nearly as much as I was thinking, it's still quite a bit. The table goes silent for a moment as I dip another cheese stick into marinara sauce and Sunny checks her face in her compact mirror.

We try to keep the conversation on Blake and his potential business, asking as many questions as we could, before Sofia shows back up with our dinners.

"Here you go," she says, then names each one as she places them in front of the diner who ordered them. "And garlic bread for the table."

She sets them in the center of the table, then Janus says a short grace before we start eating. The conversation quickly turns to how each of our dishes tastes, and once we're all satisfied that each tastes good, I try to steer the conversation toward Sunny.

"Sunny, what do you do for work?" I ask between bites of lasagna.

"I work at Kardi Home and Garden in Mapletree in the gardening department," she answers.

"Do you like it there?" I ask.

"It's okay, I guess," she replies. "It's good enough for now and pays the bills. Barely."

"Do you have any hobbies?"

"Well, if you must know," she begins, then gulps down the rest of her wine. "I'm a candy maker. Not the kind we'll be passing out at the event, but more gourmet. Saltwater taffy, caramels, and hard candies that actually taste like oranges, pineapples, and even carrots and cucumbers. Not like that bulk stuff they sell during Halloween, but aimed at a more refined, sophisticated palate."

"Is that so?" I ask, then take a bite from a garlic bread to appear more casual. "How did you come across such a hobby as that?"

"I always enjoyed cooking and candy. One day, when I was younger, my mom bought me a candy-making kit from a craft store. I learned some basics, then through online courses, I learned more about the art of confections."

Okay, the opportunity presented itself. I give a nod to Janus, and we mentally agree it's time to go into matchmaker mode.

"Do you sell them?" I ask. "It sounds there may be a market for them."

"I do, sometimes," she answers. "When I can. I'd really like to quit my job and do this full-time. My selection is limited now, but with the right opportunities and possibly an expanded menu, I think it could catch on in Oakfield and beyond."

"What sort of expanded menu?" Janus asks, then Sunny turns to face him better.

"Food probably wouldn't go too well, not at this time, anyway," she says, then lays her hand on top of his. Drat! "A drink line would work well, I think. Fruit punch, apple juice, something to complement the flavors of the candy."

"Sounds like you have a pretty good marketing plan, Sunny. At least the start of one," I say.

"Are you looking for a partner?" Janus says, and I notice his careful wording. He didn't say business partner, just partner. Nice!

"I wouldn't be against one," she says.

"Gourmet coffee and gourmet candy just may be the combination you're looking for," I say to whoever wants to take my bait.

"Maybe," they say in unison, then chuckle a little after that.

"Coffee and candy," Blake says, almost to himself.

"Candy and coffee," Sunny utters similarly.

"Where do you make your candy?" I ask Sunny.

"In the church kitchen. Everything there is commercial grade, and I have the proper licenses to be able to cook and sell food from there."

"Interesting," I say. "So if you sell on location, you'd need no extra equipment?"

"Just a cooler with ice to keep some things cool that need to stay cool," she answers.

"What flavor lattes do you make, Blake?" Sunny asks, then shifts herself to better face him.

"The usual, I suppose," he replies, then bites into his shrimp scampi. "This is delicious."

"It is," Sunny agrees, then smiles at him.

"Anyway," Blake continues. "Chocolate, salted caramel, peppermint white chocolate, even pumpkin spice. I think mine is better, as you could taste the espresso and steamed milk as well as the other flavorings. I think that's important. At many places, you could only taste the chocolate or whatever, and barely the other ingredients. That makes it simply a hot chocolate drink with extra caffeine, in my opinion."

"Sounds a lot like you and your candy, Sunny," Janus says to her. "Taking time to make sure the flavor is just right."

"It does," Sunny agrees.

"Interesting," Blake says, then refills his and Sunny's wine glasses. "Which of your taffys do you think would go well with a toasted marshmallow latte?"

"Well," Sunny thinks for a moment as she takes a sip of her wine. "I'd actually recommend a coffee-flavored jelly bean with that."

"You make those, too? Jelly beans?" I ask.

"Sure," Sunny says. "I hadn't thought about it before, but luxury coffee and my candy seem like a perfect match," Sunny says, then bites into her meal.

"This is delicious, Blake. There's just the right amount of shrimp in it."

"I agree," Blake says, then smiles at her as he takes another forkful. They look at each other as they enjoy their same dishes kitty-corner from one another, as the table goes quiet.

"If you'll excuse me, I have to use the ladies' room," Sunny says, then stands.

"I think I'll join you," I say. No, I don't have to go, but it's all part of the plan. We walk away, leaving the men behind.

They sit quietly for a short time before Blake breaks the silence.

"Your date is rather interesting," Blake says. "Have you been seeing her for long?"

"Well," Janus says, then wipes his mouth. "We're not actually seeing each other, and she's not my date. We're just friends and are on the same committee at church."

"Is that so?" Blake asks.

"It is," Janus says, smiling at him. "How about you and Saturn?"

"We're not a couple. We dated a few times, and I thought we were done. Then, out of the blue, she invited me here," he answers.

"Do you want to date her?"

"I thought I did, but right now I'm not so sure," Blake says, then looks like he's going into deep thought.

"You know, I think I have to go, too. Please excuse me."

Janus leaves and goes into the men's room alone. There is another man in there washing his hands, so Janus goes into a stall for privacy to text me.

The plan is working

I'll work it from my end

I'll stay in the bathroom until you're ready

K

"Are you having a good time?" I ask Sunny as we stand next to each other at the sink.

"I am," Sunny says. "Are you and Blake very serious?"

"Well, we dated a couple of times," I honestly answer. "Nothing serious. In fact, I'm not sure he's right for me. Don't get me wrong, he's a very nice and sweet man, but I'm not sure he's the one for me."

"Is that so?" she asks, then freshens her mascara.

"Yeah, it is. I think this will be our last date," I answer, then pretend to check my makeup as well. "I hope he finds someone more to his liking. Someone who shares his interests and life goals."

"Is he a good kisser?" she asks, then stares me down like she's trying to beat a confession out of a suspected murderer. I give her my most intense look and try not to laugh.

"He's a very good kisser," I say, which actually is true. He really is a good kisser. She smiles at that.

We finish up at the sink, and as Sunny leads us back to our table, I text Janus to wait thirty seconds before coming back.

"I see Janus isn't here," Sunny says. "I'll just take the inside seat."

Perfect! Now she and Blake are sitting across from one another.

"I know Blake wants to call his business Blake's Beans. What about you, Sunny?" I ask, hoping to get them to look at one another.

"Sunny's Sweets," she answers.

"That's a very good name," I say, and mean it.

"I'm back," Janus says, and before anybody could say anything else, he announces that he'll just sit where Sunny was, then they trade plates. "What are we talking about?"

"Names for their food service businesses," I answer.

Blake picks up the wine and starts like he's going to pour before Janus stops him.

"Blake, I think two is enough if you're driving. You can keep the bottle and have more at home if you like, but let's try to stay sober here tonight."

"Good idea," he says, then puts the cork back on. "I'll just have some of this ice water."

"So, Sunny. Do you think that coffee and candy would make a good pairing?" Blake asks her.

"There's one way to find out," she says, then places her hand on his while smiling. I find it a little obnoxious of them to act this way when they're supposed to be my and Janus's dates, but I try to put that out of my mind as best as I can, reminding myself this is what we're here for. Still, they don't know that, so… Drat! I can be too complicated at times.

They talk for a while longer as we finish our meals, and I don't think either of them realizes that Janus and I haven't said a word in fifteen minutes. Sofia comes over and asks if we'd like anything else.

"I tell you what," Janus says. "Bring those two a cannoli each. Here's a credit card to pay, add $30 for yourself."

"I'll be right back," she says, then thanks Janus for the tip.

I reach into my purse to repay Janus for the tip as I agreed, and he tells me to put my money away. Sofia comes back with a receipt, Janus's credit card, and the desserts for Sunny and Blake. Janus tells them to enjoy their treats as we leave, and I don't think they even notice.

We get outside to his truck, and we can see those two in the restaurant, looking at each other the way they used to look at us.

"Mission accomplished," Janus says.

"I think so," I reply, then take his hand.

"What now?" he asks.

"Well," I think. "We still haven't had dessert. Let's go to Cheaper by the Frozen and get some, my treat."

"Sounds good," Janus says, then leads me to his truck as we still hold hands. He opens the door for me, and before I get in, I just have to pull him down for a simple kiss. For the record, while Blake is a good kisser, Janus is even better. Hopefully, Sunny disagrees with that.

Chapter 15

Aftermath

The ringing starts again. It's Thursday morning, and after I shut the alarm off, I feel like lying back down. I don't, though. I sit up, stretch my arms, rub the sleep from my eyes, then look over to see Muffin still asleep on his comfortable little cat pillow.

"Lucky," I say to him, then sit for a moment longer as I replay last night's events in my head.

Hopefully, Blake and Sunny will find their happily ever after, or at least seek others besides Janus and me to fill that role. I also think about our dessert afterward, and what happened next. We shared ice cream, which was a good move forward, but the kisses seemed less passionate. However, he did kiss me "Hello," which was something new. I think I'm starting to overcomplicate things way, way, WAY too much. "Just enjoy the drive," I say as I stand to start the day.

I decide that last night's shower will hold over through today, so I make my way to the kitchen to see about breakfast. Fried eggs and toaster waffles seem like a good combination for today. I start to heat the pan, then put the waffles in the toaster. I pour a cup of coffee and, as usual, debate with myself as to whether or not to put a stirrer in the plain, black coffee. I do, of course, and give it a good stir.

"Perfect," I say after a loud sip, then set the cup on the counter.

I plate the waffles, add syrup, then flip two eggs next to them. I take that, along with the coffee cup and fork, to the dining table. I say a short prayer of blessing, thanking God for the food and the time I have in the morning for myself.

After saying "Amen," I notice the flowers that Janus gave me are fully – or at least fully enough – dead. I sort of want to preserve one, but I have no idea how and think it may be too late for that, anyway. Once I'm done eating and have the dishes cleaned and put away, I dispose of the flowers, wash the vase, and set it back on the table.

"He said he may bring me more," I say to Muffin. "I wonder when that may be."

I'm at work in plenty of time to get settled in for the day before the morning meeting begins. I check emails and make notes about which to answer first. When that's done, I sit back for a moment, turn my chair around, and look out the window. There is a grassy area just outside with a couple of medium-sized trees. There are a few birds and a couple of squirrels foraging for food, picking and pecking away at the ground in search of something to eat. I watch them for a few minutes, then decide I'll ask Gretchen if I'd be allowed to set up bird feeders out there. I'd tell her that I'd pay for and maintain it, but I still want to make sure that she'd be okay with attracting wildlife near our office building.

I stare a little too long and realize I'm almost late for the meeting. I scurry in as fast as I can, still trying not to look panicked, and sit at my regular spot.

"It's so nice of you to join us, Ms. Syres," Gretchen says. I wonder if the formality of the way she addressed me was some type of warning, but there's no time to think about that now. I take out my notepad and pencil and listen as Gretchen, or shall I say Ms. Gillmore, begins.

It's your typical meeting with the usual updates and assignments. I wondered if I should bring up what the owner of Cheaper by the Frozen said to me yesterday about their upturn in business, but decided not to say anything and let our own internal analysis speak for itself.

The meeting is near the end, so I'm anticipating going back to my office and going about my day when Gretchen announces otherwise.

"Saturn, we need you in the recording booth all day today. There are many political ads needing voice-overs, plus a radio spot for a local bike shop. It's a cartoon thing where the different bike parts all talk to one another, each explaining their part in helping the six-year-old girl get the bike moving. John, what are they?"

"Let's see," John says as he looks over the script. "A pedal, chain, tires, handlebars, and even the bell."

"Can you sound like a bike chain, Saturn?" she asks, and I'm relieved that we're back on a first-name basis.

"I turn the wheels when the pedals move," I say in a slightly southern voice of a little girl.

"Perfect," Gretchen says, though I'm wondering how she knows what a bicycle chain sounds like when speaking. "Frida has been informed to forward all of your calls to me or Diane. We'll make sure you get all messages and are updated on everything tomorrow."

I tell John that I'll be right there after taking care of a thing or two in my office. I suppose doing voices all day will be fine, but I just hope the political ads aren't all negative. I so, so much hate doing those. That's one part of this job I try to keep hidden from the outside world.

We do the political ads first, and time slips away as I read the scripts, trying not to pay attention to what they're saying. Of course, I end up absorbing every single one, and by the time lunch rolls around, I have no idea who I'd vote for based on what I've been reading. I will vote in November, but that's about four months away, so I have plenty of time to decide.

Karen and I go to Here and There Pizza and share a medium pie with sausage only. I talk a little about how the morning went, and she advises me on how to work the job without being too influenced by what we do.

"Of course, our job is to sell products, people, events, etc. Just use your own critical mind when it comes to what you buy. You don't buy everything you see being advertised on television, so do the same while working here."

"I'm here, at this restaurant, because of the ad," I say.

"The ad YOU created, mind you," Karen says, then laughs a little. "I'm not saying to never buy from anything we advertise. That would be silly and detrimental to our work. I'm just saying, Saturn, to do your best, trying to sell without feeling the need to buy everything you do sell. Do you plan to vote for that client for mayor?"

I'm usually uncomfortable discussing politics with a coworker, but in this case, it's a little different.

"No, I don't think so," I honestly answer.

"Are you still doing your best with his billboards?" she asks.

"Yeah, I think so. I mean, they could use improvement, but I really am trying my best to…"

"We all feel our work needs improvement," she says, then bites into her pizza slice. "But you're doing your best for a product you don't plan on buying. I know that's not one-hundred-percent what is happening, but you understand."

"I do," I say, then take another slice. "Thanks, Karen. I'll take this all to heart."

"Speaking of heart," she says, then looks at me intently. "How are things going with you and Janus?"

"His ad's coming out July first," I answer, then coyly take a bite.

"Come on, Saturn. You know what I mean," she says, then wipes her mouth and takes a sip of soda.

We spend the rest of our lunch hour talking about my love life, or at least my dating life, and hers, too. When we drove back to the agency, I was feeling better about where Janus and I are at the moment. I do a couple more voice-overs for political candidates, then we switch to the bike shop ad. Admittedly, I did have fun doing the voices for the bicycle parts. When this ad comes out, I definitely will tell Janus that all of those voices are me. If he asks about the political ones, I would fess up, but what he doesn't know won't... well, if he knew it wouldn't hurt anybody, either. I just don't want anybody to think that I really do believe that the incumbent mayor is as bad as his opponent claims him to be.

The day ends, and I'm in a much better mood than I was before lunch. That's good, because I teach the craft stick class tonight. I quickly go home, change into something more comfortable, and drive back to Andrea's Arts and Crafts in plenty of time to get things set up and mentally prepare.

At six, the class starts on time. The four from last week showed up, plus 11-year-old Samantha. The oldest student brought a friend her age, Belle White, and now looks more comfortable among all of the younger students in the class. The two newer ones went to buy the needed supplies, while the rest found their projects from last week and continued with those.

"Notice how you can't see the glue," I stated as I held up Maryann's for the rest of the class to see. "This is very good. Let's keep working on them, and they should be finished today."

"How high should we make them?" Katelyn asks.

"As high as you want," I answer. "What do you plan on putting in yours?"

"Pencils and crayons," she answers.

"Well, that's tricky," I answer her. "Pencils are much longer than crayons, so they need a higher box. Maybe you could make two, one for each. Or, if you like, make this one big enough for pencils, then I can show you how to attach another box to its side for crayons."

"I can do that?" she asks.

"Of course you could. Here's one I did."

I find one of the simpler ones I brought, and show her again how one piece could have pretty much as many attached boxes as you want. I made one when I was a sophomore in college that had about 50 boxes, but I won't bring anything that complicated just yet, so as not to overwhelm the students.

"I want one like that!" she declares, as do the rest of the younger ones in the class.

"Well, you all could," I say, smiling at what is happening. "Let's all first finish our basic boxes, then we'll move on."

As they work on theirs, I help the new students get started. I give them a similar speech as I did to the rest of the week before, then they start on their basic boxes.

Things are going well, and a few minutes before 8:00, we all start cleaning the mess. They all leave their projects behind, and after I remind them of no classes next week due to the holiday, they leave promising to be back in two weeks.

"I'm looking forward to it," I tell them as I toss a few unusable craft sticks away.

"It's catching on," Andrea says as she hands me my cut for the evening. "I'd like to start advertising. Not your class, necessarily, but the store. Or, I mean, I'd like to look into advertising the store. I don't want to sign anything now, I just want to know how much it will cost and what you'd do first."

"You mean you won't blindly trust me?" I jokingly ask.

"It's not that, it's just…" she starts, then I laugh a little and cut her off.

"No, that's fine. We wouldn't want you to until you are one-hundred-percent sure about it. It's art, so I think visual would be better than a radio ad. A small billboard or two, along with a newspaper campaign, may be what you're looking for." I hand her a business card and look around a little more. "Call the agency, make an appointment, and when you come in, be prepared to share any concepts you may have plus your ad budget."

"Do I have to come up with the ad myself?" she asks.

"Oh, no. Not at all. We can do it all for you, but if you have any ideas yourself, feel free to share them with us. You will have final say before anything gets published."

"Well…" she says, starting to hedge some.

"It's not a difficult process. I promise that, Andrea. If you don't like our designs or feel they're too expensive, it'll cost you nothing more than a little time. Just call the office if and when you're ready, and we'll guide you through everything."

"Okay, thanks, Saturn," she says, then studies the card as I leave the store.

I get home and immediately start drawing out concepts for her potential billboard. I'm not sure if she'll become a client or not, but there's no need to wait while it's all still fresh in my mind.

Ten o'clock rolls around, and I haven't heard from Janus all day. I change for bed, kneel beside my sofa to say my prayers, then lie down for hopefully a good night's sleep.

The next morning starts as any other, with an alarm ringing and me waking up on a sofa in my front room, with a slightly sore neck. Breakfast, shower, dressing, and petting Muffin all happen before I leave for work. There seems to be some clouds in the sky, and the forecast calls for possible light rain at times throughout the day. "Is that normal for around here?" I ask myself after hearing the report on the radio. After that, one of the political ads I voiced came on. As I listened, I wasn't sure whether to feel proud of my work, ashamed of what I was saying, or just shake it off and simply accept it as part of my job. After some consideration and remembering my talk with Karen yesterday, I went with option number three.

The meeting happens as usual, and we assured Gretchen that the Jack's Coffee and Pastry campaign set to begin on Monday is still on track. She didn't assign me any special projects today, but she did give me an envelope that has all of the messages from yesterday and advised me to get on them right away.

"I will be sure to," I answer. Nobody has anything else to add, so we're dismissed to go about our days.

After returning some phone calls, I looked again at the Jack's Coffee ads, as well as the billboard for

Janus's store. They all look like they're ready to go, despite my still being somewhat uncomfortable appearing on the billboard and TV ad.

I get an email notification, and when I check, I see it's a statement for my first payday with this company. I opened it immediately, and my face turned from smile to frown when I saw how much the direct deposit into my account was for.

"This must be some sort of a mistake," I say as I print out the statement. "Should I talk to Gretchen about this?"

Well, although I do love my job, I don't work for free, and while this isn't "free," it's not nearly as much as I was promised. I decide to get to the bottom of this, so I walk over to reception and ask Frida if Gretchen is available. She picks up her phone, then moments later, she tells me to go ahead into the office.

I walk in, and she is staring intently at her computer. She points to the chair in front of her desk, indicating she wants me to sit down. I do, then wait for permission to speak.

"How can I help you?" she asks, then leans back in her chair.

"Well," I say, my voice cracking a little. "I knew coming in here I wasn't going to be paid as much as I did in Chicago, and that's fine. However, I just saw my pay statement and… and… and I'm sorry to say, Ms. Gillmore, this is far less than you implied it would be."

"What do you mean?" she asks, then waits for an answer.

"I mean… If this is my pay, then I'm going to have to quit. Maybe my job is still waiting for me back home, I don't know, but… but… but…" I try to calm my emotions by taking a deep breath.

"Is that what you're talking about?" she asks as she points to the paper in my hand.

"Yes," I answer.

"May I see that, please?" I hand it to Gretchen, and she smiles and chuckles a little. "You say that your sister is an accountant and has done payroll before?"

"Well," I think, surprised by the response. "She is an accountant and does the books for the farm she lives on now. Before that, she worked in Chicago for a major retailer. I'm not sure if she's ever done payroll, though."

"I see," Gretchen says, then hands the statement back to me. "I bet she knows very little about advertising and marketing, huh?"

"That would be correct," I say, now even more confused.

"I figured so," she laughs again.

"I'm sorry, Ms. Gillmore. I fail to see the humor in this."

"Okay, Ms. Syres," she says, then leans toward me. "First, only I get to do the Ms. or Mr. bit around here. Second, I think… no, I know, that you're misunderstanding this statement."

"I can see how much it's for," I answer. "Even with deductions and whatever, it's still not even half of what I made in Chicago."

"Saturn, calm down and listen." I sit still for a few moments, and once things are settled, Gretchen calls for Frida to bring some coffee in for both of us. Once she leaves, Gretchen sips her, puts the cup down, and speaks some more.

"This isn't your paycheck. It's customary that we hold back your first check, so you won't get paid for another two weeks," she explains, leaving me more confused.

"Then what is this?" I asked, having no idea how to read a check statement.

"We know going without any pay could be difficult, so we do pay out bonuses without holding those back."

"This is my bonus?" I ask, now the numbers are looking rather big to me. "How is it this much?"

"Because, in all my time in advertising, or business as far as that goes, I've never seen anybody hit the road running as hard as you have. In your short time here, you secured a long-term contract with Here and There Pizza and brought in two new clients. Sure, your boyfriend's account may not be too big one day, but the Jack's Coffee account has the potential to be a huge grab."

"I thought you had the pizza when I interviewed," I asked.

"We had them for the one campaign. They liked it so much, they signed a two-year contract with us. That's all because of your 'Your toppings here' concept. Not to mention, and we don't pay bonuses for this, but your work here so far has been impeccable. The clients love your concepts, and the ones using your voice talents love those as well. I want you to understand something now, though, so listen carefully."

I sit still, hanging on to her every word.

"Don't expect the bonus to be this big every payday. Sometimes it may be, sometimes you may not get any bonus at all. Also, don't let the bonuses be what drives you; let your passion drive you. Are you okay now?"

"Yes. Thank you, Gretchen. I'm sorry if I offended you at first," I say, then stir my coffee some.

"No, that's perfectly fine. I'm glad you feel comfortable enough discussing such matters with me. By the way," she says, then taps some keys on her laptop, and then turns it to me. "This is what your base pay is. It's the check we held back."

I look at it and am stunned. Sure, it's not as much as Chicago paid, but it's still quite a bit more than I expected. That, with the bonuses, makes me very, VERY happy I came in here.

"Is this what you were expecting?" she asks.

"It is," I slightly lie, making a mental note to ask forgiveness from God for doing that.

"Good. Is there anything else you need?"

Since I was there, I decided to ask her about the bird feeders, then tell her about the potential for an ad for the craft store.

"Perfect," she says. "The craft store is small, but it has potential to be a client for decades with weekly ads in the newspaper and possible TV and radio spots. I feel generous. Tell her to sign with us for a year's worth of ads in the Sunday paper, and we'll toss in the first month for free. How is your sister's farm wedding thing going?"

"I talked with her, and she's still thinking about it," I answer.

"I really want that campaign, as well," she says, then goes silent while she crunches some numbers. "Tell her if she signs for one billboard for one year, we'll pay the rent for the first two months. If she adds radio ads, which we could easily record here in our studio, she'll get two months free for those, too. Do you think she'll go for those?"

"I honestly don't know," I answer. "I'll call her soon and make that offer."

"Perfect," she says. "As far as the bird feeders go, go for it. I was thinking about putting a koi pond back there, too. Buy the feeders, have a regular delivery of food, and the agency will compensate you for that expense. The filling and maintaining them will be your responsibility, and please do that on your own time."

"I'll come in early to do that," I answer.

"Perfect. I have clients to tend to. Make those two calls and email me the results. Please take your coffee, we're done."

Chapter 16
Friday Fun

I made the phone calls Gretchen wanted me to. While I talked to Venus for a little longer than I did to Andrea, as I needed a baby update from her, they both said pretty much the same thing. They liked the offer I made and said that they'd have to consider everything and would get back to me. I wait until just a few minutes before the end of the workday and workweek to email that information to Gretchen, hoping she wouldn't have a reply until Monday. Five o'clock comes, and no reply.

I say goodnight to a couple of coworkers as I start to head out the door, when I hear one call me back. It didn't sound like Gretchen, and when I turned to look, I saw that it was Karen calling me.

"Are we working late?" I ask her as she walks towards me.

"No, not in the least," she says. "I was just wondering if you had any plans for tonight."

"No, not really," I honestly answer. "I have a date tomorrow, but I am free tonight. Are we visiting a client?"

"No," Karen says, then laughs a bit. "I was just wondering if you wanted to go out tonight. There's dancing at the civic club, and I wanted to go but didn't want to go alone."

"Oh," I say, feeling a little surprised. "I don't know…" I say, hedging a little.

"I'll pay your cover charge and maybe for a glass of wine. What do you say?"

"Maybe I should go home and change first," I say as I look down at what I'm wearing.

"Nonsense, you look adorable," she says.

"I've been sort of seeing somebody," I say. "I'm not looking to date anybody new."

"Me neither," Karen answers. "We eat, listen to music, and if a guy asks one of us to dance, what's the harm? Come on… I hate going to these alone."

I think for a moment, trying to come up with more excuses, but I couldn't think of any. I agree to go, but only if we stop somewhere first and have something to eat.

We go into the downtown area to Doug's Deli. Before we go in, I look at the flyers in the window.

"Still?" she asks.

"And forever," I say, then we go inside. There are two tables occupied by two customers each, and no line at the counter. Karen looks around, nods, and then we place our orders.

We both enjoy a Doug's Deli-ght sub combo, which features a mix of grilled chicken and chicken lunchmeat, along with your choice of add-ons. We both chose provolone cheese and mayonnaise, and I added lettuce and tomatoes to mine, while she went for almost everything they offered.

"That's quite a lot," I say as we sit.

"I'm hoping to burn a lot of calories tonight," she answers.

I say a quick grace, and this time she adds a little more after I say "Amen."

"Thank you," I tell her.

"So, you say you've been to the civic club for dancing before?" she asks as she opens a bag of chips.

"Yes. Janus took me a couple of weeks ago, and I rather enjoyed it," I answer.

"And you say that you two aren't anything yet?"

I'm not sure what she means by "anything," so I answered the best I could.

"We're dating, and have been for almost a month. It's nothing serious right now, but I think it's a bit past casual dating. I'm not sure how to define it, honestly," I answer.

"Do you see a future with him?" she asks, then takes a huge bite from her sub.

"I see a foreseeable future with him. Forever? I don't know. Throughout the summer, at least? I think so."

The words almost hurt as I said them, but I realized that my quick answer without thinking was probably the most honest. I don't want to talk about it anymore, so I try to switch directions.

"I'm going to put bird feeders in the grass behind our agency. Maybe watching them will help fuel our minds," I say.

"Or delay the process if we watch for too long. I'm looking forward to that happening, though," Karen replies. "Gretchen says that it's okay?"

"As long as I maintain it on my own time, yes," I answer.

"That sounds like her," she chuckles out.

We talk a little more about not a whole lot as we finish our dinners. After cleaning up, she takes another look at the promotions in the window. She walks to the counter and asks to speak with the manager or owner. They aren't there, but an older teen who says he is the shift manager comes out to talk to her. Karen points to the window, then hands him a card. He thanks her and puts it in the cash register.

"Do you think they'll call?" I ask.

"Only if they want more than six customers in here on a Friday night."

I glance once more at what is in the windows before getting into my Volkswagen. Karen and I took our own cars, and I followed her to the civic club. After we park, I walk beside her as we make our way to the entrance. As promised, Karen pays the small cover charge, allowing us entry into the dance.

It was the same as the time Janus took me. There was the same band playing a song I recognized from last time, with lots of couples dancing, and many people eating, drinking, and even some flirting going on. I want to soak it in for a moment, but Karen takes me by the wrist and guides me to a couple of chairs where we sit.

"Now what?" I ask.

"Wait. It won't take long," she answers.

"For what?" she asks.

"Just wait," she says, winks at me, then starts scanning the room.

I wasn't exactly sure what we were waiting for until a man walked over to her and extended his hand, silently asking her for a dance. She smiles, takes his hand, and lets him lead her out onto the not-too-crowded dance floor.

The band is playing an upbeat song, and Karen and the man dance apart from one another, touching hands a few times. Another song comes on, one about the same tempo as the one before, and they dance that one, too. I sit there watching her having a fun time, not minding being alone for the time being. A slow song comes on, and upon hearing that, they nod at one another, part ways, and Karen rejoins me.

"You don't want to dance close?" I ask her as she sits.

"Not with Randy, I don't. He's a nice guy, but what we just did is as far as we'll go tonight," she answers.

"Oh," I say. "So, we wait again?"

"Not for long, we won't," she replies. "There's a good-looking one over there."

She adjusts how she's sitting in her chair, crosses her legs using the top one to subtly point to who she is talking about, and he walks over to her.

"How about it?" he asks, and she stands and goes onto the floor with him. The band is playing another faster song, and I bop along, watching as my coworker seems to have all of the right moves, both on and off the dance floor. I'm minding my own business when I hear a somewhat familiar voice asking if I'd like to dance. Oh! My! Gosh! It's Chip Flanders, the man I met at Clean as a Whistle laundromat. What do I do?

The band started playing another fast dance song, so I figured, why not? I let Chip lead me onto the floor, and we start dancing. I have a good time with him, and when the band plays another faster-paced song, though a little slower than the previous one, I stay out there with him.

The band begins playing a slow dance song. It's not an intense love song, but ironically, it's about a couple dancing together for the first time. Chip puts his hands out like he wants to continue with me, and when I see that Karen is still on the dance floor with a new partner, I stay with Chip.

He tries to pull me in closer, but I make sure to keep as much distance between us as possible without trying to come off like a prude or tease. There is probably a little less than a foot separating us, which is close enough in my opinion. That may have been a mistake, as now it gives him the perfect opportunity to talk to me.

"You never called," he says.

"I've been busy," I answer.

"You don't seem busy now," he says. "Are you here with anybody?"

"A friend," I answer, which I suppose may be correct.

"Oh," he replies, then waits a few seconds before speaking again. "When do you think you'll call?"

"When I'm not so busy, maybe," is as honest as I'm willing to answer.

"Well, I'll be waiting," he says, then tries to pull me closer.

I figure the song is about over, and more talking may get me into some trouble with him. I dance closer to him, close enough that our chests touch a few times. He stays quiet for the rest of the song, and I'm not sure if that is a good thing or not. The song ends, and I tell him that I was thirsty.

"I'll buy you a drink," he offers.

"No, thanks. I'll get my own," I say. "Maybe we can dance more later tonight."

I go to the bar, and while Karen promised to buy me a cup of wine, she's not around, so I pay for one myself. I thank the bartender, decide that pouring one glass of wine doesn't warrant a tip, then take the drink to a table. I take a small sip, then put it down and scan the dance floor looking for Karen. I see she's dancing with another new man.

"How does she do it?" I ask out loud, thinking nobody could hear me.

"She's here often, and never has trouble finding dance partners," a voice I definitely recognize answers. I look and – Drat! – It's Janus!

"Oh, hi," I nervously say, then take a bigger swig of my wine as he sits down.

"I knew you were a good dancer, and seeing you out there with Chip let me see that in a new way," he says. "He's a regular here when he's not on the road."

"I was just… umm… I met him at the laundromat a while ago, and we talked…and… we, um…" Drat! Did I just blow it with Janus?

"It's fine, Saturn. We're not exclusive, and you could dance with or even date whomever you want," he says, smiling.

"Oh, we're not dating, Chip and me. We just happened to be here at the same time," I start to explain.

"And if we ever do decide to date exclusively, you'd still be allowed to dance with whomever you want to," he explains.

"But I don't…"

"You like dancing, and that's great. You look like you had a hard day at work, so I'll let you keep your evening with your friend. I think we danced together here before, but I'm not totally sure," he says as he stands, looking her way.

"You don't have to leave," I plead.

"I'll pick you up at noon tomorrow for our date. Dress in comfortable clothes you won't mind getting dirty and possibly ruining," Janus smiles devilishly as he speaks.

"You still want to date me tomorrow?" I ask nervously.

"Of course. Have a good time here tonight. I'll be leaving soon."

Janus walks away, and as I take another sip of my wine, I see a gorgeous lady come over to him and say something. He smiles, then she leads him out to the dance floor. They dance a fast '80s new wave song together, and as I watch, I'm not sure what to think. I turn to look elsewhere and see Sunny and Blake dancing closely to a song that doesn't warrant that. "What is happening?" I mutter, then I finish my wine.

The song ends, and I see Janus say goodbye to the person he just danced with and head out the door. A slow song comes on, and I see Sunny and Blake dance even closer to one another than before. I feel a tap on my shoulder and see a handsome man with one hand extended.

"Sure," I smile, then go to dance with him.

The wine hasn't taken effect yet, so we dance close – just not too close – and when he asks for a second dance, I politely decline.

I go back to sit on a chair that's not at a table. Karen sits next to me and hands me a wine.

"I promised to buy you one," she says.

"Thanks," I say and accept it, making sure it will be my last here tonight.

"Are you having fun?" she asks, then takes a huge gulp.

"I suppose," I say, replaying the events with Janus in my mind.

"We should do this more often," she says, and I give her a non-committal nod.

Another man walks over to us, and looks like he's looking at us in the same way he's picking out a steak at the grocery store. I am relieved, and to be honest, slightly disappointed, when he chooses Karen over me. She looks at me, and I tell her to go ahead. She drinks the last of her wine, then heads out onto the dance floor to dance to a disco classic.

I only had two wines, which is well below my usual threshold for losing any inhibitions, but I still declined any other offers to dance for the rest of our time there.

When I am sure that the wine will have no effect on my driving, I tell Karen that I'm tired and will be going home.

"I'm glad you came," she says. "Let's do this again."

As she was talking, a man she had danced with earlier asked her again. She smiles back at me as he pulls her to the center of the dancing. I smile as she trots out there, give her a wave, and head out the door.

I get in my car and look at myself in the rearview mirror. I'm not sure what I was expecting to see, but I look fine, I suppose. I do a quick mental check and determine that I am fine to drive the few miles home safely.

As I'm stopped at a red light, I notice a store on the side of the road a little further down that I hadn't seen before. It's a liquor store. When the light turns green, I think about whether I want to stop and buy something. Maybe it's the two glasses of wine I've already had talking to me, but I decide to stop and check it out.

I park my car by the curb and walk inside. Once I enter, I realize that, despite all the drinking I did during my first couple of years of college, I had never actually been inside a liquor store before. In fact, besides the glass of wine I bought earlier, I had rarely ever purchased alcohol before.

It's clean, and kind of looks like a specialty grocery store inside. Of course, there are ads in here, so I look around at those first. Most are for products that they sell here. There are several posters for popular brands of beer and cigarettes. I see one for vaping products and even a couple for snack foods. There is a large poster for a brand of rum that is sponsoring a popular rock band's tour, one I don't care for so much. Too bad. There's a schedule of their upcoming dates, and besides nearby Indianapolis, they are playing in Omaha in a few weeks. I could have used that as an excuse to visit Venus if we liked their music. Oh, well. I'll have to think of another excuse now. I wonder where the wine is kept in here.

There are also signs indicating where everything is located. The employees are dressed in smart-looking uniforms, and they even have small grocery carts for your big purchases. I'm just here for one bottle of wine, so that a cart won't be necessary.

I walk over to where the wine is and immediately feel overwhelmed. The bottles have labels like Cabernet Sauvignon, Chardonnay, Merlot, Pinot Noir, and Shiraz. I don't know what's what, but I usually liked red wine when I drank it. Maybe I could ask somebody.

There is an employee who looks about my age, and I ask him for advice. He said that he's usually a beer drinker and is here only to stock shelves, so he couldn't help me find "the right wine." I thank him, anyway, and he continues with his work.

"Excuse me. Maybe I could be of some help," an older man with dark hair that's grey at the temples offers to me. "I'm quite the connoisseur of wine."

"Um, sure," I say.

"What kind of wine do you prefer?" he asks.

"Well," I say, then think for a moment. "I usually drank red."

"I see," he replies. "What will you be accompanying it with?"

"Accompanying?" I ask.

"Will you be eating anything with your wine?" he restates.

"Oh," I respond, a little surprised by how complicated this is becoming. "Popcorn, I guess. Or maybe crackers."

"Well," he says, then hands me a bottle. "Then try this. It's a Cabernet Sauvignon."

He starts talking about vintage this and pheromones that. I didn't know how boring buying wine could be. If he were a client, I'd be interested. Now, though, I just want to buy some wine and go home.

"Chill it to between 60 and 65 degrees, remove the cork, and wait for at least an hour before serving. A crystal glass, of course, would be best."

"Okay, thank you," I say, then glance at the bottle as he walks away. How much is this stuff? I'm not sure I want wine that badly. As I look at the bottle, trying to decide, another man, about my age, walks over to me.

"Hi," he says.

"Oh, hi."

"I'm sorry, I overheard your conversation. Wine snobs are something else, aren't they?" he asks.

"I suppose," I answer.

"It sounds to me like you're just wanting to drink some wine and get a buzz on while snacking," he says.

"Well, that's not exactly how I'd phrase that," I answer, then think of a better way to say that. I can't.

"It's okay. It's Friday night. Here, try this one," he says, then hands me a bottle and takes the other from me.

"Pinot noir," I say, reading from the label.

"It's good, doesn't cost a fortune, and tastes great at room temperature, but you could chill it, if you like.. It's also a screw cap, so you won't have to buy a corkscrew," he says.

"How do you know I don't already own one?" I ask.

"If you did, you wouldn't need help in picking out a wine," he answers.

"I suppose you're right," I say, and smile at him. "Thank you. It was nice of you to help, and it was nice meeting you."

"You too," he replies. "May I ask your name?"

"Saturn," I say, not wanting to say more after two drinks earlier.

"Well, Saturn, my name is Bruce. Bruce Sanford. I'm not the type who usually tries to pick up ladies in a liquor store, but if you ever want to go out sometime, here's my card. It has my business and cell numbers."

I look at it and see he's a Nissan salesman in Indianapolis.

"Well, thank you, Bruce. I'll keep this card, and maybe you'll hear from me. Thanks again for helping with my purchase."

"You're welcome," he says, then looks at me in an almost expectant way. I'm not sure what it means, but I'll try something.

I walk away, my back to him, obviously, on my way to the cashier. There's a small line, and once I make it there, I turn to see if Bruce watched me. He didn't. He's now by what I assume are large refrigerators with glass doors, picking out some beer for himself.

The line moves quickly, and I hear the cashier clear his throat, indicating for me to turn around and pay for my wine. I apologize to him, and he scans the bottle and puts it in a long, slender paper bag. I pay cash, not wanting a liquor store purchase on my credit card statement for some reason, then I drive home to see if I'll actually drink some of this tonight.

Chapter 17
Janus's Surprise

I get home a little after 10:00 p.m., which is right around my usual bedtime. After I pet Muffin and change into some night clothes, I set the bottle down on my coffee table and wonder if I should open it or not. I figure that since I bought it, I might as well at least give it a taste. I go to the kitchen cabinets and realize I don't own a wine glass. I take one out for juice, rationalizing that technically, wine is just grape juice, and use that.

I unscrew the bottle, take a little sniff, and pour what I think is the right amount into the juice glass. I make a silent toast to myself, hold the glass up in a cheers, and take a sip. I'm no wine connoisseur, but I think it's okay.

I go to the kitchen, pull a small plate from the cabinet, and pour some saltine crackers onto it. I take it back to my couch, sip more wine after sitting, then bite into a cracker.

"If I only had fancy cheese," I say to Muffin, who meows back at me,

I take another sip of wine, then turn on the television. I channel surf and come across a fishing show. I'm not sure if it's on a sports channel or an outdoor living channel or what, but I stop and watch. The ambient sounds of the water splashing, chirps in the background, and the two men fishing in a boat talking to each other remind me of my summer before going to college.

Tensions were running high between Venus and me, so I asked Mom if I could borrow the car and, using my graduation money, take a camping trip to a campground run by the Cook County, Illinois, Forest Preserve, a short distance from our house. She said that I could.

The campground provided some essential items, such as a tent and firewood, but I had to bring the rest. Because I had never camped before, it didn't take long before I realized how unprepared I was for this trip. As I was getting frustrated over not knowing how to light a campfire, my proverbial knight in shining armor came to my rescue.

A man, I presumed to be around 8 to 10 years older than me, came by my campsite and helped me with the fire. He brought some stew from his supplies, since I had only brought bologna and bread, and we had deer meat stew together that night.

We sat and talked, then he offered me some wine. I only told him I was a college student, which was technically true since I was an enrolled freshman who would be attending a few weeks from then, so he never knew my age. I don't think so, anyway.

I had a few glasses, felt tired, and went to sleep in my tent. Before that, I agreed to have breakfast with him the next morning and then go fishing with him. When I was woken up by the sun and birds chirping, I saw he was already outside my tent preparing our breakfast.

After eating, he helped me buy a fishing license for the day, and we went. As I said, I never fished before, and he made it rather fun for me. After spending the day fishing, we returned to my campsite, where he used the fish we caught that day to make another stew for us.

It wasn't long before he broke out the wine again. This time, I had five or six glasses and lost a little of my inhibitions. Although I was seeing someone else at the time, I started dancing with him to no music, and then we made out heavily. He saw that I was sleeping in a sleeping bag and told me he had an air mattress that I might find more comfortable, inviting me to sleep in his tent with him.

At this time, my body count was a firm zero. Wait, that's not entirely true. I had let boys touch my breasts before, always over a shirt or bra, and never directly, but that's as far as it went. Honest. My body count was maybe half, or three-quarters. Perhaps if you add them all together, it could be one, but however you add it, caressing my breasts was as far as it went with me. Okay, I may have cupped a rear or two and had mine cupped, but I swear, that is as far as I ever went up to that point.

At that time in the campground, I just thought Elliot—that was his name, Elliot—I thought he was only inviting me to sleep next to him, not... well, you know what. I misunderstood him, declined the offer, and slept in my own tent. I woke up the next morning with an intense fog in my head. Once that all cleared, I realized what Elliot meant. He was out fishing again, and the night before, I told him that I wanted to go hiking, and we could meet again later that day. Instead, I packed my things as fast as I could and drove home without even leaving a note.

When I got home, I had some problems. I was seeing this boy, and we were both going away to college soon. While I didn't realize it at the time, he didn't look at me the way Eric looks at Venus, but I still thought, before the camping trip, he may have been the one. I sulked around the house for a day or two before finally making a date with him. We walked around the trails at a local park, and when we found a bench, I confessed to him what I had done on the camping trip.

We both decided that a long-distance relationship wouldn't work for us, and broke up that night. It wasn't mean or nasty, just necessary. We ended our date and even kissed goodnight. Oh, who am I kidding? We kissed goodbye. We cried, kissed, cried some more, kissed some more, then finally parted and never saw each other again.

The men in the boat on television seem happy fishing together. Sometimes I wonder if Elliot and I would have been happy as well. Instead, I only have fuzzy memories of two wonderful days camping with him, never to see him again.

Will this be the end for Janus and me? I know we agreed to see other people, but will our jealousy break us up? Am I overthinking everything? It's too late to call Venus or Chloe. Drat!

I stay up for another hour watching them fish, and drink four more, I think, glasses of wine before turning off the TV and lying down on my couch to sleep.

The alarm rings at 7:30 a.m., and as I'm startled awake, I wonder why I set that blasted thing in the first place. I sit up, turn it off, stretch my arms, then rub the sleep from my eyes.

I sit for a moment and assess how I feel. While I don't have a headache, I definitely feel the same as I did most Saturday and Sunday mornings during my first year of college, with an added pain in the neck. I go into the kitchen and see that I hadn't prepared any coffee last night. Drat! I really need some right now. I prepare the coffee now, then head to the bathroom while it brews its magical potion.

After doing some morning business, I decide that a shower might help wake me up. After I lather, rinse, and repeat, I step out, wrap a towel around my unclothed body, and head to the bedroom to pick out some clothes for the day.

Janus told me to wear something I wouldn't mind ruining, so I put on some denim shorts that just about seen their last days, and a T-shirt with a picture of the planet Saturn on the front.

I go to the kitchen, pour myself a freshly made cup of coffee, and take as big a swig as I can. After my belly warms a little, I take another drink. I see the wine bottle is still on my coffee table. There seems to be a cup or two still left in it, so I put it away in a cabinet.

My stomach still feels a bit unsettled, so I eat about three-quarters of a bowl of cornflakes and take a couple of Advil with it just in case. I wash them quickly after eating, refill my coffee cup, then glance at the clock. It's around 8:30, so I need to figure out how to pass the time before Janus comes by to pick me up for our date. That is, if he still wants to go.

I turn the television set on and open the YouTube app. I see a suggestion for classic commercials from the 1990s, so I look at the description and, unsurprisingly, I turn on the just over two-hour video.

I watch the first couple and notice the nuanced details that the average consumer will notice and overlook at the same time. In some, if you turn the volume down and don't read any captions, you may wonder if it's an ad for clothing, cars, or even vacation spots or homes for sale. "Fascinating," I say to Muffin, who is unimpressed by such details.

I start working on a craft stick project for the upcoming craft fair. I still haven't an idea how well I'll do there, but once I get a feel for this area, I'll know what to work on for the next time.

At 11:30, I wonder if I should have something to eat. Janus hadn't mentioned what we're doing, but if it's going to take all day, I'm sure a meal will be involved. If he's picking me up at noon, then lunch might not be one of those. Drat! What do I do?

I figure a light lunch is best. I fix myself a grilled cheese sandwich and have that with some potato chips. I finish around noon, but still have time to wash the dishes before Janus stops by.

I get them washed and put away and return to the living room. I see that there's a part two to the commercials from the '90s, so I start that one and get back to working on the project.

Noon comes, and there's no knock at the door. That's okay. I'm sure he'll be here any minute. I work more on gluing sticks together, and fifteen minutes later, still no Janus. Now I'm getting worried. Is that it for Janus and Saturn, and now I'll have to start dating Chip? Chip does seem like a viable boyfriend, but I still want to – no, need to – see where Janus and I are headed. Or did we hit a dead end?

Twenty minutes past noon, I hear a knock at the door. I quickly attach the craft stick I'm holding, then go to the door as fast as I can. I open the door and see Janus standing there in raggedy jeans and an old concert T-shirt. I think it is, anyway, since he's holding flowers covering part of it.

"These are for you," he says, then hands me a bouquet of beautiful yellow tulips. I smile, accept the gift, then immediately take them to my table and put them in the vase he gave me.

"Thank you," I say, then fill the vase with water.

"I thought you'd like them," he says through a smile. "May I kiss you hello?"

I smile, walk over to him, and accept a simple peck on my lips. I want to do it again, but I also don't want to get too heated before our date. Besides, I had quite a lot of wine last night, and I'm not sure if that would still affect me, so I keep it at one kiss. One beautiful, perfect kiss. I decide to get it out of the way right away so it won't linger on us all day.

"I'm sorry you saw me dancing with Chip last night. It was nothing," I say.

"I told you it's fine, Saturn," he says. "Honestly. Are you about ready to go? I think you'll like your surprise."

"Just let me put a scrunchie in my hair first," I answer. "Please, have a seat."

Janus sits as I walk to my bedroom, and when I come back, I see him looking at my latest project on the table. "It's a shoe box," I answer before he asks.

"I was wondering," he says.

"It's just a big box, really. It's nothing too special."

"I disagree," he replies. "It's special because you made it. How much do these go for?"

"I ask $40," I answer. "They don't sell too well, though. I'm not sure why I keep making them."

"They should sell well here," he says, then picks up the card I got last night. "Oh, are you planning on buying a new Nissan?"

"No… well… I'm not sure…" I start to stammer and decide to come clean with Janus. "I was buying wine at a liquor store last night. A nice man helped me pick out a bottle to my liking, then said if I wanted to go out on a date with him, to call."

"Oh," Janus says, then puts the cars back down.

"I'm so sorry. I didn't mean for him to give me that card, and I don't plan on…"

"It's okay, Saturn. Honest. We talked about this. If you want to go out with him, I hope you have a good time. We're just not supposed to discuss it with each other," he says, then stands. "Can I give you something else before we leave?"

"Sure. I guess," I say, then he walks to me with a devilish look on his face.

Janus places his hands on my waist, pulls me closer than he ever has before, leans down, and kisses me with intense passion. It was as long as a single kiss we'd ever shared, and when we were done, we parted, both panting heavily. He runs his hands up and down my sides a little as we regain our composure.

"Just remember that if you ever kiss Bruce goodnight, or even Chip," he says, then releases me.

"I will," I promise, and meant it. Wow! If this were last night, I think we'd… we'd… I think we'd better get out of here before we do something we'd both regret.

"Did you have lunch yet?" he asks.

"I had a sandwich and chips, so I'm good for the time being," I answer.

"Good. This may take a while," he says as he opens the door for me.

I ask Janus where we were going, and he keeps his lips locked. We drive a short distance, and soon I think I recognize where he is taking me. He parks his pickup truck in his special spot at his shop and announces that we're there.

"Why are we here?" I ask.

"You'll see," he says, and we walk toward the front door.

He holds it open for me, and I pause for a moment. I stop and look at the entrance way, and shake my head a little.

"What?" he asks.

"You should have some ads near where people enter," I say.

"Why?" he asks.

"To let people know what you're selling in your store, of course," I answer. "They may come here for a coffee table and see you have golf clubs, glassware, and even a couple of bird cages. They may not buy any then, but will keep you in mind for the next time they need something like that."

"Can't they just see that when they come in?" Janus asks.

"Can't you listen to your advertising agent without arguing?" I joke. "Seriously, we can do that for you. When you see the success from this billboard ad, we can discuss internal advertising when you call to extend the campaign."

"If," he says, a little too seriously for me.

"When," I assure him, then we walk inside.

We greet his parents, who are working in the store area, then Janus tells them that he and I will be in the shop area for most of the day. He tells them to come get him if they need anything, then ushers me to the back.

"You can put an apron on if you want," he says as he tosses one to me. "You don't want to get your Saturn shirt messed up."

"Oh, this?" I reply as I look down. "People give me gifts like this all the time. Almost everything I own has a ring on it, except for my hand."

Oh, my gosh! Did I really just say that? Drat! Drat! Drat!

"I mean, I often get gifts with Saturn on them. Saturn, the planet, not Saturn the…"

"Are you ready?" he asks. "We have a pretty big project to finish here."

"Sure," I say. This guy must either have bad hearing or know when not to respond to my insane ramblings. I'm assuming it to be the latter.

"Great. I have this here that needs a little light refurbishing. I already got a good start on it, but since I know you like working with wood – craft sticks are wood – then I thought you may want to learn a little about working with bigger pieces of wood."

"Sure," I say. He brought me here to do his work for him. What should I be thinking right now?

He shows me where some of the wood still needs to be stripped. He teaches me how to use a heat gun, which is a tool used to help remove the paint from wood with the extra aid of a chisel. I work on stripping pieces for a couple of hours and actually lose track of time as I enjoy the work and conversation I'm having with Janus. Before I knew it, all the pieces that needed stripping were adequately stripped.

"Great," he says. "Which varnish do you prefer? Light or dark?"

"Umm," I think for a moment. I'm not sure why he's asking, or what it is we're even working on. I look between the two as Janus patiently waits, then choose the light.

"Great," he says, then puts the dark away and opens to light. "Here's the proper way to varnish."

He instructs me on how to do it, and he sounds a lot like me explaining the glue to my craft stick students. However, with varnish, dripping is never acceptable, and you must be consistent in the application. Once he is confident I can do it properly, he excuses himself to go out to the store area and check on things there.

While there are a lot of pieces of wood for this item, only a few pieces need finishing. I work on them quietly before Janus returns about fifteen minutes later. They just closed shop and said they had a typical at best Saturday.

"That'll change once your billboard is up," I promised.

"I hope so," he says.

Janus takes a brush, and we finish varnishing the pieces that need it. He then notes the time and says that it takes time for them to dry, so we should go out and get a quick bite to eat. Before we leave, he sets up special fans that he says accelerate the drying process.

"Where would you like to go?" he asks.

"Doug's Deli would be a quick stop," I answer.

Janus agrees, and we leave his store to head downtown for some sandwiches. We arrive, and once again, the place is nearly empty, with only eight others dining in, all of whom appear to be high school students.

After we order, the person running the register recognizes me from being with Karen yesterday. She asks if I work with her, and I said that I do. She asks if I could wait and chat with Doug for a moment. I look at Janus, who nods, then finds a table for us while I wait for the owner.

Doug Davis introduces himself as the owner and then asks if I have the authority to speak on behalf of Karen.

"I'm not sure about that," I answer. "But if you'd like to discuss advertising options with our agency, I can surely do that. I specialize in billboards, while she does mainly newspaper and print, but we all work together as a team at the agency."

"I hate to ask, but would you have time for a quick chat while you dine? I see you're with somebody, but if you do, I'll comp both of your meals."

I think for a moment, then I tell him to wait while I go talk to Janus about that. He agrees, and he moves from a booth to a table to better accommodate our unexpected companion.

He tells me I could wait at the table, and he'll bring our dinners out when they're ready. He comes with a tray in hand a minute later, and after he sits down, Janus says a grace, then I turn my attention to Doug.

We discuss various advertising options and what may work best for him for fifteen or twenty minutes. As we're finishing, I hand him another card in case the previous was lost, and tell him to make an appointment at the agency where we can discuss it further.

"Great," he says. "So, should I ask for you?"

"No," I reply. "Ask for Karen Keyes. She's the one who approached you first, and I don't want to take any commissions or bonuses from her."

"I will do that. It was nice meeting you, Saturn. I hope to do business with your agency soon," he says. As he stands, he nods at Janus, then walks away. I take out my phone, text Karen what just happened, and assure her that she will get the finder's bonus for this potential campaign.

"That's awfully nice of you," Janus says.

"Professional ethics," I reply. "So, what do we do now?"

"We go back to the shop. Your surprise should be ready by now."

Chapter 18
What a Difference a Day Makes

Janus starts to drive us back to his shop, and we pass one of my pizza billboards along the way. He points it out, and of course, it triggers a smile from me. It's my first, and it will always hold a special place for me.

We get back to his shop, which is now closed. He opens the back door and asks me to wait outside for a moment while he goes inside to turn the lights on. I hear the click of the switch, then the whole place lights up. Janus goes over to the freshly varnished wood pieces and touches them to make sure they're dry. Once he confirms they are, he calls me over to show me how to assemble the pieces.

It turned out to be relatively simple, especially once I learned what each piece is. It's a twin-size bed, and it's as cute as can be.

"I bet you could sell this for a good amount of money," I say after stepping back and admiring my handiwork.

"That's true," he says, then looks at me and smiles. "But I'm not selling it. It's yours."

"What?!" I almost yell. "What do you mean it's mine? I'm not sure I could afford this right now."

"Well, then it's a good thing I'm not selling it to you. It's a gift, Saturn. Please accept it," he says, still smiling.

What?! He's giving me a bed? Does he think that he'll be able to break it in with me, if you know what I mean? Is he really the type to do that?

"Janus, you can't give me a bed. It's too… too… I'm not sure it's proper for you to…"

"I'm not, Saturn. The church is. It's their way of thanking you for all your help. Really."

"What do you mean?" I ask.

"Here's what happened. Please listen, and if you don't want to accept it, then I understand," Janus says, then gestures for me to sit down. I do.

"I found this bed in the alley not too long ago. It cost me nothing as I passed it on my way to somewhere else. As I was working on it, I remembered that you don't own a bed yet and have been sleeping on your couch, complaining on occasion how uncomfortable it is."

"That's true," I say. He sold me my furniture, so he would know that. "I don't mind that at all, though."

"I know you don't, but please let me finish. I called a special meeting of the deacons, and here's what we decided. I donated this to the church, and then the outreach committee is giving it to you as a token of appreciation for your help. By doing this, I get a tax deduction for the value of the bed, which isn't much. I could sell it for a hundred dollars, maybe a bit more, since it's fancier than just a plain bed."

"I could actually afford that," I say, still waiting for the punchline here.

"I know you could. But now you don't have to," Janus explains.

"Then why have me do the work to refurbish it?" I ask.

"Oh, that?" he chuckles. "I wasn't sure if you'd prefer the light or dark varnish. That, and since I know you like working on wood projects like this, I thought you'd enjoy learning how to do this. Did you?"

"Honestly?" I ask, then take his hand. "Yes."

"Then will you accept?" he asks, then puts his other hand over mine to hold it in both of his.

"Well…" I hedge.

"Tomorrow, after church, we can go to Indianapolis, have a nice lunch, then go to a mattress store where I could…"

"No!" I cut him off. No way will I allow this! "No, I can't accept you buying a mattress for me. If you think giving me a bed and buying a mattress for me will get you into my bedroom, then…"

"Saturn," he says, and takes his hands back as he stands up and steps away. "I wasn't going to offer to buy a mattress for you. You will buy it, plus a box spring. I'm just bringing them to your apartment in my truck, saving you the delivery charge. I'm not trying to get to any place with you that we haven't already been."

"Well," I say, then stand to look at the bed closer. "I don't want to look a gift horse in the mouth, but I'll accept only on a couple of conditions."

"What are they?" he asks, then I face him.

"One, I pay for lunch tomorrow. Two, I pick out the mattress without any help. Three, once we get it installed, that will be the last time you see my bed for a long time. Are we clear?"

"I wouldn't have it any other way, Saturn," Janus explains. He then walks to me, puts his hands on my waist, and looks me in the eyes. "I like where we're at now. I'm not saying that somewhere down the line – way down the line – I wouldn't be open to a more intimate relationship with you. Right now, though, let's keep dating as we've been, and if you also want to date Chip or Bruce or whomever else, then go ahead. That's what we agreed on. Are you ready to take this back to your apartment now?"

"I suppose, just one more thing, though," I answer.

"What is that?" he asks.

I put my hands on his hips, a little lower than where he has his hands on me. I lean up for a kiss and allow him to direct the intensity of it. It isn't as intense as earlier today, but it's still a little more than I was expecting. I feel a slight urge to cup his rear, but I resist that temptation. Barely. Drat! It's like the Devil is on one shoulder and an angel on the other, both whispering to me. Listen to the angel, I keep thinking, despite the loud voice coming from the Devil's mouth.

I'm the one who breaks off from the kiss, but I continue to hold him and look him in the eyes. I think I'm starting to see it, but I'm not sure. Is he looking at me as Eric looks at Venus, or is it just my imagination? Either way, I think I'm starting to look at him the way Venus looks at Eric, and I hope Janus notices. He pats my waist a couple of times, then lets go of me.

We disassemble the bed, clean out his shop area, and take it back to my apartment. When I open the door and turn on the light, I stop in my tracks, and Janus bumps me from behind.

"Look," I say, pointing.

"What?" he asks.

"Muffin. He's inside the shoe box. See?"

Janus looks and says he looks cute in there.

"Cute is right, Janus. Be quiet, I want to take a picture of him in it."

"To frame and hang on the wall?" Janus jokes.

"Possibly," I say in a serious tone. "But also for marketing. That shoe box could also serve as a cat nap box. That might be the angle I've been searching for to help those sell better. A shoe box or a cat box. I bet if I put padding on the floor, I could sell them for $50 instead of the $40 I've been asking for them."

"You think?" Janus asks.

"If my marketing degree is worth anything, I do," I answer.

"Well, I hope it's worth a lot more than that, seeing my billboard is going up soon," Janus says jokingly.

"Oh, hush," I say, then ask Janus to stay still while I take some pictures of Muffin in the box.

After I'm satisfied with the pictures, we take the pieces into my bedroom, and I tell Janus that I could assemble it myself later.

"Are you sure?" he asks.

"Positive," I reply.

"Well, I'll see you at church tomorrow. Since we have a lunch date in Naptown afterward, should I pick you up?"

I think for a moment, then ask him to be here by 9:15. He says that he will. I walk him to the door, and before I open it for him, I look back at the tulips sitting on my kitchen table. I want so badly to make out with him on the couch, but thankfully, the angel on my right shoulder wins that argument. We do kiss, then kiss again, and yet again, before we finally let go of each other for him to leave. After one last confirmation that he'll be back tomorrow morning, I close the door behind him and prepare for my last night of sleeping on a couch in the living room.

The alarm rings at 7:30 as usual, and I wake thinking this was the last time I'll be sleeping out here on this couch. It's not that uncomfortable, truth be told, but I'm sure my bed will be more comfortable.

I have breakfast, then take a shower. Church isn't for a while, so I decide to put my scrub clothes back on and piece the bed together. It doesn't take long to do, and once I'm satisfied with its placement, I think about whether or not to bring more things in. I decide that since the mattress and box spring will be coming later, the fewer obstacles for them in the room, the better, so I leave everything out that isn't already in and will move them in later.

I pour myself a new cup of coffee and stir. I turn the TV on and open the YouTube app again. The suggestion is a compilation of McDonald's ads, starting in the early 1970s, and going up until a couple of years ago. "I have got to see this," I say to Muffin as I start the two-hour video.

I also decided that it's a good time to start the base of another "Cat bed" to be sold at the craft fair. I watch as the videos start with all of these mini-movies depicting a fantasyland where all of these McDonald's characters live. I just love ads from that era. As they progress, you could see how they adapt to the times they were intended to air. From big hair in the '80s to the grunge look of the following decade, it was all so perfect. They really should show this video as part of a marketing major course at all colleges.

Time slips away, and I notice Janus will be here in a few minutes. I quickly go to my bedroom and pick out an outfit that will work well for both church and shopping afterward. I settle on a nice slacks and a top combination, and have my shoes slipped on just in time to hear a knock. I open the door and am not surprised to see Janus standing there. He greets me with a smile, then a peck on the lips. Yes! I think we're officially at the kiss hello stage in our relationship.

"Have a seat," I tell him. "I'll be ready in a moment."

Janus sits and starts watching the video. He thought the video itself was playing an ad break, but when he realized the ads WERE the video, he chuckled and said that he wasn't surprised by what I was watching.

"When it does pause for an ad break, it's intriguing," I tell him. "Are you ready?"

"Sure," he says as he stands. "Is this going to be another cat box?"

"Yes," I answer.

He pauses for a moment as he looks around my apartment. I ask him why the delay, and he stays quiet a moment longer as he collects his thoughts.

"You say this cat box could sell for $50?" he asks.

"I think that would be about right if lined," I answer.

"And what about this?" he asks, holding a multi-compartment office supply holder.

"That goes for around $30. I've sold some for even close to $100 that had more compartments and a fancier design," I answer. "Are you ready yet?"

"Yeah, in a minute," he says as he looks around some more. "You say you only sell these at craft fairs?"

"I have at other places here and there, but mostly craft fairs and similar events. Why?" I ask.

"I was just wondering how well these would sell at my store," he says, then puts the office supply holder down.

"I've never thought about that. Let's not talk business now, Janus. I'd really like to get to church now. There is much for me to pray about."

We arrive at church well over half an hour before the service is to begin. We grab a cup of coffee, and he tries his black with a stirrer.

"I just wanted to see if it tastes different," he says before I question him.

"It doesn't," I assure. "It's only there to annoy sisters. What would Sabrina do if she saw you doing that?"

"Honestly?" he says, then thinks for a moment. "Probably nothing. I don't think she'd care."

"Then you're not doing it right," I joke, then Pastor Chalke comes over to us.

He asks if things are all set for Friday, and Janus informs him that while there are still a thing or two to iron out before then, all should go well.

"That's good to hear," he says.

"Pastor, I wanted to thank you for the gift of the bed. It was very nice, though not entirely necessary," I say, hoping I didn't sound ungrateful.

"Well, thank you for all of your help for this and future events. If this baby changing station thing works, we'll make a very positive mark in this community," he answers. "It was nice seeing you both. I'll see you at the fair if not before."

Pastor Chalke walks away, and as Janus and I chat, his parents come over to us. We talk with them a little, and at times others from the congregation come over to say hi and even a little more. At around ten minutes before ten, Janus suggests we go inside to find our seats.

We sit where we usually do, and I look around to see if Sunny is nearby. She's not. I see her on the other side of the pews, sitting rather closely to Blake.

I nudge Janus to turn around and look, and after he does, he smiles at me, giving me a "Mission accomplished" look. I smile back, then turn my attention to the choir up front, who have just started singing their prelude.

The service was nice, and the sermon was meaningful. Pastor Chalke spoke of the love stories between Rachel and Jacob from the book of Genesis, and that of Ruth and Boaz. While he was talking about how beautiful Jacob thought Rachel was, Janus took my hand and held it for the remainder of the sermon.

After the service, we greet Pastor Chalke again on our way out, then head to the community room. We have another cup of coffee, and I enjoy some homemade cake brought by a widow, while Janus stays longer than we normally do. Over half of the people leave before he turns to me.

"Are you ready?" he asks.

"To go shopping?" I reply. "Sure."

"No," he says, then swigs the remainder of his coffee and tosses the cup away. "I thought you wanted to pray at the altar with me."

"Oh, yes. Of course," I say. I throw the paper plate that had the cake on it in the trash, then Janus starts leading me to the front of the church. We're about halfway down the aisle when we hear voices calling us from behind. We turn and see Sunny and Blake standing there.

"Can I talk to you?" Sunny calls out to Janus.

"And me to you," Blake says as he looks at me. Janus and I look at each other, nod, and then we go to opposite sides of the church to listen to what our exes had to say to us.

I see Sunny holding Janus's hand as she starts talking, and I hope Blake won't do the same. He does. Drat!

"Listen, Saturn," he says in a low, very sincere voice. "I know we had something in the past. Something special. When we were on that double date, I found something in Sunny that... well... that just felt right. Feels right. I think she may be the one, Saturn. I'm sorry. I know that you wanted to give us another go, but I won't be able to date you anymore. I hope that we can still be friends."

I try my best not to laugh or even show relief. I try to play along the best I can, since he really is a nice guy and I don't want to unnecessarily hurt his feelings again.

"I understand," I say. "Yes, let's stay friends. I hope to see you here more often, and I hope that you and Sunny are very happy together."

Blake smiles, then reaches out for a hug. I figure one last won't hurt, especially since he's as good a hugger as he is a kisser. We embrace, and I feel something inside of me. No, not love or any sort of feelings like that. This is more... more.... contentment. He loosens his hug on me, but I want to embrace a little longer. He tightens his arms again, and I hold him for another thirty seconds, at least, before I let go. I take his hands in mine and look him in the eye. Why not? I think, and lean in to kiss him.

We touch lips, and I hold it for about three seconds. I'm again reminded how good it is to kiss him, and know that Sunny will be very happy with that. We let go, then he returns to Sunny, and Janus comes back to me.

"Sunny just broke up with me," he says with a sense of irony in his voice.

"I just got dumped, too," I say with the same tone, then decide to confess to him. "Then we kissed."

"So did we," he said in a matter-of-fact tone. "You know what else?"

"What?" I ask, assuming he doesn't want to talk about that part.

"She said that they're going into business together. They're going to have a table at the craft fair and sell coffee and candy, and see about getting something more permanent if that works out."

"I really do hope and pray things work out for them," I say.

"Then let's do that," he replies.

"What?" I ask.

"Let's go to the altar, and add them to the prayers we were planning to say."

He takes me by the hand and leads me to the front of the church. I wasn't sure if we were supposed to kneel or stand, and since he remained standing, I did as well.

"Heavenly Father…" he starts, then I cut him off.

"I'm sorry to interrupt. Could we please have a moment or two for silent prayer first? There are things I need to pray about, but I'd prefer to keep that between me and God."

"I also have things to pray about just between Him and me. I was going to save that for the end, but if you'd rather now, let's," he says.

"Thank you," I reply, then close my eyes and pray silently.

I pray for guidance and wisdom regarding Janus and my relationship. I pray for us to grow closer and to resist any temptations that Satan might bring our way. I pray for Eric, Venus, and her baby in waiting. I again pray regarding Janus and myself, hoping clarity will soon follow.

I'm not sure how much time went by as we silently prayed, but I guess at least ten minutes passed before I told Janus I was ready to pray aloud.

"I hope I didn't pray silently too long," I tell him.

"That's impossible to do," he replies. "Wait a moment, I still have a little more to do."

I wait for a couple more minutes before Janus opens his eyes. He lays his hands on the altar and motions for me to do the same. I do, and he starts praying. He prays for his family and the church. He prays for the upcoming event and those to follow. He even prays, heavily, for Sunny and Blake. I was anticipating him praying for us, but he never does. He starts praying, thanking God for the gifts in his life and for the gift of Jesus. He picks up a lighter at this point and lights a candle on the altar. He hands it to me, and I start praying in a similar way, then also light a candle. We stand silently for a moment or two, then when enough time passes, he takes a snuffer and puts the candle flames out.

"Ready?" he asks once he sets it down.

"I am," I say, and as we walk out, I feel something a little different come over me. I'm not claiming it's the Holy Spirit, but I'm not denying it either.

We nod to Pastor Chalke and a few others on our way out, then head into Indianapolis to continue this special Sunday together.

Chapter 19

The Day Continues

There are several ways to reach Indianapolis from Oakfield. We can take US 31, which is a more direct route, or choose I-69, which is longer in miles but might save a minute or two.

"Take the interstate," I direct Janus.

"Why?" he asks.

"There are more billboards along that route," I answer.

"Of course," he says, then heads in that direction.

He tells me that there are three mattress stores that he knows of in Indianapolis: Mattress King, Sleepy Time, and Rest Easy. He asks which one I'd like to go to first, and I suggest that we have lunch first, then decide.

As he drives, I open the YouTube app on my phone and look at the most recent ads posted for those three stores. As we get closer to the city, more and more billboards appear. Oh, they are all so beautiful, and I'd really like to have my ads on each one. I make notes of those that look like they're about to expire and send that information in an email to myself.

I point many out to Janus, and as usual, he seems interested in what interests me. He even highlights some of the nuanced details, and I'm impressed by how much he has learned from me. When he starts channel surfing for radio ads, I tell him to keep it on one station if he likes. There is such a thing as too much of a good thing, and I'm fine listening to music as we notice the billboards.

We get to a basic family restaurant in the downtown area, and he holds the door open for me to enter. No, I don't look at the flyers in the window as we enter, causing Janus to crack a joke about that.

"Do you pick up every piece of junk you see?" I ask.

"Well, I picked you up," he jokes, warranting a slap to the shoulder from me.

"I believe it was I who sent the first signals," I say to him.

"Maybe, but the moment I saw you, I just knew I had to ask you out."

As I start replaying our first meeting in my mind, the hostess comes over and asks how many will be there. Janus tells her two and requests a booth by a window.

"Right this way," she says as she grabs two menus and leads the way.

We sit across from one another and quietly peruse the menu. I'm buying, so I hope that Janus doesn't get the rather expensive steak. Actually, on second thought, I hope he does order it if he wants it. Maybe I'll prompt him.

"The T-bone looks good," I say.

"It's rather expensive," he replies without looking up.

"I'm buying," I remind him, then he looks at me.

"So, a bed frame is too expensive for you, but not this?" he asks.

"It's far cheaper than a frame," I tell him, not wanting him to know the real reason why I never bought a bed for my apartment. "I'm just saying, please order what you like without worrying about the price. I got my first bonus check, and with those and my regular pay, I'll be doing rather well financially in Oakfield once my paychecks start coming in."

"Good to know," he says. "Maybe I'll order two T-bone dinners with all the fixings. One for here now, and one for a doggy bag for tomorrow."

"Funny," I say.

Our waitress comes, and Janus orders the fish and chips. Interesting. I ordered the chicken-fried steak with mashed potatoes and the vegetable of the day. I request that no well be put in the mashed potatoes and for the cooks to totally drench the potatoes, meat, and vegetables with gravy. "I'll pay extra for that," I tell the waitress, who says she thinks the restaurant could afford another half ladle of gravy for free if that's how I'd like it. I thank her, then we hand the menus to her and turn our attention back to each other.

"So, have you decided which mattress store you'd like to shop at first?" he asks.

"Nope," I answer.

"I suppose we'll go to Mattress King first, then. It's closest," he says.

"No, we'll go to Rest Easy," I reply.

"So you want to go there first?" Janus asks, now confused.

"No." He looks at me quizzically again, and then I explain. "We only need to go to Rest Easy. They'll have what I want at the right price."

"How do you know?" he asks.

"Didn't you see the billboard on I-69?" I ask.

"I suppose. It didn't really say much," he says.

"It said enough for me," I answer. I wait for Janus to figure it out, and he never does. He asks me again, and for an answer, I do that sleight-of-hand trick I learned and make the salt shaker disappear.

"Oh, right," he says.

The waitress comes over with our food, and mine is perfectly drenched in gravy. We thank her, and I set the salt shaker back on the table. After I say grace, I'm tempted to take a picture of my dish and send it to Venus to annoy her. I don't, mainly because she's expecting my favorite little niece or nephew soon, and I don't want to unduly upset her.

We talk through lunch, mainly about the upcoming July 4 event. He says now that Sunny is going to have her own booth with Blake, he'll try to find another to take her place at the church's booth.

"I wish I could help," I say, then dip some meat into the potatoes.

"That's okay, Saturn. You've done enough, believe me," he says, then gives me another almost Eric-like look. Is it going to happen? Perhaps, but right now I should focus on the present, rather than the hopes I have for how things might be.

We end our meals with chocolate ice cream, then I leave a tip, pay, and we leave the restaurant. He wants to make sure I'm settled on Rest Easy for mattress shopping. I assure him that if I'm wrong, then we'll check the other two. "But don't count on it," I say as he puts his truck into gear.

We arrive there fifteen minutes later, and after we walk in, I stop, look around, and then give Janus a knowing look.

"I still don't see it," he says. "You're such an ad-nerd."

"If that's meant to be an insult, you failed miserably," I say with a serious expression, then laugh when I can't hold it any longer. "I see a salesman there. Let's go talk to him."

We walk up to him, and he introduces himself as Andy. We say hi, and I tell him what I'm looking for.

"Right this way," he says as he gestures, and I follow Janus as he leads the way.

We get to the area with the twin bed mattresses, and Andy says that as long as I take my shoes off, I can test-lie in any of them I want. I remove my shoes, and as silly as this sounds, I'm perfectly fine to lie down in bed in front of Andy, but not Janus. Stupid and silly, I know. Janus picks up on this and excuses himself to use the bathroom. I've no idea if he has to go or not, but I'll make sure to thank him later.

I try several, then choose the Goldilocks option—the one that's not too soft or too hard, sitting in a corner. I notice a tag on it, then I call Andy over. We start talking about the price when Janus comes back, and I signal for him to stay quiet and just watch.

"Are you the store manager?" I ask.

"I'm an assistant manager," he answers.

"Perfect. It says $149 for the mattress, and another $79 for the box spring?" I say.

"Yes, plus free next-day shipping," he confirms.

"I see," then pause for dramatic effect. "I'll give you $129 for both. I don't need delivery; we can take them right now, and I'll also take the floor models."

Janus watches, and I could see that he doesn't think I'll be able to make this deal.

"Well," he scratches his chin and thinks for a moment. "I can do that, but for $179."

"I see," I say, then give Janus a glimpse. "$138, plus you throw in a free pillow."

"Well…" he says, and I know I got him.

"This mattress has been on the floor for at least three years, which means they aren't selling too well. That, and this brand isn't mentioned in any of your advertisements, which means you've given up on trying to sell them. I'm actually doing you a favor, so take my offer or have this take up space in here for another three years."

"Fine," he says. "Sold. Let's get you rung up, and I'll help it to your truck."

I pay, and after we are loaded and Janus and I are in the truck, he just sits there and looks at me before starting the engine.

"See, ads tell you a lot more when you know what to look for," I say, then tell him to hit the road and get this to my apartment.

We're driving back, and this time he decides to take US Route 31 instead of the interstate. I'm letting the radio be our company, waiting for Janus to break. It doesn't take long before he finally does.

"How did you know that, really?" he asks.

"My degree is in marketing, not actually advertising. It was easy to spot," I answer.

"How?" he asks.

"Do you really want to know?" I ask, teasing him since we have time to kill.

"Of course," he says, then turns the radio down.

"It was mostly what I said to the salesman. When I had lain down on it, I saw a tag that said it was delivered three years ago. I would have bought it anywhere, and knew that store was where I'd get the best bargain."

"But how?" he asks. "You couldn't have known about the tag from the ads. Could you have?" he asks, then gives me a quizzical look.

"No, of course not," I say, though I wanted to tease him, saying I did. "They were the only ones offering free next-day delivery, so by us delivering it ourselves today, it gave us leverage."

"How do you know that the others don't offer that?" he asks.

"I don't. They probably do. However, only Rest Easy advertised that. They already include that in the price of their mattresses, so by taking that away, we lower the cost. That, and laying my cards on the table about its age and what I saw in the ads, just gave me more leverage. Would you have done the same thing if someone made you a similar offer for a dresser that may have been in your shop for a couple of years?"

"I probably would have," he says as he shakes his head. "Are you going to do that when you talk to Bruce about buying a new Nissan?"

"No. I'll just kiss him for every dollar he takes off the list price. Let's see, how long would it take me to kiss him 5,000 times?" I tease.

"Kiss me 5,000 times first and find out," he answers.

"Okay, but we already kissed what? About 50 times or so?" I reply.

"Oh, no. We have to start again from zero," he says, then smiles at me.

"Deal," I say, and really do hope that he holds me to that. "Then you could buy me a new Nissan."

"Well…" he says, and I sense that this teasing time has expired.

We get closer to Oakfield when I see a billboard for a home store in Mapletree. It's still a little early, so I ask Janus if he wouldn't mind taking me there so I could buy some bedding sheets.

"Did you see something on there for you to be able to talk them down in price?" he jokingly asks.

"No," I say seriously. "That only works for low-volume, high-profit retailers like mattress stores or resale shops like yours. You do intentionally put a higher price on your goods than you are willing to sell for, right?"

"We do leave room for negotiations, sure. Customers talk us down five or ten percent, then leave thinking they got a deal, making it more likely for them to come back."

"Marketing 101," I say, then Janus turns up the radio when a Lauren Daigle song comes on.

We arrive at Mapletree Home Basics around 4:00 p.m. We go inside, and it looks like a typical store of its kind. There are signs everywhere to direct you in the right direction, and of course, ads everywhere.

"Linens are over there," I say as I point, then lead the way.

As we walk, I take notice of the other items they sell there in case I need something later. I'm good for now, save for bedding, but one never knows when they'll need a new coffee maker or throw rug. We get to where the linens are, and Janus seems to have stopped short a few feet to allow me to pick out the bedding myself.

They actually have a nice selection for a store of this size in a town like this. I don't know much about thread counts or certain materials, so I stick to the more medium-priced options. I know I'll need more than one set, and two may be too few, so I decided to buy three sets today and see if that works out. I pick out a basic solid pink set since I'm a girl, a robin's egg blue since girls could also sleep on blue, and an off-white one with a pineapple pattern. I put them in the handbasket I am carrying, and tell Janus that this should do it for here.

"Ready?" I ask.

"Hang on," he replies. "I think I want a new tablecloth first. One never knows when they'll be inviting somebody over for a romantic candlelit dinner, so I want to be prepared."

"You know," I reply, "a tablecloth for my apartment would be nice. To close the deal on the Nissan with a romantic meal of our own."

Janus laughs at my joke, but I don't. He chooses a plain white one, and I go with a beige one. We make our purchases and return to his truck.

"Anywhere else you need to go?" he asks.

"Well, if you don't mind…" I hedge some.

"I don't mind at all," he says through a smile.

"Can we go to Pets Emporium, by Jack's Coffee in Oakfield? I need something for work from there."

"Sure," he says, then puts his truck in reverse.

As we drive, I remind him to watch the morning news tomorrow to see our new commercial. I wondered if I should tell him that I was in it, and I decided to, to make sure he watches it.

"I bet you'll sell a million cups," he says.

"I ordered a plain black coffee in it. I'm sure Jack would rather his customers order the fancier lattes or cappuccinos, but then again, the markup on coffee makes it almost all gross profit. Either way, I'm sure it'll be a successful campaign," I muse.

"Nobody will be paying attention to the coffee once they see you on the screen," he says.

"If that's the case, it would be a failed campaign. We're selling coffee, not sex, Janus," I reply, making him a little uncomfortable.

"No, I wasn't saying that... I didn't mean to imply..." he stammers.

"No, it's okay. Sex obviously sells. It just works better in a sports car ad, not a family-friendly coffee shop," I reply.

"Really, Saturn. I didn't mean to imply that you would…"

"It's fine, Janus. Honestly. I know what you meant, and as I said, you'd be correct if it were the right product and sexier model." Drat! I wish I hadn't said that last part. This is getting way, way, WAY too awkward. Pets Emporium is in view, so I'll get us on that.

"On the right," I say, despite Janus already knowing that. "I just need something for work."

"That's fine." Janus pulls into the lot and parks his truck. "The sign says it closes in a little over an hour, so I assume that's plenty of time."

"It should be," I say, then walk to the door and open it myself, hoping the "sexy talk" is over.

I see Peggy, the one who helped me pick out supplies for Muffin, and approach her.

"Oh, hi. How's the kitty?" she asks.

"Oh, you remember?" I say, rather impressed. "Wonderful."

"Do you need more supplies for him? Or did you find out it's a her?"

"Vet says he's a him, so I'll believe that. I'm actually here for bird feeders and supplies. Can you help with that?"

"Sure," she says, "right this way."

Peggy guides us down the main aisle to where the outdoor bird products are stored. She shows us options for bird feeders, poles to hang them from, bird seed choices, and other supplies we might need. I chose two feeders that squirrels can't access and one shepherd's crook to hang them. I pick up a couple of large bags of seed, a birdbath, and some gravel to place at the bottom for the birds to get a better grip.

I pay for the goods and make sure I get a receipt. We go back to his truck, where he jokes about how I said I couldn't afford a bed frame, but I could afford all of this.

"The agency is reimbursing me for these," I explain.

"I see," he says, and leaves it at that. "Should we take them there now and set them up?

"You wouldn't mind doing that?" I ask.

"Not at all. While we're there, would you mind showing me our billboard again? I know it's too late to make any changes, but I think I'd feel better just seeing it again," he says.

"Sure. I have keys. I'll just text Gretchen and let her know that we'll be there for a short amount of time."

I text her, and she replies using the thumbs-up icon. He purposely drives by one of my pizza billboards again, and again, I smile when I see it. I do hope that Gretchen is correct and that never gets old.

We soon arrive at the All-Ways Advertising agency. It takes two trips to get everything inside, and we set them aside before heading out into the courtyard to discuss the placement of the feeders and bath. Once we agree—even though he actually has no say—we bring the items outside and set them up.

I ask Janus to fill the feeders while I fill a pitcher with water to fill the birdbath. It takes me three – no, wait, four — trips to get it filled. I look around to see if there's a hose spigot out there, and I see none. I make a mental note to ask Gretchen tomorrow about that.

We stand and admire our work, and I take this moment to wrap both of my arms around him in a side hug, then steal a kiss while we are out there. Hoping no cameras are watching us, I let go of him and invite him inside to my office.

I unlock the door, then I take my place behind my desk as he takes a seat in one of the chairs for client consultations. I boot up the computer, and we just smile at each other awkwardly as we wait for it to do whatever it does before we can look at his account.

It seems to have taken about an hour and a half, but I'm finally able to log on. I get into a somewhat professional mode as I bring up his billboard and take out the files for his account.

"Today is June 29," I tell him. "This will go up where we discussed sometime on the first of the month, most likely before noon."

Janus sits and stares at it, and I nervously and quietly wait for him to say something. I sure hope that if this doesn't bring him any new business, he won't break up with me. We discussed before that all we can guarantee is that people will see the advertisement, but we can't guarantee success.

"I love it," he says, much to my relief. "If it works, it works, and we'll extend the campaign. If it doesn't, the store will stay open. I can't wait to see it."

"Can you, though?" I ask.

"I what?"

"Wait? Please wait until I get off work, and we can go look at it together, just like we did with my 'Your toppings here' billboard."

"I can do that," he assures. "Would you mind if my mom and dad join us?"

"Not at all," I answer, though now I'm sure a big kiss won't happen once the big reveal is made.

I lock up the office, and Janus drives us back to my apartment. I ask him to leave the mattress and box spring in the front room, as I don't trust myself right now for him to be in my bedroom with a bed intact. He agrees, and after the stuff is brought in, I tell him that it's getting late and he should go.

"See you tomorrow?" he asks.

"It's going to be a busy day at work. Let's say we make a billboard viewing date for Tuesday? One where your parents will tag along," I suggest.

"Perfect," he says, then walks close to me.

He leans down and gives me a kiss goodnight. It's a gentle one, with very little passion but an immense amount of tenderness. I can't believe how he knows how to perfectly kiss me in whatever situation. We part, and I look him in the eyes. I still don't see it, and I'm not sure what to say.

"4,998 to go," I utter.

"What?" Janus asks.

"4,998. You promised me 5,000 kisses, and we kissed twice so far. That means 4,998 to go."

"Well, I was going to kiss you once more, but I don't want to spend them all too quickly," he jokes.

"I see," I say, and then pull him down and kiss him with the passion I was expecting from him. He kisses me back, and when we part, he says that we now have 4,997 left to go.

"Wrong," I say. "The agreement was that you would kiss me that many times. I kissed you this time, so it doesn't count."

"Loophole," he says through a smile. "I like it. I also should be going before things get too… I'll see you Tuesday."

He leaves, and I make myself a quick sandwich and heat up a can of beans in the microwave for dinner. After I eat, I put the box spring and mattress on the bed frame, and put the pink sheet set on it. I move my alarm clock in there, make sure it's set, then head to the bathroom to change and do my pre-bed rituals.

I go to the bedroom, kneel down at the side of the bed, and pray and pray and pray some more for what had to have been for twenty minutes. I invite Muffin to join me, but I'm not sure that he will. I close my eyes, and with thoughts of Janus running through my mind, I drift off to sleep in preparation for a big day tomorrow.

Chapter 20

End of the Month

My alarm clock rings at 7:30 as usual, and for a moment, I forget where I am. It was my first night in my new bed, and I don't think I had as good or as comfortable a sleep since moving into this apartment. I feel refreshed, and my neck doesn't hurt. I want to stay in it a little longer, but I also have to get up and get ready to go to work. It's the last day of the month, and also a Monday. I'm not sure if that combination will make things busier around the office, but I'm looking forward to finding that out.

I sit up and start to rub the sleep from my eyes. Muffin is sleeping near where my feet were, and I reach over to give him a good morning pet. As I did, the faded dreams last night became clearer in my mind, and I'm both horrified and a little aroused at the same time.

I was with Janus, and we just assembled my new bed in here. Instead of asking him to leave when we were done, I sat on the bed and invited him to sit next to me. We started kissing, then touching, then we lay down next to each other, and we… well, I'm sure you could fill the blanks in from here.

I remember engaging in that back in college. I didn't care for my first experiences doing it on bathroom fixtures while being half to mostly drunk, with a party happening just outside the door. I did, however, enjoy the later times with men who knew how to... well, they knew how to bring that sort of pleasure to a woman. In my dreams last night, Janus was far better than any I've had before. He was tender, loving, yet also aggressive when the moment called for it. I feel guilty, very guilty, about ever dreaming in that way. However, if Janus's and my relationship ever takes that turn, I hope he is just like he was in the dream. I also hope to be able to hold off until, if not marriage, at least engagement, before we introduce bedroom activities into our relationship. There are times I miss that, but more importantly,

I'm now trying to be a better child of God and to ward off such temptations. So far, Janus hasn't outwardly tempted me too much. I hope he continues to do so.

I need to pray. I get on my knees again, fold my hands, and pray to God for forgiveness for what my subconscious has been thinking. I feel even more ashamed now as I say the words out loud, but I also know that I can't control my thoughts while I sleep. I think I'll call Chloe later, as we're each other's spiritual advisors and we try to keep each other in check when it comes to things like this.

I say amen and need a shower. Now that my insides were properly cleansed, I need to do the same to my outside. I lather my body and rinse it off with the hottest water I can stand. I towel dry myself and dress in a blouse and skirt combination that I'm sure will take me through the day.

I notice the time and see it's just about when the coffee shop commercial is scheduled to air on the local news, so I turn it on. They give a weather report and say that the festivities on July 4 should be done with a high near 80 and a light breeze. After a bit of banter with the news anchors, they finally switch to the commercials.

There are a couple of ads before the Jack's Coffee and Pastry one, and of course, I take notice. My ad finally comes on, and despite seeing it several times before, seeing it on TV brings me great joy. I see the two actors, Vince and Peg, dress differently each time they order, with Sindi delivering her lines perfectly each time. Finally, my part comes up. I watch very intently as if my whole life and career depend on it, which, in a small way, they do. I order, and Sindi asks, "What will you stir?" I tell her black coffee, then turn around with my tray. The frame freezes with me close to the camera and Sindi still behind the counter. It's the same shot that they are using for the billboard ad. At first, I feel a little uncomfortable and self-conscious, but then, as an ad for a frozen pizza brand is playing, I feel differently. If that were someone else in the ad, I'd say it was done perfectly. I get it now. As I told Janus, we're not selling sex but coffee drinks and pastries, so maybe my average looks will do just that. Besides, Sindi is gorgeous. I'm not saying she's selling sex in the ad, but she's a lot closer to that than I am. Enough with the sex talk, I really need to get to work.

I decide to skip breakfast at home and instead go to Jack's for a muffin and a drink. I arrive there and see that the sign company is in the lot changing theirs. I want to stay and watch, but they are just in the process of taking the old one down, and I don't know how long it will take to put the new one up, so I go to get my breakfast.

I walk inside, and it looks to be a little less crowded than one would expect on a Monday morning at this time. I see Sindi is behind the counter working the cash register, and I'm excited to see her now that the ad has been aired.

"Good morning," I say as I approach.

"Oh, hi, Saturn," she says. "Nice to see you here."

"You, too," I reply, and since there's no line behind me, I decide to talk to her. "Did you see the ad this morning?"

"I did," she beams. "Jack brought a TV out here for us all to watch. The customers even applauded, and a few said I looked nice and was a natural."

"Nothing about me?" I pretend to pout, but Sindi doesn't pick up on that.

"Oh, no. They loved you, too," she tried to save.

"It's okay, Sindi. I was just joking," I say. "Is it busier than a normal Monday at this time?"

"Not really," she answers honestly.

"That's to be expected," I explain. "These things take time. Next Monday will likely be busier."

"I hope so," she says. "What can I get you?"

"Umm… how about a chocolate chip muffin?" I ask.

"And what will you stir?" she replies, and we both smile at that.

"How about a white chocolate latte? I'm in the mood for a sweet drink this morning."

She puts the order in, then asks me for a favor. She doesn't think any of her friends will believe her when she says that she and I know each other, so she asks if I would take a selfie with her.

"On one condition," I say. "You take one with me, too."

She nods and comes from behind the counter. We put our arms around each other and smile for our camera phones. She asks if she could post hers to her social media accounts, and I say she could as long as I could, too. We agree, and after a few clicks, our pictures are posted.

She returns behind the counter, then hands me my drink and a bag with my muffin. I thank her, and as I walk away, I take a sip. Although I never noticed it before, after talking to Blake about it, I can taste more white chocolate than anything, and not coffee or espresso at all—or very little, anyway. I wonder if his lattes actually are better.

I go back out to the parking lot and am surprised to see that the new sign is almost up. I wait a minute or two, watching them work while sipping my latte, then after they lower the ladder on the truck, I take a picture of the new sign.

I look at my watch and, drat! I'm going to be late for work.

I drive as quickly and safely as I can, and arrive about fifteen minutes late. I walk in, cup and bag in my hands, and everybody starts to clap for me. They obviously saw the coffee shop ad, and I feel proud and a little embarrassed at the same time.

Once things calm down, which took maybe up to a minute, Gretchen reminds us that we still have our morning meeting at 9:30 and instructs us not to be late. She gives me an extra glare, then goes into her office. I take a sip from my cup, then excuse myself to my office.

I check my messages, then return a couple of calls before the meeting starts. I gulp the rest of my drink and eat the last of my muffin before I go into the conference room.

We're all waiting, chatting a little about our ongoing projects, when Gretchen enters and sits at the head of the table.

"I'd like to remind everyone that we start at 9:00 a.m. around here. Please make sure to be here on time," she says, and again glares at me.

"I was doing a client follow-up," I try to explain. "I went to Jack's to see if the ad was successful."

"Don't hand me that bull," she says rather angrily. "We all know that it takes longer than an hour for an ad like that to take effect. Now that you brought it up, what do you think?"

We discuss that ad, and decide that when we do another, I will appear in it. Gretchen seems to think that a Sindi-Saturn team may be just the right way to approach this campaign, and I'm now actually okay with that happening.

Gretchen explains that I'll have to sign an intent of exclusivity contract, meaning I can't appear in any ads for businesses that compete with Jack's in any way. I don't plan to appear in any more ads at all, save for the Jack's ones, so I am fine with that.

"We'll discuss compensation in private," she sternly says, then we move on to other business.

When my part comes, I announce that Andrea Collins from Andrea's Arts and Crafts will be in later to discuss a new campaign. Karen says that Doug Davis from Doug's Deli is also coming in today.

"Great," Gretchen says. "They will likely be billboard and print ads. Karen and Saturn, get to one of your offices and start making pitch ideas. I'd like to see at least one new signed contract by the end of the day."

"I also have a new ad for a councilman, and Karen says that the auto repair shop is ready to go ahead with their five billboards," Diane informs. "I think I could combine the two, making two ads from one shoot."

"Wonderful. Everybody, get to work now except for Saturn. Stay for a moment. I need to speak with you in private."

The rest leave, and I sit in my chair, expecting to be yelled at for an hour or two about being late. Once the door closes and we're alone, Gretchen sits back down in her chair at the head of the table and stares me down. The silence is deafening when she finally speaks.

"How is your sister's farm wedding campaign coming along?" she asks.

"Well," I say, then think for a moment since this isn't what I was expecting to talk about. "I spoke with her, told her the deal you offered, and she said she'll consider it."

"Wonderful," Gretchen says, then looks at me very intently. "There's an ad agency in Lincoln called Goode Ads and Promotions. Larry Goode, the owner, is retiring and selling his business. I told you before I want to expand west, and this is our opportunity."

"Venus lives near Omaha," I say.

"Which is just 60 miles away," Gretchen says. "Here's what we're going to do. In a couple of weeks, I'm sending you and Diane to Omaha for a week, where you will get together with the billboard and television specialists from the Lincoln office. You will collaborate on a six-month campaign for your sister's wedding business, which we will comp as long as she lets you and Diane stay at her residence for free."

"Comp?" I ask.

"Yes. We'll handle the ads, create the billboards and TV commercials, and cover the fees for both. Just a couple of billboards and some local access television. Nothing big, but still something. I want to see how things are managed at the Lincoln office and see how well campaigns like this perform in the mountain time zone before I make a final bid on the business."

"I see," I say. "I've only been here for a little over a month, if you remember."

"And fully competent to do this. At least I think you are. If you're not, tell me now so I can find someone else to work out of your office." Gretchen stares hard at me, then softens. "Saturn, as I told you before, advertisement is in your blood. You will run this office one day. Now, don't get me wrong. If this merger pulls through, I'll stay managing here and will likely retain the manager in Lincoln. You're not ready to run things quite yet. If I end up managing the Lincoln office, Diane will likely take over here for now. Or possibly she'll go to Lincoln. We'll figure that out if and when the time comes. Don't speak a word of this to anybody."

"I understand," I say. "I wouldn't want to run this agency now. As you said, I have a lot to learn."

"Like when meetings are over, and it's time to get to work. Go to your office and call your sister. When you're done, get with Karen and work on the potential art store and deli campaigns. I want three new campaigns signed today, but will accept no less than two. Now go."

I leave a little nervous and a little reassured as I leave for my office. I nod at Frida as I pass, and she hands me a memo. Good news. I shut the door to my office and call Venus. I told her what Gretchen told me and said I could send a letter of intent contract to her later that day.

"Let me talk this over with Eric, and I'll let you know later today," she says. "How are things on your end?"

"Busy," I answer. "I'd love to talk, but I have a lot of work to do. Let's Zoom pretty soon, I have to see if there's a baby bump yet."

"There's not," she says, then we say goodbye and hang up.

Before I see about joining Karen, I think more about what Gretchen said about me running this office. I try not to take it as a promise, since it might just be her way of motivating her employees. She has a lot of private one-on-one meetings with everyone here, so she may be saying similar things to everybody. With the threat of firing somebody if they say anything, it may be her way of keeping us from figuring out her little motivational tactic. While I do hope she is sincere in what she says to me, I'm not counting on that happening any time soon.

I take some files and walk over to Karen's office. We decide to meet in there and discuss the art store ads first, then the deli. We brainstorm ideas and come up with a few. We call Gene to see if he's available, and he asks to meet us in the conference room since there's more room in there.

He brings a large tablet of paper, some regular pencils, and some colored pencils, then Karen and I tell him what we're thinking. He listens and quickly sketches out what we are saying. These are only concepts, not finished designs, so his drawings are crude yet still good at the same time.

None of us is very happy with what we came up with, but we hope it's still enough to get Andrea to sign on. It's close to lunchtime, so we decide to go to Harry's Hamburgers and Hot Dogs for a quick bite, expecting a busy, if not possibly late, day after lunch.

Karen orders the hot dog special while I opt for chicken fingers. She says a short grace for us, and we pass the ketchup bottle to one another to add the condiment to our main dishes and French fries. She squirts some ketchup on her hot dog and onto the side of her basket to dip her fries. I take the bottle and squeeze it all over the top of all of my food. She tells me nobody around there adds ketchup to their chicken like that. I tell her that where I come from, putting ketchup on a hot dog is considered a crime that many would want to put you in jail for ten years for committing. We both chuckle at the banter, then start talking about the ads again.

"I still don't know," I say. "I don't know Andrea too well, but these don't seem to be her taste."

"Do you think she'll buy one of the designs?" Karen asks.

"Possibly," I answer. "That's the best we could do."

As we're talking, I notice the table next to us with a young mother and what looks to be a kid about three years old. He's having the chicken fingers, just like me, and even squirts the ketchup all over his food. I don't bring that up to Karen, but motion to what he is doing.

The mom, I presume, brought a coloring book for the boy and a small package of crayons. He is coloring the way most kids do at his age. He's not trying to color anything the proper color, and is more scribbling than anything. We quietly watch as he goes between eating fries and coloring a horse red and green. I think what would happen if Venus were his big sister, and as I let out a faint laugh, the mom looks over at us.

"Rembrandt started somewhere," she says, then proudly hands her son a yellow crayon. I almost spit out my food after hearing that.

"That's it!" I whisper-yell to Karen.

"What?" she asks.

"Excuse me," I say, then walk over to the mother.

I introduce myself and ask if I can buy that picture from her. She declines, and I ask if I could join them for a moment. She reluctantly agrees, and I sit closer to the mom than the child.

I explained to her what I was thinking, and once she understood, she said that I could have the picture for free. I thanked her and asked for her contact information. She hands me a business card, and I smile, put it in my purse, and return to our table.

"What was that all about?" Karen asks, and I start wolfing down some of my now-warm chicken fingers to finish our lunch on time.

"I'll explain back at the office," I say through a full mouth, then cram three mouthfuls of fries into my mouth at once and drink about 12 ounces of soda to wash them down.

"Does Janus know you do that?" she asks.

"Who do you think taught me?" I joke, then tell her to hurry so we can get back to the office to get our pitch together for Andrea before she comes.

"Do you really think she'll go for this?" Karen asks after I explain it in my office.

"If not, we have three backup plans. But I saw her shop, and I truly believe this is it for her."

"If she does, then you may be the best rookie advertising professional out there," Karen muses. "With the pizza 'Your toppings here' and the extra mile thing for Cheaper by the Frozen, you seem to get very lucky about being at the right place at the right time. You did say that the pizza ad was inspired by you remembering your mom pointing out a different billboard, right?"

"That's the way I remember it, yes," I say.

"Well, let's see if lightning does indeed strike a third time. Andrea should be here any minute now. I'll be waiting in the conference room. In fact, I'm going to invite Gretchen in there, as well. She has got to see this first-hand."

Chapter 21

Pitches and Prepping

I wait for Andrea to show, and she does a little earlier than expected. I ask if she'd like a coffee or water before we go into the conference room, and she declines. I tell her it's okay, it's not unprofessional if she accepts. She again says that she is fine and she'd do better without a drink in hand.

I lead her into the conference room and first introduce her to my partner for this campaign, Karen Keyes. After, I introduced her to the owner and office manager, Gretchen Gilmore. Once we all know each other's names, Gretchen and Karen take seats at the back of the table, and the presentation begins.

I begin by giving a brief disclosure to Karen and Gretchen, telling them that I have recently started teaching a class at Andrea's craft store. Gretchen says that there's no conflict of interest in my doing that and tells me to proceed.

"We thought about this and wondered which direction we should go," I start, indicating Karen as I speak. "We believe that a billboard campaign paired with a mailing would work best for you. While we know that many fine artists and crafters already shop at your store, we tried to figure out a way to bring new customers in, and possibly get customers for life."

"I would like to see that," Andrea says. I look at Gretchen, who is looking stone-faced back at me, and continue.

"What do you think of this?" I ask Andrea as I show her the coloring page I got from the hamburger shop.

"Well…" Andrea says, looks at me, then at Gretchen. Gretchen looks at me, then Karen whispers something in her ear. Gretchen whispers something back, then motions for me to continue. Andrea asks, "Are you planning to use this in the ad?"

"Yes," I say. Now all are quiet, so I nervously continue.

"This is part of the 'Everybody started somewhere' campaign," I say. "This concept is simple. We take people who are new to art, mainly young kids, and take a picture of them next to their work. Take this coloring page, for example. It was done by a boy, I believe, around three years old. We'd have him hold this up to the camera and smile. The caption would be something like 'Rembrandt started somewhere' or 'DaVinci started somewhere'. Whatever the medium, we name a famous artist using that caption."

"So if it's a sculpture, it would say 'Michelangelo started somewhere,' or if it's a watercolor, it would say 'Albrecht Dürer started somewhere'?" Andrea asks.

"Yes, but we'd want to keep it with someone who is more well-known, like Claude Monet," I answer.

"I see," Andrea says, and thinks. "So you want to use only kids for this?"

"No," I answer. "We'd want to show that even adults could be new at art. I want to ask Gloria from the craft sticks class if she'd like to be a model for this. She's in her thirties, and definitely a newbie at art."

"Who is a famous craft stick artist?" Andrea asks.

"Saturn O Syres," Karen shouts from the back, and I give her a look.

"Honestly, none that I know of. For her, the caption could be 'Everybody started somewhere' or 'You could start somewhere.' We could put six photos on one billboard and one mailer, the same pictures in the same places for both."

"How much will the models cost?" Andrea asks.

"That's the best part. If we obtain permission from the parents, our legal team will provide the proper paperwork and releases for them to sign. Typically, they'd do so for free, as they would like to see themselves or their kids in an ad or on a billboard. You may offer them a gift certificate or some free supplies if you like, but that would be totally up to you."

"I see…" Andrea says, and looks more at the coloring sheet I brought.

"We have several other concepts for you to see if this one isn't for you," I say. "I can show you now if you like. Karen and I worked all morning on these."

I hold up a couple of drawings that Gene made for her to see. She looks between them and the drawing I had since handed to her.

"What is the cost for these?" she asks.

I tell her what a six-month campaign would cost, mentioning that the agency will cover the first month's billboard rent. I also added, without Gretchen's permission, that if she signs up for a year-long campaign, the billboard can be changed once halfway through, without charging for new photos to be taken. Additionally, four different mailers will be sent out, again without charging for new photos. I see Gretchen glare at me as she tends to do, and take some notes. She says nothing, so I continue, trying not to look nervous.

"I see," Andrea says, and looks at the campaign concepts Karen and I had Gene draw up. "If the 'Everybody started somewhere' campaign fails halfway through, can we switch to one of these at no additional cost?"

I look to Gretchen for an answer, and she just stares stoically at me. I look at Karen, who does the same. Drat! It's a test.

"Well," I say, and Gretchen is watching me even harder now. "If you don't see a 5% increase in sales six months after the campaign officially starts, we will be able to do that for you."

"Well, then I think I'll do it," Andrea says, still looking at all of the concepts.

"Have you decided on which one?" I ask. "If not, call us whenever you're ready."

"I have," she says as she stares at the second drawing that Gene made. "Go with the 'Everybody started somewhere' one. Will I be able to decide on the art being depicted and the artist mentioned?"

"Yes, you can," I say. "I'll advise, though, to make sure to name artists that are commonplace. We'll be here to advise every step of the way on all aspects. We can possibly have this up and running on July 21. A lot of that depends on the acquisition of models."

"Well, thank you. When can we get started?" Andres asks.

"Right away, if you're able," Gretchen says as she stands. Andrea says she has time for that. "Perfect. Karen, please take Ms. Collins to your office. Tell Gene to join you and start getting those mailer concepts going. Saturn will be with you shortly; I just need a word in private with her first."

Handshakes are made all around, then Karen leads Andrea out and closes the door. Gretchen motions for me to sit, and I do so. Gretchen sits across from me and stares silently for way too long.

"How are you planning on covering the expenses if we have to switch campaigns in six months?" she asks me, then stares.

"I'm not," I answer. "I am absolutely, 100% confident that this will be a successful campaign, so we won't have to."

"Are you?" Gretchen asks and goes silent again.

I wait for her to talk some more, and when she doesn't, I break the silence.

"Absolutely," I confirm. "We could have targeted the established artist, but the established artist likely already shops there. Will every child, or new artist, who buys supplies there, become an artist for life? Of course not. But enough will to easily hit the 5% mark."

"Probably more," Gretchen says, then smiles at me. "That was a brilliant idea, Saturn. Twenty-four pictures, four mailers, two billboards, a brief explanation of what the store is, along with those captions, is pure advertising genius. How did you come up with this?"

I told her about our lunch at Harry's Hamburgers and Hot Dogs and my talk with the mother. I said I know I was just lucky to overhear that, and if I hadn't, we would have had to use another campaign.

"The photographer who takes a picture of Niagara Falls didn't put the water there," Gretchen says. What? "You were at the right place at the right time. I'm glad you acted on that. Was the kid who made this drawing cute?"

"I suppose so," I say.

"Terrific. Call this mother and see if she wants junior on the ads."

"I will. Are we done?" I ask.

"No, something else," she says, then starts glaring again. "If you didn't go with that campaign, which of these three were you favoring?"

"Oh," I say, and look at them again, then point to the second one. "Probably this one."

"Good choice," she says. "That's my second choice, too. Keep up this good work, Saturn. How are the sub shop ideas going?"

"Honestly, we hadn't even started yet," I answer.

"Well, if I were you, I'd go get Ms. Collins set up, then hustle on that one. He'll be here before you know it."

"I will. Thank you," I say, then stand.

"One more thing," Gretchen says. I just look and wait. "Did you make that pencil holder you have on your desk?"

"I did, using craft sticks," I answer, hoping it was all right to have it there.

"Do you think you could make one for me? I really like it."

I smile, nod, and leave the conference room. I join Andrea, Gene, and Karen in her office, where she is finishing the contracts, and Gene already has a rough billboard concept sketched out. I only hope that Doug's Deli will be as easy.

Andrea leaves happy, and afterwards, Karen and I high-five each other. It's a short celebration, though, as we have mere moments to discuss a plan for Doug's Deli. I look out the window, and there are no more birds out there than before. Peggy says that it usually takes several days for birds to come to feeders and birdbaths, so I just look at what's out there, trying to picture what it will look like next week.

"I suppose you want to recommend a billboard," Karen says.

"Sure. Nothing too flashy, though. Sub sandwiches are simple, so the advertising should be as well. Do you agree?" I ask.

"How simple?" she replies.

"I'd go with very simple since he'll be here any minute," I answer, then start drawing on a sketch pad.

I'm no Gene, something that has been long established here, but I could still get my concepts on paper before the real artist fixes everything about it. I draw out an idea, and Karen looks at it.

"Are you sure?" she asks.

"Do you have better?" I reply.

Karen looks at it some more. I see no reaction at first, then a faint smile begins to show.

"This just may work as a print ad, too," she says, then looks up at me before looking back down at the pad. "If he doesn't like this, we'll go the opposite with something over-the-top flashy."

"Deal," I say to her.

We work on the concept a little longer before Frida informs us that Doug Davis is there. We ask her to bring him to Karen's office, and seconds later, he's sitting while I'm standing and Karen sits behind her desk. Karen nods at me, so I begin.

"We usually do a big show for a presentation, but instead, for you, I'll just show you." Karen looks surprised by my bluntness, and after I give her a 'What could we do?' shoulder shrug, I show Doug our sketches.

We show him what would be a plain white background, with the words "Doug's Deli" in large block letters, and below in smaller letters of the same font, "Delicious food that's above sub-standard." Then, below that in smaller letters, the address and phone number.

"I see," he says and stays quiet for a minute as he stares at it. "It doesn't show any sandwiches."

"Yes," I say. "All of your sandwich selections are made to order. We didn't want to show any and have potential customers think that's the only way they come."

"Interesting," he says.

"We could show your chip selection as well as the drinks you serve," Karen adds. "We can put them in the corners."

"That would be your choice, Mr. Davis. We can have our artist draw those options, or others if you like, to help with your decision," I say.

"Though something simple like this would probably work best for a business like yours," Karen says. "We're recommending a billboard and newspaper campaign, with coupons in the paper."

"What kind of coupons?" he asks.

"That would be up to you," Karen answers. "As a first-time client, if you sign on with us, we're prepared to offer you a three-month campaign with, say, three weeks of billboard rent on us. We will run it in the Sunday newspaper, and will change the coupon to your specifications each week, included."

"Three months, you say?" he asks.

"That is standard for a business like yours. You could look it up if you like, or call another agency," Karen answers.

"And once this runs out, I would pay full if I renew?" he asks.

"We will offer this a second time, Mr. Davis. Once that campaign ends, we can discuss better deals for longer campaigns. For now, though, let's talk about the next three months," Karen says, and I'm totally impressed by her professionalism.

"Can we do six months now?" Doug asks.

"Let's do three," Karen answers, and I'm surprised until I find out why. "We can do the three we're discussing, and if it's successful, we will do the same again. Actually, it would be a little cheaper since you wouldn't have to pay for a new billboard design unless you want one. If we go with six now, it would be the exact same deal as if you did three twice. This gives you a better out, Mr. Davis, in the case this campaign doesn't work well enough for you."

"Interesting," he says. "Is there a reason why this campaign wouldn't work?"

"Not all ads do. That's the reality of it. However, we do believe that you will see increased business after the first Sunday paper comes out. In fact, since you're a first-time client, I'll give you a better out now. If you don't see increased business by the end of the second week, we will cancel the campaign, and you'd only have to pay for the two weeks. If we go with that deal, you can't just say you didn't, but you would have to allow our accountants to look at your books to ensure no gain has been made. We usually don't make that offer to new clients. We just signed Jack's Coffee and Pastry, as well as Ring's and Sons Restoration and Resale Shop, and didn't offer that."

"Well," Doug says. He asks again what it would cost, and we break down the numbers, including the projected sales boost that would result from this. "When will it start?"

"We can launch it on July 14," Karen says. "In early October, we can discuss either extending or cancelling the campaign. In the meantime, I'll leave and let you and Saturn discuss which billboard locations are available and will suit you best."

Karen shakes his hand, then I usher him to my office, where I find several billboards that are either ready now or will be by the time his campaign starts. We narrow it down to three before he leaves, promising to mull it over and let me know by the end of next week. We shake hands, and he leaves. I turn to look out the window and see two birds on one feeder, pecking at each other while trying to eat, ignoring another that is close by.

"Why don't they each eat from their own feeder?" I ask myself. It's almost five, and it couldn't get here any sooner. Drat! What a day, but I still love every bit of it!

Since that last meeting gave me a taste for it, I stopped by Doug's Deli to get a basic BLT sub with mayonnaise, then realized I could make it a custom order like we discussed with Doug not too long ago. I ask for cucumbers and, since I won't be kissing anybody tonight, extra onions to be put on my sandwich. The workers assembled it as if my request was no big deal, and handed it to me in a bag with regular potato chips, then gave me a cup of root beer. I take a small sip before I leave the store, and notice that it seems rather busy for a Monday night. I hope our increased business promise doesn't come back to bite us in the proverbial rear.

I drive home with the radio turned up and not paying much attention to the ads I pass along the way. I open my apartment door, and Muffin immediately meows and then comes over to greet me. I bend over to give his chin a nice scratching, then I put the bag on the table next to the tulips that Janus gave me.

I open the wrapper the sub is in and use it as a plate, placing the sandwich near its edge, then dumping my chips on it. I set the napkins provided next to the wrapper, take a little sip of my root beer, then say a short grace before I start eating.

I eat quietly, reflecting on everything that's been happening to me recently. Muffin walks over, lets out a faint meow, and rubs his face on my leg. I break off a bit of bacon and drop it to him, figuring a little taste won't hurt. He sniffs it, bats it a time or two, then daintily eats his treat and meows for more. I break off one more little piece, and Muffin repeats what he did before.

I finish my dinner and clean the mess. I go to my living room and set up my craft sticks on the coffee table. Time is getting close, and since there's a lot of waiting for glue to dry while doing these projects, I decide to work on three at a time. I'm going to make two large cat boxes and a multi-compartment pencil and office supplies holder. After getting some bases glued together, I figured it's a good time to call Chloe on a Zoom call.

"How have you been?" she asks, then sips from a glass of soda.

"Pretty good, I suppose. I'm just getting some final pieces together for Friday," I answer.

"Will you be bringing a lot?" she asks.

"All I have, except for the clock tower," I reply. "I've no idea how people in this town will react to these, but those who saw them so far have taken a liking to them. My boss even asked for a pencil holder for her office."

"That's great, Saturn," she says, and takes another sip from her cup. "I know you have more on your mind than the craft fair. Let's not play the beat-around-the-bush game tonight and just get to it."

"Sounds good," I say, then pick up a bottle of glue and dab some on a stick.

I tell her about how my relationship has been going with Janus. She patiently waits, knowing that the good stuff is coming. I tell her about my dream last night, and do so in vivid detail. As I said, neither of us is a perfect angel, yet we're trying to get our lives back on a more Godly track. We confess many of our sins and try to hold each other accountable for them. When I'm done, Chloe just stares for a moment before speaking.

"Wow!" she exclaims. "That was some dream. Do you think he's like that when he actually… well, does that?"

"Chloe!" I shout. "Don't encourage me! While I do hope to find out one day, you're supposed to help me in delaying that for as long as possible."

"You're right, and I'm sorry," she answers. "It's just that… that… wow."

"Chloe!"

"Okay, fine," she says, then takes another sip. "You already know the answer, Saturn. If you don't trust yourself, then don't put yourself in a situation for that to happen. Do you trust Janus?"

"I suppose so," I answer. "It's been what? A month or so? So far, he hasn't tried to get me into bed, despite having a few opportunities so far."

"Do you know if he's ever…" Chloe starts before I cut her off.

"I don't. We never discussed that. I mean, I assume he has, but it's just that. An assumption."

"We all have pasts," Chloe answers, then gulps the last of her drink. "1 Corinthians 6:8 says, 'Flee from sexual immorality. Every other sin a person commits is outside the body, but the sexually immoral person sins against his own body.' Read 1 Corinthians chapters 6 and 7."

"I will," I say, and take a note.

"In fact, read all of 1 Corinthians, and all of the Bible for that matter," Chloe says with a straight face.

"I'm working on it, Chloe," I answer.

"Just hold out for as long as you can, Saturn. We all fall short of the grace of God and are tempted by the pleasures of the flesh. Just do your best, my friend. If you fall, beg for forgiveness and try a little harder. We're not perfect, none of us is. Make sure of one thing, though."

"What is that?" I ask.

"If you do invite him into your bedroom before you're married, at least make sure you love him first, and he loves you."

"I'll try," I promise.

"Then tell me if he was anything like your dream," Chloe says, which lightens the mood.

"Chloe!" I exclaim again. "I will not!"

"Yes, you will, and you know it," Chloe states. I smile and nod, knowing she is probably right.

We talked some more about how life has been going with her, and she said not a whole lot. She hasn't dated anyone in a while and has been considering relocating.

"I'm not sure where," she says. "It's nice here, I suppose. I've just been craving a change lately. I've been looking around and had a few bites. All in Indiana. I don't want to stop being a Hoosier."

"Good call," I say, and we talk about that a little more, though she doesn't reveal much more than what she just said.

Gretchen promised we could take off early on Thursday, July 3, or we may even all get the day off. Chloe says that she also has the day before Independence Day off, and will be coming into town that day.

"I expect some pizza with my toppings there," she says, her way of complimenting my first billboard.

"I'll even show you one of the signs," I answer.

"You'll show me all five, little lady," she says.

We again confirm her coming and staying on my couch now that I have a bed, and she's staying until Sunday. We say our goodbyes, and I log off the computer. After putting away my craft sticks, which I made good progress on during the call, I brush my teeth and ready myself for bed. I kneel beside the bed and pray my nightly prayers. I confess my sins, asking for forgiveness, thank God for friends like Chloe, boyfriends like Janus, sisters like Venus, and parents like mine. I thank Him for putting it into Janus's heart to acquire this bed for me, and ask God to bless him overnight. I say amen, then tuck myself under a blanket. As I drift off to sleep, I add to the prayer, asking God not to allow those dreams to be replayed in my mind tonight. Muffin jumps on the bed, lies in a ball, and then I drift off to sleep, looking forward to another wonderful day tomorrow.

Chapter 22

Phonies and Friends

The alarm rings at its usual time, startling me awake and causing Muffin to jump off the bed. I stretch my arms and rub my eyes. I sit and think for a moment about my sleep. I do remember waking and repositioning myself a time or two throughout the night, but I don't remember any dreams. I do remember having them, just not what they were about. I take that as a good sign, then get up to face the day.

I arrive at work early to tend to the bird feeders and birdbath. I think when Gretchen has the koi pond installed, which actually may not happen, it'll add something special to our client consultations and meetings. There is something so soothing about watching birds around feeders, and I'm happy to make this a part of my day.

I finish with them and check any messages I may have received since last night. I had none, which means that Janus's billboard will be going up today as promised. I can't wait to see it, but I'll keep my promise to him and wait for all of us to see it for the first time together.

The morning meetings go pretty much as expected. I get congratulated on the art store and sub sandwich restaurant accounts, and I make sure to share the credit with Karen. I also informed Gretchen that my sister, Venus, is still considering our offer. Gretchen tells me to lean on her harder. I'm not sure if she knows it or not, but the harder you lean on Venus, the harder she pushes back. At least she was when we were teens. Eric and marriage really softened her, so she may not push back as hard as she once did. Still, I'll call her later to see about that and how other things are going.

"We have a shoot today at Quick Change Oil and Repairs in Oakfield," Diane says. "I have a local politician who wanted a campaign showing her as a person of the people. She wanted to do something at a local establishment that people would frequent, and since the repair shop wanted a billboard, we decided to combine them. Radio, TV, and billboards for the councilwoman, and a billboard shoot for the shop. This may even urge them to do a TV campaign if they see how well we do ads for that medium."

"Wonderful," Gretchen says. "When is this scheduled for?"

"10:30," Diane answers.

"Wonderful. You, Saturn, and Karen get on that. Saturn, it looks like your day is booked. When you get back, get into the studio and do voiceovers for all. Gene and John will cover any clients you have for today. Please don't disturb me unless it's absolutely needed today. I'll make that phone call to, what is the name of your sister's business?"

"Brown Farms Weddings," I answer.

"Very Nebraskan," she says, though I'm not sure how. "Get ready for your location shoot. I don't want to have to come in on Thursday, so let's make sure we all get a nice, long weekend."

We try not to noticeably celebrate as we're leaving the office. I look back at Gretchen and wonder how she and Venus will do on the phone with each other. I hope Gretchen doesn't upset her too much, as the baby does not need to be upset this early in their development.

I get a few things settled in my office, hoping this day doesn't go into overtime. Diane knocks and asks if I'm ready. I say I am, and she suggests that we all drive ourselves for this one. I say I'm right behind her, and after a quick check of my email, I log off and am out the door.

We get to the repair shop a couple of minutes before expected. We unload the equipment from the van that Karen drove and get everything set up. Diane explains the concept to me, which is relatively simple.

"The councilwoman is up for reelection, and she wants to be seen at a place relatable to most of her constituents. The repair shop wants billboards showing their mechanics at work. We simply take photos and videos of the mechanics at work, some with the councilman closely watching, some without. There are no speaking roles for the TV ad; you'll dub them in later. Radio is radio, which you'll also do later today with John."

"So we just take pictures and film of them doing their normal work and edit it this afternoon?" I confirm.

"That's it. Karen and I will run the video cameras, you take the stills," Diane says, then hands me the camera.

"I have never done this before," I say as I look at the camera.

"You took pictures in your life before, surely, and know what billboards look like. That is your specialty, right?" Diane asks, sounding a little agitated.

"I suppose I have, and do," I answer.

"Fine. The councilwoman is here. Call her Ms. Patterson, and treat her with kid gloves. She is something else," Diane says, then walks toward the client. She is dressed in a sharp gray business pantsuit with her hair up, looking around as if she's never been to a place like this before, accompanied by two handlers dressed like they're secret service wannabes, dark sunglasses and all.

We all gather in the parking lot near the bay where the shoot is to be done. Bud Aubry, the owner, wonders which car we could use. We all look around before I speak up.

"If you're going to do actual work, my Volkswagen needs an oil change," I say. "It's $39.99 for that and a full inspection, correct?"

"That car looks a little..." Kelly starts to say before one of her handlers speaks up.

"Perfect, Ms. Patterson," he says as he adjusts his glasses. "It's a common car used by the common man."

Should I be insulted by that? No, I don't think so. It's quite true if you think about it.

"I suppose," she says. Once it's agreed, I hand my keys to Bud, and he pulls it into the bay.

We set up the cameras and some lighting. We ask a mechanic, who doesn't want to be shown in the ads, if he'd like to hold a lighting rig for us. He says that he will.

As we're prepping to take pictures, I look over and see the councilwoman being helped by one handler, taking off her suit jacket, and another handler takes a large letterman-style jacket with the logos of a local professional sports team all over it and helps her put it on. It says 'Indiana Pacers,' which I think is the basketball team from Indianapolis. I'm not 100% sure, and something tells me that the councilwoman also has no idea what she's wearing, either. I want to call out her phoniness, but I remember that we're here to put an ad together for her, not question her professional ethics.

"Whatever," I mumble to myself as I get ready to take pictures. Lots and lots of pictures.

Diane asks Ms. Patterson if she'd like to take a seat so Karen can touch up her makeup. Kelly insists that her makeup is already perfect, and there's no need for that.

"Can we just get on with this?" she asks. "I have important things to do today."

I hope she's talking about work for the city. While getting reelected is important to her, it's more important to us citizens that she do the job she was hired to do without worrying about a next term.

Three mechanics who are actual employees of the shop take their places. Diane instructs the councilwoman where to stand, and she doesn't seem to like being told what to do. After a nod from a handler, she listens and stands where instructed. We start the video cameras rolling, I begin snapping pictures, and the mechanics get to work on my car.

Diane directs Bud to point to things under my car's hood, and asks Ms. Patterson to do the same. The handlers direct Diane and me to make sure we get good pictures of the logos on the jacket, and we assure them that we are.

It takes about ten minutes for my oil to be changed and other fluids to be checked and topped off. A mechanic then asks the councilwoman if she wouldn't mind stepping aside, as she is right where he needs to be to continue the inspection of my car, which is something I wasn't expecting them to actually do. She huffs a little, then steps away. She asks if we're done using our cameras, and when Diane says that we got enough, she immediately removes the Pacers jacket to put her own back on.

The handlers ask Kelly what to do with the jacket, and she says that since I looked like a common person to just give it to me. I shrug, accept the gift, and decide to maybe watch a basketball game next time one is on. This is July. When does the basketball season start up again? Never mind, I'll find out later.

We start to get our equipment put away as the mechanics finish with my car and pull it out. I walk inside to pay, and they do charge me the full price for the oil change. That's fair. It needed one, and I would have had to pay for it anyway. I slide my card in the reader, then Bud prints the inspection report.

"One thing, Ms. Syres," he says.

"Saturn," I correct, then listen.

"We found a slight leak in your exhaust, the battery is a little on the old side and will need replacing soon, your tires are just about near the end of their lives, and you'll need to replace those brake pads soon."

"Oh," I say as I look at the estimate for repairs.

"Nothing is urgent as of this moment," Bud says. "If you don't believe me, please take it to another repair shop for them to do an inspection."

"And this is the cost to fix all of this?" I ask, pointing to where the total obviously is. Bud just nods with a pity smile on his face.

"I can also offer you around $2,000 for the car as-is. I'll do the repairs and sell it used in my lot out there. $2,000 is about half of a down payment for a cheaper new car. A Kia Soul or Nissan Versa comes to mind, both of which are comparable to your Volkswagen."

"Nissan, you say?"

"I'm not recommending any car for you, Saturn. I'm just helping you with options. We can, of course, fix your Beetle, and you could keep that for far cheaper than a new car. However, more repairs are around the corner, and new cars do come with some pretty good warranties and maintenance packages." Bud continues. "As I said, these repairs aren't urgent, just recommended to get done within the month, but definitely before the winter season comes."

"So it's still safe for me to drive home now?" I ask.

"For now. I'm not a hard sell businessman, Saturn. Go on back to work, get my billboard set, and if you have any questions, come back or call. It looks like your team is waiting for you."

I turn to see that the van is loaded and Karen and Diane are ready to return to the agency. I thank Bud for the information and say I'll be back in touch with whatever my decision is. I don't think I'll need to take it to another shop for inspection since I can't imagine this car being in such high demand that a car shop owner would go through that much trouble to buy it from me. Still, before I leave, I do a quick check on what the trade-in for a car like this would be. Just around $2,000, exactly what he said. I feel a little better now.

I decided to stop at Here and There Pizza for a little earlier than normal lunch. I'm just looking for a couple of quick slices, nothing made to order, and see that the freshest they have ready is one with only pepperoni. I ordered two slices, French fries, and a drink. I pay for my order and take a table near the center of the dining area. It's not too crowded. That doesn't mean that the billboards aren't working, but it could just mean that a Tuesday just after opening isn't their normal busy time. I'm glad, too, as now I can enjoy my meal in peace before what is promising to be a hectic afternoon.

I return to the office, and Frida assures me that my calls and clients are being taken care of. Diane is finishing her lunch in the break room, so I go into the recording and editing room to mentally prepare for doing the voiceovers.

Diane comes in, along with Gretchen. She again assures us that the other could handle our clients for the afternoon, and she wants to be in there with us to assist with the editing.

It's pretty straightforward. They captured about twenty minutes of video from each camera, and we watched all of them a couple of times before editing began.

From all of that video, we need just sixty seconds to bring out the best in our client and help her get reelected. I try to put aside any personal beliefs about her and do my best to assist in making a TV ad. I'm still new at those – still new at making any ads, actually – and if nothing else, I'll get a good education from this.

We get the footage together in no time, making sure to show the sports logo many times without making it the primary focus. We also make sure to get the councilwoman's best facial features, ones where she looks quizzical about what's happening and appears she really wants to know about this stuff. We zoom in a couple of times to show a close-up of her face, which is rather attractive for a woman of her age. Once we're all satisfied with the sixty seconds of video, Diane gets the sound recorder ready for the voice-overs.

I go into the sound booth with the script in hand while Diane and Gretchen talk about something. I read the script, and it's your basic bullet points about why we should keep her as our councilwoman. I see her list of accomplishments that she's claiming, and I am rather impressed. I put the headphones on and adjust the microphone. Thirty seconds later, Diane is counting down to me, prompting me to start.

I speak in a slightly lower voice than usual. The trick to these is to read the script within the allotted time. In a sixty-second ad, you want to leave one second at the beginning and end, so fifty-eight seconds is my goal. I know we can edit it later, but much like my high school graduation salutatory speech, I want to get this as close to exact as I can.

I end up reading and recording it five times, using a slightly different voice each time. The client was insistent that a female voice only be heard, so I didn't do any of the male voices I have done so many times before. I nail most in the time allotted, and I congratulate myself on it since neither Diane nor Gretchen did.

I stay there and record a few radio ads. For these, Kelly wanted it to sound like a conversation between a man and a woman, where the smart woman explains to the not-so-smart man why Councilman Patterson is the best person for the job. These are her words, not mine. They're written right here on the script. I record them, even having one sound like a mother talking to a little boy.

"Kids don't vote," Gretchen says through the microphone right into my ear. "Stick with adults for this."

"Fine," I say, probably with too much attitude. I thought it was cute, and could convince many working and single mothers to vote for her, which is what a lot of her campaign is running on. This is Diane's ad, though, so I do as I'm told.

When we're done recording and editing, we go into the conference room to pick out a photo for the billboard. Gretchen called the staff artist, Gene, to join us. Gretchen also said to make sure to include the sports team logos, but not the logo of the car. I'm not sure why, and I'll make sure to ask her later about that.

The billboard is simple. It's just going to be a picture of the councilwoman and mechanic looking under the hood of my car, with the caption "Reelect Kelly Patterson for Councilman-at-Large." Straightforward. Nothing fancy, no slogans – just a picture of them on the billboard, and a message telling you what to do. The five for the auto repair shop is also straightforward. We show a couple of mechanics working on my car, with the name of the shop, a slogan, and the location. The five billboards are already reserved for this one.

"This should just about do it," Diane says.

"I think so," Gretchen agrees. "When is the councilwoman's campaign starting?"

"ASAP," Diane says. "I'll contact the radio and TV station and see what time slots are available. Saturn, go see which billboards in the city proper are available now, or will be soon. She wants this on as many as possible."

"I know of maybe three that are available now," I say.

"Try and find more," Gretchen demands, then looks at Diane. "This goes until election day, right?"

"Yes," she answers.

"Great. Any time one opens between now and then, let us know. Keep selling others, too. I hired you to get our name on every billboard in the area, and so far, you're doing a great job at that. Better than your predecessors, for sure. Election season is always good for the advertising industry. I talked to your sister—she's in. You and Diane will be heading out there in a few weeks."

"You what?" I ask, shocked. Not at her quick change of topic, as that seems to be a trademark of hers, but the context of the quick change.

"She's a rather smart lady, Saturn. She's an accountant and knows numbers. I talked numbers with her. Oh, and don't forget to pack your blue jeans, because she agreed only if you worked on the farm during your free time there. I said that you and Diane both will.I'll talk to you both more about that later."

Gretchen leaves the room, and Diane and I just stare at each other.

"Do you think you could handle farm work?" I ask Diane.

"I worked on a farm during the summers when I was in high school. It helped pay for a lot of my college. Gretchen already knows that. How about you?"

It was then that I realized I was only on a farm once in my life, and that was for my sister's wedding.

"I never have, and frankly, I'm a little scared."

"Why?" Diane asks.

"If you knew Venus Birchard Syres the way I do, you'd be scared, too," I answer.

Everything went quickly without a hitch, except for that Venus bomb dropped at the end. I want to call Venus to yell at her or send her an angry text or email, but since I'll get a paid week to spend with her in Nebraska, I might just hold off on that. She will be getting a call soon, though.

I'm back in my office just after 4:00 p.m., with just under an hour in the workday left. Karen and Gene took care of my clients for the day, so I checked on what happened and am satisfied that anything there is to do can wait until tomorrow. I then do a little research on Councilman Kelly Patterson, not for the ad but for personal reasons. I want to see just how honest those ads are.

After some light reading, I discovered that everything she claimed is true. She's not only honest about her accomplishments, but she may have even held back on some. Interesting. Sure, wearing that sport-themed jacket is a bit pandering, but she is trying to win an election. The sports team you cheer for shouldn't be a factor; just your record should be. Sure, in a perfect world, that would work. However, this is the world of politics, where every vote counts. I'll do some further research, but so far, she has gone from last to front-runner for the candidate who earns my vote come November.

It's 4:30. I've nothing to do, and since looking at the billboard with a first-time client could be considered work-related, I tell Frida that I'll be leaving now for a client meeting.

"Going to check out your boyfriend's billboard?" she asks in a knowing way.

"It still counts as a first-time client follow-up," I retort. Technically, it is. I leave the office and head to my Volkswagen. Now I'm a little nervous to drive it, but I put that to the back of my head and decide to go to Cheaper by the Frozen first for a tasty treat before the billboard viewing.

I get there, and the parking lot seems more full than usual. I go inside and see that it's well over half filled. They have a large, professionally made sign behind the counter that says, "It's worth driving the extra mile for." I smile at that, then place my order when it's my turn. I stare at the sign some more as I wait for my Sundae, and when it comes up, I thank the young lady and take my tray to try and find a seat.

I stand, looking around, as it seems there are many families with young children there at the moment. I think about finding a table outside when I swear I hear my name being called. I look in the direction where I thought I heard the female voice and see Sunny Knight sitting alone at a booth. I nod and smile at her, then look around some more.

"Saturn! Saturn!" I turn and look at Sunny again. "Come sit by me. Please. I'd like the company."

I look around again and reluctantly walk over there. I sit across from her, silently looking as she takes a bite from what appears to be a root beer float. I take a small spoonful of my Sundae, not knowing what, if anything, to say. I don't have to, as Sunny breaks the ice.

"I am so happy to see you, Saturn," she says. I force a smile back and eat some more from my bowl.

"I know that you're upset with me over the way I treated you, and you have every right to be," she says, sounding sincere. "Please forgive me."

"Well…" I say. I will, but she isn't going to get off this easily with just a simple apology. She has to beg.

"The way I treated you was uncalled for. I still wanted to date Janus, and thought I had a chance until I saw him with you. I wanted to break you two up, and… and now I know the truth."

The truth? What is the truth? I have to know. "What truth?"

"The truth is, Janus no longer wanted to date me. I knew that, but I thought if I was persistent, he'd wear out and I'd win. Blake did the same with you."

"Blake?" I ask, surprised by this turn.

"He told me everything, Saturn. You date a couple of times, he saw a future, and you didn't. He was as persistent with you as I was with Janus, and he got fired from his job because of that," she admits.

"That sounds about right," I say and nod.

"We know now that you two weren't right for us. I actually knew when I first saw you and Janus together. He looked at you in a way he never looked at me. I was jealous. Deeply jealous. Now, even though it's been mere days, Blake looks at me the way I wanted Janus to look at me. The way he looks at you."

This woman does have a flair for the dramatic, that's for sure. I'm not sure about this looking thing, since I haven't been seeing it. Maybe that's it, though. Maybe others see it first. Maybe I saw the way Eric looked at Venus before she noticed. No, that's a bad example. They were deeply, DEEPLY, in love the moment she first brought his name up to the family. Still, that doesn't mean she saw the way he looked at her like I did. Geez, now I'm having that dramatic flair about me. What do I say to break this awkwardness?

"I'm glad we all found each other," I say.

"No, that's not how it happened," Sunny replies. "We didn't find each other. That dinner was a set-up. Admit it."

I smile, nod, and say that it was.

"Thank you. From the bottom of my heart, thank you," she says. "We're going into business together. Listen to this."

She talks for the next ten minutes all about their plans for their coffee and candy operation. She sounded a lot like Blake did with me, so maybe those two were made for each other. I smile as I listen, some because of what she's saying and some because my Sundae is so good. We finish our treats, and she finishes her story.

"Come by our booth on Friday," she says. "Taste for yourself how good they are."

"I will," I promise, and mean it.

"Oh, and one more thing," she says, then wipes her mouth and starts cleaning up. "Do you forgive me now? Can we be friends?"

I look in her eyes and see the sincerity looking back at me. I assure her that she is fully forgiven, and I'd love it if we were friends. We exchanged phone numbers and liked, shared, and friend-requested each other on all our social media accounts. She leaves with a wave of the hand, and I stay back for a moment. I look at her Facebook account, see her status is "In a relationship," and it's plastered with photos of her and Blake together. I scroll down enough to see some of her and Janus together, too.

They did look happy together, especially the one of them kissing. I can't wait to show this to him and get a little fun ribbing out of it. I saved that picture to my phone, then left to go pick him up from his store.

Chapter 23

New Billboard Day

Because of the delay caused by Sunny, I'm a little late getting to Janus's resale store. I'm there around 5:20, and the store closes at 5:30. His dad, Jesse, is on the floor while his mom, Angela, is behind the counter by the cash register. We greet one another, and I assure them that their billboard went up sometime today and will remain up for the duration of the campaign.

"You can renew at any time," I remind them. "The sooner the better, though. You don't want to risk it having to move because somebody else rented the sign before you renew. It will be put back on the market one month before the campaign is set to end if you don't renew."

"And you say this is going up for six months?" Jesse asks. I confirm. "So we should let you know by mid-December?"

"That would be best," I answer. "We can discuss other media, like radio or TV ads, before then if you want. You won't have to wait for this campaign to expire."

"We'll keep that in mind," Angela dismissively says.

"And we'll do it if we see the increase in business that Saturn projected," Janus says from the doorway of his shop. "Hi, Saturn."

"Good afternoon, Janus. Are you ready?"

"Just about. Let me clean up the shop first. We close pretty soon, and we'll leave then."

Janus returns to his shop area. While I'd like to see it again, I'm not sure he'd appreciate me going in without an invitation. I wouldn't want him barging into my office without one, so I'll give him the same respect. I stay out with his parents and ask if there's anything I could do to help with the closing of the store.

"We just turn the lights out and flip the sign to closed," Jesse says.

"We sweep the floor, too," Angela adds. "I'll take care of that, though. You don't have to do any extra work."

"I don't mind, really," I say. "Where do you keep the broom?"

"You really don't have to…" Angela starts to say.

"Over there," Jesse points to the corner of the store. I smile at him, and then at Angela, and grab the broom and dustpan.

I start sweeping, though there's very little dust and debris on the floor. I ask if the day has not been so busy, and Angela tells me that they sweep several times throughout the day to keep their store clean.

"That's good business," I say. "Presentation is so important for a business like yours."

"How is your new bed?" Jesse asks.

"Comfortable. Thank you for it. I've been sleeping a lot better these past couple of days," I answer.

"That's good to hear," Jesse replies, then sees Janus come out of the shop. He looks at his watch and says it's about that time. I finish sweeping the floor while Jesse flips the sign. After locking the door, Janus decides to ride with me in my car, and his parents to follow in theirs.

I drive down 5th Street, which leads to downtown, and when I pass Chesapeake Avenue, I find a spot by the curb where we can easily park both of our vehicles. I pull over, and Jesse follows.

We get out, and I ask them to please keep their eyes covered until I say to open them. No, this isn't what I'd do with a regular client, but this is for Janus. I not only want to play this game just to have fun, but also to see if Janus will trust me to take his hand and lead him while he has limited vision. I take Janus's hand, he takes his mom's, who takes his dad's. I led them a couple of hundred feet or so down the sidewalk to where I think will give them the best first look at their billboard.

"Ready?" I ask as I release Janus's hand, and the rest follow. They all say they are, so I start a countdown. "3... 2... 1... OPEN!" I say, and they do.

They all stand there, looking up, not saying anything but just taking in their ad. I stand there waiting, nervously, needing somebody to say something – anything – even if it's that they hate it. I look at each one, seeing how they all make similar faces as they stare up at the sign.

"So that's our billboard?" Jesse asks, even though it's obvious.

"It is," I say. "Is there something wrong with it? It's just how we discussed."

"No," Jesse replies, then smiles widely. "It's perfect. It should double, even triple our business in no time."

"Ummm…" I nervously say, Not sure what to say about that. "While it should give you increased traffic and revenues by the end of the campaign, I wouldn't expect it to double, let alone triple."

"Dad knows that, Saturn," Janus answers, then puts his arm around my waist. "He tends to be overoptimistic at times. While that would be great, a huge increase like that, he knows that likely won't happen."

"Janus is right," Jesse says. "I remember what you said. This, plus more word of mouth, should have us seeing an increase of at least 5% in six months."

"I'd even expect one of 10-15%, which would then taper off by the end of the year. From there, more advertising may not increase revenues, but it should keep them so they wouldn't waver, neither," I state. "That's how business and advertising work sometimes."

"Is that so?" Angela asks.

"We discussed this in detail, Mom," Janus says to her. "She showed me the numbers, and they made perfect sense. If this works, we'll see about doing TV ads."

"Who would we hire to act in them?" Angela asks.

"It would make more sense for you and your family to," I answer, and see her start to object. "But let's cross that bridge if we get to it. I recommend waiting three months. We'll conduct an analysis for you, then discuss your advertising needs. There's a chance all you'll need is this billboard."

"Why would we need more?" Jesse asks.

"If you do regular TV ads and/or newspaper ads, you could include current inventory in those. As I said, Mr. Rings, let's discuss that when the time comes, and we have more information."

"For now, let's just enjoy this billboard. The big, beautiful billboard," Janus says, then wraps his arm around me tighter as he stares up at the sign. I'm in heaven in so many ways right now.

We stand there silently, looking up at the sign for at least three minutes. Janus finally sighs loudly and suggests that we break it up before the police arrest us all for loitering. We all laugh at his joke, then his parents leave. Janus asks me what's next, and I suggest going to Taco Tom for dinner.

We both ordered the basic taco dinner. Janus goes to fill our drink cups while I wait at the counter for our order to come up. I sit across from Janus at a booth by the window, and he sets our drinks in front of each of us as I place our meals on the table. We look at each other, then Janus bows his head and says grace for us.

He squirts a liberal amount of hot sauce on his tacos while I opt for the mild. He calls me a wimp, and I say that his choice may have cost him a kiss goodnight.

"You wouldn't really do that to me, would you?" he asks.

I give him a devilish smile, but never answer. "I saw Sunny today."

"Oh?" he responds, apparently over the kissing conversation.

"I went for ice cream before coming here…" I start.

"And you didn't invite me?" he asks, then takes a huge bite from his crunchy taco shell.

"It was probably best I didn't," I answer in a serious tone. "Sunny and I had a rather interesting conversation."

I tell him all about it, and how we are going to try to be friends now.

"I told you she isn't so bad," he says when I finish.

"I hope that's true," I reply, and truly mean it.

"She voted 'Yes' for your bed. One other voted 'No' at first, and despite the 'Yaes' having it, she fought for it to be unanimous and won," Janus explains.

"No kidding?" I ask, surprised.

"She likes things like that to be unanimous, as she thinks it makes our decisions look better."

"Really?!" I ask again, still surprised by this. "She said for me to make sure to stop by their booth on Friday for some coffee and candy."

"I hope you go," he answers. "It really is good candy. How is your booth coming along?"

I'm glad he took my bait and asked this, as I need to discuss something with him.

"Chloe, my college roommate, should be coming in on Thursday and help with finishing some of the pieces, then running the booth."

"I'm looking forward to meeting her," Janus says.

"Who says you will?" I jokingly ask.

"I'll just stop by your booth to buy something and introduce myself to her," he cleverly answers.

"Touché," I say. "Sunny says that she and Blake are going into business together, selling their coffee and candy."

"I remember them saying that," Janus says, then scoops some Spanish rice.

"That brings me to something I need to talk to you about," I say, then take a small bite of a taco. I wipe my mouth and look Janus in the eyes.

"That may work for them, but I don't think it would for me," I start, then continue before he can say anything. "I like you, Janus. A lot. A whole, whole lot. However, I don't think it's the right time for us to go into business together. I appreciate your offer, Janus, but I won't be putting my craft stick pieces in your store."

Janus finishes the first of his tacos, then bites into his second, leaving me waiting for an answer. He reaches across the table, asks for my hands, so I give them to him.

"I like you a lot, too. A whole lot. I don't want you to get into something that you're not ready for. I thought they'd be a nice touch in my store, but if you're not ready for that yet, I'm good with that. Blake scared you away with his persistence, and I don't want to do that. Am I still allowed to shop at your booth?"

"Of course, you goof," I say, then yank my hands away. "There was no need to get all dramatic over it. A simple 'That's fine' would have done."

"Maybe someday," Janus says, then sits and looks at me. His eyes are sincere, and his faint smile is saying more than he may know. I look back, and he sees me in the same way. "Or maybe your billboard will drive customers away, and we'll be out of business before the six months are over."

He laughs at his comment, and I pretend to be insulted. Maybe I was a bit too dramatic about the whole craft sticks in his store thing, but I didn't want a repeat of what happened with Blake. We talk more about the upcoming event, and about his store and possible ad campaigns in the future. We finish our meals, then I say I'll drive him back to his place so I can get back to mine and glue a few sticks together before bed.

We stand outside his store in the parking lot, looking at each other under the light of the streetlamp. I go to kiss him goodnight, and he initially refuses because he had hot sauce on his tacos. I grab him, plant a big kiss on his lips, and ask that we not go out again until the event on Friday, saying I have a lot of work to do with my crafts. He says he's fine with that, and I kiss him again. As I drive out of the lot, I notice the marquee for his store. "He should change what it says," I say to myself, then pull into the street and drive home.

I work on my craft stick projects, three at a time, since time is short, and I even stay up a little later than normal. I wake up the next morning again feeling extra refreshed, sleeping in this refurbished bed with a new mattress. My first thought isn't on Janus or Chloe or even Venus, but on work. Okay, for me, that's not all that unusual. What is, though, is my hope to get twice as much done today as normal, so we all get the four-day weekend that Gretchen promised her staff.

I show up early and get the bird feeders filled again. I'm surprised by how much they eat, and I may be doing this twice a day if they attract more birds. I'd be happy if that happens, but also happy if it doesn't. Maybe I'll buy a book from the pet shop to help me identify which birds are which.

The morning meeting was typical, where I told them how the Rings and Sons Restoration and Resale account is doing. Professionalism was evident, thank God, and no one asked me about my relationship with the son of that business. Gretchen recapped the oil change shop ad, combined with the councilwoman's, and told us all to try to combine ads like that when the possibility comes along.

"Don't force it, though," she says. "It's not likely to happen too often, but when it does, roll with it."

Roll with it? I think. This must be our equivalent of a casual Friday, as Gretchen isn't like that too often. As I internally chuckle at her, she dismisses us, telling us again to work hard today so we earn that long weekend.

We all leave having little to say to one another. I'm glad that neither Diane nor Gretchen asked me to return to the recording booth. I walk to my office as quickly as I can without making it look too obvious, and shut the door tight, hoping it stays that way for the rest of the day.

I send emails and take calls at the same pace as a regular day. I don't rush anyone off the phone, and if they request a meeting for tomorrow, then what can I do? Lunchtime comes, and so far, no appointments have been made for tomorrow.

Karen knocks on my door just before noon and asks what I am doing for lunch. I told her that I packed a lunch and planned on eating at my desk, taking an abbreviated break.

"Suit yourself," she says, then she and Frida head out for lunch to wherever they are going.

I didn't care. I was happy with my ham and cheese sandwich with a baggie of chips and an apple. I look over accounts in progress as I eat, and am satisfied with how things are going.

I spend my after-lunch searching for more billboards for Kelly Patterson's councilman reelection campaign. I find three more that will be available soon and do what I need to do to get her sign up. I sent her an email informing her, with a BCC to Gretchen. I receive positive replies from both, and I am glad for that. I don't find any more available, but I will keep looking as long as this campaign runs.

A little after three comes, and curiosity gets the best of me. I call Rings and Sons on their business phone and ask to speak to Janus. He answers, and wonders why I didn't call him on his cell. I had no good answer for that.

"How is business?" I ask.

"Are you asking if the billboard is working?" he asks back, knowing what I was really asking. I confirm, and he answers. "Actually, we had three customers come in saying they saw the billboard. I'm not sure if they were new or not, but at least it was seen."

"That's a good thing," I say. "Did they buy anything?"

"The third one that came in bought the table shown on the billboard," he answers, and I could hear the pride in his voice.

"That's wonderful," I say. "We can't change the sign at no charge, but you already knew that."

"What about your idea for newspaper ads with new inventory each week?" he asks.

"I'll tell you what I'd tell any client," I reply. "Let's not get too excited after just one day. While I think a newspaper ad would work, I'd recommend seeing how the billboard does first. Give it at least two weeks, but I'd even suggest waiting a month before considering other options."

"Is this because you're the billboard specialist and not the newspaper?" he asks.

"No, Janus," I say, maybe sounding a little flustered by that. "Yes, I am the billboard expert here, but I have every ability to create a successful newspaper ad, just as Karen made rather good billboards in her time and still could. It's not about that. It's about getting you the most from your advertising investment."

Silence follows, then Janus sounds upset when he speaks.

"I'm sorry, Saturn. I didn't mean anything by that. I was just excited that the billboard is already working. I didn't mean to question your professional ethics," he says.

"No, it's okay," I say after calming down a little. "I know what you meant. Believe me, I'm excited, too, over somebody noticing the billboard. Like I say, let's just wait and see how the campaign goes. That is the advice I'd give anybody, not just my boyfriend."

Drat! I just referred to him as my boyfriend, and to him! Drat! Drat! Drat! What do I do?

"Thanks, Saturn. I'll let you get back to work, and will see you on Friday."

I say goodbye, hang up, then drat myself some more over saying he was my boyfriend.

At 4:50, Gretchen calls everyone into the conference room. We're not sure what she wants. It could be confirming we earned a four-day weekend, or she could be telling us we're all working late on a grocery store ad that just came in and is to start on Monday. Sometimes it's hard to tell with her.

She tells us that we're not to come in tomorrow, but we also don't have the day off.

"I expect you all to check your email and phone messages once an hour, from nine to five. You are to return calls, reply to emails, and treat the customer like it's a normal day at work. Most of our clients are also taking tomorrow off, so I wouldn't expect too many, if any. Go get ready to close for the long weekend. Oh, and Saturn…" I look at her with a silent voice and dead eyes. "Make sure to take care of the birds during the time off. I've really been enjoying them."

"I will," I say through a smile, and we all close our offices and leave for the long weekend.

I drive straight home, and once inside, I feed and water Muffin and clean out his litter box. I make macaroni and cheese for dinner, and have that with a hot dog. After cleaning the dishes and kitchen, I go out to my living room and prepare to work on my craft stick projects some more.

First, though, I need to find something on TV. I searched the YouTube app and found videos made by amateur bird-watching enthusiasts. I click play on the first, then get my projects set up on the coffee table and get to work on them.

I again work on three different projects while keeping half an eye on this middle-aged lady demonstrating how to get the most out of your bird feeders and baths. I make a lot of mental notes as I watch hers and a few more after that.

I look out the window and see that it's now dark outside. I look at the clock and realize I totally lost track of time, and it's just after 9:00 p.m. I won't be going to bed soon, and after about three hours of gluing sticks together, I need some fresh air.

I walk outside and hear the ambient sounds of the neighborhood. It's quiet for the most part, as I mostly hear the occasional car driving by, dog barking, or other general sounds of the outdoors. I look up and see the stars shining brightly without a cloud in the sky. I think, why not? I go inside to get my telescope and set it in the courtyard behind the apartment building.

I try to remember how Dad taught me how to do this. I take my phone out, look up a thing or two, and adjust the telescope. I look through it, get it in focus, and see where I aimed to. It's Janus. No, not the man whom I've been dating, but the moon of Saturn. I look at it very closely this time. It looks like a stone you'd find in an alley somewhere.

I readjust the telescope and look at Venus. It's blobby at first, but once it comes into focus, it has an understated beauty about it. It reminds me more and more of my sister. No, not the flashy teen who ruled the hallways of our high school. It reminds me of how Venus is now. It tries to appear plain, but if you look really close, you'll see all of the near-hidden beauty shining through. That's Venus, my sister. She now wears flannel shirts and blue jean overalls, and little to no makeup. However, when you look closely, you could still see what she is trying to hide from view. A beautiful person inside and out who will soon give birth to a beautiful baby.

I look at Saturn through the telescope, studying it closely. It has stripes and rings around it. Unlike Venus, it seems like it's trying hard to be noticed, to be beautiful. But is that really what's happening, or am I just seeing my sister and me in the planets? I'm unsure of what I see, and I think I should start getting ready for bed.

Before I pack it up, I take out my phone and text my sister. I just sent "I miss you," and I wait for a reply. I peek through the telescope again, this time trying to see just what's there, and see Saturn for what it really is. The sixth planet from the sun in our solar system, and the reason why I have the name that I have.

I look some more, and when I realize I won't be getting a reply from Venus, I take my telescope inside and get ready for bed. I say my nightly prayers, asking God for guidance, for Chloe to have a safe trip from Michigan City, for Sunny and me to become good friends, and for success with my craft stick art at the event on Friday. I add a little about Venus, thanking God that we were able to mend our fences and become as close as we are in our adult lives, and thank Him for sending Eric to her. I confess my many sins and ask Him for forgiveness for them, and thank God for sending His son to pay for my sins as he hung on the cross to bring me salvation and a promise of everlasting life in God's Kingdom of Heaven. I say amen, make sure my alarm clock isn't set to ring at 7:30, then try to drift off to sleep with Muffin by my feet.

Chapter 24

Chloe Comes to Town

I sleep in on Thursday morning. Not too late, just until about 8:30 a.m., which is just an extra hour. I stayed up later than normal last night, so it's really more of a shift in sleeping time, not more sleep. Still, I take sleeping an hour later as some sort of weird victory and celebrate that by not having to turn my alarm clock off.

I stretch my arms, then look at my cell phone. I did get a reply from Venus. It's a smiley face. I smile at that, thinking this is the perfect way to wake up this morning.

I give Muffin a little pet, and he purrs, then takes a few steps away and goes back to sleep. I get up, and since he looks so comfortable lying there, I decide to make the bed later.

I do sit on the edge of the bed to say my prayers, again thanking God for this bed to be able to sit on. I pray for safe travels for Chloe coming into town today, and add my general prayers that I do in the morning.

I start the coffee maker, then go and take a nice hot shower. I let the water pour all over me, nearly hot enough to cause first-degree burns, and I savor every moment. I even wash my hair three times, just because the feel of the water running over my scalp feels heavenly.

Reluctantly, I turn the water off and get out of the bathtub. I dry myself off, wipe the fog from the mirror hanging on the bathroom door, and look at myself. I may be average looking at best, but I do like what I'm seeing. I see myself for who I really am, maybe noticing a little extra that the BMV doesn't need to know about to change on my driver's license.

"Maybe I'll join a gym," I say to myself. "I'm sure there's one around here somewhere."

I dress myself in clothes I'd generally wear on a Saturday, then go into the kitchen. I pour some coffee and add nothing but a coffee stirrer. I feel a little gimpish, so I take a picture of it and send it to Venus.

"Such a waste," she texts.

"I love you too, Sis," I say, but don't text back.

Since I have the day off, I decided to make homemade pancakes for breakfast. Okay, fine, pancakes from a box of mix. I still have to add eggs and water, so it's homemade-ish, at least.

I make them with a side of breakfast sausage, and after I plate them, I smother the pancakes and sausage with syrup, and bring the plate along with a cup of coffee to the sofa I used to sleep on. I move a couple of projects I've been working on to make room, and I set the plate and cup down. I say a short grace, then turn the TV on.

I again turn on the YouTube app and find a one-hour-long video of commercials that were exclusively shown in the Florida and southeast markets. I still find it fascinating how the same products are sold in different ways depending on the location. If the agency buys that branch in Lincoln, I wonder if we're going to have to work on ads for there and adapt. We will for Brown Farms Weddings, I'm sure. I'd actually like to do that, doing ads for different markets.

Look at this commercial for a global fast food chain, for example. In Florida, they show people eating a signature item before heading out to surf. The same company has a similar ad running in the Midwest now, but instead of surfing, they show people hiking on trails. A homeowner's insurance ad follows, emphasizing the importance of hurricane insurance. The same ad here would be similar, except they'd promote tornado insurance instead of hurricane insurance.

"I could watch these all day," I say to Muffin, who has since come out for his breakfast, and I have done so several times when I was a teen living at home.

While I could, I won't. I clean up the breakfast mess and notice it's ten o'clock. I do as Gretchen instructed and check my email and voice mail messages. There's nothing that can't wait until Monday, so I make a note of it and log out.

I find commercials from the southwest region, and start that ninety-minute video. I then get my craft sticks near me and start working on the projects I hope to be done for tomorrow's fair. I work on three at a time, and when these are done, I'll probably just take what I have and not rush to make any more.

I lose track of the next ninety minutes, and before I know it, it's nearing lunchtime.

I text Chloe to see when she thinks she'll be in town. She says that she'll be leaving in a couple of hours, and expects me to take her out for dinner once she gets here. I send a "k" back, then think for a moment. I call Janus's store, and his dad says that he's out on a delivery now and shouldn't be too long.

I don't want to leave a message or wait. I call his cell, and he answers.

"Hi, Saturn," he says instead of hello.

"Hi. Your dad said you're making deliveries?" I ask.

"Yeah. And before you get too excited, these were arranged before the billboard went up, so don't go start taking credit," he jokes.

"I won't," I answer, pause, then add "yet."

"Ha!" he replies. "Do you need something? I have a busy day ahead of me."

"Well," I say, "I wanted to see if you wanted to have lunch with me. If you're that busy, I could pick something up for us, and we could eat in your shop. That is, if you allow food in there."

"I was going to grab leftovers from my apartment fridge, but if you're offering, I'm accepting. Be there at one?"

"Do cheeseburgers from Harry's Hamburgers and Hot Dogs sound good?"

"Sure," he answers. "Load mine up. I have to finish my deliveries now, so I'll see you then."

Janus hangs up before I get a chance to say goodbye. He's at work and in a rush, so I guess that's understandable. I start another YouTube video, this one of an orchestra from California playing a Tchaikovsky symphony, and have it playing in the background while I work on my craft sticks some more.

At 12:30, I'm satisfied with the progress and see I have very little more to do. I make sure that Muffin's bowls are full, then grab my purse and go out the door.

I drive to Harry's for our lunch and resist the temptation to look at the ads in his window. I just go to the counter, order two cheeseburger meals loaded with colas to go, and head back out the door and to my Volkswagen.

I try not to think about what the mechanic said as I drive to Janus's store, but I will have to do something about it soon. I go inside, and Janus isn't there yet, but Jesse greets me as Angela sweeps the floor.

"Just take that into the shop and set it out," Jesse says. "Janus should be back any minute."

"Are you sure?" I ask.

"Just don't touch anything," Angela yells from a distance. "There should be a cleared off table in there. Use that."

I smile at her and go into the shop area. I feel a little awkward being in here alone, but I get over that rather soon. I set our food out and fight off the temptation to look around at all of his tools. Okay, I do look around while sitting, but don't touch.

There is a screwdriver on the table in front of me, one with a head I've never seen before. I pick it up and take a closer look at it.

"It's a Torx screwdriver," Janus says as he appears in the doorway.

"Oh, sorry," I say, and gingerly put the tool down.

"It's okay," Janus says. "Maybe after lunch, you could stay and help me some more? You could touch more tools that way."

Janus looks sincere in his invitation. I tell him that I may have a little time, but we should eat first. I say grace for us, then we both pick up our hamburgers and take big bites, Janus a little bigger than me.

"Mmmmm," he says through a mouthful of beef, bun, cheese, and vegetables.

"You could say that again," I say, and take another bite.

We enjoy our meals, eating more quickly than I usually do, and mostly comment on how good the food tastes. When we're done, I clean up the mess and tell Janus that I'll go now and leave him to his work.

"Oh, no," he says.

"What?"

"You promised to stay and help. This old recliner still needs some fixing up. I got most of it fixed; we just need to finish the job. You'll be able to use that Torx screwdriver when we get near the end parts."

I smile and say that I'll stay for no more than two hours. Chloe is coming into town today, and I need to be home for her.

"Perfect," Janus says. "Now, here's what we need to do."

"Actually, first I have to check my messages," I inform him. I do as I say as Janus waits quietly. I have no phone messages needing immediate replies, but I have one email I decided to tend to. I send a reply to a client assuring them that their campaign is on schedule and will start as scheduled. I put my phone away, then tell Janus I'm ready.

Janus begins to show me how he does his work, taking chairs and other furniture that look like trash and have been thrown away, and restoring them to almost new condition. It's a fascinating process, and takes a lot of skill and patience. I remember when I first talked to Janus in the coffee shop, and I questioned him about whether or not this is a real job and if he should be pursuing more out of life. After an hour working with him, I understood. This is a real job, and this, combined with his degree in business from the University of Notre Dame, is what keeps this business going with rather good profits.

"Just use this and turn that screw to tighten," he says as he hands me the now-famous Torx screwdriver. I do, and after I tighten the screw, I smile.

"It's a good feeling, isn't it?" he asks.

"What?" I question back.

"This chair is done. I found it in the trash, we fixed it, now I can add it to my inventory after I give it a good upholstery cleaning." Janus smiles, then stands next to me, takes my hand, and we stare at the chair.

"It does look comfortable," I say.

"Have a seat. That is, if you don't mind a little dust," he offers, then releases my hand.

I think for a moment, and figure why not? I have a seat, bounce on in gently a couple of times, then start to rock it.

"It squeaks," I say.

"Does it?" Janus asks, then walks to a cabinet and takes a can out. "Take this."

I do, then Janus asks me to stand and take a step back. I do, then he puts the chair upside down.

"Just take that can, and squirt it here, here, and here," Janus says while pointing.

"What if I put too much on?" I ask.

"That can't happen. Just squirt a liberal amount at each spot I showed you."

I do, then hand the can back to Janus. He puts it back where it belongs, and I think about how my mom would approve of his methods. He then sets the chair upright, rocks it a couple of times, and then takes my hand to urge me to sit again. I do.

"Oh, the squeak is gone," I say as I rock.

"There. Now, once we get it cleaned, how much should I ask for?"

"I'm not sure," I say.

"Well, I'd say about a hundred and fifty dollars. I'd go as much as twenty-five dollars lower, but I think I can get the asking price for this piece, especially now that this store is famous in the area," Janus says.

"Well, one billboard hardly makes it famous, but we'll get you there," I say.

"I hope so," he replies, then helps me out of the chair.

I tell him that it's been fun, and I really enjoyed learning how to fix furniture. He smiles and says that he'll see me at the event tomorrow, then kisses me goodbye. Nothing much. Not much more than a kiss after a first date, but it was still nice. Every kiss from him, no matter how he does it or with any amount of passion, is nice. I won't count this toward the 5,000 for the new car.

I go to my car and check my messages again as Gretchen directed us. Okay, I may not have been checking every hour on the hour, but close enough. Nothing is pressing at the moment, but I am looking forward to a busy Monday when we all return to work.

I get home and decide to relax a little by putting on the flip-flops I bought about a month ago and working more on the Shafer Bell Tower project. It's just about finished, and maybe, just maybe, Chloe and I can have it finished by the time she goes back home.

I decide to work in silence, just allowing any ambient sound from the outside to sneak in to keep me company. I look at the plans that Chloe made and see that they and the results are close. Close enough to call it a success. I set a can of cola on the end table on a craft stick coaster and sip that as I glue sticks to the tall tower.

I hum a little as I work, and wonder what I'll do with this once it's done. It's scale, standing approximately six feet high, and it isn't too light. I'll worry about that later, though. Right now, I'll just concentrate on the here and now, wondering when Chloe will be knocking on my door.

Just before 5:00 p.m. I received a text from her. It says that she just pulled into town and asked that I wait for her outside my apartment building for her to show up. I wondered if I should first change my footwear, but keep the flip-flops on my feet.

I bring my purse outside with me and stand by the main entrance to the parking lot of Bluebird Apartments. I wait a bit, checking my watch, wondering why it's taking her so long. Chloe finally arrives, and I direct her to the few spots available designated for visitors of residents. She gets out, and we wrap each other into a tight hug that seems to have lasted for hours. It didn't, but I would have been totally fine if it had.

She grabs a suitcase out of the trunk and tells me to grab the other plastic bags.

"I stopped at a grocery store I saw after I texted you," she says as she closes the truck. "That's what took me a little longer, as I wanted to bring some food for us."

"That was totally unnecessary, but nice of you," I reply as I look into one bag. "You are staying until Sunday after church still, correct?"

"Probably more like after lunch after church," she answers.

We go inside my apartment, I introduce her to Muffin, then I put the groceries away as she pets him.

"I like your place," she says as she looks around.

"Thanks. I'd give you the grand tour, but basically, what you see is what you get. You're sitting on your bed right now."

"It'll do just fine," she says as she tests the springiness of the cushions. She stands and walks over to where the bell tower replica is standing. "This looks great."

"Thanks," I say, smiling over the refrigerator door. "It's your design."

"But your work," she says as she touches it. "Is it done yet?"

"Not quite. I was hoping we'd be able to get it done tonight," I say, then close the door.

"Oh," she says, sounding surprised. "Were we going out to dinner tonight?"

"If you like. How does pizza sound?" I ask.

"Are you talking about the place you made the billboards for?" she asks.

"I am."

"Then I'm in. I saw one of the billboards coming in, and it looked nice. Can I see them all before we go?" she asks.

"Absolutely. Just let me change back into my tennis shoes, and I'll drive us."

After we both give Muffin a little love, we head out to my Beetle. I drive us around the county showing her all five billboards. I am still very proud of my work with them, and she could tell as I talked about them as we passed them.

We get to the restaurant and agree on a medium pizza to share, with her choosing the toppings. She went with fresh tomatoes and sausage, and I liked that idea. She also orders fried mushrooms as an appetizer for us to share, and asks for extra dipping sauce.

We chat a little about how our jobs are doing before we get to the topics we both want to discuss.

"So, how have you and Janus been?" she asks.

"Good, I suppose. We're still in the 'seeing each other' phase, but I hope for that to change soon," I answer.

"Why don't you make the first move for that?" she asks as the waitress sets the mushrooms down.

"I'm not sure how he'd feel about that," I answer honestly. "We never talked about our pasts. I'm not sure what he thinks the next phase would constitute. Would we just continue dating exclusively, or would he want to take our relationship into the bedroom? I'm not sure."

"You told me that he's a good church-going man who is also a deacon, right?" she asks.

"Yeah," I answer. "But, we both know that doesn't mean he's never... or wouldn't want to... I'm just not sure." I sigh, and she sits there quietly, which is something she does often during these types of conversations.

"Just because he invites you into the bedroom doesn't mean you'd have to join him," she finally says.

"I know, but you know just how weak I could be, especially around somebody like Janus. He seems so perfect in so many ways. I even had a dream about that, remember?" I remind her.

As I told you, Chloe isn't an angel, neither, and also has a past when it comes to men and relationships. We do our best to keep each other in check with God, but we can't control each other's actions twenty-four-seven.

"Well, if he's anything like you described he was in the dream..." Chloe says, then raises an eyebrow.

"Chloe!" I shout almost loud enough for everybody in the restaurant to hear. By the way, it's over seventy-five percent full, and I think the billboards have something to do with that.

"Good, you're still thinking with your head," she says, smiling, then dips a mushroom in some sauce using a fork. "What will you do if he does want to take it to the next level? If he does want an exclusive relationship with you?"

"I want that, too," I say, smiling back.

"Then there you go. You answered your own question. Now for a harder question," she says.

"What is that?" I ask.

"What will you be doing with the bell tower once it's done?"

I tell her I've been thinking about that for a while, and I haven't come up with anything. The waitress brings our pizza, and after Chloe says grace, we enjoy our dinner while discussing what to do with it. We finally decided to see if Ball State University would be interested, and if not, then possibly an alumni group would like to own it.

We finish our meals, and despite my objections, Chloe insists on paying for both of us. I let her, and she wouldn't even allow me to leave a tip.

We go back to the apartment, and I put on another one of those blocks of regional ads on YouTube, this time ones mostly from Southern California. We work on the bell tower, and the added distraction of my explaining to Chloe what the ads would look like had they been run in Central Indiana was a welcome distraction. She even started noticing what I was talking about and made a few good observations of her own. Is advertising that easy, and can anybody do it? No. I'm just a good teacher, and she's a quick learner. That's all. I wonder how well I'd do trying to learn civil engineering. At first I think lousy, but then I step back and look at the tower and the work I mostly put into it. It was by Chloe's design, but I was still able to read them and build from that. Maybe I could do that job. Maybe I could, but I wouldn't want to. I was born to be in advertising, and that's where I'll stay.

Chloe steps back, looks at it, and says what we're both thinking.

"One more stick to go, and it's done."

"You are right," I say, then pick up a stick and dab some glue onto it. "You do the honors."

"Are you sure?" she asks.

"Absolutely," I answer.

She smiles at me, walks to the tower, and attaches the last piece. Finished! After a couple of years, it's finally finished! We hug each other in celebration, then notice the time. I tell Chloe that she could use the bathroom first while I make up the couch for her to sleep on.

She comes out ten minutes later and announces that it's open. I thank her, then we face each other, take each other by the hands, and say our prayers before retiring for the night. She starts, I add, she adds more, then I bring it home, making sure to say "Amen" before we pray all night. I'd be fine with that happening, too, to be honest. Maybe tomorrow night. Tonight, though, we need our sleep. The big craft fair is tomorrow, followed by fireworks. It's going to be a long day, so we need a long night first to get our beauty sleep in.

Chapter 25

Independence Day Music, Food, and Crafts Fair

I set my alarm for 7:30, and it rings, waking me from a delightful dream. No, not that delightful like the one I had to discuss with Chloe, but delightful anyway. I don't have time to discuss it now, though. I get up, will save my prayers for later at the breakfast table, make my bed, then go to the bathroom before going out to the front room.

Chloe is sleeping on the couch with Muffin by her feet. I hate to wake her, but this is important. I think about whether I should be gentle or jarring, and since I need her up and at full attention quickly, I go with jarring. I pick up a pillow, throw it as hard as I can at her face, and… BULLSEYE! I got her!

"What the…" she mumbles as she comes to, trying to remember where she is.

"Rise and shine," I say in a singsong voice.

"What time is it?" Chloe asks, looking for her watch.

"Time to get up. I know it may be a little early, but I needed you to see something on TV."

"What?" she asks as she sits up, then gives Muffin a good morning scratch.

"This," I say, then turn on the local news.

It's your basic stuff one would expect on a Friday morning that's also a holiday, and after the anchors play a feature about the Independence Day Music, Food, and Crafts Fair, they go to commercials.

"What was I supposed to see?" Chloe asks.

"This," I say as I turn the volume up on the television.

"Oh, ads," Chloe says through a yawn. "Of course."

We sit through a couple of simply fantastic ads when one comes on for Jack's Coffee and Pastry. I point to the TV, make a "Shush" sound, and Chloe wipes her eyes and pays closer attention.

Suddenly, she scoots closer as she sees me on the screen ordering a black coffee after Sindi asks what I will stir. She chuckles as I turn and face the camera with the tray in my hand.

"So, you star in ads now?" she asks with a hint of pride in her voice.

"Just this one, and a billboard," I answer, trying to hide my pride. "It was my coworker's idea. I didn't mean to appear in it."

"Now your dream has come true, appearing in one," Chloe says as the news comes back on.

"My dream was making them, and it still is. I had fun appearing in that one, but that will be it. Well, unless we do a series of them, which that idea has been floated."

"Saturn O Syres, the new infomercial queen," Chloe says, then stands.

"Hardly," I say. "I've no intention of doing any of those. Now that it's over, go ahead and use the bathroom, and I'll start breakfast. Will a triple-double do for you?"

"Sure," Chloe says, then waddles into the bathroom.

I start making that triple-double breakfast, which is just two eggs, two breakfast sausage patties, and two pieces of toast with butter substitute for each of us. I have some cereal, too, if that's not enough for Chloe – or for me, truth be told.

I have them plated at just about the same time as Chloe comes out of the bathroom. I put the plates on the dining room table along with two cups of coffee, then asked Chloe if she'd like to say grace for us.

"Dear Lord, as we begin this day, I pray for strength to tackle the tasks before us. Please empower us with the energy we need to be productive and successful. May we approach every challenge with a spirit of perseverance and faith. May Saturn's work not only on the craft sticks but also for the church be noticed, and may her blessings spread to others throughout the day. Amen."

"Amen," I say, and give her a little smile.

As we eat, we discuss more of the plans for the day. It's my first craft fair here, and we don't know what to expect. I'm hoping to sell well, but also for some slow times to occur, so we could take turns looking at what the others have to offer. Usually, that does happen, so I can't see how the Oakfield craft fair will be any different.

We finish eating and then do the dishes right away. We put them away, then we start bringing the craft stick pieces to my car. We wondered if we should bring the bell tower along, but since it's not for sale, it didn't seem like the work would have been worth it. We place the pieces for sale as gingerly as possible in the back seat and trunk, along with a table, portable canopy, a couple of folding chairs, my sign, and a cash box.

"Is that everything?" Chloe asks.

"I sure hope so."

We're both dressed casually, each wearing almost knee-length denim shorts. She's wearing a plain yellow T-shirt, and I'm wearing the green one that says "Craft Life" with the yarn, scissors, and other crafting items on the front. It was the shirt I was wearing when Janus first asked me out, and I'm hoping the good luck from wearing it continues.

As we leave, Chloe asks me about the coffee shop billboard. "Why didn't you mention that before? Like yesterday?" she asks.

"I suppose I forgot," I shrugged off.

"Well, take me to it now, then to the fair," she demands.

It's not too far out of the way, so I drive by it, pointing to it, though that wasn't necessary. Chloe looks, smiles, and says I look beautiful and nobody will even notice the blonde girl behind me.

"You did," I point out.

"Well…" she says, and nothing more. I turn to go to the park.

The fair doesn't officially start until 11:00 a.m., but vendors are allowed to set up early while the workers get the stage set up for the bands to play on. I show my registration form to a security guard at the main gate, and after he checks "Saturn Sticks" from his clipboard, he shows us where to go.

I wasn't aware of this before, but vendors are allowed to park their vehicles at their designated spots to sell. I follow the numbers, and when I find the one assigned to me, I pull in, pop the trunk, and then Chloe and I get to work.

I see others are there, and I am relieved that there are no other craft stick booths. I'm not sure why I felt that relief, as there have never been any others before. The lady on one side of me is selling handmade potholders and placemats, and the other is selling homemade jam. I make mental notes, knowing of at least two booths I hope to shop at before the day is over.

I see Oakfield Second Christian Church starting to set up about a block away from where we are. I have a little time, and I ask Chloe if she doesn't mind waiting as I'd really like to go and visit them before the fair opens.

"How is it going?" I ask as I walk up.

"Oh, good morning," Pastor Steven Chalke replies and points to their baby changing area. "It's nice to see you here. Is this how you envisioned it?"

"It looks good," I answer, although they are just getting started setting up.

"Do you think this is enough diapers and supplies?" Janus sarcastically asks as he opens the tailgate to his pickup truck, which is filled with diapers, wipes, and other baby-changing supplies.

"I sure hope so," I say and walk over to kiss him. We pecked lips, then, remembering where I was, I turned and looked embarrassingly back at the pastor.

"Kiss him again," he says. I think he was sincere, so we pecked lips once more.

"Well, we won't get anything done if we keep kissing," Janus says. I agree, then I start to walk back to my area.

"Saturn," Pastor Chalke says as I'm a couple of steps away. I stop, then walk over to him.

"How are things between you two?" he asks softly enough for only me to hear.

"I'm doing the speed limit," I answer.

"That's good to hear," the pastor says, then turns me around to have our backs facing Janus. "I also understand you helped with Sunny finding someone new."

"Well," I start to hedge, then decide to be straight with the man of God. "We both thought that our sort-of exes would be good for one another. It seems that they are. They are happy, we are happy, and everyone is happy."

"As am I," he replies. "Where is your booth located?"

"Right over there," I point, and he squints to have a better look.

"Well, I'll make sure to visit it later. I heard some good stuff about what you do, and my office just may need a new office supply holder or plant pot holder," he says.

"And I'll make sure to give you a good deal," I reply.

"I'm sure that your asking price is fair enough. I'll let you tend to your business now, Saturn. I'll be going to help set up our tent now."

With that, Pastor Chalke walks away, and I return to our booth. I see how Chloe has everything set up, and I like it. I check to see that the prices for

everything are correct and easy to see. They are. There are twenty minutes to go before the fair starts, so Chloe and I sit on our chairs, being mostly quiet, enjoying the heat from the sun as we wait to see how Saturn Sticks will do in these parts.

As the event start draws near, I am pleased to see that Blake's Beans & Sunny's Sweets is nearby. I point this out to Chloe, and we agree to get some coffee and treats at the first moment as we're able. They look our way, and I give them a wave. They wave back with huge smiles, then Sunny takes Blake by the hand as they go to their places in their respective area. They look so happy together, and I couldn't be happier for them.

The event starts, and as expected, it's very slow at first. The fireworks show isn't until sundown, around 9:00 p.m., so we have a long day ahead of us. We expect it to get busier as the day passes, and I hope to have everything, or at least almost everything, sold before then.

"Look, Mom, it's popsicle sticks," I hear a girl of about 10 say.

"It is," the mother says, and they both come over. The Mom gives me a curious look that I've seen many times, and she asks the question that usually follows. "Why Saturn Sticks?"

"My name is Saturn," I answer. "Saturn O Syres."

"Oh," the mom says and picks up a big box. "What is this?"

"I have been selling them as a shoe box," I answer. "But I got a kitten recently, and he started sleeping in them, so it could be used as a cat bed."

"I bet Ginger would like this," the girl says.

"How much is it?" the mom asks.

"I usually ask for forty dollars, but since she looks so excited and it would be the first time I sold one as a cat bed, I'll let you have it for thirty," I say with a smile.

"I tell you what," the mom says as she digs in her purse. "I'll split the difference and pay thirty-five."

"Thank you," I say as I accept the payment. "Would you like a bag for that?"

"Oh, no thanks. I may be able to use this as a bag itself. I see Cloris is selling her pot holders again. I bet they would make a good liner for these."

I thank the mom and whisper to Chloe to keep that in mind. I only have a couple more of those, but recommending them to be lined with the pot holders is a genius idea. Also, crafters supporting crafters is always a good thing.

As 12:30 comes around, the business and craft fair remains relatively slow. I imagine that with the amount of food and craft vendors here, more people will start coming out for this. I see some people on the stage getting that prepared, as well as a dance floor in front of it, and I look at my schedule of events. A band is supposed to perform at 1:00, then more bands throughout the rest of the day. I think that this would be a good time for Chloe and me to have our lunch, as it may start getting busier after 1:00.

"I see that Harry's Hamburgers and Hot Dogs has a truck here. Would a hot dog be okay with you?" I ask Chloe.

"Make it two, with fries or chips and a diet soda," she requests, then turns her attention to a middle-aged couple who motions to get her attention.

I let Chloe tend to the customer and make my way to buy our lunch. There's no line, and after I get the four hot dogs and large fries for us to share, I load our dogs with toppings and take the food, along with two sodas, back to our booth.

"I sold a couple more coasters," Chloe says as she shuts the cash box.

"And I bought lunch. Looks like a break-even," I joke, then set our food in the back of my car.

We enjoyed our lunches quickly, and no customers stopped by as we ate. After tossing the trash away, we move to the front of the booth, hoping to attract more customers simply by being noticed.

At 1:00, the band starts. They start playing what sounds like a country and western song, and when I look at the event schedule, I see that they are named "Mark and his Mountain Men." I'm not a big fan of that type of music, yet I don't hate it. It's nothing I'd tune the radio to, yet when I hear it, I tend to enjoy it.

As the band plays, a few couples start dancing, and more people start coming. Not in big droves, mind you, but the event is starting to get filled up. It's held at a city park, and it's a rather large one for a city of this size. Kids start swinging on swings and sliding down slides as one parent stays to watch and the other goes shopping.

As the event gets more crowded, I explain several times why the booth is called Saturn Sticks and what the shoe/cat box is supposed to be. Most people handle an item or two, say they're nice, but don't buy. That used to frustrate me, but I soon realized that it is just part of how these fairs work. Many look, some buy. The ones who don't buy aren't saying that what you have is bad, just that it's not anything they need or want at the moment. That's fine. I plan on looking around later, too, and not buying something from every booth that I visit.

Around 2:30, the country band stops, and the next isn't scheduled to start until 3:00. I look at the schedule, and I think it's the same band that plays at the civic club on Friday nights. I'm glad. I like them, and more people will likely come out to hear them.

During a lull in business, I hear a familiar voice calling out my name. I turn to look and see Janus walking toward our booth. I say hi to him and introduce him to Chloe.

"I heard a lot about you," Janus says as they shake hands.

"I can say the same," Chloe replies.

"These are nice," Janus says as he picks up an office supply box. "My offer still stands."

"I know," I say, smiling at him, then turn to Chloe. "Would you mind if we looked around for ten minutes or so?"

"Sure. I'll run a buy-one, get one free promotion while you're gone," Chloe says through a smile.

"Funny," I say, then Janus takes my hand, and we start walking around.

He tells me that so far, two mothers have changed their baby's diaper in their tent, and the tent itself is attracting far more attention than in previous years.

"I'm glad it's working," I say.

"You are a marketing genius," he replies, and I just give him a 'whatever' eye roll, though I didn't outright deny his claim.

We look around, and just as I predicted, I look at a lot of stuff but don't buy much. In fact, I didn't buy anything, though a pot holder and a few jars of jam will be purchased later. We look at about half of the booths, and I notice that we've been away for far longer than ten minutes. I suggest that he go back to his church's booth, and I go back to Saturn Sticks.

"Not before we buy something from there," he says, pointing to Blake and Sunny's booth.

"Of course," I say, then take his hand and lead the way.

They greet us with great joy and point to their menu board. They have a much bigger selection than most coffee booths have at these, and I wondered if the quality would be lower because of that. I look, and since everything is $5, which is good marketing on their part, I order a banana and cream latte.

"What would you recommend to go with that?" I ask Sunny.

"How about a strawberry and orange mix of jelly beans? Sip the latte, then eat a few beans. Don't only eat one flavor at a time, but balance them," she answers.

"I will," I say.

"I want a mint chocolate latte. What candy do you suggest?" Janus asks Sunny.

"Vanilla bites. One flavor to complement that drink," she says.

We pay her $20 for our treats and take them to my booth. I apologize to Chloe for taking so long, and she jokes that it's okay since she pocketed half of what was sold.

"That's fine," I say.

"We sold a few more coasters and a plant box," she says. "We're doing well."

I agreed, then took a sip of my latte, expecting it to be average at best. I was stunned by what I tasted. Blake was right. I could not only taste the bananas and cream in my drink, but also the espresso and steamed milk. I took another sip, then quickly followed it with a few jelly beans.

"Holy cow!" I exclaim.

"What?" Janus asks.

"Give me your drink and candy," I say, then take the drink from his hand without waiting for an answer. I take a gulp, then eat a few of his vanilla bites. "Oh! My! Gosh!"

"Chloe. Taste this," I say, and hand her my coffee and jelly beans. She does, and the expression on her face is priceless. "Go over to that booth and order a latte and ask the woman what candy to get with it." Chloe gives me a look, then takes ten dollars from her purse and goes to their booth.

She comes back shortly with a tangerine and blueberry latte, with a mix of pineapple and mango jelly beans. I take her drink, gulp, and follow it up with the candy.

"Amazing," I say, then decide to run an experiment. I sip from my cup and eat Chloe's candy. It's good, but not as great. I then sip from her cup and try Janus's vanilla bites. While it's very tasty, none of the combinations I tried match up to the way Sunny suggested.

"You guys try that," I insist. Janus and Chloe were at first reluctant to drink from each other's cups, but I told them that since I kissed both of them on the lips before, there shouldn't be any cooties between them. Immature, I know, but I need to know if it's just me or if it's real.

They exchange looks, then cups and candy. They both taste and have the same reaction as I.

"Now mix and match," I say, and they do, agreeing that while it's delicious, it's not as good as the recommended way.

"Excuse me," I say, and leave Chloe and Janus at the booth. I see Janus leave after me to return to his church's booth as I walk back to Blake's Beans & Sunny's Sweets.

"You say that these are all homemade?" I ask Sunny, motioning to her candy inventory. She says that they are.

"And these are all your own recipes?" I ask Blake. "You didn't steal any from Jack's?"

"While they are similar, yes. All lattes would be, they are my own recipes that took me years to perfect," he answers with great pride.

"Perfect," I say, then take a business card from my purse and hand it to Blake. "Call the agency when you're ready to expand. We can help you with flyers, your sign, and even a better logo."

"What's wrong with our logo?" Sunny asks with a hint of attitude.

"You just combined your two businesses' logos. You just overlapped them, it seems. A good logo is key to attracting customers. You have the name. You have the products, no doubt. You just need help with advertising and marketing, and we could do that. Blake, you said that you wanted to go national, possibly worldwide, right?" I ask.

"Well, yes. We both do," he answers, then looks at Sunny, who nods.

"You won't get there with this," I say, pointing to their signs. "Seriously, we can help. Don't expect to be nationwide, or even statewide, too quickly. With the right pacing and advertising, you could be nationwide in ten years."

"Well…" Blake says as he looks at my card.

"Feel free to call another agency, but make sure you call someone if you want to expand. I have to get back to my booth now, but first... Blake, mix me another latte, and Sunny, pair that with candy. Here's ten dollars."

Sunny takes the money, then they discuss what they should make. They go basic and make a simple vanilla latte, and Sunny hands me some chocolate saltwater taffy. I thank them and return to my booth. We try the drink and candy, and have the same reaction.

"I can't believe those two are able to make something this perfectly delicious," I say to Chloe.

"What?" she asks.

"Never mind," I say. We start bopping along with the music as more customers come to check out just exactly what Saturn Sticks is.

The day goes on, and I'm happy to say that by 6:00 p.m., we were officially out of inventory and had sold out.

"It looks like you were a hit," Chloe says.

"I couldn't have done it without you. Had you not shown me how to make these like an engineer, they would have just still been things cluttering up my apartment."

"Oh, phooey," she replies. "Don't start that again. Let's get cleared out of here. I still haven't had much of a chance to look around."

Chapter 26

Looking Up at the Sky

Chloe and I get our booth put away and leave the car where it is after packing it. Chloe says that she wants to shop at some of the booths, and I wanted to go and see how the baby changing booth is going. We agree to part ways, find our own dinners, and meet up at the church's booth around 9:00 for when the fireworks start.

First, though, I buy some jam and a pot holder from our neighbors' booths, put them in the trunk of my car, then go to the Oakfield Second Christian Church booth.

I see some familiar faces, and a couple I don't recognize. The pastor introduces me to them and says that Janus is out shopping at the moment. I turn and see him looking over a booth that sells earrings, necklaces, rings, and other types of jewelry. I allow him his privacy as he shops, and ask the pastor if their booth needs help.

"We wouldn't deny it if you're offering," he answers.

I smile, then ask if I could help run a game where you pick up a rubber duck, and whatever number is on the bottom, that's how many pieces of candy you get. I try a piece for myself. It's store-bought, out of a bag similar to what you'd buy for Halloween. It's good, but nowhere near as good as Sunny's. Still, that doesn't stop me from having three pieces before I stop to make sure that there will be enough for any kids who stop by.

Deacon Brynn Keigh is there, and I ask her about how many have used the baby changing area so far. She said that she's been there just over an hour, and so far, no one has during that time. She said that throughout the day, maybe five people have used it, or so she's been told. That's not disappointing, I tell her. In fact, it's encouraging as I expected maybe three, at the most, to use it, and they're on track to double that number.

I stay at the booth a little longer, getting a kick as the kids' faces light up when they win any amount of candy. We pass out the flyers that my agency helped design, and tell anybody who asks that they are always welcome to attend services at the church.

Janus returns around 7:30 and tells me that he's seen me there for a while and assumes that I am hungry. He hands me a chicken dinner from one of the restaurants out of Mapletree that is there. He jokes that their flyers didn't look so good, and suggests that I go over there and have a chat with them. I consider that, but also consider that it's my day off, and while advertising is my job, it's not my job to recruit every business I see to sign on with the agency. Please don't tell Gretchen I said that, as she may have a different opinion from mine.

Chloe finds us and walks over as she's chomping on a huge turkey leg. She sees the tent and is impressed with what they are offering. I introduce her to Pastor Chalke, and Chloe tells him that she's looking forward to attending on Sunday.

"Saturn speaks highly of you," she says through a mouthful of dark meat.

"Well, I hope she speaks highly of me speaking highly about our Lord," he jokes, and we all smile.

We stand and chat for a while when we hear the band start playing songs from the early 2000s. Janus asks if I'd like to dance. I wasn't sure I'd want to leave Chloe behind, then a man from the church named Ezra Hatch asked Chloe to dance. She smiles and says that she'd enjoy that.

We all go to the dance floor and start moving to the beat. A second song comes on, and we switch partners. I have fun dancing with Ezra while Janus and Chloe chat a little as they clap and dance to the music. When a slow, romantic song starts playing, we all feel a bit uncomfortable. I switch partners, wrap my arms around Janus, and start swaying. Chloe looks at Ezra, and since the song has already started and we're all in the middle, instead of disturbing everyone by leaving, they each put one hand on the other's waist and hold the other hand, dancing with each other as far from each other as possible.

The slow song ends, and an upbeat one begins. I wasn't sure if Chloe wanted to stay on the dance floor, switch partners, or walk away. She answered without answering when she kept hold of one of Ezra's hands and started leading him in a fast dance. I did the same and danced one more time with Janus.

Once the song ended, we all left the dance floor. Ezra excuses himself, then goes to where their tent is and brings back four bottles of water for us. We all happily accept, then find a picnic table nearby to sit down.

Ezra and Chloe chat a little, but I could tell that they're both being guarded with their words, as they may not want to start a relationship with each other since they live so far apart. Still, one night of dancing, then watching fireworks, and possibly a little kiss at the end, never hurt anybody. I won't press Chloe either way, but I certainly won't stop her, either.

Time gets away from us, and soon it's 8:00. We all return to the church's booth to pack everything, then find our spots to watch the fireworks show. Chloe and Ezra remain close to each other, but not too close, as we work at tearing everything down.

At a little after 8:30, the job is finished, and we all take a chair to claim our spots. We set them all side-by-side, close to where other groups are sitting, then chat a little more about how we're looking forward to the Independence Day fireworks. Pastor Chalke mentions that he was disappointed that he never had a chance to see our booth. I assure him that there'll be more, so there's no need to be upset.

A classical symphony takes its place on a bandstand. They all sound a little disturbing as they warm up their instruments independently from one another. Before that goes on too long, the conductor taps his baton to his stand, and the musicians silence their instruments and look towards him. He raises both hands, waves the baton as he counts, then the band starts playing.

It's quiet at first, and the band slowly builds its music as the fireworks show builds anticipation. We all say "Oooh" and "Ahhh" as the fiery flowers explode in the sky right before our very eyes.

Soon, the band starts playing Tchaikovsky's 1812 Overture, and we all know what happens next. The band plays the familiar tune, and in place of cannons, the explosions in the sky take care of those parts. I feel my insides vibrating as each bomb explodes, and I am still in awe at the sight of the colored display happening in the clear, night sky.

The fireworks end with one last display of a crude version of the American flag in the sky. The orchestra begins playing the National Anthem, and everyone stands, places their hands over their hearts, and sings along. After the song finishes, we all cheer loudly and then start packing our things to head home.

"What a perfect finish to a perfect day," Chloe says, then glimpses toward Ezra.

"Easy now," I whisper to her. "Don't start something you can't finish."

"Who says that I can't finish it?" she asks, and I'm not sure what she means by that.

"You're staying at my apartment tonight, alone on the couch," I tell her.

"Oh, I wasn't talking about tonight, Saturn. I got a job offer from Kardi County, which I'm seriously considering. I didn't want to bring that up before this event, but it looks like you and I will have a lot to talk about over the next couple of days."

I am stunned by this news. I don't know what to make of it, and there's no time to think about it now. I look up at the night sky, and despite all of the smoke from the fireworks, it's about as clear as it can get.

"Do you have plans for tonight?" I ask Janus, who looks confusedly at me. "Come back to my apartment if you have time. I want to show you something. Outside," I say, adding that part at the end so he doesn't get the wrong idea.

"I suppose I could turn in a little late tonight," he answers. "After all, it is a holiday, and a wonderful one at that."

I tell Chloe that we're going to be leaving now, and she asks for a moment to speak to Ezra. They take a few steps away, she takes his hand and says something to him, then leans up and kisses him on the corner of his mouth. He smiles and says something else. She smiles back, takes his cheeks in her hands, and leans up again to give him another kiss on the lips that was quick yet still nice. They smile at each other, then Chloe comes over to me and hops in the car.

"I haven't kissed a guy in a while," she tells me. "That was long overdue."

"I wasn't going to say anything," I lied. I was, but her explanation will have to do for now.

We get back to my place, and I park my car in its designated spot while Janus parks his truck next to where Chloe's car is parked. I tell Janus to wait outside as I have something inside that I have to bring out. He asks me what that is, and I tell him a surprise.

I go inside and tell Chloe to make herself at home. I'll be outside with Janus for the next half an hour or so. She says that she's fine with that, and turns the TV on while I go and find my telescope.

I carry it to the main apartment building door, and when Janus notices me struggling with it, he quickly comes over to hold the door open for me. I thank him, and he offers to carry the telescope, but I tell him I'm fine carrying it and ask him to follow me to the center courtyard of the apartment grounds.

I get the telescope setup as he patiently awaits. While I'm sure I know what he wants to see, I decide to do a little teasing first.

I adjust the telescope and get it focused on an object in space. I tell him to look through it, and by the look on his face, I know what he expects to see. He smiles as he puts his eye to the lens, then the smile quickly goes away.

"What is that?" he asks. "It's grey, lumpy, and quite ugly."

"You said it, not me," I laugh, then he looks at me. "That's Janus, a moon of Saturn."

"What?!" he shouts, then takes another look. "On the other hand, it is ruggedly handsome."

"That is true," I agree, for both the moon and the man.

"How about showing me a planet?" he asks.

I adjust the telescope again, and by how far I move it, he knows I'm not aiming it where he wants. He looks anyway.

"What is it?" he asks. "It looks a little plain and fuzzy."

"Adjust the focus," I say, and show him how to do it. "Oh, now it's pretty in its own way. It looks like it's trying to be fancy through its plainness, but when you look hard and close enough, you see it for what it really is."

"Yep," I say. "You nailed it. That perfectly describes Venus. Both the planet and my sister."

"It does?" he asks, then looks at it again. "It is amazing, but you know what I want to see."

I do, and I decide not to tease him any longer. I point it back to close to where I had it the first time, and focus on that ringed beauty floating around some 886 million miles away. I tell him it's ready. He asks me if I'm sure, no teasing this time. I promise it is, and tell him to go ahead and look.

He gives me a face, and I smile assuredly at him. He looks into the lens, adjusts the focus a little, and stares. He looks for a long, long time, not saying anything, but a smile on his face grows bigger and bigger.

"So that's Saturn?" he asks, already knowing the answer.

"It is," I answer.

"Saturn. It's one of the most beautiful things I've ever seen, and I'm not talking about the planet."

He surprised me with his words; he looked at me and then back into the lens. We stay quiet for another minute as he stares, and I silently bask in what he just said.

"Would you like to see something else in space?" I ask, trying to break the silence except for the crickets chirping in the background.

"No. This is perfect, Saturn. The planet and the you; they are both perfect."

He looks at me with a smile, then reaches into his pocket and pulls out what looks like a small box for jewelry. Oh, no! He's not about to propose, is he? I look at him closely, trying to see if he looks at me the way Eric looks at Venus. It's dark, and hard to tell. No! This can't be that. We never even said those words to one another, so this can't be what it looks like.

"Saturn," he says, then takes me by the hand. "My world turned upside down when you entered it. The moment you walked into my store, I just knew that there was something about you."

"Janus…" I say, and he keeps talking.

"I wanted to ask you out, as you know, but I didn't for professional reasons. I am so, so happy we literally bumped into each other at the coffee shop."

"Me, too," I say through a chuckle as I remember that moment.

"I know it's been barely five weeks since we've been seeing each other. It's been five of the best weeks of my life. When I saw you dancing with Chip the flautist, or how Bruce the car salesman gave you his card, asking you out, it nearly killed me on the inside. I know I have no right feeling that way, but I did."

"There's nothing between me and those two. There's nothing between me and anybody else, for that matter. I promise," I say.

"When we were at the craft fair today, I found this. I'd like to give it to you," he says. I don't think they'd sell that kind of jewelry there, so I'm relieved. Just a little, because it still may be. I don't know.

He lets go of my hand, steps back, and thankfully stays standing on his two feet and doesn't kneel. He opens the box, and what I see stuns me.

"This is a locket of the planet Saturn," he tells me as he takes the necklace from the box. "It opens, and you could put pictures on either side of the planet. I didn't put any pictures in, as I didn't want to be so presumptuous."

This took a turn, I think to myself, and let Janus continue talking.

"I'd like for you to have this, and wear it," he says. "That is, if you accept the terms."

"What terms?" I ask, really having no idea what is happening.

"We've been dancing around this for a while now. I'd like for us to see each other exclusively. I know I haven't been seeing anybody else, and you told me that you haven't been. I'd like to make that official. If you accept and wear this, then we agree to be a couple. I only date you, you only date me. I promise, Saturn, that is the only term of this. I'm not asking for you to do anything with me that we haven't so far, except to only do them with me. That is, for you to and for me to…"

"You're rambling," I say, cutting him off. "I know what you're saying, Janus. May I see the locket?"

I reach my hand out, and he hands me the chain and keeps the box it came in in his hand. It's pretty, and it looks very close to how the planet looks. While I've received many gifts before with the planet Saturn on them, I was never once offered anything quite like this with terms like that attached.

I hold the chain by its clasp and inspect the locket as well as I could in the dim lights of the courtyard. It's beautiful. I look at Janus, who has since gone quiet and waits in anticipation. I give him a serious look, then ask him to hold his hand out. He does, and I gently place the locket back in his hand.

"Is that a no?" he asks, sounding disappointed, and starts to put the locket back in the box.

He goes to close it, but I stop him. I smile, hold my hair up, turn around, and say, "Put it on me."

He does, and after it's secured, I hold the locket in my hand and slowly turn around. I let go of it and wrap my arms around his neck and pull him down for a long, passionate kiss. It was our first as an official couple, and I wanted him to remember it. By his reaction, I'm sure that he will.

We stand there, under the moonlight, next to my telescope. We hold each other's hands as we face one another. I lean up, give him another kiss that is nothing more than a peck this time. I step a half step back and look him in the eyes. I look deeply into his eyes. He looks deeply into mine. While I can't be certain in the dim lighting, it looks like he's looking at me the way that Eric looks at Venus. That's good, because I think I'm looking at him the way she does Eric. I stare into his eyes a moment longer, holding the locket with my right hand as I do. I tell him that it's getting late, and maybe we should part ways. We kiss once more, and I tell him that I'm fine taking the telescope back in, and he can go home now.

He gets out of sight, and I clasp my hands together in prayer. "Dear Lord, as I begin this new journey in a relationship, I ask for Your divine guidance. Lead us according to Your will, not by our emotions or expectations. Help us make decisions that honor You. Let our connection be rooted in love, mutual respect, and purpose. I pray all of this in Jesus' name. Amen."